TEMPER

NICKY DRAYDEN

HARPER Voyager

An Imprint of HarperCollins*Publishers*

HarperCollins books may be purchased for educational, business, or sales promotional use. For information, please email the Special Markets Department at SPsales@harpercollins.com.

Harper Voyager and design are trademarks of HarperCollins Publishers LLC.

FIRST EDITION

Designed by Paula Russell Szafranski
Map by Eric Gunther. Copyright © 2018 Springer Cartographics LLC.
Background art for half title and title page © ririro/Shutterstock

Library of Congress Cataloging-in-Publication Data has been applied for.

ISBN 978-0-06-249305-7

18 19 20 21 22   LSC   10 9 8 7 6 5 4 3 2 1

Praise for Nicky Drayden's THE PREY OF GODS

"This dense and imaginative debut is . . . a book like no other, with a diverse cast that crosses the spectrum of genders and races, and a new idea (or four) in every chapter."

—*B&N Sci-Fi and Fantasy Blog*

"You'll need to clear your schedule as soon as you get your hands on a copy of Drayden's debut novel! . . . Drayden has certainly made herself an author to watch out for."

—RT Book Reviews, $4^1/_2$ stars, Top Pick

"*Prey of Gods* delivers on every promise in beautifully unexpected ways that leave you breathless, a little dizzy, and wanting more. . . . Exquisite, fast-paced, and excellent fun."

—Fran Wilde, award-winning author of *Updraft, Cloudbound,* and *Horizon*

"Drayden's delivery of all this is subtly poignant and slap-in-the-face deadpan—perfect for this novel-length thought exercise about what kinds of gods a cynical, self-absorbed postmodern society really deserves. Lots of fun."

—*New York Times Book Review*

"Drayden has knocked it out of the park with this novel. . . . An excellent piece of fiction that is levels above any of the summer reads coming out."

—New York Journal of Books

"Thanks to a rip-roaring story and Drayden's expansive imagination, it all coheres into the most fun you can have in 2017."

—*Book Riot* (Best of 2017)

"Nicky Drayden's debut novel *The Prey of Gods* is a surprising cornucopia of genres and characters taking place in a futurist South Africa. . . . It's a little bit surreal, a little bit weird, a lot of fun and wholly impressive."

—*Kirkus Reviews*

"A fantastic mix of science fiction, horror, fantasy, and humor, *The Prey of Gods* is a unique novel that defies categorization. . . . Fun and engaging, *The Prey of Gods* is an unforgettable read."

—Bustle

"Ancient gods, gene-tech, and gripping action—I love so much about this book."

—Cat Rambo, author of *Beasts of Tabat* and
Neither Here Nor There

"One of the biggest pleasures of this book is the plurality of its voices and story lines, and the way Nicky Drayden skips and weaves between them. . . . It's a book full of energy and momentum, strange wit and sensitivity. It is a LOT. And it is wonderful."

—Vulture (Best of 2017)

"*The Prey of Gods* was a very entertaining novel filled with wonderfully imaginative ideas, and it was very competently written. . . . I really enjoyed reading it, and I would definitely recommend it to whoever is looking for a diverse novel full of action and inventive creations."

—Black Girl Nerds

"*The Prey of Gods* is an ambitious blend of folklore, bioengineering, and science fiction. . . . With luck, readers will remember Drayden's novel when nomination season rolls around."

—SF Site

"You may wonder exactly what kind of speculative fiction it is. . . . Trust me: This stuff is good, call it what you will."

—*Seattle Times* (Notable Book of 2017)

"In this debut novel from accomplished short story writer Nicky Drayden, the mythic and the mechanical mesh as smoothly as servo gears in a security droid. That's due largely to Drayden's understanding of the creatures that occupy the space between those two: human beings."

—*Austin Chronicle*

To Noel,

the most outstanding boss

in the Field of Excellence

CONTENTS

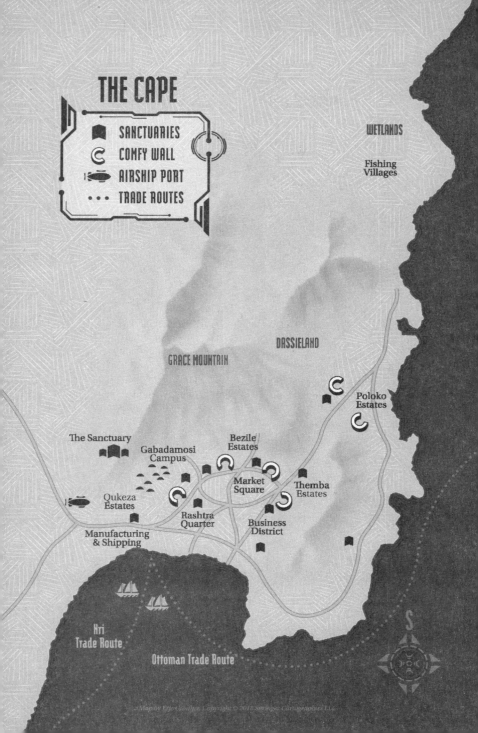

VAINGLORY

The queasiness of a proximity break drains from my gut as I spy Kasim through the glass door of his classroom. Relief overwhelms me as my stomach settles. In the classroom, Mrs. Okoye paces in salt-stained boots, her facial features as precisely angled as the writing across her chalkboard: HEED THE NARROW SEASON, AND A FRUITFUL YEAR RENEWED. Her holiday greetings may be merry, but the lines drawn on the foreheads of her students are not. Eyes gaze down at paper, and pencils scribble furiously. Despite the crisp chill of the season, sweat drips from worried brows. Finally, Kasim feels the tug of my proximity and sighs in frustration. He places his test pencil on his desk, then glares at me.

What? he mouths.

I'm going out for a smoke with Nkosazana. Meet us when you're done, I mouth back.

What? he says again.

We may be twins, but he can't read lips for shit.

I'm—I point to my chest—*going out.* I make exaggerated swings with my arms and walk past the door. When I peek back in, a few other students have taken note of my presence. I draw a handful of smirks. *For a smoke*—I take a puff on an imaginary sanjo cig—*with Nkosazana*—I pop open the top three buttons of the drab gray-and-white ciki jacket we all wear, cup my hands beneath my muscled chest, and sashay like I've got the rack of a vice mag centerfold. This gets stifled giggles from some of the students, and the mellow brown of Kasim's cheeks flushes red beneath.

Mrs. Okoye stops her pacing, and as her eyes dart to the door, I dive out of sight.

"Concentrate, class," I hear her say. "This exam will count for fifty percent of your final grade, and partial answers will not be accepted."

I heave a sigh, thankful that I'd drawn a biology teacher fresh out of university, and a religious one at that. You could tell how uncomfortable he was with science, like every single word of it left oily residue over his tongue. He'd skimmed through so many chapters that we'd had our final exam weeks ago—all multiple choice. I'd aced it, of course, but then again, it had been so easy nearly everyone did.

"Mr. Mtuze," booms a deep voice from behind me. I look up from the floor and panic when I catch a glimpse of Principal Boro's reflection in the glass, bulky arms folded firmly across a delicate lace lapel revealing eir even bulkier chest. With all that muscle packed onto eir tall and curvy physique, it's hard not to get intimidated this up close and personal. I'll admit, I'm a little envious, too, but somehow I resist the urge to ask for eir workout regimen.

"Principal Boro," I stammer, then jump to my feet. "I was just—"

Boro plucks the cigs peeking out of my jacket pocket. "Getting back to class," ey finishes for me. "And button up your uniform. You're in violation of dress code."

"Yes, Principal Boro. Right away, Principal Boro." You've never seen buttons get fastened so quickly. I'm out of there and running down the narrow hall so fast that Boro's voice has gone quiet when I hear that baritone "Walk, Mr. Mtuze!" chasing after me.

I don't walk . . . and I don't return to class either. The narrow season has already started as far as I'm concerned. As soon as the soles of my worn loafers hit pavement outside the school, my proximity with Kasim breaks and the queasiness is back. The emotions that Kasim's closeness had tempered come raging forth so quickly, I pitch over from their impact in my gut. I feel my anger welling up, and all those things I'd wanted to cuss at Boro fill my saliva with bitterness. Muscle-headed know-it-all stole my cigs, and is probably smoking them now. I grab the collar of my ciki jacket with both hands, and tug until the buttons pop loose, all the way down to my thighs. I shrug it off, ball it up, and toss it up onto the tin awning.

"*Yes*, Principal Boro! Right *away*, Principal Boro!"

Sometimes I hate the person Kasim makes me, but left to my own devices, I'd be sitting in detention right now, or probably worse.

Nkosazana's waiting for me on the school's front steps,

standing in a thin sliver of sunlight in the midst of the long
cool shadows of the late afternoon. She looks annoyed. Nkosazana shakes her head when she sees me, shirtless and shivering despite myself. She whips her long silken braid over her
shoulder, blinks thick come-hither lashes, and stares me down
with kohl-rimmed blue eyes the shade of the ocean just before
sunset. It's all a facade, of course. Aisle three of whatever posh
cosmetic store she frequents. But what can I say, I'm a sucker
for vainglory in all its forms. Especially the female form.

"Want to borrow my jacket?" Nkosazana asks with a grin.

"It's not that cold."

"That's not what your nipples are telling me." She flicks
me, and the pain shoots through my body and settles into
my nether regions. "And your mom is going to flip when she
has to buy you another uniform."

I shrug. I'll swipe one of Kasim's and let out the hems.
I've got a month before I'll have to worry about that anyway.
No more school until after the year renews, which normally
I would be excited about, but Nkosazana and her twin sister
are escaping the cold, rainy season by going north to Nri
for the holidays. Her parents are the type who can afford a
better school, but send Nkosazana and Ruda to the Bezile
School of Fundamentals on principle. They are even okay
with her dating a poor boy from the comfy—*as long as you
stay chaste,* her father had stipulated to me privately after
the most decadent dinner I'd had in my life. Endless plates of
lamb with foreign spices, pure white rices, and several odd
and meaty vegetables that I'd never seen or even heard of.
With my best manners, I'd smiled, and said my "Yes, sirs,"
and put on a good show, and then stipulated Nkosazana very
thoroughly later that night.

"You're sure you can't tell your parents you don't want to go?" I ask her. Not for the first time. Or the tenth. This narrow season promises to be particularly bitter. I'll miss the anticipation as my pebbles plink against her bedroom window in the cold of night, and the warmth she brings between the sheets.

"I would if I didn't want to go. But I do. You would, too, if you'd seen the swim costume I've picked out. Completely sheer, besides a few carefully placed rhinestones."

I growl under my breath. We'd been dragged along on family trips with the cousins, of course, and though Kasim and I had never stepped a foot outside the country, we knew all about the carnal pleasures associated with the beaches of Nri—tropical drinks, exotic dishes, and the dark, bulging muscles of men who can break coconuts open with their bare hands. "Well, I hope you don't get sand stuck where the clouds don't roll." Lie. I totally hope she does, and spends her entire posh holiday walking funny.

Nkosazana screws her lips at me. "You know you and Kasim are more than welcome to come. You don't have to act like a jerk."

"I don't want to be your dad's comfy puppet, paraded around all of Nri to show just how progressive he is to his welshing buddies."

"Dad wouldn't do that."

"Please. *You* do it sometimes."

Nkosazana's posture whips to attention, and in less than a second, she's in my face, hands on her hips, somehow managing to make our androgynous school uniform seem both feminine and fashionable.

"What?"

Anger rims her voice. She's the only one I know whose temper is anywhere even remotely close to being as quick as mine. "Auben Mtuze, you take that lie back right now."

I shake my head. "It's not a lie. Last weekend, when we were out shopping, and your friends Nyiko and Tiwa came by—"

"Nkule and Sindi," Nkosazana corrects. She must see where I'm going with this, because her brow has loosened.

"When you introduced me, you said we went to the same school."

"We do go to the same school!"

"But why did you have to tell them? Why couldn't you have introduced me as your boyfriend and left it at that? They know you go to a comfy school. And they could probably smell it on me anyway." The queasiness in my stomach shifts, pulsates. There's more I want to say to her, scream at her, but I can't allow my temper to drive me. I shove my hand into my pocket, carefully fondling the shards of broken glass I've started carrying with me, letting them pierce my fingertips in succession until the pain eases my anger back into submission.

Later, a voice whispers, then crawls across my neck, down my back—soft and delicate like a silk scarf. My mind falters. These past few weeks, I've been hearing things—whispers in the wind, laughter in the distance, cusses beneath the baying of street dogs at night—but the voices have never been this close, this clear. I shiver, and not from the cold.

"Auben?" Nkosazana says, staring up at me through those thick lashes. "Are you okay?"

"Huh? Yeah. Never mind, it was stupid."

"If something's bothering you, we should talk about it."

"Less talk. More making out." I tug Nkosazana close,

and she squeals. Our tongues wrestle, her mouth artificially sweetened by a blend of coconut-lime-flavored beeswax with a touch of something fishy, leaving her lips unnaturally shiny and shimmering. She is perfection incarnate. That it comes at the expense of hours upon hours of primping and priming only makes her sexier. Nothing could dampen this moment.

Except . . .

"Seriously, Nkosazana? Out here in front of the whole school? Classy." Ruda, Nkosazana's allegedly greater half, shifts the waistband of her ill-fitting uniform, then takes a hard seat on the steps next to us and picks at the dirt beneath her gnawed fingernails.

Nkosazana shudders, then concludes our session with a prim and tight, off-center peck on my lips. She's gone prim and tight all over in fact, and any hopes I'd had for a frolic in the tangle reeds are squelched cold. Nkosazana dabs away our slobber with a frilly kerchief, then takes a moment to reapply another layer of gloss upon her lips before settling down next to her twin.

They look nothing alike. Act nothing alike. I know that's not uncommon for twins, but if you lined up a hundred random girls and had to rank the likelihood that each had once shared a womb with Nkosazana, Ruda would come up dead last. Every. Single. Time.

I've heard the rumors. Ticket twins. As in their mother was open to any man willing to pay the price of admission. One mom, two daddies. Not so uncommon for twins in the comfy, and apparently even high-class snobs party a little too hard sometimes.

Nkosazana wedges her arm beneath Ruda's and lays her

head on her sister's shoulder. "Sweetie, could you give us ten minutes?" she coos.

"I've got a headache. I need proximity," Ruda hisses. Likely a lie. Ruda may be the greater twin, but duplicity and greed run hot in her, even when Nkosazana is close by. Lie or not, Ruda pulls out a small vial of one of her medicinal oils and rubs her temples until the whole area smells like Mother Nature's breath after a night of binge drinking. "In any case, humility is neither of your virtues, so no reason to start acting like it now. Play tonsil slalom all you want. I don't care."

I raise a brow at Nkosazana, not above taking Ruda up on her offer, but Nkosazana shrugs me off like chastity is suddenly her middle name. I've got to get rid of Ruda. There's no way I'll make it through the school break if we end our eight-month romance like this. I moan and pitch forward, rubbing at my own temples.

Nkosazana is immediately up, her hand rubbing along my back. "Are you okay?"

"Yeah," I seethe. "It's just a proximity headache. Nothing to—" I wail out in agony.

"Must be contagious," Ruda mumbles under her breath.

"Do you want me to get Kasim?" Nkosazana offers.

"No, I don't want to disturb—" For the win, I start to pant, staring glassy-eyed off into nothingness like I'm about to snap off from a permanent proximity break. It's a ridiculous display. My acting is worse than when Kasim and I used to play snap offs in the primary school playground. Our vice scars were still new then, still scabbing over in fact, depicting the seven vices split between all twins. I'd been branded with six from shoulder to elbow, now garish raised keloids. Kasim had gotten only one—greed—now a faint scar, more like a discoloration, easy to miss unless you're looking for it. But back then, before we really had an idea of the repercussions of being a lesser or greater twin in society, it was all fun and games. We'd spend hours feigning the symptoms of terminal twin separation, then enact the ways our vices and virtues would be our undoing. My favorite was death by vainglory, preening forever in a mirror, turning down Kasim's offers for food and drink, until my body succumbed to malnutrition in a fit of dramatic and highly ostentatious death throes. Kasim's favorite was conscience, in which he fell into a spiraling loop of moral balance, debating and judging the rightness and wrongness of every action, word, and thought until his brain exploded all over the blacktop.

Fun times.

"I'm getting him," Nkosazana declares, then races off back inside the school.

My performance ends as soon as the door shuts behind her.

"I think you missed your calling," Ruda says with a smirk. Duplicity recognizes duplicity. She nods, her unwieldy and unkempt afro nodding a half second later. "We're always looking for honest males to fill roles in theatrics. We're up to our eyeballs with finemisters and laddies."

Finemisters and laddies? I flinch at her use of those outdated gender slurs, her crudeness catching me off guard. Sure, maybe I've been known to call gender chimeras, or kigens for short, out of their name when my temper is running hot, but coming from perfect goddess-of-the-earth Ruda, with her five clunky virtue talismans hanging from homespun hemp rope . . . Color me intrigued. I forget all about my plan of bribing her for a little alone time with her sister and pry deeper.

"Honest male," I say, flexing my chest muscles. "I don't think anyone's been called that since my grandfather's time."

"Just got out from a brutal history exam, and my head's still buried under a mountain of antiquated terms. Had to write a two-thousand-word essay on the effect that the Bankole Sex Revolts had on each of the four sexes for the past century and a half. So I really do have a headache. Just not a proximity one."

"Friendly Lemurs Make Greasy Gravy While Flying Big Great Colorful Kites."

Ruda raises a bushy brow. "Did you hit that pretty head of yours today?"

"It's a mnemonic for remembering kigen nomenclature from the rise of Branch Institutionalism to the Bankole sesquicentennial," I say with a shrug. "I made up a mnemonic for all of the recognized sex and gender permutations there were during the pre-Institutionalism era, too, but I gotta warn you, it's forty-seven words long and a fair amount of them are cusses."

Now she looks at me like I've got horns growing out the sides of my head. "Mnemonic. Sesquicentennial. Permutations. Those are big words for—"

"A lesser twin? Is that what you're going to say? Because last time I checked, intelligence isn't linked to vice and virtue."

"I was going to say 'for someone whose library study sessions turn into make-out sessions about one hundred percent of the time.'" Ruda looks me over closely, then snorts. "Maybe I should apologize for all of those nasty things I've said about you."

"You've never said anything nasty about me." Rude, yes. But not nasty.

"Not to your face." Ruda steps right up next to me, and I catch her scent. Like boiled cabbage and wet burlap, and for some strange reason, it does not completely disagree with me. "So, Auben Mtuze, what do you want to ask me, out here, just the two of us?" Her lips part. Full, chapped lips that look like they'd cut if I tried to kiss her. Not that I'm thinking about kissing her. Not that I'm *not* thinking about kissing her.

Taste her, the whisper says. The hairs on my back rise, and despite my unease, other parts of me start to rise as well.

"I, um . . ." I swallow the hard knot in my throat. "Maybe, I was hoping that you ladies wouldn't be in such a rush to pack for Nri. You could come over to our place. Maybe stay for a bite of something. You know. Get the 'full comfy experience' beyond the wall, so you can brag to your friends over umbrella drinks on the beach."

"Full comfy, huh?" She pretends to consider my offer, especially, I'm sure, the draw of diving farther into our section of the neighborhood—a pocket of sin situated within the posh Greater Bezile suburb. "Can you promise we'll see wu mystics and holler whores, and eat mealie pap and fried chicken feet, and wash it all down with a heavy quart of tinibru?" Her tongue is sharp and accurate, but I don't take offense. Sometimes stereotypes are stereotypes for a reason.

"I'm afraid we only have light tinibru in the icebox, fewer gristly bits. But yeah, something like that."

"Sounds repulsive. But, sure. I'm in."

I smile at Ruda, right as proximity kicks in. I look over my shoulder and see Kasim, a big fat frown on his face. "You and Ruda are getting along? Nkosazana was right. This is an emergency." He glares at me with a temper that never ignites beyond mild irritation. "I had to leave my test early for this. I left two answers completely blank."

"Sorry," I say. "It was touch and go for a minute, but Ruda gave me some of her nature's teat oils, and now I feel better."

Nkosazana looks at Ruda for confirmation. "*You* shared your homeopathy with *him*?"

"What? You asked me to be nicer to him. What could be nicer than keeping him from snapping off? Besides, last thing I want to do is spend the entire narrow season listening to you whine about how you looooost your first true looooove . . ."

Nkosazana manages to flush through the shellac of her cosmetics. "Ruda!"

"Sorry. I made that up. Nkosazana never said anything of the sort." Ruda raises a duplicitous brow at me. "But we'd better see the guys home. I don't think Auben is in any kind of condition to walk after what he just went through." Ruda puts her clammy hands up to my temples, lifts my eyebrows with her thumbs, and peers deeply into my eyes. "I think he's lost a significant amount of brain cells, and he didn't have a whole lot to spare in the first place. Isn't that right, Auben?"

She's so deliciously vicious, and I can't even imagine how much trouble I'll be in if I let myself fall for her. "Yeah," I say with a lecherous grin. "Yeah, that's right."

Nkosazana hails us a rickshaw. Rickshaws, rather. The first three aren't up to her particular standards. The first has a cabbie with an unsightly hunch. The cushions are too thin on the second. The third seems perfect to me—fluffy cushions, solid wooden wheels, a respectably good-looking cabbie with thighs that were made for pedaling up and down the cobbled streets of the city bowl. But apparently, the brightly colored shweshwe-print canopy clashes too much with Nkosazana's uniform, so . . .

Finally, I'm directing a cabbie deep inside Lesser Bezile, into comfy life within the U-shaped wall that divides our neighborhood, keeping the destitute and vice-ridden twins out of view from their wealthy counterparts without the risk of proximity breaks. We weave through a maze of jewel-colored storefronts with dusty windows crowded with displays of secondhand clothes and thirdhand furniture. Blocky cement tenements scrawled with tribal graffiti loom, almost leaning into us, it seems, like intimidating street thugs daring us to misstep. I breathe easier as we enter a bustling vice trough, and are greeted by the soothing smell of cheap tobacco, comfy-distilled spirits, and great vats of home-brewed tinibru. An oryx-drawn carriage speeds past us, hooves clopping steadily, then it swerves, cutting sharply into our lane. The carriage nicks the side of our rickshaw, sending our cabbie into a fit of cusses, all of them in the Rashtrakutan tongue. I don't speak it myself, but any vice-ridden teen raised in this cultural melting pot knows how to swear in at least seven languages. I suck my teeth at the back of the carriage driver's head, and add a few foreign cuss words our cabbie had left out, most notably pointing out their fondness for licking the sweat from a lizard's bristly scrotum.

The girls are rattled, but not shaken enough to call off our adventure. It takes us a good fifteen minutes to find an actual holler whore, with Kasim protesting the entire way. Even from the rear seat, I can see that Ruda is disappointed there hadn't been one on every corner. Still, she's the first out of the rickshaw when we do spot one. Ruda jingles coins in her fists as she scurries toward the makeshift stage. I hop down and sprint after her, grabbing her wrist and pulling her back.

"That's not how it's done," I whisper into her ear.

"I've been studying to audition for Daughter Sarr in *A Thousand Glass Nights* next quarter. I think I know a thing or two about holler whores." Ruda puts both hands on her hips, and as her eyes catch up with her mouth, it becomes obvious to her that real life in the comfy is a lot different than theatrics. "Whoa," she says with a pant, watching the holler whore's graceful moves and the stares of her small audience of three men, two women, and a fem kigen. They hold small glass bowls filled to the brim with various shades of edible pigments, and sit stone still as the holler whore passes within a breath of them, taut, muscled skin covered in all the colors of the rainbow and nothing else. She licks a deep blue from her wrist, then dips her finger in the glitter-gold a woman is holding and paints bangles upon her arm. Her movements are painfully slow as she contorts, licking bright purple from her inner thigh, tongue exposing an undulating track of dark brown skin beneath the oily pigment. She shudders as she replaces it with the kigen's blood orange.

Nkosazana and Kasim have joined us now, though Kasim's more interested in the pill bugs he's nudging with the toes of his loafers.

Nkosazana's eyes go wide as the holler whore's tongue mops away a swatch of white paint next. "So it is true," she stammers. Her clammy hand catches itself in mine. "She really can lick every inch of her own body. That's so disgusting."

"It's beautiful," Ruda whispers.

"It's tragic," Kasim adds, louder than he should. He draws

the holler whore's attention, her stare like that of a lost, feral creature, then she's back to preening herself.

"Only you would think a naked woman was a tragedy," I say, knocking him in the ribs. "Ruda's chaste, and even she can appreciate the beauty of the female form."

"Not that," Kasim says. "She's being tormented. Dying a slow death. Her body sustained only by the scant nutrients in her paints. Maybe she was a beautiful person once, but you can't call this art. It's lechery in its most vile state, and I'm not—"

The holler whore wails, her head arched so far back her neck looks like it's about to snap. The note is chilling, drowns out everything but my most pressing thoughts. Kasim covers his ears. Nkosazana presses her head against my chest. The pitch isn't substantial enough to break glass, but it does manage to break something within me. They say the average holler whore has thirty-seven orgasms per hour, and up until about eight seconds ago, there's no way you could have convinced me this could possibly be a bad thing.

"Thanks for ruining this for me," I say to Kasim as quiet reclaims the streets. On our way back to the rickshaw, I notice how much closer we all walk together. I can't help but wonder how that holler whore snapped off. Had her twin died? Or was there someone out there, beyond the bounds of proximity, suffering in some equally unpleasant way?

We're right in the center of Lesser Bezile, farthest away from the comfy wall, and closest to actual danger. It's danger I normally wouldn't think twice about, especially during the day, but seeing it through the girls' eyes, you start to notice things . . . like the prevalence of stray dogs, mange cutting through the chimeral stripes along their backs. The constant wail of hungry babies from tenement blocks, like the music score to a theatrical play about my life. And the abundance of wu mystics, wrapped up in traditional divining cloaks, thick plumes of incense smoke rising from ivory-carved pipes obscuring their kohl-painted faces. Kasim, of course, doesn't believe in wu, or anything spiritual for that matter. He finds the whole concept offensive, especially versa wu. Five djang will get you a small bag, enough to reverse your vices for a full hour. Vainglory becomes humility, duplicity becomes sincerity, envy becomes conscience, and so on, and so on, and so on, and so on. Virtues do the same. Maybe it's real. Probably it's not, but I must admit, I'm a little piqued to see chaste Ruda's propensity for lechery.

"Who's in? I'm buying," Nkosazana says, approaching the mystic. His cloak spreads open with the whip of a prey bird's wings, revealing a portable apothecary of glimmering crystal wards, viscous potions in glass decanters, and fragrant herb sachets tucked neatly into a myriad of pockets.

Ruda seems more taken with the mystic himself, rather than the spiritual paraphernalia curated from a dozen lands and cultures. She observes his subtle movements, the flick of his sharp eyes, the urgency in his hand gestures as he tells us to hurry up and buy. It's like she's his understudy in one of her upcoming productions.

"This is ridiculous," Kasim says from the rickshaw, arms folded across his chest. "At best, that stuff won't work, and at worst, it'll knock the senses out of you, but the whole idea that one's vices and virtues are interchangeable is incredibly naive."

"I'm in," I say. "It's the start of the narrow season. What's the harm in a little fun?"

Nkosazana buys each of us a bag of versa wu, though Kasim refuses his. Sure he's socially awkward, but he's not usually a drag like this. He's probably still mad about my ruining his test. I jump into the rear seat next to him, hang my arm around his shoulder. "Look, I'm sorry about pulling you out of the exam early, and I want to make it up to you. Let's go back to the way we did it before and get our classes together next quarter. You can copy off me all you want. I was miserable this quarter. Too many proximity breaks."

Kasim gives me a pained smile. "Honestly, Auben, I kind of enjoyed the break."

My gut sinks. "What?"

"My test scores are better. I've finally started making friends. Don't get me wrong, I love being your twin, and your proximity makes me whole. But sometimes, it's nice to be just me. You know?"

It's impossible to get mad at Kasim with him so close, but it doesn't stop me from feeling like I've been kicked in the teeth. Getting through this quarter was hard enough. I can't imagine enduring this sort of strain for the rest of my life. I've seen the distance that's crept between Mother and Aunt Cisse, and their love-hate relationship that's a lot more of the latter. Bickering. Sideways compliments. The kind of guilt trips where you need to hire a porter to carry all the baggage. They're tethered to each other, and even though they try to keep it from the kids, we see the contempt through their plastered smiles.

"Sure. Yeah, I know what you mean," I say, putting on a fake smile of my own, then I notice Ruda's still chatting up the mystic. He hands her a pair of compact wooden dolls wearing dark blue-and-red cikis with gold twine and cowry shells as accents. I swallow. I'm not afraid of versa wu like Kasim is, but proximity hitches make me go cold all over.

"Earth, water, wind, spirit," the mystic intones, voice throaty and almost lyrical. "Bind each doll by the essence of its human mate, and a proximity break shall never be your fate."

"How much?" Ruda says, eyes wide and greedy. She turns the dolls over, and back again.

"You don't want to mess with that," I say. "Proximity is not something to play with. We just saw what can happen if you snap off." I groan. I sound so much like Kasim.

"Relax, they're just for show. It's not like I'm going to use them."

"Seventy djang," the mystic demands.

"Forty," Ruda counters.

"Seventy djang," the mystic repeats.

"Forty is all I've got," Ruda says. She pulls a short stack of blue-and-silver bills from her pack and offers them. "How much for one?"

"The hitches must *never* be separated." For some reason, the mystic locks his pale haunting eyes with mine as he says this. Like I'd be caught dead with those wicked things. I've been through enough temporary proximity breaks with Kasim that I can't even fathom risking a permanent break. All that pain, all that longing.

The mystic plucks the dolls from Ruda's grip, and shoves them back into the blackness of his cloak. I breathe a sigh of relief, and it takes all my might not to lean into Kasim's shoulder to calm my anxiety. His words still bite at me, but I try to ignore them. Twins grow up and apart all the time. Maybe I thought our bond was different. Our proximity binds us tighter than most twins our age. Despite the physical limitations, it was something I was always proud of.

Now, I'm not so sure.

My eyes flick to the depths of the mystic's cloak. If Kasim wants space, I can give him space. All the space he wants. Plus, if I can impress Ruda in the process, all the better. I look at her, so sad and pitiful. I'd be rude to let her leave disappointed and unsatisfied. I'd promised her the full comfy experience, after all.

I grit my teeth, jump out of the rickshaw, snatch her bills, and approach the mystic.

They're just dolls . . .

. . . just pieces of carved wood . . .

. . . nothing to be afraid of.

The whisper crawls across my collarbone, then slips down to my navel and beyond.

I wouldn't be so sure about that . . .

"What about obi powder?" I ask, my heart in my throat, and my mind trying to chase out the doubt. The voices.

"I have my own loose incense," Ruda grates at me. "Certified organic."

"Trust me—you want some of this. Just wait until you smell it."

The mystic is eager to make the deal, and opens his cloak. I see the wu dolls tucked in there, right near his body. He hands me the jar, takes my money. I smile as I twist off the lid. Breathing it is supposed to ward off demons and sickness. I inhale, too deeply. The scent is earthy—sharp and cloying. My nostrils sting, my lungs tickle, and I sneeze. Hard. Obi powder goes everywhere, and soon we're all hacking and coughing, bumping and colliding with one another, trying to get out of the incense cloud. I'd be laughing at the comedy of it all right now if it didn't feel like my lungs had caught fire.

Finally, Ruda and I make our way to the rickshaw, and settle into our seats. I've got tears in my eyes, phlegm in my throat. My sinuses are raging.

"Let's go," Ruda says to the cabbie, and he pedals out of the alley, fast enough to whip my head back.

"Well that was a waste," Kasim says to me. I know what he's thinking. Forty djang could have bought us food for the whole month.

"I'm sure her daddy's pockets are plenty deep," I snap back at him. If I didn't know better, I could have sworn I'd caught something like envy in his eyes.

I slip my hand into my own deep pocket, and shiver as I touch the wu dolls I'd pinched in the commotion. My eyes slit at Kasim. I wonder what he would think of me if I told him about the voices, and how the queasiness in my stomach has been getting harder to ignore. It hurts that I can't share everything with him like I used to, but his holier-than-thou attitude lately rubs me in all the wrong ways. It's like he thinks the balance of vice and virtue is no more real than wu. Like I should be responsible for my own actions and not blame my lechery/vainglory/envy/duplicity/doubt and least of all my temper that's dragged him into trouble as much as his grace has bailed me out of it.

Like any of this is fair.

No one I know has six vices like I do. Even those with five vices are few and far between. Nkosazana is one of half a dozen at our school. All of the other lesser twins have four vices. All of the other lesser twins have at least a sliver of hope that one day they'll stack their shoes at the edge of the comfy wall, and say goodbye to comfy life forever. But me and my scars, we'll be lucky if we can land a job pedaling a rickshaw after I finish school, while Kasim will diligently work his way around the wall until he's on the other side of it. He'll establish his new life—a modestly affluent home, a virtuous wife, polite children who never bicker or pick their noses or forget which silver spoon to use when supping on water flower stew. I'll be out of sight, out of mind, separated by a thick wall of brick, but just close enough not to bother him with the hassle of proximity headaches . . .

Anger brews as I think about the future and quickly turns into resentment. If he wants to live his life his way, fine. I'll show him the vice I'm capable of, even under the burden of his proximity. I go to pull the wu dolls out, and I don't know which I'm more excited about—impressing Ruda or disappointing Kasim—but before I can do so, the cabbie slams the brakes.

I look up to see that reckless carriage again, pulled by a pair of dehorned oryx approaching us head on, cutting off our exit in the narrow alley. Our cabbie rings a bell and shouts, but the coach doesn't stop. I seize up, readying myself for a fight, but as they draw nearer, I recognize the passengers all too well.

Kasim and I roll our eyes, then get out to greet our cousins, younger by a year—physically at least. Emotionally, they're a couple of spoiled toddlers. Chimwe and Chiso are tall pillars of muscle, the both of them, filling out their designer ciki jackets—a mesmerizing pattern of silver and lightning blue, each drawn together with a peach-colored silk sash. Shorn hair dyed rust red, skin the same copper brown. Looking at them, you'd have a hard time guessing which is the fem kigen and which is the andy. Chimwe is the feminized male, I think, and Chiso the masculinized female, but they've both got the same sparse chin stubble, and the same slight bulges that hint at breasts. Mother claims they swapped so much genetic soup in utero that they're practically identical. In any case, they annoy me equally, so maybe that's true.

"Brothers Mtuze. I thought I smelled something a bit off," Chimwe says, smiling wide with those big straight white teeth that had taken half their dad's salary to get that way.

"Likely it's your top lip," I say. "Or perhaps it's dinner's leftovers, caught between those oryx teeth of yours."

Chimwe's teeth disappear behind pouty lips, and ey looks at Chiso for reassurance. Chiso eyes my bare chest. "Is Aunt Daia so burnt-out now that she's resorted to letting you run around the comfy half-naked? I'm sure we can have one of the house servants put together some hand-me-downs for you. Think Mama still has those matching jumpers from when we were in primary? They might fit."

"I'm sure," Chimwe says. "The ones with the little blue elephant stitched on the bib?" They laugh their deep, throaty laughs, and punch one another in the chest, double-fisted. "Hey, Kasim, you always were particularly fond of elephants, weren't you?"

Kasim, ever the easy target, smiles with the grace we all expect. "You're referring to the time you pressed my face into elephant dung when we spent the narrow season at the animal preserve."

"The way I recall it, you tripped and fell," Chimwe says.

"The way you recall it is a lie," Kasim says.

"You're calling my sib a liar?" Chiso grates.

"Yeah, you calling me a liar?" Chimwe echoes.

"I don't have to call you anything. It's written right there on your arm." Kasim nods at Chimwe's arm. Ey has five vices, too, but we'd never connected over it. Not like Nkosazana and I had.

Chimwe flexes eir biceps and laughs. "Anyway, we're in the presence of fairer company. Why don't you introduce us to your ladies?"

"They've seen a hundred mangy dogs this afternoon. I doubt they'll be impressed by meeting two more." Kasim says this, one of his sideways insults, one of his belligerent truths. He'd never dare call someone out of their name directly, but he marches right up to that line, and then spits upon it. It's one of the things I love most about him.

"Cute, cousin." Chiso steps forward. "I've missed that about the comfy. Seeing all those bitch mongrels walking around, teats dragging along the ground. Always in heat. Poked so many times, she has no idea of who her pups' father is." Chiso pauses, barely long enough to insinuate that ey is segueing to a different topic. "And I've been meaning to ask, how is Auntie Daia doing these days, anyway?"

And there it is. Ey's calling Mother a promiscuous bitch, and us little fatherless bastards.

Don't let him get away with talking about Mother like that . . .

Temper tightens my gut so hard, my vision goes misty.

Kasim lays a hand on my shoulder, and my rage immediately ebbs into something manageable. He steps between my cousins and me, for the sake of all of us. "She's doing great," Kasim says. "Thanks for asking."

The cabbie rings the bell again. I look back, and Nkosazana is standing up in the rickshaw, hands on her hips.

"Should I call the sanitation department?" she says. "Because it sounds like you guys are talking a lot of shit. I don't want any of it landing on me, if you know what I mean."

The tension bends, but doesn't break.

"We're leaving now," Kasim calls back to Nkosazana, but his gaze remains set upon Chiso. "I wish I could say it was good to see you two," he says to our cousins, so much earnestness in his voice.

"Umph, the grace on this one," Chiso says. "It's almost no fun. Even with a mouth full of elephant shit, he pretends everything is right as spice." And then ey flicks Kasim right in his teeth.

Kasim's smile stays genuine, and I swear his skin takes on a golden hue, like he's glowing from within. He will not be pressured. His temper will not flare. He is the coal that refuses to become diamond, the sand that refuses to become glass. I, however, do not have an ounce of grace within me.

"Touch my brother again and lose your fingers," I snarl, even before the whisper has a chance to goad me. I may love or hate him depending on the time of day, and even though we never see eye to eye, blood is thicker than virtue, thicker than vice. I would die for Kasim. I would kill for him, too.

Good boy.

Both Chiso and Chimwe back up, like they've been spooked. Behind the fog of my temper, I wonder if they see something aglow within me, too.

I hate holding Nkosazana's compact while she primps. And compact is a misnomer. It's a big-ass mirror. A portable vanity, is more like it.

"You're sure your mom won't be home until later?" Nkosazana asks as she tousles her hair, combing her fingers through the roots as she flips her luxurious store-bought mane from side to side.

"We'll be lucky if she comes home at all," I say. "Relax, we've got the place to ourselves."

Nkosazana bats her lashes, then dusts her cheeks with powder, relines her eyes with smoky gray kohl, and sets another layer of shimmery wax upon her lips. Enticing contours form before my eyes, but they fail to stir me like they once did. Once you know a magician's secret, the veil of awe lifts, and you can never go back.

Unless you find yourself another magician with a new trick.

My eyes flick across our cramped living room to Ruda, who's frowning at the contents of her glass of tinibru, probably wondering if this chalky mix of mashed yam, fermented star apples, and pungent spices could possibly taste as awful as it smells. I'm eager to get her alone so I can impress her with the bulging treasure I've got for her in my pants.

Those little wu dollies, of course.

When I'd poured their tinibru, I'd spiked hers and Nkosazana's with the versa wu. Nkosazana took hers well, with a little coaxing and a pretty straw. But the wu won't work unless they both drink up. Then their vices will reverse, and suddenly Ruda will have to tend to the flames of a new hotness erupting in her pants. Flames I will gladly help her to extinguish.

"Maybe we can move this party to the bedroom?" Nkosazana says, tugging my eyes back to her. As she talks, I see the perfect facade, superimposed on the imperfect reality beneath. The narrowness of her beauty bores me, although bedding twins on the same night would stoke my vainglory quite nicely.

I nod my head. "I'd love to."

I take her by the hand, and wink at Kasim as we slip away into our room with giggles. He rolls his eyes, and I catch a twinge of envy again. Envy of what? I wonder. But the look has disappeared from his face already, and he's back to sipping his tinibru in that annoying way he does, pinky finger out, like he's too sophisticated to let the reek get to him.

One thing Kasim and I do share is our obsession with cleanliness. Not once has our mother had to tell us to clean up our room. Kasim's need is driven by grace, and a need for his surroundings to reflect the calm of his mind. I see the bedroom as an intimate extension of self, an outward expression of ego. Beyond that, our tastes in decor are the opposite, but we coexist well.

That said, his comment about being his own person, needing his own space, still stings though. I don't know, maybe deep down I thought we'd be the kind of twins who shared a room as bachelors. Him on the top bunk, me on the bottom, chatting about how awful our bosses were, about the new dive in the city bowl that served *the* best chutney over braised beef, about the girls that came into and out of our lives and how no love could come close to touching what he and I shared.

Nkosazana runs her finger along the chair rail that divides our halves of the room. I'd gone hungry for a month, and had sold my subsidized meal card at pennies on the djang to save up for the most luxurious golden-velvet wallpaper that lines the bottom half of the room. Kasim painted the upper half a crisp sky blue. The warm wood trim of our windows and doors ties everything together, though apparently I'd never noticed that I'd hung so many mirrors. Eleven? Really? In any case, we might not have much, but it's a place we can be proud of.

"So this is where the magic happens each morning? Where Auben Mtuze yawns and stretches and decides he's going to be the most handsome man on campus."

"Every day, up at the crack of dawn." I'd meant to say ass crack, the same way I always do, but the word had somehow skipped right over my tongue. "Two hundred pushups, three laps along the inside of the comfy wall, then I sneak through the gym's service entrance for a good steam shower to open the pores . . ." I stop myself before I get into my daily preening rituals. I've already shared too much. I like to keep my tricks close to my chest.

"Really? You always say you wake up looking this good." She grins and lays a hand on my thigh, then leans in close for a kiss. I oblige. The fog of lechery stirs. I wait for it to fill me from toes to ears, pushing out all other thoughts in my head except those needed by a doting lover, but the fog doesn't thicken, just swirls loosely, never rising above my shins. I grit my teeth and concentrate with all my might. My knees prickle, my thighs. It's slow coming, but I'm getting there, and just when I manage to get the fog to rise to where I need it the most, a knock comes at the door.

"Auben," Kasim says through the door. "Ruda says she's bored and wants to go."

"Well then act like a person and entertain her," I say through gritted teeth, trying to maintain my concentration.

It's never been this difficult. Lechery has always been my go-to vice. Definitely my favorite.

"Entertain her with what?" Kasim asks.

"Talk to her, you dolt."

"About?"

"I don't know. Flowers or deep-fried desserts or ancient princesses from Nri. Keep changing subjects until something interests her."

"Maybe I can talk to her about ant colonies?" Kasim whispers. "They have queens."

"No ants, no spiders, no crickets, no roaches." Even my temper struggles to ignite, but the effort is enough to cause my fog to shrivel up and retreat down to my ankles. "Forty fatty fritters," I mumble under my breath.

"What?" Nkosazana says.

"Nothing. Just something Kasim says when he's frustrated." Instead of dropping a couple of f-bombs like I would.

"Even with all the grief you give him, you really love him, don't you? Back there, with your cousins, you surprised me. You put your neck out for him."

"I didn't do anything special. He's my brother. You'd do the same for Ruda."

"I don't know. I mean, sure I'd speak out, but nothing that would risk messing up this face." Nkosazana smiles her flawless smile, and eases in for another kiss.

I wince. Suddenly her saliva in my mouth tastes of soured milk. I try not to think about it, and make another attempt to get the fogs stirring, but she and Ruda literally share the same blood. Maybe the in utero crossover didn't run as deeply between them like it does between Kasim and me, but still, that's no excuse. I tug back.

"What's wrong?" she asks, cheeks flushed.

"What you said really bothers me." I bite my tongue. My head spins. I'm pretty sure I'd meant to say "Nothing." Eyes narrow. Auben Mtuze does not say "forty fatty fritters." He doesn't think eleven mirrors is excessive, and he definitely doesn't have any sort of issue with getting it up. "You slipped us versa wu, didn't you? Me and Kasim?"

"Just a little bit in your tinibru. It will wear off soon. I have to know. Before we go any further, I want you to tell me that you love me."

Oh, the little she-devil. Bested at my own game. I hold the truth between my teeth. I don't love her. I never have. Never will. She is just another accessory, one that looks good on my arm, and kisses even better. As soon as I open my mouth, the evening will be over. The truth will have her bolting out of the apartment, with Ruda tagging along behind. I can't lie, but maybe I can channel my inner Kasim, and slip her a sideways truth.

"Honestly, Nkosazana, if you walked out that door right now, I'd be devastated." I smack my lips. I never thought the truth could taste so bitter.

She smiles at this, but I can already tell my answer isn't sufficient. "That's so sweet. But I want to hear the actual words. Ruda says I'm a fool to have fallen for you, and that I can't trust a word that slips off your forked tongue. But I know deep down, beneath the duplicity, you have real, true feelings for me."

"I'm not going to lie. I couldn't if I wanted to," I say, my mouth moving carefully around each syllable. Maybe I can still pull this off. But I have to make it believable. "Love is such a strong word, one I'm not ready to use. But I do know that all my heart will be in Nri this narrow season, aching for the smile of a certain rich, wonderful, amazing girl from Greater Bezile."

"You forgot beautiful," Nkosazana says, bobbing her penciled-on brows.

"I did," I say, thinking of Ruda. Natural beauty. I don't know how I've managed to go so long without seeing it. "You know, with this little plan of yours, I'm chaste now?"

"Only for the next thirty minutes or so." Her hand rubs over my doll-stuffed pocket. "Oh! Or maybe sooner."

I smile to myself, a little pang of vainglory tickling at my ego. Yes, even under the magic of versa wu, I am this good. "Don't get excited yet," I say to Nkosazana. "Those are just the wu dolls I stole to impress your sister—" I clap my hands over my mouth seconds too late.

I cringe and cover my soft bits, waiting for her to enrage. Nkosazana is always keeping tallies—if I stared a second too long at a cute girl passing us in the hall, or if I talked too enthusiastically about how the lunch lady must like me since she'd piled an extra helping of mopane worms and onions on my tray (even though it was mostly onions), I could expect a knee to the groin or a punch in the chest. But neither of those things come. "I'm highly disappointed in you, Auben," she says instead. Her eyes widen. "Why can't I get angry at you?" Wider. "You slipped us versa wu, also? No, no, no. This is all in our heads . . . it has to be."

But if it's not, that means both Nkosazana and I are chaste. Which means that . . .

Nkosazana and I take a panicked look at each other and then rush to the bedroom door. Neither of us can open it fast enough. There they are, on the couch, half-naked. Kasim on top. More slobber migrating between their lips than I've ever seen in my life. Ruda's fingers rub over the chimeral stripes on Kasim's back—the dark brown of my skin embedded into the light brown of his. It is the only thing I have ever envied about him. They are regal, better even than mine, and I think quite highly of mine. And now Ruda is stroking them with such tenderness, when she should be stroking me. I catch a hint of her breasts peeking from beneath the press of Kasim's chest.

Finally, he comes up for a breath and looks me dead in the eyes. "I figured out a way to entertain her," he says, my lecherous smile on his lips. It does not last long, however, because the very next second, the sound of metal on metal comes from the front door.

"Mother's home," Kasim and I say simultaneously, with equal terror.

This isn't the first time Mother's come home early to catch me up to no good. We assume our roles. I rush to the door to stall Mother, while Kasim herds the girls back into our room and down the fire escape. I've never seen them move so fast. In our frantic state, I almost forget that I am no longer armed with my lies. I smile wide as Mother steps into our home. I kiss her on the cheek, right as I hear the bedroom door shut.

"Mother, you're home early," I say carefully. I can't mess up like I did with Nkosazana.

Mother kicks off her boots, sets her work bag next to her slender and stately striped ebony writing desk by the living room window, then plucks diminutive yellow ribbons from her mussed hair and discards them into a glass jar that sits upon the window sill.

"Where's your shirt?" Mother says, taking a scant moment to look up at me as she glides gracefully to the kitchen
as if she hadn't been on her feet for the past ten hours. She
stokes the coke coals in our cast iron stove, and the front
grill alights with a devilish, red-orange grin. Then she tosses
her hot comb onto a burner. "I won't have you running
around all narrow season looking like I can't afford to have
you properly clothed. And what's with all the glasses? How
many times must I tell you boys not to dirty up a cup every
time you're thirsty? I get paid to clean up after filthy slug-
gards all day, and you can bet your ass I'm not going to come
home and do it for free."

"Yes, Mother," I say, gathering up the glasses and rinsing them out in the sink. Our kitchen is small, and we stand
shoulder to shoulder. She smells of orange blossoms and
harsh cleaning chemicals, a scent I always long for, though it
tickles my nose and stings my eyes in the most horrid way.

"Where is that brother of yours anyway?"

The truth shall set you free . . .

"He's . . ." in the bedroom, helping a couple of girls out
of the apartment so that you won't be angry and kick us out.
Yes, we'd be free, but we'd be homeless, too. ". . . tidying up
a big mess in the bedroom," I say with a sigh.

But Mother's already lost interest. She's beyond agitated,
opening and slamming the cabinets, cussing under her breath
as she looks for something. "I can't believe she's doing this
to me. Again. Like I can afford to take time off from work!
With two hours' notice! If I end up losing my job over this,
she'll be paying our rent until I find something else, because
there's no way we're moving in with them. No way!"

"Aunt Cisse again?" I dare.

"Of course it's that inconsiderate sister of mine! Who else would it be? Your uncle's traveling to important meetings all through the first week of the narrow season, so she wants us all to come up tonight to celebrate. One of her big impressive dinners. Two full-time cooks, and she has the nerve to ask me to bring a dish! Go put on some clothes. Something nice."

I don't waste time getting out of that room. Kasim's alone now, sitting on the top bunk. I close the door behind me and lock it. Outside the still-open window, the girls' rickshaw pulls away from our tenement block, and with it, all hopes of starting the narrow season with a little warmth. "Everything okay in here?" I ask, scrambling up onto the top bunk and sitting next to him.

"Not really. Everything okay out there?"

"Not really. Do you want to talk about it?"

"I've never lied to you, Auben. And I don't want to start now." From the tone in Kasim's voice, I can tell his temper is running hot, and if it's anything like mine, I don't want to cross him.

"And I don't want to mess things up any more by telling the truth," I say. We both laugh at this. "But I am sorry for being such a horrible brother."

"You're not horrible," Kasim says too fast. "Shit. So much for never lying to you. Okay, you're horrible, but horrible in the best possible way." He lays an arm over my shoulder, tugs me close, like I am his and he is glad to have me. I study him, the way his eyes beam off into a future of limitless possibilities, the comfort in his crooked smile, every imperfection masterfully placed—a reflection of the flaws of humankind. He is the magnificent one. Always has been. I've just been too cocky to see it.

I hang my head, humbled to say the least. "Thanks, Kasim. I wish I could say I'd try harder . . ." But we both know that'd only last for as long as it takes the versa wu to wear off.

"I'm ready to put an end to this awful day."

"Oh, yeah, about that. Mother says we're going up to Greater Bezile tonight."

"Aunt Cisse's place?"

"Yep. She's pretty pissed about it, so I'm sure it'll be a lovely evening all around."

Kasim shivers, like a cool breeze has caught him by surprise. Or perhaps the sudden touch of a silken scarf across his skin. He leaps down, feet padding softly against the floor like he's immune to gravity. He slings shirt after shirt out of our closet, until he holds up just the right one—deep red shweshwe print, gaudy rhinestones lining the collar and along either side of the button-down front, stiff black lace ruffling the bottom.

"That one's mine," I say, wishing I hadn't when I see something wicked flash behind his eyes. Panic crowds my throat. I've had my whole life to learn to tame my vices. I've seen how bad Kasim was at wielding my lechery. I can only imagine what he'd do with the brunt of my temper at his fingertips.

"I'm borrowing it for the evening. Don't want to bloody up one of mine." He flexes his hand, then balls it into a tight fist. "Hurry and get dressed. I've got an appointment with Chiso I don't want to miss."

ENVY

K asim, Mother, and I are in the rickshaw, not even close to turning the comfy wall, when the versa wu wears off. In that exact instant, Kasim looks down in horror at his flamboyant ensemble, then back up at me. "I feel ridiculous in this thing," he mumbles.

"Well, you look ridiculous," I add, being helpful.

"Why did you let me wear this?" He holds out his arms, gaudy cuffs slightly too long, and he's absolutely swimming in my tribal print pants. "I thought we looked out for one another."

There was nothing stopping whatever was behind those eyes, but I don't tell Kasim about how badly he'd spooked me. I want to forget all about it myself. "Maybe if you hadn't spent a half hour primping in the mirror, we could have gotten there in time for you to slug Chiso in the jaw."

"Boys!" Mother says, not bothering to lift her eyes from the posh magazine she's fallen into, probably lifted from the dustbin of one of her clients. "None of that talk. I want you to behave tonight. No tiffs with your cousins. Let's all act like we love each other."

"Yes, ma'am," we both drone.

Kasim touches the crisp, tight curls atop his head. He'd emptied half my jar of pomade onto that petite fro of his. The edges of his hairline are sharp enough to cut glass, his jaw as smooth as a baby's bottom. I've never seen him so uncomfortable in his own skin.

The funny thing is, he actually looks great. He just doesn't have vanity in him to realize it.

The rickshaw's cabbie starts to strain as we make the ascent to Greater Bezile. He cusses, and then punches the pedals until he gains momentum. My eyes widen as the grounds come into view. We've been up here to visit the cousins dozens upon dozens of times, but the vista never fails to amaze me. Entrenched in the flats of the comfy, it's easy to forget that we live in what has got to be the most beautiful place on Earth. Up here, the cloud-blanketed ridge of Grace Mountain is unobstructed by the cram of tenement buildings. The mountain's arc embraces the city—exactly like a comfy wall—except what lies behind it are a few fishing settlements and then the rest is unspoiled nature as far as the eye can see.

The homes here are made of steel, and glass pane or glass brick tinted every shade of blue, paying tribute to the beauty of the ocean vista beyond. Narrow season decorations adorn the streets and houses: tea candle flames dancing in every window, oversized vice-catchers hand-strung by children hanging from tree branches, and ornate, demon-faced chimney pots puffing cinnamon-scented smoke up into the air. The narrow season is the season to be heeded, but I've always found comfort in the sights and the scents and the spectacle of it all.

Aunt Cisse's house finally comes into view. Mother's proximity is back as well, easy to tell because she stops swearing so much under her breath. Their house sprawls, boasting bold angles, a luxuriously curved roof, and brightly colored windows in every conceivable shape, like the architect had detonated a bin of children's play blocks to send shrapnel through those pristine, white walls.

It's hard not to be envious, though I'd never want to live in a home as gaudy as this, and I especially wouldn't trade all the sand in the world for the horrid neighbors they've got. But it's so freeing to be able to stand outside and breathe—to look up at the stars and delight and wonder and wish without worry over being mugged or mauled or hustled. Starlight fills Kasim's eyes as well, and even Mother looks up from the pages of her magazine to enjoy the splendor of the night sky. The pages go slack, and a pamphlet falls out, inked with images of overlapping circles and gears and strange writing. Rashtrakutan lettering, I realize, based on my experiences ordering mutton saag and freshly baked naan from the menus of the Rashtra street carts roaming our comfy. But great food wasn't their only import to Mzansi, and I am pretty sure I am looking at the other thing they are known for smuggling into our country.

Machinations.

I'd seen a machination once, in the Greater Bezile Bazaar, an upscale world market that meets right on the other side of our comfy wall once a month. I'd dragged Kasim out there to look at hookahs—well, that's not what I told him, of course—but we were there, in a tent belonging to an Ottoman couple, when the raid happened. Kasim was busy marveling at the weave of a luxurious carpet, and I was pretending to browse calligraphy sets while trying to figure out how to stuff an entire hookah into my jacket. The shop owners had a falcon that perched up high in the corner of the tent, watching me with those fiery eyes. It reminded me of one of those Ottoman firebird pilots we'd learned about in history class, gliding into the sails of enemy ships and setting them ablaze. That falcon looked like it wanted to drive me away, sink its talons in my neck to teach me a lesson, but there was no way I was about to be intimidated by a bird. I was just about to make my move when the patter of foot soldiers' boots broke through the singsong vendor calls of the market. Everyone outside went silent. I dared to peek out from the tent, and not ten feet away, the Rashtrakutan vendor next door was swarming with officers. They ransacked the place, spilling crates of betel nuts, knocking over bottles of sesame oil. Delicate muslins were strewn about, some of them whipping off into the wind like kites.

Moments later, they were hauling out crates upon crates. They looked like the ones displayed out front, piled high with dried betel nuts, but then one of the soldiers banged a crate's corner. Wood splintered, and out came crawling a bug the size of my fist, something like a scarab, but it glittered gold all over and was inset with small rubies and sapphires. It hit the ground, skittered toward the carpets Kasim had been browsing, and slipped into the stack.

Kasim looked at me. I shook my head vehemently, but dared not utter a word. I didn't want to draw attention. But

Kasim has a fascination with bugs, and he slipped his hand inside, pulling the machination out. Tiny gears whirled and twirled, making wings spin and legs twitch in a stutter step. It was small. Harmless. Cute, even. Nothing like those war machines the Rashtrakutans had used all those centuries ago to expand their empire into Northern Bharat and the countries beyond. Kasim petted the bug between its clockwork wings, then smiled at me. About two seconds later, he was broadsided by a foot soldier. He nearly got carted away for possession of a machination, but my tongue is slick, and I'd convinced the soldier that we were just a couple of kids in the wrong place at the wrong time—which, oddly for me, happened to be fairly close to the truth.

A shiver rips me from my memory. The gears on that bug machination looked a lot like the diagram on that pamphlet, though Mother would never risk getting caught with such contraband. I go to pick it up, but Mother snatches it from me, rolls it up, and stuffs it in her purse.

"What—" I start to ask, but Mother's intense stare shuts me down. She discards her magazine on the seat next to her. Arms crossed, legs crossed—an impenetrable fortress of attitude.

Aunt Cisse is upon us before the rickshaw slows, arms spread wide, wearing a precariously balanced cheetah-print turban with matching floor-length cape whipping behind her, like she's a winged monstrosity. Mother says I favor her, but I don't see it. I do see the way Aunt Cisse struggles to be graceful, every move calculated, trying to emulate what comes so easily to our mother. Mother pays and thanks the cabbie. She is aglow in her vibrant yellow-orange dress, like she's sunlight peeking through the clouds. Beaded fringe sways with her each step, all the way down to her ankles. Pure grace. Her mouth on the other hand . . . well, it's graceful when the situation calls for it.

"Well, you have some nerve, you inconsiderate bitch," Mother snaps at Aunt Cisse.

This, apparently, is not one of those situations.

"I had plans for the evening."

Aunt Cisse opens her purse and tips the cabbie before he pulls away. His eyes light up, and he offers her a hearty "Thank you, ma'am!"

Mother's eyes ease into slivers. "I paid him already. More than fairly."

"It's the narrow season!" Aunt Cisse announces, twirling as if she's the belle in a theatrical production. "Smell the fine bush in the air. Taking a few hours off to celebrate won't hurt anything. You work hard. You deserve it."

I nudge Kasim when I see a gray frock of tangles through the glass panes of the house. My heart skips with excitement. Uncle Pabio has come out of his basement. He's not our actual uncle, but the twin of Chimwe and Chiso's father, though we claim him just the same. At least I do. Kasim is a bit indifferent, but he comes willingly when I tug at his elbow. Even Uncle Pabio's antics are better than listening to catty bickering. Drifting apart is one thing, but I hope that Kasim and I never become like Mother and Aunt Cisse.

"Uncle Pabio! Uncle Pabio!" I yell as I run into the kitchen. He's bent over, head shoved all the way into the icebox. When he stands, his scraggly mustache is white with mafi guzzled straight out of the carton. He smiles.

"Auben! Kasim! Good to see the both of you!" He tousles

my hair, and though he mentions both of us by name, his eyes only speak to me.

"How is your children's book coming along?" I ask.

"Fine! It's finished, in fact. Would you like to see it?"

"You know I would!" I clasp my hands together as Uncle Pabio leads us down the stairs and into his basement apartment. It's cold and clammy, dark and dingy, smelling of insanity and washing detergent. Uncle Pabio's work area is in shambles—half-stretched canvases, papers, colored pens, inks, and quills all strewn about. He hands me his creation, written and illustrated by himself. I take it carefully, like it's aglow with the brilliance bound inside. *Obio the Happy Octopus* reads the title.

Kasim looks over my shoulder. Even he cannot resist the draw of this guaranteed disaster. We have an ongoing bet on which will be worse, the story or the illustrations.

I turn to the first page and read aloud. "'Obio the happy octopus lived in the sea.'" A simple start. The illustrations are fabulous, as always. Color patterns are bold and mesmerizing. Linework crisp and evocative. I squint at the picture of the octopus. "Are those mouth herpes?" I ask.

"Yes!" Uncle Pabio says with a grin. "Do they look realistic? Because I was going to go with genital herpes, but I wasn't sure how to draw an octopus penis. I tried adding a human-looking one, but then it looked like the octopus had nine legs, and I thought that would be confusing to kids." Uncle Pabio blinks his drowsy eyes and scratches at his crotch.

"That was probably a wise decision," I say, then whisper to Kasim, "I've got dibs on illustrations this time."

Kasim shakes his head. "I might as well pay out now."

"'One day, Obio the happy octopus got fired from his job for being sexually inappropriate at work, and was forced to go to his greedy brother, Jeboah, for help.'" Our uncle's name is Yeboah. It is pretty much impossible not to read anything into this. "'Jeboah said that he was tired of paying for Obio's shit-headed mistakes, and opened his big maw and swallowed Obio whole.'"

Kasim grimaces at the page, and nudges me in the ribs. He might have a chance of winning this one after all.

"'Obio the happy octopus was content to live in his brother's bowels, subsisting off the scraps that entered. But one day, Jeboah met a lazy shrew named Casse, and swallowed her whole, too. She lived there in the bowels with Obio, took all of the good scraps and constantly berated him. One fine day, she gnawed her way out of the bowels and swam around Jeboah's innards until she found his scrotum and filled herself with his seed. She birthed a man heifer and a girlie bull, each so foul-tongued that they spat prickly cactus every time they talked. They were particularly cruel to Obio the happy octopus, even though he tried to be a good uncle to them and didn't tattle when they got drunk off their asses on tinibru in his basement. Finally, Obio the happy octopus decided he was fed up with their shit, and skewered himself with cactus quills until he bled out, and flowed down into one of his brother's anal polyps where he rested, undisturbed, for eternity. Happy.

"'The End.'"

"Anal polyp for the win!" Kasim whispers to me, then says out loud, "I have to say, Uncle Pabio, I can tell you really worked hard on this. These illustrations aren't half bad." I catch the sideways truth in his words: they're not half good either.

"You did an amazing job with this," I say. "Hands down, my favorite of all your stories. Better than any story ever written!" Oh, how he beams at my bold lie. I get warm fuzzies all over. Of all of the glitz and glamour Chimwe and Chiso were born into, I envy them most for having an uncle like Pabio.

"This one only took me three years," he boasts. "The story flowed from me, like I sat down and opened a vein."

I hand the book back to Uncle Pabio.

"No, I want you to keep it. I have more copies."

"At least let me pay you for your hard work," I say. "I insist. How much are you selling them for?"

"Eighty-eight djang," Uncle Pabio says. "But for my favorite nephew, I can do forty."

I jingle the sparse change in my pocket. "How about seventy-five cents."

"Sold!" Uncle Pabio says.

"Sign it, please? I can't wait to add it to my collection." This will be the third of his books I own. There's also *Rhonnie Rhino and his Red Razor Blade,* which resulted in all the sharp objects being taken out of the basement for several years, and *The Dopey Little Puppy,* in which Uncle Pabio had gotten high for "research" on his book about a little street dog who accidentally ingests bad mushrooms and then goes on to have a very trippy adventure that involves porcupine whores of all four sexes, public defecation, and a whole lot of scrotum licking. There is something to say about the diligence that goes into illustrations drawn by a man who spends four years hopped up on hallucinogens. Very detailed work.

Very detailed.

Uncle Pabio scribbles his infamous signature on the cover, dates it, then raises a brow to Kasim. "How about you, can I interest you in a copy?"

Kasim's mouth opens and closes futilely. There's no bending his way out of this lie. "Dinner must be ready by now," he says. "I'll go check."

Uncle Pabio's shoulders slump like he's deflating. I hang an arm over them. It's my job to pump him back up, and not because I'm obligated by loose family ties. I love him. He's been something like a father figure to me. At least as close to one as I'm ever going to get.

"Kasim didn't mean anything by that, Uncle Pabio. He's not into the arts like we are. He wouldn't know brilliance if it bit him in the ass."

"Ah, it's okay. I'm used to it. Yeboah and Cisse didn't have many kind things to say about it either. I'm just glad you enjoyed it so. You make this whole process worthwhile." He gives my forehead a hard kiss, then sighs. "All this excitement has caused me to work up an appetite. Let's go see what's for dinner."

Uncle Pabio grabs his jacket, the old gray one with the black-and-white cheetah-print lapel. It smells of sanjo smoke and is patched over with green corduroy on the left elbow and maroon suede on the right. The satin lining is a bright cherry red, and I spent many a childhood afternoon with it tied around my neck, pretending to be royalty, pestering Kasim about how one day we would escape comfy life and live as kings.

Uncle Pabio looks back when I don't get up to follow.

"Auben?" he asks. "Come on. I know how you and Kasim don't like to be sep—" He pauses, looks me over head to toe, drinking me in with his crazed eyes. "Oh." His shoulders slump again.

Is the heartbreak on my face that obvious? "Can we talk down here? Just for a bit?"

"Sure, sure," he says, and all of a sudden, the roles are reversed and he's comforting me. "What's going on between you two? Is it a girl?"

"No, nothing like that . . ." I say. Well, *something* like that. I can't get the images of Ruda and Kasim kissing out of my mind. I'm practically crawling out of my skin with envy. But what's wrong with Kasim and me goes way deeper. "I think we're drifting apart."

Uncle Pabio shakes his head emphatically, like a street dog trying to rid itself of a wet coat. "No, no, no. Not you and Kasim. It's impossible." His eyes spark, and he pulls a switchblade from his jacket pocket.

I stiffen. I love my uncle with all my heart, but Rhonnie Rhino flashbacks pummel my thoughts, filling me with unease. *So much red ink.* "Uncle Pabio, does Aunt Cisse know about that knife?"

"I could fill a book with what Aunt Cisse doesn't know," he grumbles as he walks over to a bin in the corner of the basement. He opens it and pulls out a long thin yam. With a sweep of his arm, he clears a spot on his worktable, sending papers, quills, and inkwells scattering across the floor. Then Uncle Pabio slams the yam down onto his workspace. "Here," he says. "How many yams do I have?"

"One," I say.

I barely get the word out, when he stabs the knife into its center, then twists until it pops in two. "Now how many yams do I have?"

"Two halves," I say with the certainty of a remedial math prodigy.

"Wrong!" he shouts. "That's what your eyes tell you. It's what your mind tells you. It's what the Rashtra would have you think. They could talk all day about the scientific reasons behind the prevalence of twinning in our lands, pointing to our diets or anomalies within our genes. But they don't twin like we do, so they can never know what their eyes and minds do not tell them. Two halves are *not* the same as one whole."

Slowly, he slides the yam pieces back together. I'm filled with an odd sort of tension as the pieces move closer and closer, then a strange calm overwhelms me as I watch their orange flesh touch. I suck in a small, involuntary gasp of air.

His eyes drill into mine, and he nods. "You felt that, didn't you?"

The calmness soon fades, and a proximity ache hits me right in the gut. Sharp and precise, like I've been stabbed with a knife. Uncle Pabio puts his hand on my shoulder, and with the other, he smudges a tear from the corner of his eye. Judging from the pain Uncle Pabio and I are trying to hide from each other, maybe the bonds in his blood run as strongly as the ones in mine. The way he and Uncle Yeboah fight, I would never have guessed.

"I'm starving," Uncle Pabio says with a pat to his belly. "Aren't you?"

I nod, knowing exactly what he means. Starving for proximity.

When we arrive in the dining room, I gag on the scent of cinnamon, two tea candles in each window, twenty windows opened to the ocean vista. This room could swallow our meager apartment up whole, but somehow it seems cramped with all these egos stuffed into it. Aunt Cisse orchestrates Mother and the servants as they set the table and bring steaming dishes of lamb stew and pig trotters, pumpkin fritters, and loaves upon loaves of beer bread. Uncle Yeboah's aged mother and her twin have arrived as well, both of them dressed in lofty felted wigs and their finest netted shawls, both last fashionable around the time they'd witnessed Uncle Yeboah and Uncle Pabio take Discernment some forty years ago. They give Chimwe and Chiso slobbery kisses and handfuls of gold coins, gushing over how they've never seen a firmer finemister or a prissier laddie, kigen slurs common back in their day. Chimwe and Chiso flush as Aunt Cisse corrects the bigoted old hags with more socially acceptable terms, but her efforts, as usual, go ignored.

Uncle Yeboah always says that it's impossible to change what's ground into someone's moral fiber, probably the one thing he and I see eye to eye on. People can't help the vices they're dealt. We play the hand as best we can, is all. That said, both Great-aunts Anenih and Mensah seem to enjoy getting a pass for lack of tact. It's one of the perks of living as long as they have. They're a mess, the both of them, but they're the nicest bigots you'll ever meet. I press my shoulder against Kasim's, feeling whole again, as the great-aunts shower us with handfuls of gold coins, too, calling us handsome little bastards.

Aunt Anenih pinches my cheeks. "Look at you, little Kassir. Oh, this dark chocolate skin, I could lick it off you right now. And Arwin," she says, turning to Kasim. "You're a nice hunk of warm caramel. You must drive all those comfy girls crazy, leaving a trail of little bastards behind you, no?"

"No," Kasim says. He scowls and discards his fistful of newfound wealth onto the table.

I scoop up his coins. They clatter and jangle against the ones already in my pocket as I try my damnedest not to feel like a charity case. I turn and catch snickers from Chimwe and Chiso, wearing different cikis of course, with bold diamond-print skirts down to their calves—untouched by the taint of the comfy. "Cousins," I greet them with a childish stick of my tongue. "Good to see you, as always." I can't believe I'm even related to these jerks.

"Glad you've made it up here for a taste of the good life," Chimwe says.

"Don't boast," Chiso says. "Comfy life is perfectly fine. Sure they might not have the freshest foods, or the servants at their beck, or the best schools, or the spending money. But they've got their pride." Chiso scrunches eir nose. "And sewer rats the size of a small dog."

"Children!" booms Uncle Yeboah's voice. The room goes quiet as he makes his grand entrance through the high arches leading from the living quarters. Even the servants stop dead in their tracks. Uncle Yeboah looks something fierce in his turtleneck ciki jacket—the elasticized python skin dyed indigo, cobalt blue, and gold. I'd been drawn to something similar at Liddie Ameache's, and had barely turned the price tag over when the sales attendant shooed me away. Sixteen hundred djang. Uncle Yeboah steeples his fingers and brings them to his chin, looking pleased with himself as he approaches the table. His rigid brow eases. "We're here to celebrate the narrow season, not pick each other apart. Butts in chairs, now."

Chiso and Chimwe straighten up and snap to, finding their seats at one end of the sprawling mahogany table. The great-aunts have already seated themselves at the opposite end. Kasim raises a brow, silently asking if we should seat ourselves next to the bigots or the assholes.

"Bigots, definitely," I say, louder than I should. I get a stern look from Uncle Yeboah. He seems like he's bent on taking a reed to my rear, but grits his teeth at me instead. He's so full of himself, and unabashedly so. Mind as narrow as this damned season. He almost makes me thankful that we'd grown up fatherless.

Almost.

"The narrow season is upon us," Uncle Yeboah says, taking his seat at the head of the table. "Ol' Icy Blue's eyes are keen this time of year, so it is important that family stays close and twins stay closer, tempering each other's vices and virtues alike, lest that great frigid devil set whispers of evil into your mind."

"Hush, Yeboah," Aunt Cisse says, finally settling into her seat across the table from her husband. Mother takes her seat as well, and the servants buzz away. "Speaking that old devil's name is as good as inviting him into our home! Why don't you do something useful with your mouth, and say the bless—" Aunt Cisse's eyes go wide and watery. "Good Grace, what is that smell?" Her eyes track to Uncle Pabio, and her lips purse. "Pabio. I could have sworn I threw that filthy jacket out."

Uncle Pabio looks up from doodling upon one of Aunt Cisse's cloth napkins and gives her an innocent shrug. Aunt

Cisse scowls at Uncle Pabio, like he's taken a shit in one of her immaculate flowerbeds, then she turns to Chiso sitting to her right. "Chisomo! Don't cross your legs. You'll crease your ciki," Aunt Cisse says, flicking Chiso in the forehead. "And Chimwemwe, you little mongrel," she growls, with a vise grip on Chimwe's earlobe. "If you slouch like this at the sanctuary next Tiodoti, I swear I'll disown you!"

A caterwaul of whining ensues from my cousins. These two are so coddled, they couldn't punch their way through a wet paper bag without complaining to their mother about it first. Aunt Cisse tunes them out as she checks that her turban is perfectly balanced upon her head, then tucks the edges just so. She looks the picture of a patron donor, until she rises from her seat, leans forward, and slams her hands down onto the table with all the grace of a mouthy fishwife slinging cod at the docks. "For the love of Grace, Yeboah, can you say the blessing so we can eat already?"

Uncle Pabio whispers into my ear. "I know this is a nice holiday from school for you, but me, I'm counting the days until they ship those whiny brats back to Gabadamosi Prep." He pats the flask tucked into his breast pocket, then eyes my glass. "I'm not sure there's enough spirits in the world to make this dinner go by any faster, but we can try, right?"

I smirk, sneaking my glass to Uncle Pabio as Uncle Yeboah closes his eyes and leads us in prayer. His voice is full of the charisma and charm that landed him his cushy job. "And let vainglory be tempered by humility. Let the outwardly wants of envy be tempered by the inward introspection of conscience. Let the duplicitous tongue be moved to truth and absolute sincerity, and the lecherous heart be guided into chastity. Replace doubt with due diligence, and let greed beget charity. And above all, let Grace shine down upon us all, banishing temper into the icy depths of the shadowlands. Can I get a 'Hallowed Hands'?"

"Hallowed Hands!" the great-aunts shout, their hands thrust high in the air. Chimwe and Chiso follow along, albeit with significantly less enthusiasm. Aunt Cisse nods appropriately.

"And what are we going to do with these Hallowed Hands?" Uncle Yeboah asks.

"Praise Grace! Praise Grace! Praise Grace!" the great-aunts sing, fingers a-wiggle.

Uncle Pabio slips me his napkin, strewn with illustrations in a soupy purple ink depicting Uncle Yeboah holding a huge flaming sanjo cig hand-wrapped with paper from the Holy Scrolls. A plume of smoke drifts over into Chimwe's and Chiso's open skulls. Uncle Pabio is as talented at weaving conspiracies as he is at drawing indecent picture books. He thinks Grace and Icy Blue are just clever inventions for branding morality, and that all schools, especially religious schools, and *especially* Gabadamosi, were designed to separate us from nature, from our tribal communities and cultures, and from critical thinking so that we could wholly tolerate this unjust and unnatural system instituted by a bunch of wealthy Nri immigrants fearful of growing Nationalism and the Mzansi elite who pulled their strings.

His words, not mine.

Sometimes I want to believe him, to think he knows something that the rest of us don't, but then he'll start ranting about "death traders" skimming around the ocean in their sailing ships, and their "skin the color of sun-bleached bone" and how centuries ago, they "almost nearly could have brought an end to the Nri empire spread out along the west coast of the continent *and* the Ottoman empire on the east, and all the lands like ours caught in between" and it all just gets to be a bit much to swallow.

The praises continue, then start to peter out. Just when I think we're through the thick of it, just when I think I can't stand staring at all this food going cold in front of my eyes for a second longer, Uncle Yeboah says, "And you, Kasim. What are you going to do with those Hallowed Hands?"

Mother's posture goes stiff. "Yeboah, you know my stance on religioning," she warns. "We will respect your observances, as long as you don't infringe on our right to respectfully decline involvement."

"You said it. It's *your* stance. The boys are old enough to decide for themselves now." Yeboah clasps his large and intimidating hands. "Well, boy?"

"I . . ." Kasim glances at Mother.

"Look here, boy," Uncle Yeboah demands, pointing at his own eyes. "Your mother doesn't know whether or not Grace dwells within your heart. What say you?"

"Hallowed Hands do not move me," Kasim says. "My virtues and vices are my own to act upon."

Oh, the humility on this one. Kasim could have said "vice" in the singular. But all the humility in the world couldn't stop his words from causing the great-aunts to go into one of their conniptions. They pray loudly and inappropriately for his "little bastard soul."

"And you, Auben. Tell us all how Grace touches you." You could hear a pin drop as all eyes drill into me. It is not often I have the chance to be seen as the greater twin. I could easily spin a deft lie, say how Grace guides me in my every step, is above me while I sleep, beside me as I sup, to school and from school, always there, always watching. Our narrow season dinner would go on to be its normal absolute disaster. I could lie, but right now, all I can think about is how family obligation is a huge pain in the ass, and a huge waste of time, and I'm done pretending. So for once, I tell the truth.

"There's no such thing as Grace," I say. My heart goes rigid, worried that I've gone too far, and at the same time, that I haven't yet gone far enough. I turn to Uncle Pabio for strength and reassurance, but he's already lost in another napkin drawing. Still, he nods, almost imperceptibly, and it's enough to fuel me. "Or Icy Blue. They're figments to stop people from treating each other like crap, but apparently no one in this family has gotten that memo."

"Daia!" Uncle Yeboah booms. "You'd better control that boy of yours before he says something he'll regret!"

Mother smiles, and I nearly melt from the pride I see stretched across her lips. "You asked him a question," she says. "He answered."

"You've raised these boys and denied them Grace. I should never have—"

"They're my boys and I've raised them as I've seen fit. You'll have no hand in their upbringing, hallowed or not."

"My corset!" Great-aunt Mensah says with a wheeze. "Help me out of my corset!" Usually the great-aunts do not begin to disrobe until after the rum desserts have been served, but Great-aunt Mensah seems overly anxious to free herself from the miracle of a contraption that keeps her body from wiggling like the jellied currants waiting so deliciously for me to take a taste. "Please! I can't breathe."

Yes, she's all kinds of awful, but the woman needs help,

so I take Aunt Mensah's arm as her breathing becomes strained, guiding her to a comfortable position on the floor.

"Hail an ambulance!" I order into the brimming chaos. I keep my wits about me, willing myself to remember what we'd learned about this in the homeomedics class I'd just had a test over. Check the airway, I say to myself. No obstructions in her throat. Her pulse has gone thin. I tune out the screaming behind me and place my ear to her mouth, listening for signs of breath. There is none. I focus on her pale pruned lips, ready to press mine against them.

She doesn't deserve your help, the whisper tells me. I ignore it.

She tastes of hard liquor and hard candies. I blow once, twice, her chest rising beneath me. I go to blow once more, but something other than my breath slips coolly over my lips, falls into Aunt Mensah's mouth. Her skin ashens, her lips go blue and cold as ice.

Uncle Yeboah tries to restrain his hysterical mother, but she claws her way to her fallen twin and begins beating me with her coin-filled purse. "You filthy, filthy devilish bastard! You've killed her!"

"I'm trying to save her!" I say, but then I take a jawful of designer leather, and I back off. She's gone now, anyhow, lying there, eyes staring off into nothingness. I've never seen death before. So serene, so surreal, so detached from everything. The body once full of life, now an empty husk, and already the world has started to move past it.

Kasim catches my hand out of nowhere. "You tried," he says, then bends down to close her eyes. Upon his touch, they flick wide open. Her cheeks flush, and she takes a loud, ragged breath. Kasim stumbles backward, looks at me. I've never seen so much disquiet in his eyes.

"I hear they do that sometimes," I say to him, later that night, after the ambulance has come and gone, hauling dear Aunt Mensah's body to the morgue. "The recently deceased. One last involuntary spasm before they kick it permanently."

"Yeah, that's probably what happened," Kasim says with a grimace, and I can tell he doesn't believe his words any more than I do.

Great-aunt Anenih goes three weeks later, and after the funerals are all said and done, we are in the peak of the narrow season. The chill seeps through the windows of our bedroom, beneath our covers, into our bones. Even Mother's resorted to putting tea candles on the sills at night, though she claims it is purely for decoration, and in no way tied to diverting Icy Blue's breath from our home.

It pains me to admit it, but I envy Chimwe and Chiso. I envy their privilege. They already have their entire lives written out for them. They're a year younger than us, and look how much they've accomplished—going to Gabadamosi Preparatory, the premier boarding school in the Cape, and probably the country. Pedigree drives admissions there, and I've heard even the offspring of royal families from Nri have been turned down. Our cousins will spend their last year and a half there, then will have Primways University knocking at their doors to bring them on, then six or eight years later, Chimwe and Chiso will be co–vice presidents at their father's firm, hauling in more djang per day than Mother makes in a year.

It's not fair. Mother works damned hard. It hurts to never see her, and when we do see her, it hurts to watch her struggle to raise us all on her own. Two jobs every day so that we can afford to pay tuition at our crappy secular school. There are a dozen religious city schools that we could attend for cheap or free, but she'll have none of that.

Still, it eats at me. I'd heard Mother mumbling a couple months back, when we brought home letters about next quarter's tuition increase. "Grace will provide," Aunt Cisse had said, when Mother had made the mistake of complaining about it over our weekly family dinner. Mom had gritted her teeth so hard, she'd cracked one of her incisors, but what if Aunt Cisse was right? She and her family were certainly well provided for.

Mother had done her best to keep religion out of our home, but Uncle Yeboah had spoken the truth. I'm old enough to decide for myself now. Besides, if I open my heart to Grace, what's the worst that could happen? If I feel His Hallowed Hands moving me, I can convince Mother to let me do my religioning in one of the free public schools where I can learn to silence the voices bidding me toward vice. And if I go out into the world and find that Grace doesn't exist, well . . . there are other ways for a vice-ridden teen to scrape up a few djang. Either way, this is something I have to figure out on my own.

Only thing is, I've never done anything on my own.

I slip out of bed, the cold driving deeper into me, so deep, I worry I'll never be able to rid myself of it. I dig in the closet until I find the wu dolls I'd stolen for Ruda. My heart twists, but I try to ignore that failed stage of my life and concentrate on bringing upon a newer, better one.

The little black-faced dolls stare at me with their heavy-lidded eyes and their lips puckered in a kiss. The wood is rough, and much of the artist's knifework can be seen and appreciated. Dangling from each of their necks is a strand of white beads with a tiny crystal virtue token attached—a plus sign to signify the greater twin, and a minus sign to signify the lesser.

"Earth, water, air, and spirit," I mumble under my breath, careful not to disturb Kasim's sleep. *Body essences,* the wu mystic had mentioned. I pluck a piece of my hair for Earth and twine it around the lesser doll's head. I spit upon the doll's face for water, breathe into its chest, and then wave it around, hoping that will satisfy my spirit.

Now the hard part. Collecting the essences from Kasim without waking him. Lately, he's warmed to the idea of sporting his fro in a pomade-crusted helmet, so plucking a hair from his head is out of the question. I trim a toenail instead, his body cringing as I pull up the blankets to do so. For a moment, I entertain a thought of the fun it would be to dip his fingers in warm water to make him pee himself. Wu is all about collecting bodily fluids, it seems. Blood, tears, urine, semen. I take the easy route instead, and carefully set about harvesting a touch of drool from his gaping, snoring mouth.

A soft dab, perfect. I go to place the spittle on the greater doll's face, but Kasim's hand catches mine.

"What are you doing?" he says, eyes still closed.

"Going to Grace Mountain," I say, tugging free and applying the water element to the doll. I wave the thing in front of Kasim's face, certain his impending verbal attack will satisfy both air and spirit.

But Kasim just yawns. "Go back to bed. It's way too early for your foolishness."

"I'm serious. I need to go. Now."

"You're not dragging me along on another one of your

midnight escapades. It's freezing outside. And that climb isn't safe, even during the day."

"Well, it's not something you need to concern yourself with, because you're not going."

"Huh?" Kasim rubs the sleep from his eyes, sits up, then raises a brow. "Those are wu dolls, aren't they?"

"Yup." I bring them close to one another. The lesser doll jumps out of my hand, and locks face-to-face with the greater doll. I tug once, and they do not come apart easily.

"I'm not even going to ask how you got them."

"Good. You'll save me a lie." I throw on a coat and shove the dolls deep into a side pocket.

"You can't use them. They're not safe. If proximity breaks—"

"You're the one who wanted a break, remember? You should be glad I won't be dragging you down for a change. Besides. It'll work. If I feel even the slightest tug, I'll rush back here before either of us can snap off."

"So your Plan B is to run down a near-vertical mountain face in the dark with your vices unchecked. Great. And here I was concerned that you hadn't thought this through." Kasim rolls his eyes and crosses his arms. "What could possibly be so important that you'd willingly put the both of us at risk? Seriously, we just saw what happened to Great-aunt Anenih. Humility did her in. She was literally nothing without Aunt Mensah. She refused to eat, not feeling worthy of even the most basic sustenance. She wouldn't accept help or condolences. She felt like nothing, Auben. And that's how you're making me feel right now."

"Get over yourself. They were eighty years old."

"I'm not going to let you do this," Kasim says in a near

shout. He jumps down from the bed in that weightless way that he does, feet padding on the floor.

I feel a shift in the pit of my stomach, right where the queasiness lives. "I'm going."

"Then you leave me no choice. I'm telling Mom."

"Hit him." The words slip out of my mouth in a chilled rasp. They are not my words, but I know who they belong to. Temper whips through me, so fast and so hard, not even proximity can quell it. My fist connects with Kasim's jaw. He backs up, holding the gash on his lip, shock deeply etched into his face.

I may walk a tough walk, but I've never hit anyone, not like that. Not hard enough to draw blood. Now I've done it to the person I love most. It takes everything within me to break his pained stare and not apologize a million times over. But I have to do this. I *need* to do this. Grace may be the only thing that can drive out the evil afflicting me. I have to find Him.

I timidly step out into the night. Every twenty steps I reassess, waiting for the queasiness to snap back into place, and waiting for panic and whatever foulness follows in its wake. I reach the edge of our comfy, where the wall of brick becomes one of stacked shoes. The stench of weather-worn leather marks the turn, symbols of those who'd managed to leave the comfy life for a better one beyond. Aunt Cisse's shoes are in there somewhere, same as Uncle Yeboah's. Same as Kasim's will be someday, and maybe even mine. Nkosa-zana once asked why no one ever took the shoes, seeing as there were so many people in the comfy who were in need. It was almost over for us right then, the shock warring with my temper at the stupidity of her question. At the time, though, I was coming off a lecherous high, and so I was able to restrain my anger and told her that taking them would be like stealing our collective dream, erasing the tales of those who trekked through vice and poverty, who persevered and made it out despite the odds. Seeing all those shoes stacked up high, just as formidable as the brick wall next to them, gives us a sliver of hope that we can do the same.

I make the turn, sure that this is as far as Kasim and I have ever been apart all seventeen and a half years of our lives. It seems like the proximity hitch is working. I don't feel a strain in my gut, and all my vices are holding steady. No flaring temper or lecherous desires or crippling doubts. I pat my pocket and start to run, overcome by my secondary concern of getting back home and into bed before Mother wakes up to go to her morning job.

I breathe the cold air in through my nose, out through chapped lips, keeping a steady rhythm in my run, and trying to look as inconspicuous as I can out here in the middle of the night. Hardly anyone is up this late, and those who are probably want to remain inconspicuous themselves. Either way, I encounter no one and finally reach the base of Grace Mountain, where the city's cobbles ease into scrubland sprawling with all varieties of scratchy-leaved fine bush and invasive pines tough enough to withstand the harshness of the Cape's southeasterly winds. I take a rest, bent over, hands on knees, looking at the trek I have before me. My eyes are quick to adjust to the light of the half moon. The stars themselves seem brighter and more abundant.

The slope is manageable for the first few hundred paces, then becomes more treacherous as vegetation gives way to sheer rock face. I take my time, planting my feet, double-checking my holds before continuing. I hear the scurrying of small wild things taking cover beneath clumps of foliage, like I'm some kind of predator and not a mere boy risking his life to find Grace. I consider what I might say to convince the animals that I am no threat, but then I hear the choppy bark of a caracal. We get them in the comfy sometimes. Sickening what those claws can do to an unsuspecting street dog—a few hundred centuries' worth of pent-up feline frustration being released until all that's left are bloodied tufts of fur.

I hasten my climb.

The summit welcomes me nearly two hours later. It's dizzying up here, staring down into the bowl of the city spread out before me—a dozen comfy walls like little moon crescents encircling canopies of trees and tarred roofs, the choppy sea battering the shipping boats in the harbor, clouds bunching in the distance threatening to drop bucketfuls of cold rain. I fall to the ground in a heap and look up to the heavens, taking it all in. But I didn't come here for the view, as spectacular as it is.

"Is anyone out there?" I yell. "Are you watching?" My voice echoes hollow against the night. "If you're real, give me a sign."

Then I wait. When you're desperate to find meaning in something, you can find meaning in almost everything. A stiff wind blows past me. A star shoots across the sky. An owl hoots in the distance. "Whooo? Whooo?"

"You! Grace. I'm on your mountain. I've met you half-way. Now it's your move."

But nothing happens. Nothing other than ordinary nature. Maybe this is the sign I needed. A sign that there's no such thing as Grace. I flush warm against the cold of the narrow season, feeling foolish for even attempting such a thing.

What did I expect? For Grace to show up in the flesh before me, welcoming me into His arms? Whispering into my ear that I am really a good boy, despite the inadequacies that stir my heart?

I peel myself from the ground, then shout to the heavens, "There! You've had your chance, and you missed it!"

A chilled wind blows past me again, though this time it feels more . . . significant. I brace myself against it, turn my back and squint my eyes. Something white litters the ground. I kneel down. Thousands and thousands of delicate white flowers have pushed through the ground where I'd lain, forming my silhouette. I stand up, take several steps back, rub my eyes. Yes, it's there—the stature of a young man, perhaps a little thinner and shorter than me, but there I am.

"Okay," I say, eyes wide. "This is a sign I can work with."

Mother is wrong. Grace is *real*. In the morning, I'll press her to enroll me in a city school, where I can start my religioning by whittling down my vices into tiny nubs that no longer exert power over me, and honing my sole virtue, charity, until it's the sharpest tool in my arsenal. And I, myself, will be a tool in those Hallowed Hands.

The close growl of a caracal snaps me from my reverie. It's a lean beast, all muscle and attitude—tawny coat, those oversized ears and their furry tufts that look like the horns of some greater beast. The false smile on its face draws back, and pointed teeth become my primary concern. I take a stance, and pull a knife from my pocket. I didn't come here completely vulnerable. It's a smallish caracal, just an oversized housecat, really. I can take it.

Then I watch as the ground goes to ice under its paws, spreads toward me. My concern turns to terror as the man-shaped field of flowers frosts over and wilts away into rotten mush. The ice is at my toes when I look back up to the caracal, but another beast stands there instead. Same feline form, but now my size, with fierce and cunning eyes, whiskers like blades, fur a ragged steel blue, row upon row of nightmarish fangs . . . and what once were questionably ears are definitely horns. There's no such thing as demons, I try to tell myself, but then it gnashes its fangs at me, and those definitely aren't figments. It bolts into the air, claws aimed in my direction. I don't waste time, only taking a second to get traction on the ice before scurrying to dry ground. I run, fast as I can, in a near free fall, pushed by gravity and fear. Down the mountain I go. Sharp rock jabs at me, slices up my coat, my hands, the soles of my shoes—and all I care about is the thing behind me. The growl isn't getting any farther away, but it doesn't seem any closer either.

A sudden cramp stabs my stomach, so hard I retch right there on the mountainside. Seconds later, my sick slicks over with ice. My hand darts to my coat pocket, ripped down to the seam. One of the wu dolls has fallen out. One remains. I look frantically for the missing doll. Under the moonlight, I catch the gleam of golden twine fifteen feet back up the mountain. Fifteen feet beyond that, the demon pads down toward me. Without Kasim here to temper me, my vices bubble up, and boil over. Thoughts cram to the front of my brain, toxic thoughts I can normally rein back. *I can slay this demon,* my vainglory whips me. My temper flares out of control. *How dare this beast threaten me?* I brandish my knife and go for the kill.

The demon laughs in my face as it pounces. Its breath chills the air between us, and I go rigid with cold, frozen over, unable to move. It's not just any demon, is it? It's *the* demon. The one Uncle Yeboah is always warning us about. Maybe I should have listened a little harder.

Claws extend like sickled blades, slash at me. They catch me in the throat. I go down hard. I struggle against the frozen confines of my own body as Icy Blue pries open the flesh at my neck, but nothing is as severe as the pain of missing Kasim. The demon digs deeper, his gnashing, ravenous maw disappearing into my throat, then his head, his body, and finally his seductive feline tail with a final whip.

He fills me, every bit of me, a cruel, cold pleasure that makes me shiver all over. He whispers sweet nothings as the stars spin high above, promising me that this is only the beginning.

Perhaps unsurprisingly, I recognize the voice.

I wake up in a cold sweat, grasping at my throat. I'm in my room, in my bed, safe as safe gets. I heave a ragged sigh, and try unsuccessfully to shake off my nightmare. I slip out of bed bleary-eyed and pad into the bathroom.

As I empty my bladder, a fog of white mist manifests on the surface of the water, tendrils slowly rising out of the bowl. I stagger backward, rush to the mirror, drag my finger along the fresh scar at my throat. I try to cry out to Mother, to Kasim, but my voice rasps. In my reflection, my index finger moves to my lips and a sustained shush prickles my skin all over.

I stumble back to bed, take a seat, shivering as tears turn to miniature icicles on my lashes.

"Glad you made it back safely," Kasim says from above.

"I told Mother everything. She'll have it out on your hide when she gets home from work." The top bunk creaks as Kasim rolls over. White petals flutter down past my face, graze my cheek, give me hope.

Uncle Pabio once spent a few months in a whackhouse, so I've heard the horror stories. If I go around telling people that I've been possessed by Icy Blue, I'll end up in one in no time flat, and not the kind that drugged-out thespians frequent when their careers fly north. I have to be subtler than that. I need answers, but Mother has kept all traces of religioning materials (propaganda as she calls it) out of our house. No Holy Scrolls, no defting sticks, no virtue charms.

There has to be a way to drive that wicked devil from me, but I have no idea where to start. Visit a sanctuary? Talk to a Man of Virtues? A counselor at a city school? The scrolls are ancient, and I can't be the first one in all this time to be accurst by evil in this manner. There must be precedent, some sort of incantation or prayer that can cure me . . .

My planning stops dead in its tracks.

Can Icy Blue hear my thoughts?

My throat constricts painfully against scar tissue.

I am your thoughts.

Well, shit.

The proximity dolls sit atop the dresser, bound together once more, but I'm not going that route again. My stomach is still sore from our proximity break. With Kasim and me caught so far apart, with so violent an onset, there hadn't even been time to call upon my vices and virtue to soothe the pain. Besides, I have a feeling that walking into a sanctuary, alone, mind full of lecherous and deceitful thoughts, would only invite more trouble. Whatever my plans, they will have to involve Kasim from the get-go.

"Are you awake?" I say up to Kasim, my voice still a knotty rasp. I know the answer. The lack of snoring is evident.

"Yes."

"Are you mad at me?"

The silence stirs. "Yes . . ."

"Well, I'm sorry I hit you. I was out of line. Maybe out of my mind."

"It's okay, I forgive you. Though it was nice to see you show a little diligence. Even if it was misdirected."

My guilt eases, and I pop out from under my covers and scramble up onto the top bunk to join Kasim under his, like we used to do when we were kids, back when vices and virtues were imaginary concepts that neither of us really understood. The bed used to hold the both of us fine, but now we're pressed close out of necessity. Yes, I realize I'm more man than boy these days, but I can't deny, absolute proximity soothes me like nothing else in this world.

Kasim smiles at me, split lip not all that bad after all. "Did you find what you were looking for?" His breath smells faintly of sick. I wonder if he'd felt the break as hard as I had. I wonder how close we'd come to it being permanent.

I nod. "And something I wasn't looking for."

"That's the way it always is, isn't it?"

"Hands to Grace, I hope not." My breath goes cold. Kasim recoils.

"You sound like Uncle Yeboah," Kasim laughs, then his finger traces along my neck at the ridge of my scar. "When'd you get this?" he says.

I shrug. A lie can't come between us. There's no room when we're like this. "Grace."

"Huh?" he asks.

"That's what I was looking for. Up on the mountain."

"And you found Him?"

"In a way. I think He's been with me all along."

"Now you really sound like Uncle Yeboah."

"He's full of shit. But what if he's right about religion and Mother is wrong? We're old enough to figure this out for ourselves." We're nearly nose to nose now, and I have Kasim's undivided attention. "I want to go visit a sanctuary. And I want you to come with me."

"Oh, Auben," Kasim says. He puts his hand to my forehead.

"I'm not sick," I hiss. Suddenly, I feel cramped and wrong next to him. I pull away, but he holds me tight.

"I'm kidding, bro. Of course I'll come with you. It's only natural that our interests will vary, but I'll support you and you'll support me. Just as we always have—for the most part. You can leave me out of your wu doll escapades from now on, though." Kasim throws the covers off us, jumps down to the floor, and disappears into our closet.

My mind flips back to the evening we'd had the girls over. I can still taste the earthy grit of the versa wu on my tongue, the hot spice of the chicken feet we'd snacked on, the tang of the can of expired tinibru I'd sipped. But there is one taste I'd failed to partake of. One that Kasim had—his lips dutifully upon Ruda's, eager to make up for a chaste adolescence. I cringe, thinking of what would have happened if Nkosazana and I hadn't walked in on them.

"Maybe we should have taken the girls up on their offer

to join them in Nri," Kasim calls out like he can read my mind, tossing an old pair of swimming trunks my way. "Warm weather. Less drama . . . More skin." I can practically feel the lecherous arch of his eyebrows. We've had this kiss-and-tell conversation dozens of times, but I've never been on this end of it.

"Yeah, like you could get me on an airship. And besides, I thought you hated the beach," I say, tossing the trunks back. Summer seems like a bleak improbability this deep into the narrow season.

"I could make an exception," Kasim says. "For the right incentives . . ."

"Sooo . . ." The quiet stretches. We're twins. I know exactly what he wants me to ask, but I don't know if I can handle his answer. All I can think of is how it should have been *my* lips pressing upon hers. "How was she?"

"Aggressive. Sweet. Soft. Very uninhibited." Clothes hangers clang like they're being moved about in frustration. "Nice." His voice quavers. In that moment, I know that she is lost to me, and yet envy still sinks its icy grip into the marrow of my bones. Which isn't all that surprising—that's how envy works.

Kasim comes out, pant legs ending at his ankles. I laugh and he flushes. "This is odd," he says.

"So what? You shrunk your pants in the wash again. Throw on a pair of mine."

"These are your pants." He tugs the extra material at the waistline. So they are. The same ones I'd worn to narrow season dinner, in fact.

I jump down and stand next to him. For the first time

in our lives, I find myself looking up into his eyes. "Growth spurt?" I ask with a shrug.

"Four inches overnight is a pretty significant growth spurt."

"Four inches closer to Grace." I purse my lips. "And yes, I know who I sound like." I remember how Uncle Yeboah would pat our heads when we came to visit a little taller and a little smarter than we had been since the last time that we'd seen him. He'd actually seemed proud, and it's one of the few fond memories I have of him. I shake my head and slip into a pair of pants, a shirt, and a coat. "Come on, let's get going."

"I can't go out in public like this!" Kasim says. "I look like a fool."

"Fine. We'll stop at the Saintly's on the way."

"Ehhh. I was thinking maybe we could stop at Liddie Ameache. Look around a bit?"

Liddie Ameache is where I steal all my best clothes, but I know the thought of theft would never cross Kasim's mind. "You've got the money to shop at Liddie Ameache?"

Kasim reaches down into the buttoned pocket on the side of my pants and pulls back a handful of the old gold coins our late and great-aunties had given us. I frown. Half those coins belong to him, and the other half I probably owe him for busting up his lip. "Whatever," I groan. "Let's just make it quick."

He's not even close to quick.

Nine billion pairs of pants later, Kasim comes out of the dressing room, eyebrow raised. "I think these are the ones," he says, trying to catch a glimpse of how his ass looks in the infinite accordion of reflections in the store mirrors.

"Great. They look great. Let's go," I say.

"I don't know. They look good now, but what if they shrink in the wash?"

"I'll wash them. They won't shrink." We're wasting so much time. The sanctuary is going to be closed by the time Kasim finds the perfect outfit, and then I'll have to spend another night with this demon stuck in my head. I grit my teeth, biting back a growl. My own, not Icy Blue's. "I'll wash all your laundry for the rest of our lives if you buy those pants right now!"

"I think I can go an inch longer. Just in case my spurt isn't quite over."

I raise a hand to hail the dressing assistant to fetch the next length, but then Kasim digs his hands into his pockets, jiggles things around a bit.

"I think I liked the relaxed fit better. These seem tight in the crotch. And the color . . . ehhh . . ."

I throw my hands up, and storm out of the dressing room. I've been shopping with Nkosazana dozens of times, clutching her monster-sized purse in my lap while she complains about pocket lines and hemlines and panty lines, but not even that terror compares to Kasim's incessant primping and preening.

"Where are you going?" Kasim asks after me, but I can't take it any longer. I go as far as I can, right up to the slightest strain against my gut. I take a seat next to an older gentleman and heave an exasperated sigh.

"You look just about how I feel," the old man says in a loud, gruff voice. "Hate shopping?"

"I love shopping. Just not with that prima donna."

"Ha. I got ya. How much time ya done today?"

"Going on two hours! Like I didn't have things I wanted to do."

"Ha, boy. You haven't even scratched the surface. Four and a half hours for me. Now that's true love. But I don't get what's so special about finding 'the one,' anyway. A dress is a dress is a dress. Women, right? Grace willing, we'll get home before supper."

"Grace willing," I say, trying the words out in my mouth. If our sanctuary visit won't be happening for another two and a half hours, then maybe I can start my research here. With regular people. "Speaking of Grace, do you attend a sanctuary? Have you studied the Holy Scrolls? What about defting sticks, are they easy to use?"

"Whoa, whoa there, son. That's a lot of questions. Is there something you're getting at?"

"My mother raised me secular. All I know about religion I learned from schoolyard rhymes. I guess I'm sort of curious how it all works."

"Ah. The Hallowed Hands are moving your heart. That's good for a boy your age to start seeking out faith on his own. It's more real that way. I attend sanctuary three nights a week, and I've read the Holy Scrolls backward and forward, upside right, and reverse in a mirror. Grace has spoken through the defting sticks to me on many an occasion. I've seen His work."

"And the work of Icy Blue?"

The smile drops off his face. "Of course," he whispers. "But you don't want to go messing down that road."

"It's just that I've . . . got a friend I'm worried about. I think Icy Blue's got his grips on him. He's hearing voices. Whispers. His hands are doing things he doesn't intend them to do, and his thoughts are no longer all his own."

"Sounds like what your friend needs is a simple exorcism."

I perk. Maybe this sort of thing happens all the time. "Yeah. What do I . . . I mean what does he need to do?"

"All he needs is five hundred djang and a willing sanctuary, and they'll rid him of his affliction. Takes maybe an hour. Two tops, if it's a difficult case."

My shoulders slump. So not so simple. "My friend doesn't have five hundred djang."

"Well, you might catch a discount during the narrow season. Maybe four hundred fifty. That blue bugger gets up to no good this time of year, particularly."

"There's no other way?"

"I suppose you or your friend could go to a city school and study up enough to do it yourselves. Either that, or get on special with a Man of Virtues."

I raise my brow. "On special? Like some kind of apprenticeship?"

The old man laughs. "In a sort. Think more along the lines of lechery."

I clench all over. No way. I'd rather be Icy Blue's plaything. "I thought Men of Virtues were all virtues."

"No one since Grace and Icy Blue has been born with all virtues or all vices." The old man perks, smile drawing cavernous laugh lines across his face. "Speaking of vices, here's my lady now." He nods at an elderly woman followed by a dressing assistant scurrying behind her carrying four shopping bags imprinted with the Liddie Ameache logo in a fancy script. The old couple embraces, then shares an uncomfortably intimate kiss. Beyond disgusting, but I feel a pang of jealousy. It'd be nice to have what he has. I know it's wrong, but I catch myself imagining Ruda and me at that age, gray and achy all over, me falling victim to her homeopathy, her wry jokes, the scratch of her chapped lips against mine. My heart skips.

"How long have you two been married?" I ask with a wan smile.

"Married? Goodness, no." The old man leans in close to me. "Beah and I have been screwing around these past four months."

"Do you have any idea how much your voice carries?" Beah says with a wretched frown. "It's been seven months. And my name is Keita! I thought you said you were over and done with that bitch."

"I am, honey. I am. You're it. I swear, you're the one," he says, not bothering to mask the air quotes around "the one." He takes the bags from the assistant, turns back to me and winks. "Come on. Let's get home and see what pretty things my hard-earned money has bought you."

I laugh. Lechery recognizes lechery. He's right. Nobody is without vice.

"What's so funny?" Kasim asks, walking toward me with a debonair swagger. He claps his hands, then presents his pants to me in a grand fashion. White flowing linen with a drawstring tie. Quite possibly the most high-maintenance pants he could have chosen.

"Between the wrinkles and the dirt, you know you'll never be able to sit down again, right?" I say.

"But I look good, yeah?" He turns slowly and gracefully,

allowing me to take in the whole experience. He's treated himself to a new shirt as well, a white button-down that just so happens to let the striking deep brown chimeral patterns on his back show through. Humility my ass.

"You look very nice," I say.

"No lie?"

"Not a one."

Kasim smiles, like he knows that he's not worthy to wear such finery. And that he knows that I know that he doesn't think he's worthy. I don't know how he does it. On my face it comes off as vainglory, on his it's as humble as shit pie. Right now, he's probably inwardly thanking the designer for the grace of his design, the diligence of the fair-trade workers who sewed it, the conscience of the buyer who foresaw the need for such exceptional work, and the charity of the store owner that made all their jobs possible. "Thanks, Auben," he says to me. So sincere. So annoying. "Ready for the sanctuary?"

"Actually, I need to stop back home first," I say. "I need to scrounge up four hundred and fifty djang."

"For what?" he exclaims.

"You wouldn't believe me if I told you."

The majority of my clothes sit upon my bed in a pile. Even if I sold them all to the Saintly's, I'd get a hundred djang if I was lucky. I need more, but our belongings are sparse, and what we do have is so well used, nobody would want it anyway. I could get a job, but it would take me months to get that sort of money, and by then, who knows how deep Icy Blue will have sunk his claws into me.

"Hey," I say to Kasim, his nose buried deep in a Liddie Ameache catalogue. "Be my lookout."

Kasim looks up and blanches. "You're not going out to steal something, are you? Because I don't want any part of that."

"No, I'm not going out to steal something. Now will you help me or not?"

"Promise?"

"Yup," I say with a duplicitous smile. "But it's a two-man job, in one of the scariest places I've ever been. So will you help?"

"I guess." He dog-ears a page, lays the catalogue on his pillow, then jumps down. "Where are we going?"

"Mother's room."

Kasim shakes his head. "So you're 'staying in' to steal something?"

"Borrow, technically. Something she won't miss for a few months. I need something to pawn. I'll get a job and get the money to buy it back." I bid Kasim with an innocently raised brow, but he's steadily backing away. I'm losing him. Not just physically, but I can see it in his eyes. He wants nothing to do with me.

"Why are you acting like this?" he says.

"I wish I could tell you." The demon shifts beneath my skin, and I feel him laughing. "But I can't. Not yet. You have to trust me."

"Proximity hitches. Four hundred fifty djang. This sudden interest in Grace. You're planning something. Something big." Kasim blinks, shakes his head. "Some sort of pilgrimage? A holiday alone? What, are you running away to Nri?"

"I swear, this isn't about chasing after a couple of girls! This is serious."

"Couple of girls?" Kasim's face draws in on itself until it's as tight as a knot. "What do you mean by that? Tell me what you mean by that, and I want the truth."

I clench my teeth tight. There's still plenty of room for me to lie my way out of this, if I tread carefully. "I'm . . . in love with Ruda," I declare in a voice that isn't mine. I grip my throat, and my scar pulses icily against my hands.

"You're what?" Kasim says. I don't know if Icy Blue's playing his beat upon my eardrums also, but I could have sworn I'd heard temper in Kasim's voice.

I try desperately to speak, to tell him the whole truth, but nothing comes out but a constricted rasp.

"You know I like her!" Kasim yells.

"You fooled around with her on the couch. Once."

"No, I've always liked her. Ever since she first came to our school. In alchemic studies, she was so cute, so smart. Knew the answers to just about everything. I kept catching her staring at me through the scratched lenses of her goggles, and then I got caught up in watching her watch me. We had to evacuate the whole class one time when I was paying more attention to her than the brimming beakers in front of me. We're both chaste, so I never thought anything would come of it until you started dating Nkosazana. With an excuse to be around Ruda, I thought I'd work up the nerve to ask her out. And when I finally got somewhere, here you come trying to swoop her out of my arms."

I didn't see any of that. I had no idea. I try to apologize. "Well, I'm sorry you got your hopes up. And in any case, you should be thanking me and Nkosazana for dosing you guys with versa wu, or else you would have never gotten the nerve to kiss a girl." I cringe and lick the ice crystals from my lips.

"Idiot. Wu isn't real. We *saw* you guys sneaking it into our drinks. We poured it out."

"But your tongue was down her throat. You're *chaste*."

"We were kissing. That's all we were doing. I'm human. I have needs, too."

He needs to be put in his place . . .

As my hand balls itself into a fist, I hastily turn and leave before Icy Blue gets a chance to make things worse. Mother's doorknob is heavy in my grip, but the breach of confidence is a necessity now. I've got to scrape up the money for an exorcism by any means necessary. There must be something of hers that holds value. Nothing immediately jumps out, though—when you live in the comfy, the most valuable things are intangible—a family that makes sure no one goes without, a brother who has your back no matter what. Don't have that, so here I am, desperately searching for trinkets and baubles. Finally, I venture deep into her closet, find a small, dust-covered box with a lock. I make short work of it, and the wooden lid pops open. Inside, two crystal virtue charms hang upon a gold chain. I laugh at the thought of Mother wearing such a thing, though I suppose she must have been raised religious. Still, for her to hold on to such things speaks volumes. Unfortunately, the crystals are pitted and low quality—not good for warding off anything other than potential buyers, and the gold chain an insignificant sliver. Next to worthless. I push them aside and dig farther into the box. A black velvet bag seems promising. I open the drawstring and my breath catches as the contents tumble out into my palm. It's a metal sphere with that same odd script I'd seen in that pamphlet Mother had dropped nights ago. My hands shake, and my heart is aflutter. I give it a twist, and it starts to hum. Inside, I can hear the faint whirring of gears. It's some sort of machination. Priceless, and at the same time, worthless, except among the shadiest markets with sharp-tongued, steel-eyed vendors that make my demon-filled thoughts seem as scary as a caracal pup. I quickly twist it again, and it goes silent. My mind turns over and over, trying to piece together why Mother would risk possessing such contraband, when my eyes flick back to the box and catch a glimpse of perhaps the most prized treasure of all.

The Graceful Gazelle, the storybook reads on the cover in one of Uncle Pabio's ridiculously ornate fonts. The paper inside is brittle and yellowed, so I turn it delicately with a bit of slobber at the corner of my mouth. I've never seen this one before. It must be nearly as old as I am.

Gaia the Graceful Gazelle frolicked across the savanna, happy as could be. Her every movement was an enchanting dance, whether it be how she licked water from the stream, nibbled at dainty flowering shrubs, or simply pranced about.

One day, a clumsy meerkat named Mabio happened upon her and was instantly mesmerized. He was taken by her beauty and watched her in secret, so envious of the ease with which she moved. Mabio desired nothing more than to ride upon that graceful gazelle, the wind blowing through his meerkat fur. He swore that one day, he would ride her and ride her until his loins grew sore, and then some more until Gaia happily exhausted herself. He imagined it would be the most pleasurable experience—

I shut the book, wincing at the sting of vomit at the back of my throat. I flip back to the signed cover and take note of the date: the year I was born. My mother Daia is obviously the graceful gazelle. And the meerkat Mabio is obviously . . .

No.

Could he be?

Uncle Pabio?

"Kasim!" I yell at the top of my lungs. "I know who our father is!"

DUPLICITY

Crammed into Mother's closet, her best silk dresses brushing at our cheeks, Kasim and I argue over whose hands are trembling the least. He ends up winning, and is entrusted with turning the pages without damaging them. I can't believe Uncle Pabio is our father. And yet, I completely believe it. It explains why he's always doting over us. The resemblance is there, too, now that I think hard about it. And maybe that's why I've always felt some sort of deeper connection to him. But why did my mother want to keep this from us? Because he's a little bent in the head? Was she embarrassed? We keep turning pages, hoping to find out.

Our mouths hang open at the next illustration—Gaia the Graceful Gazelle, shot down, two gaping wounds in her abdomen.

"'One fine evening,'" Kasim reads, "'Mabio was watching Gaia the Graceful Gazelle's tongue lap from a bubbling brook, when out of nowhere, two bullets struck her. The woods went silent, except for the victorious cry of a hunter crouched nearby. "Hallowed Hands! I have brought down this magnificent creature with my mighty shot, and now no one shall gaze upon her gracefulness again!"'" The hunter is not named, but his likeness has been stolen hair for hair.

It is Uncle Yeboah.

Kasim and I look at each other. I shake my head, and press my fingers over twin bullet wounds inked onto the page.

"Not him," I whisper. "Anyone but him." I go numb all over.

We read silently after that. The meerkat soothes the gazelle's wounds, tries to nurse her to health, but her wounds only grow larger. Eventually, a kitten and a baby sparrow gnaw their way out of the bloody tangle of ruptured flesh. The wounds never quite heal, and the gazelle never reclaims the grace she once had. She denies the meerkat's offers to help rear the helpless creatures that had emerged from the wounds, but she does so with respect and without laughing. Mabio still dreams of riding her on occasion, but is content to be her friend.

Kasim closes the book. Puts the book back into the box. Closes the box. Puts the box back onto the closet shelf. Closes the closet door. Closes the door to Mother's room.

But we can't close our minds off to what we had read.

"It's a children's book," I say, leaning over Mother's desk to crack open the living room window and let out the stuffiness plaguing the air. I tug at my collar, breathe deeply, but it doesn't help. "It could mean nothing."

"It could mean everything."

"Well, what should we do? If Mother finds out that we know—"

"She can't find out!" Kasim snaps.

"It's not fair. Uncle Yeboah has never given us a single thing. What about last narrow season when we nearly froze because we couldn't pay for coke?" My fists ball. My lip trembles. My voice shakes so hard, I'm not sure how long I can keep it together. "Or all the dinners we've spent scrounging through the cupboards for stale bread and expired jellies? Or how we never get to see our own mother since she's busting her ass all hours to raise us on her own? He owes us, Kasim. He owes Mother." And a whole lot more than the four hundred fifty djang I need to rid myself of these voices.

"What if he doesn't even know we're his?" Kasim asks. "What if we come out with the truth and cause a rift in our whole family? We have to keep this quiet. It's going to stir up too much pain."

"You of all people want to bury the truth," I say. "That's rich."

"You shouldn't have dug it up in the first place," Kasim spits back at me. His eyes are wide and bloodshot. His nostrils flare. He's the one who's supposed to be talking me down, telling me everything will be all right. He's not, though, and there's something—*off* about it. Kasim is upset about this, but there's something else that's been weighing heavily on him. Something bigger than discovering that our father is our asshole uncle. My pain becomes secondary, and I lay a hand on his shoulder as he has done for me countless times, hoping there is some speck of grace within me to soothe his temper.

"What's wrong?" I ask him. "You're not behaving like yourself."

"You wouldn't believe me if I told you!" he shouts, shrugging me off. The front door slams a minute later. And a minute after that, the queasiness sets in.

I let the matter drop for the time being. I've gone seventeen years without a father. I can go a few more days, no problem. Since the incident with the great-aunts, we haven't exactly been welcomed back into the Mazibuko home. That's all fine and good. I'd rather confront Uncle Yeboah at his office anyway, away from the strain of family drama. But I will confront him. I need to know why he left us to fend for ourselves. He knows. Sometimes we lecherous folk pretend like we don't, but we do. Nice smile, nice eyes, thanks for the prize, and eight months later, she's at your doorstep, a bundle under each arm, claiming that if you'd just take a peek, just hold them for a few moments, you'd see how much they look like you . . . but you don't look, don't hold them, because you're not the father, and can't be because you're too young, and can't even remember the girl's name anyway . . . you know. It happens.

You can't let an asshole like that off, no consequences. You've got to fight tooth and nail to get to the truth. To get him to acknowledge his responsibilities and to support his obligations. To get him to explain how he could so easily abandon his children.

"Kasim?" I call up to the top bunk, two nights before school starts back up and this horrid month-long break comes to an end. He avoids me as much as he can during the day, but he has to sleep.

For a long while, nothing comes except the chirp of crickets, the echoing barks of street dogs in the distance, and the unquiet of my own mind.

"What?" he finally says, voice punching through the darkness.

"I hate us being like this. Why don't we take some time and talk about things tomorrow. We could go to that new Rashtra place . . . you know what I'm talking about? What's it called?" I say, feigning a slight lapse of memory.

He doesn't fall for it. "You know what it's called."

"Right . . . Bhagesh Palace. I hear they've got a red curry that's so spicy, it'll make your whole face go numb."

"That's not a selling point."

"Come on. I'm paying. It's my narrow season gift to you. Or a peace offering, or whatever. Please. I want to make things up to you."

"You want to make things up to me by taking me to a restaurant a block and a half over from Yeboah's office? How convenient for you." The missing "uncle" doesn't go unnoticed.

"Oh, yeah. He does work around there, doesn't he?"

"Yes. He does. What were you going to do, excuse yourself to the restroom and then slip out to go beat the truth out of him while I'm left to foot the bill?"

"No!" I lie, so easily. He's not buying, so I quickly bolster it with another. "I would have come back for you . . ."

The bed creaks as Kasim rolls over and settles for sleep. "You know, the best thing about holding this lie within me, Auben, is that I've gotten a whole hell of a lot better at spotting yours."

Shit. My tongue is definitely the sharpest tool in my duplicity arsenal, but it isn't my only tool. People look down on lesser twins. Maybe they claim not to these days, but looking around, you notice things. Sure there may be plenty of lesser twin teachers, but administrators, forget about it. We're store clerks, but never shop owners. Foot soldiers, but never ranking officers. They tolerate us like impish children, encouraging our aspirations, and yet firmly reminding us of our limitations. Reach, but don't reach *too* high. Even though they're far from flawless, they're always looking to chastise us for our lechery, or for our greed, or for our lies. They expect our lies. What they don't expect is the truth.

And truth in the hands of a duplicitous person is perhaps the most dangerous weapon of all.

Kasim thinks he's won, but I'm going to get him to come with me so I can give Uncle Yeboah the shakedown, and I'm going to do it without telling Kasim a single lie. Without telling *anyone* a single lie.

"Can anyone name the Seven Holy Wars in order by year?" Msr. Ademola asks the class. When ey gets no response, ey tips eir glasses down and peers about the room, eyes hungry for blood. Students keep their gazes aimed at their worn desks, at the pencil-pocked ceiling tiles, at the broken concrete schoolyard outside the windows. They look anywhere, except back into Msr. Ademola's eyes. It's only the second day of class. How can ey expect anyone to know this already?

"This is a secular school," a mousy fem kigen with a slight Nri accent says from the back of the class.

"Being secular doesn't exempt you from history——" Msr. Ademola looks down at eir class roll "——Msr. Egwu, is it?" Ey makes a hostile mark on the page. "Anyone else?"

I raise my hand, stare Msr. Ademola down. My stomach churns.

"Yes, Mr. Mtuze?" ey says directly, without referencing eir roll sheet. "Perhaps you're in need of a bathroom break already?" My reputation precedes me. So maybe, on occasion, I've left class to use the restroom, only to come back twenty minutes later reeking of sanjo smoke or worse. This is definitely going to be an uphill battle, but Msr. Ademola's reputation has preceded em as well——a bitter, hard-as-nails Gabadamosi Preparatory reject who apparently got the boot for giving poor marks to the wrong Mzansi noble. Eir default attitude is one of defensive indignation and offensive hostility.

Fortunately, I've come prepared for war.

"No, Msr. Ademola. I wish to answer the question."

"Fine. Proceed." Eir lips prune up like ey's sucked the life from a lemon.

"First, there was The Benevolent Legion War. Then The Great——" My cheeks bulge. I take a moment to gather myself, then continue. "The Great Hurt."

"Are you okay, Mr. Mtuze?"

"Fine, Msr. Ademola. I think it's something I ate." Maybe the steaming double portion of mala mogodu I had this morning——beef offal stew with pap, spinach, and a handful of raisins for sweetness. Traditional comfy food. Kasim had lapped his up, then happily went back for seconds and thirds, but it has never agreed with me. Something about the chewiness of the offal and the grittiness of the pap, the slipperiness of the cooked spinach, and the squishiness of those bloated raisins—it's like all the best parts of a sinus infection sneezed into a bowl. I'd forced down spoonful after spoonful, slicker on my tongue than all the lies I've ever told. And now my stomach churns and gurgles loud enough to draw a look of disgust from the kid in front of me. "As I was saying——" My cheeks bulge again, and this time they do not remain empty. I place my hands over my mouth.

"To the infirmary, now, Mr. Mtuze!" Msr. Ademola slings a hall pass around my neck, a big block of wood attached to a tarnished chain, then ey shoves me out the door.

At the end of the hallway, I lose my mogodu in the waste bin, and my stomach eases after a long drink of cool water. I walk high and tall, taking a detour past Principal Boro's glass-fronted office, a place I know all too well. My fingers play against the worn edges of the words HALL PASS branded into the wooden stick, just as the mark of duplicity had been branded upon me after Discernment. I stiffen once I realize that my free pass is not foolproof. What if Principal Boro asks me where I am going? I can't say to the nurse, because it would be a lie, and if I tell em I'm off to the theatrics department to learn how to orchestrate a mammoth ruse on my brother so that I can confront my deadbeat father, well . . . sometimes the easiest truth is that of avoidance.

"Lechery consumes me, and I it . . ." Ruda bellows into the auditorium filled with dark recesses and empty seats. The stone-faced theatrics teacher sits alone, front and center, clipboard and pen in hand.

Chaste Ruda moves gracefully within the confines of her lie, all the undulations we had witnessed with that holler whore come to life under the limelights. Colorful, skintight leotards reveal every curve of her body, every pucker and detail. She might as well be naked and covered in paints. I steady myself against lecherous thoughts. Kasim is in love with her, and for whatever strange reason, she's into him, and I can't come between that. Ruda continues to play out the audition with unexpected ruefulness. Damn, I feel for her. Could have sworn she'd spent the last four years on a street corner, consumed and consuming, twinless.

The teacher stands as Ruda's head drops and the scene ends. "Magnificent!" he screams, and a smile cracks through his stoic face. He stuffs his clipboard and pen under his armpit to give Ruda a brisk ovation. "We have found our Daughter Sarr!"

The four other Sarr prospects standing in line with me, also clad in near nothingness, clap politely, though they are visibly disappointed. They offer hugs to Ruda, and Ruda accepts them with such humbleness. Then she comes to me, the last in line. She looks me over, tugs at my black wig, pinches at my blaringly bright leotard.

"What are you doing here?" she asks, unable to contain her amusement.

"The sign said 'open auditions,' and I was open." I offer her a shrug and an apologetic smile. "Sorry about how our evening worked out last year."

"If I had a djang for every fourth-story apartment I had to suddenly evacuate via fire escape . . ." She rolls her eyes. "Seriously. That wasn't even the worst part of our narrow season. Not even close."

"Same here. That wasn't even the worst part of my day. Bad time in Nri?"

"Our whole family is officially banned from the beaches, so . . . yeah."

"Do please tell!"

"Nkosazana got sick right after we left your place. I offered her some feverfew to help with the chills, but she refused, and was miserable and cranky our whole trip. We got into a fight. Proximity was broken. Sea cucumbers were put where no sea cucumbers ought to go. Paramedics were called. Paramedics were bitten. Law enforcement was called. Sirens. Glass bottles. Tear gas. I got sixteen stitches." She points to a reddened scar along her jawline. "Lovely time. Highly recommended."

"Whoa."

"Seems like you have a story there yourself." She runs her finger along my neck scar, and her touch lingers a couple seconds too long.

"Oh, you know. Fight with Kasim. Broken proximity. Climbed a mountain. Attacked by a caracal that I'm pretty sure was the devil. Found out who my dad is." My words are light and airy, but their weight bears down on me hard. "Typical narrow season antics."

"Sooo typical. Almost boring, really." Ruda laughs the pain away, right along with me, but I catch a hint of hesitation in the corners of her eyes and at the turn of her lips. "So back to my original question . . . what are you doing here?"

"I want to write a play and I need your help."

Ruda perks as if we've started speaking the same language. "Please, dear sir. Step into my office . . ."

We find a quiet nook backstage among the mountains of old wooden set pieces, and sit cross-legged, facing each other. Thick velvet curtains help to dampen out the intonations of actors auditioning for other parts and the scrape of heavy stage props being moved about. I feel like I'm caught in the aftermath of a typhoon that cut through a fairy tale. Upturned houses, trees lying on their sides, donkey parts everywhere, a flattened oryx-drawn coach, man-sized mushrooms. All hand painted with the same diligent care. It's dizzying.

"So," I say, focusing my senses, leaning into my knees with my elbows. "Basically, I want to scare the shit out of Kasim. Get him so wound up and out of mind with worry that he'll do anything I say, and go anywhere I want to take him—specifically our uncle's office building. He can't get suspicious either. We'll have to incorporate it into our daily routine somehow."

"Then all the world is our stage . . ." Ruda's lips part to reveal a duplicitous smile.

"Exactly. But my budget is tight. Not a lot of money for props or actors, but I can work it off. Maybe help build sets or sew costumes or whatever."

"Not necessary. We've got tons of stuff we can borrow from the department. And I can call in a few favors from a couple fellow thespians who owe me big."

"Hmm. Well, that was easy. I thought I'd have to sell you my soul to get you to cross your little love buddy." I make an appropriately inappropriate gesture to match what had gone down on our couch during their make-out session. My eyes fall to the curve of her lips. *Aggressive,* Kasim had said. *Nice.*

"Ugh, don't remind me." She laughs cruelly, then looks up at me and catches the shock on my face. "Don't get me wrong! Kasim's a nice enough guy, but it was either listen to him talk about the endemic dung beetle species of Mzansi for another two hours, or find a way to shut him up. So I found a way to shut him up."

Ruda doesn't like Kasim? My mouth hangs agape as I mull the possibilities. Should I break things off with Nkosazana first? Or keep Ruda as my secret lover? Definitely break things off first, I think. Ruda deserves better, though if I played things right, Nkosazana could be my side piece. I clamp my jaw tight, and stiffen my brow, realizing I must look as overwhelmed as a doe-eyed fawn. My heart flutters with delight, and then drops like a stone as I realize . . . Ruda doesn't like Kasim.

He'll be crushed.

"So, you want to scare Kasim," Ruda says, her rough hands rubbing together like sandpaper. "What's the thing he's the most afraid of?"

Losing you, I think.

But I say, "Wu. He tries to hide it and pretends he doesn't believe, but that stuff makes him super nervous. Did you see how he was about to bolt when we pulled up to that mystic?"

"Brilliant. Are you familiar with Biobaku?"

"Sure. That fancy dish with the swordfish wrapped in seaweed."

Ruda shakes her head. "No, no. That's briabaka. Biobaku was a playwright several centuries ago who wrote over a hundred plays. I'm guessing you and Kasim don't get out to the theater much?"

"Not a once."

"Well, in any case, Biobaku wrote a play called *The Five Curses of Akerele.* We put on a production of it a couple years ago. It's about an ostentatious socialite—renowned for throwing lavish, gluttonous parties. He gets cursed by a wu witch, as they used to be called, and loses the ability to enjoy the finest pleasures in life, one sense at a time, until left with nothing, he gnaws off his hands and feet, and takes a donkey as a lover."

"Mmm. Bestiality. Just what I was aiming for . . ."

"It's a lot more complicated than that. Biobaku was a genius. Anyway, we'll just use the second act. After the setup, and before the downfall. The part where Akerele is driven to insanity by the wu witch's antics."

I nod. "And speaking of driving, we're going to need a coach to get us across town fast." Excessive? Maybe. Ruda seems like she's all in, though, so why not reach for the stars?

"Yeah, yeah. Mind tricks. Coach races. This is going to be so much fun," Ruda says to me. She scoots closer and begins to go into detail about the play and how it can be translated into our open-air production. We sit there through the remainder of her theatrics class. When the bell chimes, neither of us budges a muscle. Shortly after, the lights go out, all but a single dingy yellow light hanging above us like a moon. I look up into the rafters and see a set of silver-painted stars dangling from rope. It's almost romantic.

The knots in my stomach untwist, my nerves steady. It's like Kasim is here, except instead of my lechery being tempered, it presses harder. My heart knocks so loudly against my ribs, I'm sure Ruda can hear it. Maybe this is what falling in love feels like. I bite my lip, wondering if I should make my move, but my finger is already tracing over lips first claimed by my own brother. Ruda smiles, looks down bashfully.

My hand moves slowly, almost on its own, until it finds the curve of Ruda's breast, and in the dim light, her nipples pucker through the rainbow leotard. I inhale her spicy sweetness, and a chill fog rolls over my mind, through my body, numbing me to everything except the hard ache in my mouth. I move to kiss her, but her forehead blocks me, catches me right in the bridge of my nose.

"Oof," I say. I blink away the pain, and turn, suddenly fixated with detangling the long scraggly black tail jutting out from the ass-end of three-fourths of a wooden donkey. "Sorry about that. I sort of thought . . ."

"No, I'm sorry. I just have a weird thing about kissing."

I'm about to confront her, to call her on her lie. She hadn't had this "weird thing" with Kasim, but then the back of her hand grazes my chest, works its way down. My mind fogs up again, and on the next strong pump of my heart, I hear the strain of my leotards, crotch fabric suddenly pushed beyond reasonable limits.

I press Ruda down onto her back. I am not gentle. She laughs nervously, not knowing what I am capable of, and at this point, I'm not so certain what I'm capable of either. My nails scratch like claws against her tights. They break open, revealing smooth brown skin beneath. She flinches as my hand slips into the tear, nervous, eager.

Saliva pools in my mouth, sharp, acidic.

"Auben—you're drooling. All over the place." I think she's concerned, but all I can see are those lips. Full, pink, chapped.

Kiss her, the voice commands, digging harder into my mind than it ever has before.

"Auben, I'm flattered. Really." She pushes futilely against my chest. "But this was a bad idea."

"If your lips go numb, and your tongue does, too. If your breath freezes over, and a shiver runs through . . ." My cool whisper slips into her

ear and gives her gooseflesh all over, the old schoolyard rhyme rushing to the front of my mind, one I haven't heard in years.

"This isn't funny, Auben." She peers into my eyes. I do not know what she sees, but I can tell it wasn't what she was looking for.

"If your body aches with chills, but doctors don't know what to do. And if your heart stops cold, then you've been kissed by Icy Blue."

She slaps me. Hard. My mind clears, ever so briefly.

"Don't," I yell at Icy Blue. But he is back upon me in no time, riding me so hard. My muscles strain. It's impossible to deny him. Ruda screams so loud, Daughter Sarr's own hollers would pale in comparison. All I need is a couple seconds, enough to let Ruda escape. I reach for the glass shards I keep in my pocket, but I touch only the smoothness of my nylon-covered thigh. Shit. My pants are in the dressing room, along with any hope of driving these urges back into the icy depths. My lips move ever closer to Ruda's.

KISS HER.

I spy a bent nail near a pile of dust-covered props. I move my hand, inch by inch, against the strain. My fingertips touch it.

Give her what she deserves.

I clench the nail in my hand, point digging into the skin of my palm. I press hard, until I feel my flesh pierce. The fog recedes to the shadows and the blood rushes back to my head. My heart strikes my chest a million times a minute. I ease off Ruda. She looks as terrified as I am, but we both manage to pull nervous smiles from the dark pits of denial. Icy Blue laughs from within.

"You totally believed that, didn't you?" I say, holding my bloodied hand behind me, and helping her up with the other. I brace myself as the knot in my stomach returns with a vengeance, and press through it. "Oh! Look at me! I'm Icy Blue."

"That was intense, Auben. Too intense. Next time give me a heads-up first." She tugs against the gap in her nylons and laughs, but only to give the impression that she is no longer afraid of me. "We can start tomorrow if you'd like. Quick and dirty and done with." Done with me, she means.

She hadn't resisted. Not at first. She was as much into me as I was into her, but all of that is gone now. I've got a bad feeling that we're dealing with more than a simple exorcism. Icy Blue is growing stronger with my every breath, and soon he'll be capable of much worse than putting an end to an already awkward and ill-advised love quartet.

"Yeah, tomorrow would be great," I say. "The sooner, the better."

ACT TWO, SCENE ONE: AKERELE GETS CURSED BY A WU WITCH

With a wu mystic on every busy street in the comfy, the new one on the corner of Qukeza and Jeso doesn't stir suspicion. He opens his thick woven cloak to us as we near. Bottles and vials and dolls and sticks and bags of dried herbs are tucked neatly into dozens of little pockets.

"An offer of wu for you and you?" the mystic calls to us. His beard is thick and matted, his face painted with kohl markings, his eyes are wild and an unsettling blue.

"No, thanks," Kasim and I say together, as we always do.

"Tik and tuc, half off for willing hearts," the mystic's head cocks, his too-white smile inviting. "A little cheer in the new year?"

"No, thanks."

"Perhaps a stick or two of incense fine? Cherry adder, agapanthus, sandalwood?" the mystic presses, practically in Kasim's face.

"We said no thanks!" I give Kasim a hard nudge. He bumps into the mystic, who stumbles backward and lands hard upon the sidewalk.

Kasim stands next to me, visibly shaken. "What did you do?"

The mystic slowly stands while growling a barely audible incantation, interspersed by loud and sudden claps and the stamping of worn boots.

"I think he's vexing us," Kasim whispers to me, a raspy tremble.

"They're just words," I say, pushing Kasim along. "Words can't hurt us."

ACT TWO, SCENE TWO: THE CURSE OF THE INSIPID TONGUE

Braised Sheep Stew, Kasim's favorite meal, is the perfect way to see off one of the last cool nights of the narrow season. Mother left the pot in the icebox for us to heat up, upon my request. I'd slyly slipped a half container of salt into the flavorful stew before placing it upon the burner. I give it a stir, and watch the root vegetables comingle until steam rises off my concoction.

The smell is divine, and lures Kasim out of his funk. He gives me a half smile. "Finally, something is going my way," he says, unable to keep the saliva in his mouth.

I serve a bowl to each of us, then we sit across from each other, alone in our dining hutch as usual. "Still rattled by that wu mystic?" I dip my spoon into my stew and take a long, luxurious sip. It takes all my effort to bite back the saltiness and not let it show on my face.

"Nah. You're right. They were just words, and wu isn't real anyway." Kasim laughs, then takes his own taste and immediately spits it back out. "This is disgusting!" He scrapes the remnants off his tongue with his spoon.

"A few too many potatoes for my liking, but it's warm and will fill my belly fine." However briefly. I've got a date with a porcelain goddess tonight. I take another spoonful, and shrug.

"It tastes like ocean water. How can you stand to eat this stuff?"

"Mother spent a long time on this, and meat isn't cheap. The least you can do is eat it."

Kasim squints at me, looking for lies that I have not told. He then dips his spoon into my bowl, and takes a taste. Lips pucker. He sighs, then goes for a loaf of bread.

"Good idea, some bread to cleanse the palate."

"I'm making a sandwich."

"But you'll waste the stew."

"Then you eat it."

I do. With gusto. Kasim throws a frustrated look my way, then takes a bite of stale bread with a smattering of currant jelly.

ACT TWO, SCENE THREE: THE CURSE OF THE SCENTLESS GARDENIA

At the center of every sibling relationship is the fight for bathroom time while getting ready for school. I wake up early to claim the first spot, take a twenty-minute shower, and then sit upon the toilet, making not-so-subtle grunting and groaning noises and dropping soft chunks of boiled yam into the toilet bowl with satisfying plunks. Kasim is beyond annoyed. He'll only have five minutes to get ready before we need to go. Plus, maybe I've been known to have bowel movements that don't exactly smell of roses, shall we say. Though, lately, things have been so acidic I've had to find elsewhere to do my business, or else risk further damage to the bowl's finish.

When Kasim knocks for the third time, I hastily flush, watching the yam bits swirl away. "Phew!" I say, opening the door, fanning my face. "Sooo sorry. Maybe you were right. Something about that stew didn't sit well."

Kasim cringes, expecting a fecal-scented back draft, but surprisingly nothing comes. He takes a timid step in.

I wash my hands. "Here, a little cologne couldn't possibly make it smell any worse in here." I select one of the colored glass bottles from my neat collection on the counter—now all filled with water—and spray liberally until I'm satisfied. "Better?"

"It's fine. I don't smell anything."

"Well, lucky you." I step out of the way and let Kasim in.

The door closes promptly in my face. From this side, I hear Kasim give a cologne bottle a single spray, then he takes a futile whiff and sighs.

ACT TWO, SCENE FOUR: THE CURSE OF THE WANING TEMPO

We walk to school our usual way, nothing out of the ordinary. It's early yet for most wu mystics, but Kasim steers clear of the ones we do see. Halfway to school, we pass a street musician, blowing breezily across the string of a goura. He keeps tempo with a tap of his foot, but the characteristic squawk of the instrument, reminiscent of the sound of a tenacious goose, does not carry over the air.

I nod my head absentmindedly from the other side of the street, carrying on with my conversation. "So Msr. Ademola is giving a test tomorrow. Fifth day of class. Six chapters. Who does that?"

Kasim stops me short, then turns me toward the musician. A businessman walks by and drops a coin in the musician's upturned hat. The musician smiles and puts a little more pizzazz into his step.

"You hear him? Playing music?" Kasim asks.

I can't lie, but I can parry his question. "I don't know if I would actually go as far as calling it music, but I've definitely heard worse musicians." Another man drops a few djang into the hat, and the panic builds on Kasim's face. I place the back of my hand to his head. "You're feeling all right, aren't you?"

"My senses are all out of whack. First the stew last night. Then your cologne this morning. And now this. I don't hear him, Auben. Not a single note. I think . . ." Kasim shakes his head.

"What's wrong?"

"I think this might have something to do with that wu mystic from yesterday."

"I highly doubt it. What about your sinuses? Allergies?"

"Not during the narrow season."

"I'm sure it's nothing. Come on, we're going to be late

for school." I tug at Kasim's arm and feel him shivering. He's taken the bait, and now it's time to reel him in.

ACT TWO, SCENE FIVE: THE CURSE OF THE MISLAID BARONESS

Apparently lechery was alive and well in Biobaku's time. However, we haven't an actor willing to fully commit to the role of the lusty baroness, and even if we had, Kasim wouldn't be willing to engage in such an explicit act, and even if he were, there's no way I'd want anything to do with figuring out how to numb his sensitivity in that particular area, so this scene has been abridged from our production.

ACT TWO, SCENE SIX: THE CURSE OF THE MIRRORED EYE

We're a few blocks away from school when the final scene starts. In the morning, the streets are lousy with students in indistinguishable dingy school cikis, walking to school or piling up by the dozen onto some poor rickshaw cabbie's cart to share a fare. One of the bustling students knocks Kasim's shoulder as he passes. He looks back and says a quick "Sorry, sal," so fast, I worry Kasim won't have time to process what he's seen. I keep my face relaxed, no sign that anything is amiss.

"Did you see that?" Kasim asks.

"I know, rude, right? It's like he did it on purpose."

"No." Kasim grips my bicep. "It was the wu mystic. Neck down, it was a student. But his face . . . the matted beard, the kohl markings. The piercing eyes."

"Do you hear yourself right now, Kasim? We can hail a rickshaw if you think you need to see a doctor." No one I know owns their own oryx-drawn coach here, but there are a few to hire in case you need to get somewhere fast, though they're mostly for people with business on the other side of the wall.

A woman pushing a stroller passes us next. She wears a long flowing dress, and her hair is pulled back into neat afro puffs. Her face is dirty with kohl markings, chin covered with a tangled beard, eyes ice blue. She pays us no mind, singing sweet lullabies to her child.

"There. That woman," Kasim whispers in a panic. "And that guy, and that kigen, and there—walking the dog."

I raise a hand into the early morning traffic. Seconds later, a coach drawn by two haggard oryx bucks with muddied hooves settles against the curb. The shabby driver greets us with a bitter purse of the lips.

"How much to the nearest hospital?" I ask.

"Twenty djang," he says, looking us up and down. "You pay now."

"Fifteen djang, and we'll pay when you get us there."

The driver scowls, then pets the knife sitting along his dash. "No funny business from you two," he says. "Get in."

"There's another one," Kasim moans, eyes fixing on an elderly woman across the street.

I tug him into the coach, wincing at the throbbing gash on my palm from that rusted nail. With the way it's starting to pus, I wish we were actually headed to see a doctor.

Kasim is so out of it, he comes without a fight. "And another. Auben, why is this happening to me?"

"Whatever you're seeing is not real. Just keep focused on me." I look Kasim deep in his eyes, which are terrified, darting. With the rhythmic clop of oryx hooves, the comfy turns to the city proper. Coaches go from being unreliable transport to shiny symbols of status. Buildings go from cramped, gray, and unimaginative to massive glass displays of ingenuity. People go from poorly dressed assholes scurrying about to dapper assholes scurrying about.

An oncoming driver honks at us behind the reins of a candy red, cloth-top Nnamari. "Share the road, asshole," the man curses at our driver, full of road rage as he barrels past us, dressed in his clean, tailored business ciki. His face, however, bears the signature markings of the wu mystic.

This drives Kasim over the edge. I do everything I can to keep him from jumping out of the coach. He's screaming at me, at the world. Ranting and raving and repenting. Perhaps I've gone too far. "Stop the coach," I demand of the driver. But he doesn't stop. Doesn't slow down even. Keeps speeding forward, dodging traffic.

Following the script.

I see Uncle Yeboah's building, the early morning sunlight reflecting off foreboding golden brick columns, blue glass front blending seamlessly into the cloud-heavy sky. The finale. But Kasim is so out of his mind right now, I don't think he can't handle it. "Don't turn around," I beg the driver. "For the love of Grace, don't turn around."

He does. The driver gives Kasim the nastiest smile, his face now bearded and marked with kohl. Glass contacts turn his eyes icy blue. He cackles and screeches, right up until the point Kasim screams like a holler whore and punches him in the face. The driver holds back handfuls of blood gushing from his nose? A busted lip? There's so much of it, it's too hard to tell. His surprised eyes dart to me for explanation.

"It's not real, Kasim!" I say. "It's all fake. I made this all up. Calm down."

But Kasim is lost to logic, and I'm sure he can't hear me above his wailing. When I try to subdue him, he fights me off, then climbs over the driver's seat and snatches the knife. He and the driver grapple over it for a moment, but Kasim prevails.

"Stop haunting me," he says to the driver. "Leave me alone. I didn't even do anything to you!" He drives the knife into the driver's abdomen. Over and over.

"Kasim! Please!" I scream. Tears in my eyes.

The driver slumps against slack reins, motionless. Finally, Kasim settles back down, wipes the blood from the blade with his fingers, and smiles viciously at me.

"What have you done, Kasim?" *What have I done?* I tremble all over.

He holds the knifepoint to his own chest, presses hard. I take a helpless breath and feel my soul slipping away. He stabs himself, again and again, laughing. No blood. No wound. Nothing. A stage knife. He slips his hand into his pocket, pulls out a piece of folded paper, and tosses it to me.

It's a playbill. Specifically, *The Five Curses of Akerele*. My lungs gasp for air, and relief rushes through me. Then anger. "How could you do this to me?" I scream. "I thought you'd—"

"How could I plot an elaborate setup against my own brother? Is that what you really want to ask me?"

But it's exactly what I want to ask. I search his eyes, unable to fathom how my brother—the one so full of virtue—could be capable of such deceit. My hands shake, and my throat goes dry. I try to snap out of it, to laugh it off. But the image of Kasim sinking that knife into the driver's body and then his own—I thought I'd lost him, and that feeling of nothingness washes over me like all of the space between the stars. I lose it right there. I can't keep the snot in my nose, or the tears in my eyes. In the span of seconds, I'm a blubbering mess.

Kasim's wicked smile goes soft, his arms wrap around me. "It was fake, Auben. You know that, right?"

I nod into his chest, but the warm tears stream down even harder.

"Oh, Auben." He pats my back. "Let me make it up to you. I'll take you to that Rashtra place. It's right around the corner."

My mind manages to string together a few words, *Thanks, but no thanks,* but they come out in an indistinguishable smear of wet syllables.

"Don't feel bad. I've seen the play. The mystic's costume was taken straight from it. Really, you could have made a little more effort. And maybe paid your actors better. A couple of homework bribes was all it took to get my revisions worked into the scene."

"We were on a budget," I sulk. "And since when have you been to a play?"

"I've been to every single one of Ruda's dress rehearsals for the last two and a half years. Made an excuse to get out of class."

"*You* skipped class?" I sit up straight, wipe the wet from my face with my sleeve. "So you're saying my plan didn't work because you're a lying, lecherous, no good cheat of a brother?"

"Eh. That, and you kept mumbling act and scene numbers under your breath."

"Speaking of skipping class, can we call this a scene?" the driver says, sitting up and peeling off his beard and smearing the blood off his coat. "I've got a quiz second period, and I've still got to get this coach cleaned up and back home before my dad notices."

"Yeah, sure," I mumble. "Can you drop us at school on the way?" I glance sideways at Kasim, my head still spinning. He's drifting away, so far, so fast, right when I need him the most.

"Actually," Kasim says. "I feel awful, and with all the effort you went through, I see how important it is for you to speak with Yeboah. I still think it's a bad idea, but if we do it now, we can avoid any future theatrics, can we not?"

"I promise, my stint as an actor is done. No more lies between me and you."

Kasim rubs my back. "That almost sounded sincere."

"It was."

I've always imagined that one day I would meet my father. He'd come home to us, one rainy evening after a meager supper, a figure in a dark leather ciki jacket hanging down to his calves and a wide-brimmed hat cocked to the side, standing mysteriously in the doorway. He'd look up, and I'd catch that first glimpse of his face. Handsome, his skin a rich shade of brown exactly between Kasim's and my own, daring eyes, hard chin covered in rugged stubble. "Sons," he'd call out in the smoothest baritone voice that'd drop my heart to my feet.

My father would apologize, saying he'd been away on a secret government mission all these years. It pained his every breath to be apart from us, but even the slightest contact would put us in mortal danger. He would then pull Kasim and me into his arms, his chest broad enough to accommodate the both of us—and all the missed birthdays, all the shame taunts inflicted by my classmates, all the nights we'd gone to bed still hungry would become nothing more than abandoned memories. Then he'd whisk us all off to our real home, in a big glass house with a view of the ocean and servants and meat at every meal and shoes that got replaced well before the soles wore away.

My fantasy played out a dozen different ways: a famous explorer, an opera singer touring the world, an aquanaut who'd established a secret colony on the ocean floor, even Grace himself, come down from his mountain to partake in a vice or three. But my wildest delusions pale against the truth.

"We're here to see Yeboah Mazibuko," I say, my voice echoing in the chilled air of the atrium of my father's building. Workers stream in, clutching their cups of steaming coffee, trying to ward off this narrow season that refuses to quit.

"You have an appointment?" the receptionist asks, though we're greeted only by the top of her green silk turban, since she apparently can't be bothered to look up from the pages of her word scramble.

"No appointment, but—"

"Sorry, he's not available. If you'd like to leave a message, feel free." She pushes a yellow pad of paper to us. It's titled WHILE YOU WERE OUT and has a selection of boxes and corresponding contact options. She doesn't bother to provide a writing instrument, but I get the feeling our message would end up in the trash bin shortly anyway.

I press the pad back to her. "I think you can make an exception. You see, we're his—"

"Nephews," Kasim breaks in, rubbing at the tear stains I'd left on the front of his ciki, like streaks of bleach.

"I was going to say nephews," I whisper to him.

"Oh, you're his nephews! Why didn't you say so?" She looks up, shoots us a tight-lipped smile. "There's a *special* form for that." She scrawls a box under the printed ones, and next to it writes the word *nephews.*

I heave a sigh. "Thank you for your time," I say.

"Whatever," she mumbles.

Cusses swim about the saliva in my mouth, but I swallow them back. My temper won't do us any good here.

That's only because you don't know how to wield it properly, the whisper says enticingly.

I shove my hand into my pocket as we walk away, and grab a fistful of glass shards. Squeeze. The pain inflames against my existing wound.

The whisper recedes, along with quiet ideas of burning down the building.

"Auben!" Kasim says, pointing to my pant leg. The haze of agony parts, and when I look down, there's a bloodstain blooming below my pocket.

I pull my hand out, a pulpy red mess. Kasim takes it gently, and rushes me through the atrium as we leave a trail of blood droplets behind us. We enter the restroom, and he runs my hand under cool water, washing and rubbing and rinsing away the blood with his hands. Bright red swirls circle the drain, and the pain must have me on the verge of hallucinating, because I swear my blood is sort of . . . glowing.

Kasim shuts off the faucet, pats my hands dry with a towel. I look at my palms, nearly completely healed, minus a few shallow scratches no more significant than paper cuts. But it was not paper that cut me.

"It must have looked worse than it actually was," Kasim says with a shrug.

Maybe, but my nail gash from two days ago is completely healed over, and ten minutes ago it was well on its way to a full-blown infection. "I thought we weren't lying to each other anymore," I say straight at him.

Kasim mouths at words that he can't find.

"It's okay. I'll go first," I say. "I've been changing lately, in strange ways that are hard to explain. I suspect that something similar is happening to you. Have you been hearing—"

"Voices," Kasim admits. "I heard the first one two months ago."

"Me, too. Telling you to do things?"

Kasim nods. "All the fucking time." He exhales, and it's like the weight of the world has finally dropped from his shoulders.

"The lechery, the lies, the cheating, the cussing. I knew something was off with you, but I was so caught up with my own mess that I hadn't even thought that something could be driving you to vice. You can't imagine what I've had to endure . . . that voice is what made me punch you. And that isn't even the worst of it." I think of Ruda and the terror behind her eyes. "Just now it wanted me to burn down this building. I've been resisting as hard as I can. Pain helps."

Kasim goes stiff. "I've been resisting, too, but it's not like that." He won't look at me directly, but manages to meet my eyes sure enough in the reflection of the mirror before us. "The voice in my head is telling me I can do better. That I can be better. Nothing is good enough, and there's always room for improvement. It's bad, Auben. It's analyzing my every thought for deficiency, judging not just my actions but also my precise intent. I'm not even safe in my own dreams."

"So you've basically got Mother living inside your head."

I shudder. I'd take Icy Blue over that any day. "Any other tricks up your sleeve? Besides healing?"

"Well, there's this . . ." Kasim climbs onto the granite countertop, then jumps. Something catches him inches before he hits the ground.

He hangs there, floating in the air, like he's made from cloud vapor. "Whoa," I say. "I guess that explains your cat-like dismounts from the top—"

The door to the restroom swings open. Kasim glances back, then drops to his feet.

The silhouette of a man fills the door. He is wearing neither a leather ciki nor a wide-brimmed hat. He is not handsome, and is a brown closer to that of dried mustard. His eyes are beady, his chin clean-shaven and weak. But his voice . . . his voice is a smooth baritone that stands my hairs on end. "I got a page from the receptionist. She said someone came by claiming they were my nephews, then left a blood slick over the floor."

"Just a bad paper cut," I say, holding up my hand. I might have sworn never to lie to my brother, but that doesn't mean I can't lie to my own father.

Uncle Yeboah suspiciously eyes the bloodstain on my pants. "Well, you've already ruined my morning agenda. Might as well come up to my office."

"I take it your mother finally told you," Uncle Yeboah says, all business, as soon as the double doors to his corner office are shut behind us. It's like we've stepped into a hunting lodge. Floor to ceiling, the entire office is lined with a rich deep red zebra wood. His conquests hang on the walls neatly,

like trophy mounts from a safari: his Gabadamosi Preparatory Certificate, his degree from Primways University, an oil
painting of Aunt Cisse, one of his family, and one of Grace
Mountain. Like he needs a painting of Grace Mountain with
the view he's got of it outside his window.

"No," I say. "She doesn't know that we know. We found
one of Uncle Pabio's books."

"I thought I'd burnt all the copies," Uncle Yeboah grumbles. He heads to his liquor cabinet, pours himself a glass
tumbler of Effiong, and plunks in three ice cubes. He takes a
long and loud sip, then exhales against the sting as he sets
the drink down on his desk. Uncle Yeboah looks at us, like
he's ready to entertain all of our questions, but my mind is so
busy processing what had happened in the restroom. What
is this I'm feeling? Envy because the demon possessing Kasim
is more badass than mine?

"Does your family know?" Kasim asks.

"No, and they can't find out. It's senseless to ruin a family over a single mistake eighteen years ago." Uncle Yeboah
clears his throat. Even he realizes how insensitive that was.
"*Indiscretion* would be a better word," he adds, though there
are no apologies to accompany it. He goes to the framed oil
painting of Grace Mountain and swings it to the side. There's
a wall safe behind it. Uncle Yeboah fidgets with the dial until
it clicks open. He rifles through stacks of paper.

As he does so, I look at the ice cubes in his drink, thinking back to my night upon Grace Mountain and how all
those flowers had frozen over. A neat enough trick. I've spent
nearly all my life trying to hold back the queasiness in my
gut with a steady flex of ab muscles and mental energy. I
release, giving the thin leash I hold upon Icy Blue a bit of

play. My insides go cold, and his smile slides across my lips. I press my hand on Uncle Yeboah's desk. A narrow slick of ice crawls across the surface until it reaches the glass tumbler. It frosts over, nice and cool. I look to Kasim, raise my brow. He's noticed my quaint performance, and his eyes have gone wide. I take a silent bow, as I flex muscles back into place. They're weaker now.

Uncle Yeboah shuts the safe door, spins the dial, and returns the painting to its original position. He holds a thick envelope in his hands. Even from where I'm standing, I can see it's filled with money.

"We didn't come here looking for a payoff," Kasim says, definitely not speaking for the both of us.

"We don't want this secret out any more than you do," I say, playing along, "but we do deserve the truth." I keep my chin held high, hoping my voice won't start to quaver. "How could you let your own flesh and blood suffer like we have?"

"This isn't a payoff," Uncle Yeboah says.

He hands the envelope to me. I flip through. Most of it is large denomination djang, but there are several yellowed Money Mate certificates among them, dated at the year of our birth. A dozen of them in all, each tucked in their own thin envelopes. I take one out. It's addressed to Mother, with RETURN TO SENDER written in the script I've learned to forge so well over the years.

"I want you to understand: I *tried* to do what was right in this tough situation, but your mother didn't want me involved as a father, financially or otherwise. I wanted to come clean to Cisse, too. We were just married, and didn't have the kids then, and yes, it would have been hard to bounce back from, but there was a possibility that things could have worked out. Your mother dragged her feet for so long, though, afraid of the backlash, afraid it would end their relationship. You should have seen them back then. Close as twins can be. By the time your mother worked up the nerve to tell the truth, Cisse was pregnant, and I couldn't risk losing another set of kids." Uncle Yeboah clears his throat, and goes for his drink. When he tilts it back, the whole frozen mass slips out and clinks against his teeth. He looks at it, more irritated than perplexed. "In any case, the money is yours. Three hundred fifty djang set aside for every month you've been alive. For each of you."

Kasim and I gawk at each other, each of us doing the arithmetic in our heads. Nearly seventy thousand djang. *Each.* When I'd put together this plan, my goal was to squeeze a couple thousand djang out of Uncle Yeboah—enough for an exorcism and a little pocket change left over.

I've never held so much money, and yet it fails to excite me the way I thought it would. It feels wrong in my hands. Sure, we could invest it, live off it for fifteen or twenty years easily. Buy nice clothes, nice toys, a nice place to live. Sneak some to Mother, of course, without raising suspicion. And now there are dual exorcisms needed, and I've got a feeling that a run-of-the-mill, buy one, get one fifty percent off exorcism won't be sufficient for either of us. Voices and strange visions, sure, but levitation and healing and ice powers . . . not so much.

But the money feels wrong. The ice, though . . .

The ice feels *right*.

Maybe we shouldn't be so hasty to try to rid ourselves of these afflictions. Maybe we need to learn more about our demon possessors. With the proper resources, we could learn to quiet our minds, and still be able to use these powers, and perhaps learn how to tap into others. There's only one place I can think of that has the knowledge to get us there, and that gives me an idea.

"We don't want your money," I say.

"What?" Uncle Yeboah asks.

"Yeah, what?" Kasim parrots. He snatches the envelope from me and holds it against his chest, no longer high and mighty. I guess everyone has their price.

"We want you to get us into Gabadamosi Preparatory instead." I point at the gold pin on Uncle Yeboah's lapel with tiny cut jewels that represent the great stained-glass symbol of his alma mater. Of the school Chimwe and Chiso currently attend.

"I'm afraid that's impossible," Uncle Yeboah says.

"And completely unnecessary," Kasim adds. "If you don't mind," he says to our father, "my brother and I need a private moment."

Uncle Yeboah sucks his teeth and busies himself in paperwork. Kasim grips my shirt and drags me to the far corner of the office.

"What are you doing?" he says, slamming the money into my chest. "We're going to take this. He owes us this. There's so much good we can do with this money."

And so much evil, come the thoughts in my mind. At this point, I am not sure if they are mine or Icy Blue's. "We could take this money, fix whatever has gone wrong inside of us," I say, "and then go on to lead comfortable yet unremarkable lives. Or we could learn to manage the voices and use our *powers* for good. You think seventy thousand djang could help people? Imagine what these could do." I take his hands in mine. "Heal the sick, the wounded. What price can you put on that?"

Kasim's mind churns over this. He does not agree with me, but he can't disagree either.

"Gabadamosi has the biggest library in the Cape," I tell him. "There has to be something there that can help us. And if we can't figure it out, or if the voices become too strong, we can go straight to the Sanctuary, the one with the capital S." We've heard the cousins talk—our half siblings, it now hits me—about the Sanctuary, a place that still uses blood sacraments instead of wine, and defting sticks made of human bone instead of wood or ivory.

"But Yeboah said it's impossible. You remember how frantic he was, worrying if he'd be able to get Chimwe and Chiso admitted, and they went to the best private schools. How in the world is he going to get a couple of comfy-educated secular boys in?"

"He's the one that runs a multibillion djang corporation," I say, gesturing to his panoramic view of the fog-blanketed coastline. "We'll make that his problem to solve. All we need to do is add the proper motivation."

Kasim's eyes look one off, and I'm willing to bet his voices are speaking to him. He curses under his breath, and then concedes. "So we're going to blackmail him?"

"The best kind of mail. Won't even cost us a stamp."

DOUBT

feel like a drone in an ant colony," Kasim whispers to me as we follow the curve of a gravel pathway, weaving through swarms of students and passing the big brown mounds of school buildings set into the base of Grace Mountain. Knowing Kasim's fixation with bugs, he doesn't mean this as an insult, but I'm sure taking it that way. This is Gabadamosi? I'd expected something grand. Big glass buildings, daring feats of architecture, a place that exuded knowledge from every nook and cranny. This place looks so ancient, so tribal, and not in a good way. Doubt hits me like a punch to the ribs. What have I gotten us into?

My satchel hangs like a noose around my neck, holding the entire extent of the personal belongings we are allowed: two long-sleeved cikis and two short, all ruddy brown linen with orange jacquard embellishments around the collar and cuffs, with the school crest upon the right shoulder. Two matching sets of pants. A few pair of underwear. A sleep gown. Three notebooks filled with twice-blessed paper. A set of defting sticks. A cup, a bowl, a spoon. One comfort item, and a note from home.

For my comfort item, I've chosen a pocket mirror, not to stoke my vainglory, but as a quick source of glass shards should the need arise. Kasim has picked a whole carton of individually wrapped Jak & Dee's dehydrated samp and beans. He eats them right out of the packet when he's stressed. And instead of a loving note from our mother, we'd both gotten a slur of cusses, punctuated with "how could you?" and "I raised you better than this!" I wanted to explain to her why we had to leave, but how could we tell the woman who birthed us, who raised us the best she could, that her sons were beset by demons? And yet beyond her anger and disappointment, the way she looked at us, it was like she could *see* those monsters inside us as she slammed the door in our faces. Yes, it stings, but Kasim and I have to focus on figuring out a way to quiet our minds while wielding our powers. Then we can make it up to her.

We draw sharp stares from all directions. There is an unspoken social order about things, the way students move in packs, the paths they take, who yields to whom when those paths intersect, but it is well beyond my grasp. We wear the clothes, but we definitely do not walk the walk. And I can barely stand to walk at all, the way these loafers pinch at my toes. Kasim stumbles along as well, scratching at his collar, like his grace has been left behind along with the rest of our possessions. He walks so close to me that our arms brush. The proximity is like a breath of fresh air. We may have next to nothing, but we have each other, and that's more than enough.

We near the administration building, another brown mound of old brick and thin panes of dingy glass, evoking images of the simple wooden huts our ancestors once dwelled in. Don't get me wrong, the place is immaculate, but the buildings cannot escape the burden of their age. We ascend a short set of stairs, our heads passing directly under a Welcome to Gabadamosi Preparatory banner. When I open the door, the dimly lit rotunda is abuzz with school staff scurrying across the packed dirt floor, flitting in and out of the glass doors of offices carrying stacks of precariously high paper and wearing impossibly wide smiles. That all grinds to a sudden halt as each and every eye falls upon us disappointedly. Whispers stir about as we pass, referring to us as *those boys* before we even get a chance to identify ourselves. Apparently, Uncle Yeboah had called in a huge favor from one of his welshing buddies who sat on the school board. Together they pushed through a Religioning Exchange Program that took poor secular kids from the comfy and immersed them in Grace's shadow for a quarter. He'd spent many multiples of the money he'd offered to us to pay our tuitions via "scholarship," bribe the proper officials at Gabadamosi, and keep his name from it all in any shape or form.

One quarter. Or what's left of it. Ten weeks is all the time we have to learn all we can, and hope that it's enough.

I place my hands on the front counter and nervously touch one of the pens held by a gilded cup bearing the school's crest—a bird-faced cheetah with a snake for a tail, wielding a long knife. "Hi. We're Auben and Kasim Mtuze. It's our first day."

The receptionist behind the desk forces a smile upon
eir face, but would have had an easier time squeezing water from a rock. "Welcome, new students." The receptionist
smacks eir lips like the words have left a disgusting aftertaste. "Munashe!" ey calls out, annoyed.

A smallish wooden door opens, which I'd thought was a
maintenance closet, and out comes a young woman dressed
in a high-quality yet ill-fitting blouse, neck adorned with a
chunky kola nut necklace, and slacks with their cuffs skimming the floor. Her hair is pressed and fashionably unkempt,
though I get the feeling that this was not her intent.

"Hello," she greets us, face aglow with the compassion-
ate gaze of a child's doll. She looks a few years older than
Kasim and me. "You must be Auben and Kasim. I'm Munashe,
recent Gabadamosi alum, class of '09. They couldn't get rid
of me, and now I'm a new student liaison. I can show you
around and answer any of your questions. I'm at your beck
and call."

We shake hands. She seems sincere enough, and her
face doesn't have that look like we're polluting up the place,
which makes me both trust her and feel immediately warier
at the same time.

"You should get along with the tour, then," the receptionist says briskly. "We'll send all of the necessary paperwork over to your dormitory." Ey brushes me away with a
finger flick, then sets about polishing the spot on the desk
where I'd leaned . . . and tossing the pen I'd touched. The
receptionist straightens the remaining pens, shuffles paperwork, neatens eir tight afro with a pat, waxes on a smile.

"Don't mind them," Munashe whispers to us. "I wish I
could say they usually aren't quite this awful, but then I'd

be a liar." She gives us an impish smile, then bids us to follow
her to the exit. "It's just that everyone is a bit on edge. Gueye
Okahim is paying a visit to Gabadamosi today. It's all very
exciting. Rumor has it that he's seeking out an apprentice.
Perhaps one of our students will catch his eye."

"Gueye Okahim?" Kasim asks.

Munashe stops so quickly, I run right into her back.
"Seriously? You don't know who Gueye Okahim is? For the
glory of Grace, this exchange program couldn't have been
any more prudent. Gueye Okahim is the Man of Virtues at the
Sanctuary. The man who stands directly in Grace's shadow.
Who has been thoroughly touched by those Hallowed Hands.
Who speaks His word. Also a Gabadamosi alum, I have to
add. Class of '71."

Munashe takes Kasim by the hand and eagerly bids us
forth. "Come on. We don't want to be here when he arrives. I
can't even imagine the extent of the school's embarrassment
if his first visit in nearly five years involved a couple of sec-
heads. No offense." Munashe pushes open the front door,
and stiffens as she looks out. Coming up the stairs is a man
clad in dark purple sequined robes that kiss the ground, his
thin black thighs peeking from the slits upon either side. A
collar of stiff pheasant feathers frames his head like a lion's
mane. Hints of age dance lightly about his wizened eyes,
though no evidence of his years exists anywhere else upon
his chiseled face. His hair is shorn, except for a smooth bald
band straight through the center, where the symbols of the
seven virtues have been branded front to back. The one for
grace overlaps onto his forehead.

Munashe immediately falls to her knees and makes the
quick gesture we have seen our uncle do enough times.

Kasim and I exchange a worried glance, and in the instantaneous language shared by twins, decide that we should at least make a minimal effort to fit in. We also go to our knees, but refrain from the religious gestures.

It soon becomes apparent to the three of us that we have chosen to show our respect right in the doorway to the building so that it is impossible for the Man of Virtues to pass. I slowly start to stand, but Munashe tugs me back down by the collar of my uniform. "We can't move until he's passed," she rasps to us. "Or until he's addressed us to do so." Unless the Man of Virtues intends to step over us, it will have to be the latter. He will have to speak directly to Kasim and me, and we have no idea what to do or how to respond. "Don't look at anything besides his feet. Say nothing other than 'Yes, Amawusiakaraseiya.'"

Say *what*?

My eyes stay fixed upon glimpses of bare feet peeking from beneath Gueye Okahim's robe. The feet stop inches away from us. I hear the amused smirk on his face as he says, "Arise, my children," in a voice full of intonation and power.

We comply thoughtlessly, like puppets pulled by strings.

The scurrying of many feet fills the rotunda behind us. I dare to part my glance from Gueye Okahim's feet to see the small army of school administrators with horrified faces.

"Amawusiakaraseiya," Munashe says, a quivering mess. "I am incredibly sorry you have been inconvenienced by these students. Please—"

"There is no inconvenience. I am here to be among the students and to witness how the Hallowed Hands have touched the minds and souls of our young ones. You," Gueye Okahim says, lifting my chin up with one of his ageless fingers. "I trust this fine institution is seeing to your religioning in an adequate manner?"

"Yes—" I try to get my mouth around the title, but the syllables refuse to cohere. I do the next best thing I can think of "—sir."

I swear I hear Munashe gritting her teeth at me.

"And you." Kasim's chin is lifted as well. "Do you feel your time here has brought you closer to Grace?"

Kasim grimaces, his mind churning over one of his sideways truths. "It certainly hasn't brought me any farther away, Amawusiekeseiya." The word slips effortlessly over his lips.

The air in the room is sucked thin by a collective gasp.

Kasim flushes. "What? I said that right, didn't I?" he whispers to Munashe.

Her mouth gapes, then opens and closes like a dying fish. "I throw myself upon your mercy, Amawusiakaraseiya. It is my fault. These students here do not know any better. They are exchange students sent over from a secular school in a nearby comfy. They do not mean any offense."

"None is received. It is a good thing for His hands to reach into the hearts that need Him the most. It is good to meet you both. I am called Gueye Okahim by birth, Amawusiakaraseiya by His hands. You may call me Gueye if it is easier for you." He presses both of his hands around mine.

"I'm Auben, Gueye. Auben Mtuze. It is an honor to meet you."

"Likewise," he says with a major helping of humility.

"I'm Kasim Mtuze," Kasim says. "We're brothers. Twins." He stands next to me, his arm pressed against mine. It is like we are a united front in Gueye Okahim's presence, and together we might get through this unscathed.

"Kasim? It is interesting that parents raising a child in the secular way would give him such a highly religious name. *Controller of temper* it means in ancient Sylla."

"There were a dozen *Kasims* at our former school," Kasim says with a shrug. "I think it was a popular name at the time."

Munashe stands tight-lipped, her wide eyes drilling into Kasim's. I think a "Yes, Amawusiakaraseiya" was meant to go there. Sweat beads prickle upon her forehead, and I'm sure she's stopped breathing.

Gueye Okahim looks us over intently. We have caught his eye, and definitely not in a good way. "Yes, perhaps," he says with a short bow. "May Grace walk with the both of you."

And then he takes his leave. As soon as he is out of sight, Munashe hyperventilates. She attempts to speak at us between her quick and desperate breaths, but all that comes out is a broken string of indistinguishable consonants and airy vowels.

"That was an absolute disaster," she finally wheezes. "But it's all my fault. It's always my fault. Sorry, boys. I've got a mess to repair. Here are your class schedules." She shoves crest-embossed folders into each of our hands. "There's a map tucked inside. Come to me if you have any questions . . . just not today!"

10:30 A.M. INTRODUCTION TO ANCIENT SYLLA

As a work of art, our map is a masterpiece, hand inked onto a fine piece of parchment, detailed down to the leaves on trees and the rock-trimmed borders of the pathways. As a tool for traversing the sprawling campus, it is absolutely useless. Each rotunda building is indistinguishable from the next. Munashe has written some notes upon it that I'm sure were meant to be helpful, but her penmanship is completely illegible. Our only saving grace is that the classroom rotundas are open-air, and as we pass, we catch bits of the instructor's lectures. History, scriptures, literature, some stilted antiscience version of biology. Finally, I hear words that do not cohere, and Kasim and I duck inside.

We catch the instructor midconjugation, stabbing a long piece of chalk against the words on his chalkboard. "Jomealah Mtuze *na* Jomealah Mtuze," he says, and introduces himself, I think, as Jomealah Aguda. His tongue whips Sylla at us, and I can only infer that he wants us to take a seat. Desks full of students wrap around the edge of the rotunda, and of course the only two empty ones are right next to Jomealah Aguda's desk.

Back at our old school, you could always tell the first-year students by the look of overwhelming confusion in their eyes. The first-year students at Gabadamosi are not like that in the slightest. They beam as Kasim and I wedge our way into the undersized desks. They introduce themselves warmly, despite the blatant interruption we've caused, and then listen intently when the instructor resumes the lesson. But there is a silent ferocity moving behind their eyes, and even though the majority of them barely come up to my chin, you can bet I won't be swirling heads in any commodes anytime soon.

We are already two weeks into the quarter, and everyone has partnered off, so Kasim and I are paired together for exercises, and that's fine with us. We take turns asking the question "How are you?" and responding with a set of replies.

"*Sedu ka e moro?*" I ask Kasim.

"*Nari em mmadi,*" he replies for the billionth time. *I am well.* "*Sedu ka e moro?*"

How am I? I feel like we're adrift together in a sea of stilted conversation. I put my hand upon Kasim's, wondering if he feels the same crippling bewilderment I do. I know it will pass, but right now all I see is an endless horizon of watery swells and no way out but down. I want to tell him that, but Jomealah Aguda rewards the mother tongue with a lash of a ruler across our knuckles, so I respond in the few words of Sylla that I do know. "*Nari em mmadi.*"

Our next exercise involves a worksheet and conjugating various common verbs: *eat, sleep, play, walk,* and *run,* among others. Pencils scratch busily upon paper. After ten minutes of staring at the foreign words, the letters start to blur into one another. I sit up and try to wipe the haze from my eyes, and notice a note being passed among the students. The note is carefully unfolded, read, and silently recreased and passed along again. Coarse glances are shot in our direction. More specifically, in Kasim's.

"Everyone is staring at you," I whisper at Kasim during our next partnered exercise.

Kasim has noticed, too, and looks pained. Before he can respond, Jomealah Aguda is upon me. "*Nagi gei Sylla biko, Jomealah Mtuze!*" His wooden ruler raps across my knuckles, and stings more than I thought it would. Though I was the offender, he gives Kasim a tight-lipped scowl, then flits off. His skin is as dark as mine, but he looks of Rashtra descent. His nose too sharp, his hair too straight, his face too pointed. He tries to hide it with layers of scarves, but here he is, a foreigner from a whole nother continent, telling me how to speak the language of my ancestors and having the nerve to tie my tongue so I can't console my own brother.

My tongue may be tied, but I can help lighten the mood. I flip to the glossary of our textbook and look for cuss words. Of course in a first-year intro course, there are none, but that doesn't stop me from improvising.

"*O bu kume apka oke*," I say with a smirk, enunciating like a four-year-old. *He's a ball sack.*

I watch with delight as Kasim looks up the words. He smiles devilishly at me, then starts flipping through the glossary for his response, his fingers zigzagging along the page. "*O bu qeajiji kume apka oke*," he says. *He's a hairy ball sack.*

Kasim and I play back and forth like this for the duration of the class. Honestly, it's the most fun we've had together in a long time. When the bell tolls, I'm sad to pack our things away.

"Which one of you is Kasim?" comes a high-pitched voice from behind us. We turn to see the sweetest sliver of a girl, golden-brown afro like a halo about her head, so much of it that it probably weighs close to what she does.

"*Nagi gei Sylla biko*, Chimealeh Ibore!" Jomealah Aguda calls from his desk as he grades our exercises.

The girl harps back at him, one hand on her hip, in what sounds like decent Sylla. Definitely better than what she could have picked up in the last couple weeks. Jomealah Aguda rolls his eyes at this, and immerses himself in his paperwork.

"I'm Kasim," Kasim says, looking down his nose at her with interest. As he does, I notice that three other students have stayed behind after class, and are slowly packing their satchels, trying to look inconspicuous. Her crew, no doubt.

"So are the rumors true?" the girl asks, all limbs and cuteness, like a baby antelope, though her jackal-esque stare speaks otherwise. "You called Gueye Okahim a false prophet? Right to his face?"

We literally stepped on campus a little over two hours ago, and we're already rumor worthy.

Kasim's brow rises. "I addressed him by the proper title."

"It's Amawusi*akara*seiya, not Amawusi*ekeke*seiya. Maybe it sounds the same to your Sylla-deaf ears, but there's a lot of difference between *Divine Prophet* and *False Prophet*. I only hope you didn't manage to tarnish Gabadamosi's reputation in the process." The girl sucks her teeth at us, then stomps off, her entourage falling in line behind her.

"Well, that's a relief," I say to Kasim as I stuff my book into my crammed satchel. "Here I was worried about sticking out for being a poor kid from the comfy, when I should have been more concerned about the tongue of my blasphemous brother."

"That's not funny, Auben. They hate me, not you."

"We're in this together, brother. If they've got a problem with you, then they've got a problem with me." I look down at my schedule. "Looks like we've got our lunch hour." My finger traces over the map. I find the cafeteria situated on the opposite side of campus. "Looks like a hike."

"I don't really feel like eating right now." These are words I've never heard come out of Kasim's mouth. Gluttony has always been the one way Kasim allowed his greed to shine through unabashedly. He's not doing well. A lot worse than he's letting on.

"Is it the voices?" I whisper to him.

He nods. "They're getting harder to push back. Almost

an indistinguishable blur." He winces, puts his fingers to his temple.

Icy Blue has been uncomfortably quiet, but I feel him lurking in the shadows, like he's hoping I'll forget about him and lay down the tattered reins I've been gripping at so desperately. Between Kasim and me, I'm feeling more and more like coming here was a big mistake. But if we throw away this opportunity, we won't be getting another. We need to focus all our efforts into the reason why we came here in the first place.

"Let's go to the library, then. We can start sifting for answers," I say, both thrilled and terrified of what we will find there.

The last breath of the narrow season should have passed by now, welcoming the new year and the spring, but the cold, wet air lingers. Still, I catch a few students brave enough to wear their short cikis, tempting the weather to finally change. Trees are bare, paths are thoroughly swept. Native fine bush surrounds the buildings, and even though it's been tamed and pruned, I get the feeling that this whole place would be swallowed back up by nature if left unattended for a season or three. We trudge uphill, past a garden of grotesque glass statuaries, and to the last set of rotundas before the campus butts up against the base of the mountain and eases into wilderness.

"Auben," Kasim exhales in defeat. The larger of the buildings is the school's sanctuary, and the smaller by several factors, the library. The place doesn't look big enough to hold the answers to silence an inquisitive toddler, forget about the answers to silencing the demons that plague us.

"Well, we're here anyway. Who cares if they have ten books or ten thousand as long as they have the one we need?" I nudge Kasim forward up a short set of stairs, and under the dark lip of the dome. Double doors greet us, and we step inside. The small room is filled with floor-to-ceiling shelves, eight rows of them, I count, crammed with hundreds of red leather-bound tomes. I pull a book from the shelf, open it.

The Holy Scrolls
    As Divined by Amawusiakaraseiya
    Transcribed by the Hallowed Hands of
Jomealah Attah,
    Third Year, Gabadamosi Preparatory
    1003 S.S., the year of the Adamant Huntress

I pull another book. Another. And another. The names and dates vary, but they are all hand-written versions of the same text. I look around. At the edges of the room, students sit hunched at recessed desks, quills dipping into gilded ink, filling page upon page with meticulous holy script.

My mind spins and I go numb all over. One book. A whole damned library filled with a single damned book. A book we could get for free from any sanctuary in the Cape. "I'm sorry, Kasim," I say with a pained exhale. "We should have taken the money."

"What money?" says a familiar, irksome voice.

I look up, wipe the wet from my eyes, and see Chimwe standing before me, satchel loaded down with books. My heart lurches for my half sibling, so unexpectedly, it's all I can do to keep the truth from leaping out of my mouth. My eyes dart to eir eyes, nose, lips, lobes, looking for traces of myself, traces of Kasim. My tongue goes dry and sour from realizing exactly what this lie has stolen from me—Chimwe is so close to being mine, tied together by blood and vice alike. "Nothing," I manage to say, locking my feelings away, and ignoring the ache in my arms from wanting to hug em, and to finally put the bad blood behind us. "Hello, cousin."

Ey shushes me, then looks Kasim and me over. Sighs. Chimwe does a maneuver with my jacquard collar that makes it lie flat, then repeats it for Kasim. Sighs again. "Please tell me you two got dressed in the dark. With both arms tied behind your back." When Chimwe's taunt fails to rouse us, ey purses eir lips. "What's wrong? You two look like you got the snot kicked out of you."

"Why'd you lie to us?" Kasim asks. "You always brag about how amazing Gabadamosi's library is. This—" Kasim gestures at the holy books "—is far from amazing."

"Well, religious insult aside, this isn't the library. It's the antechamber, which houses the largest collection of Holy Scrolls in the world. Some date back over four hundred years, which I think is pretty amazing." Chimwe purses eir lips at Kasim. "But if you're looking for the library, I guess I could show you. But you have to promise to forget we're cousins for however long it takes you to wash out of here. It's taken me three years to build up the little reputation I do have. No way I'm going to be dragged down by the likes of a blasphemer. *False Prophet,* Kasim? Really?"

My temper swells. It is bad enough I have to deny ey is my sibling. Now I have to deny all traces of our bloodlines? I send Chimwe a tight scowl. "I'd disown you for a dozen lesser reasons."

"Do you want to see the library or not?"

"Fine."

"This way," ey says, leading us back through the stacks. We come to a meticulously carved wooden wall. A massive door, I realize, when I see the enormous brass knocker, threaded through the cast of the chimeral beast that adorns Gabadamosi's crest. Chimwe knocks twice, the action taking both eir hands and a significant amount of body weight put behind it. Nothing happens for a long while, then the door swings open. A pair of armed guards in dark robes greet us. Each wields an impressively ornate scythe with what looks like a human skull at the base of the blade. I know these are meant to intimidate, but they spark me with infinite hope. There's something in here worth protecting. Maybe that something will help us.

"I bet all of their books get returned on time," Kasim says to me.

The guards' beet-red eyes turn on Kasim. Their scythes slice the air inches in front of his face.

"They're okay, Yomelela. They're with me," Chimwe flashes an embossed leather badge.

One of the guards grunts, but they both slowly pull back their weapons. We push our way through a short dank hallway and steer well clear of the scythes. Then the hall opens up into a cavernous room brimming with shelves several stories high. The air is dry and dusty, and upon my first full breath, I begin to cough. My eyes water. I quickly rub them clear. It's like a whole city excavated from the mountainside. Long thin windows are set into the earth. A prism of color shines through the stained glass, motes dancing about the beams. Hundreds of students bustle about, flipping delicate pages of leather-bound tomes, chattering in hushed whispers.

Lithe librarians dressed in lavender-colored linen frocks expertly scale precariously high shelves, fingers grazing along leather spines, pulling books, slipping them back into place.

Chimwe spreads eir arms out for us to behold. "*This* is the library. Some of the books date back over eight hundred years. The library houses the largest collection of ancient texts, not just from the Mzansi, but from all over the world." Ey wafts eir hands in front of eir face and breathes in deeply. "What you smell is literally knowledge—tiny disintegrated paper particles adrift in the very air we breathe. Of course, you can also have the librarians pull actual books for you and read them. I find the knowledge sticks better that way."

"Thanks so much for getting us in here," I say. Then the awkward silence begins.

"So, uh, your teacher's already given you homework?" ey asks.

"We're here for personal reasons," Kasim says, trying to be helpful, but sometimes his half-truth vagaries just bait additional questions.

"Personal reasons?" Chimwe asks. "What kind of personal reasons? Are you looking for anything in particular? The books are stacked according to the Anikalopi Numbering System of Ratios. ANSR for short. Give me the category at least, and I can point you to the right ANSR."

I have no doubts in Chimwe's ability to do so, but I don't really see a way to tactfully broach the subject of demon possession and superhuman abilities. "I think these are the kind of answers we need to seek out on our own," I say. "You know. *Alone.*"

"Oh!" Chimwe says, surprised at first, then a scowl settles upon eir face. "And here I was thinking you two had changed. You can take the boy out of the comfy, but you can't take the comfy out of the boy."

"We're grateful, really!" Kasim pleads.

Chimwe shrugs us off. Footsteps echo softly before ey starts up a ladder tall enough to reach Grace.

"Well, that went about as well as it always does," I say.

"We really could have used a point in the right direction," Kasim admits, chin up, overwhelmed by books shelved up to the rafters. "There are millions of books. Tens of millions. Where do we even start?"

"On the ground, preferably," I say, my neck straining. "How many accidents do you think they have here every year?"

Kasim hangs an arm around my shoulder. "They have to get their skulls from somewhere," he says with a grin.

And so we pick a stack and start to browse, too intimidated to ask anything from anyone and desperately trying to act like we know what we're doing. The first stack is filled mostly with texts written in Sylla. Curiosity gets the best of Kasim, and he pulls a book so tall, it is shelved lying down on its side.

Usura nidu nke Mzansi ani ohya, the title reads.

He stifles a cough as he cracks the book open to the middle. There are several disturbing hand-drawn illustrations of an eviscerated elephant. Skin and muscle pinned down to the sides, revealing the bone structure beneath. It is both foul and mesmerizing at the same time. Kasim flips a few hundred pages and a similar image greets him, this time that of a caracal. My gut stirs.

"We're in the biology section, I guess," I say.

"Ha, look." Kasim points to the inset diagram of the cat's reproductive organs, skin of the scrotum flayed away from a pair of impressive testes. The only familiar word on the page jumps out at me. *Apka*. Sack.

I laugh. "Looks like we're well on our way to being fluent in Sylla," I whisper.

"Ahem," comes a voice from behind us. I turn and see one of the librarians standing there. She holds a pair of thin leather gloves out for each of us. "These are required for all encounters." Her words are scratchy and faintly audible, but her mouth moves plainly as if this were her regular tone of speech. I notice a small scar on her neck, right about where her larynx is.

"To protect the books from the oils in our hands," I say, removing my finger from the cat's ball sack. I grimace at the smudge left behind.

"Yes, and sometimes to protect you from what lies within the books." She folds her arms across her chest and waits for us to don our gloves. When she is satisfied, she pads off, and scales the nearest ladder like a tree-bound primate seeking security among the leaves.

Three stacks over, we're greeted with titles such as: *A Brief History of Malted Toure*, *Eighty-five Unique Ways to Serve Goat*, *The Complete Guide to the Chocolate Delicacies of Pre-War Rashtrakuta*. I heave a sigh. Culinary section. No wonder there are so many books here. Nearly every title reaches deep into some obscure microniche of a topic. I throw my hands up in surrender twenty minutes later when I come across *A History of Tines: A Four-Century Examination of the Dining Utensils Used by the People of the Lalam*

Province. "Come on," I say to Kasim. "We're going to be late for our next class." Kasim doesn't answer. He's got his nose buried in a book. "Did you find something?"

"Something," he says flatly.

I look over his shoulder. On the page, an illustration of a man battling a cat-like demon. The man doesn't appear to be winning.

"Nothing about powers or exorcisms as far as I can tell, but there are dozens of personal accounts of the people of a small Pre-wars tribe in Nri being possessed by demons."

I perk. Kasim allows me to read the text on my own. We're huddled together, like we used to do over the penny pages Mother brought home when we were younger. I'd learned to read a full year before Kasim got the hang of it, and would read the stories to him, and we'd laugh at the comic illustrations together. The closeness is nice, but there is nothing to laugh at among these pages.

The Personal Account of Omehia Sebiko

I was bundled up one night against the cold of the narrow season, when I heard a scream from the sty. The hogs were riled, and that happened sometimes when a wild dog preyed about, so I didn't think much of anything when I went outside in my sleep clothes and an old coat thrown over me, wielding a Long Knife while barefoot and still half asleep. A set of blue-white eyes snapped me out of my fog. I stuck the knife out in front of me. From the corner of my eye I saw all nine of my hogs lying dead, guts torn out of their stomachs, but not eaten. It was then that I realized that this was not a wild dog, and the hogs were not the intended prey.

The demon pounced upon me. Slipped inside me.
Made me rape and murder my wife, while I watched
from behind my own mind. I kept praying and praying
for him to murder me as well, but then he left as
quickly as he came. Left me kneeling there in her still-
warm blood . . .

I tear back from the book, trying to wipe my mind of
images that feel closer to memories than they should, with
unnamable cravings tugging at the roots of my teeth. "What
happens?" I ask Kasim. "Did the demon return?"

"Didn't get the chance. Omehia Sebiko was beheaded
shortly after his statement was given. As were all of the people in this book." Kasim flips the cover for me.

Confessions at the Scimitar's Blade, An Account of
Nri's Possessed

I must look as faint as I feel, because Kasim grabs me by
the shoulder. "It's just an anthropology book. It's not the
answer we're looking for. We'll find it, Auben. Just maybe
not today."

2:00 P.M. ELEMENTARY DEFTING

For the first time today, Kasim leaves my side. The exercises in our Elementary Defting class require groups of
students, and we're separated and put into two smaller established groups. I find myself in a group with a familiar
face—that too-cute girl from our Sylla class.

"Oh, perfect. We get the good one," she says to me as I sit

down. She rolls her eyes, then pulls her defting sticks from a black velvet sachet. My dealings with defting sticks involved exactly the twelve minutes that it took to pick out the cheapest set from the store, but even I can tell the quality and care that went into crafting hers. Each stick is hand carved from a bone sliver, just thick enough to inscribe with gold encrusted lettering down each side. My own are chunky and an offensive shade of blue, with flaky white lettering. My set came with twenty-four, hers with thirty-six.

Unlike the other classrooms, the defting room is completely enclosed, devoid of freely circulating air. It's dusty and stuffy and claustrophobic, and my eyes keep darting to the door, counting down the minutes until I can escape. Our instructor, Msr. Bankole, is a bit more on the flitty side than what I'd expected from a teacher at Gabadamosi: ostentatious gold loop earrings, colorful dyed yarns weaved through eir chunky braids, and a haphazard wardrobe that looks like it was pulled blindly from the bottom of a Saintly's last chance bin. Ey is bright-eyed and kind, and goes into detail for Kasim and me, explaining things many instructors would have assumed we knew without shaming us for our secular background. Ey even sells me on the concept—balancing the sticks, and trying to get them as high as possible without falling. The closer to Grace the sticks rise, the more detailed His message is, deciphered by constructing words from letter pairings at the intersections where the sticks meet.

"Sesay, could you please demonstrate?" Msr. Bankole asks the too-cute girl.

Sesay lights up. Her nimble fingers clear a spot on the packed dirt in front of her and she lays the sticks script side down. She takes two and balances them on their narrow ends without a thought. She places another across their tops, then builds two identical structures so that a triangular base is formed. She continues up, four stories, before her placement becomes nervous and more deliberate. The structure is precarious, and Sesay stops shy of placing the next to last stick.

"There," she says. "If I am deft enough in hand and in spirit, let the words of Grace be told." She backs up, barely breathing. Chalk and scratchboard in hand, she notes down the letter groupings at the intersections starting top down. Finally, she looks upon the scratchboard, filled with her perfectly penned script. A smile curls her lips.

"You can share Grace's message with your cohort if you deem it appropriate," Msr. Bankole says.

"Greatness will soon knock. Be prepared to answer." Sesay turns the board to us, as Msr. Bankole spot-checks the work against a few of the deft tower's indices.

"Excellent work, Sesay," Msr. Bankole gushes. "I am positive greatness will soon be knocking at your door. Let's all take a few practice builds before we start the incantations."

I've built quite a few stick forts in my childhood, so the concept isn't completely foreign. I am interested to see what Grace has to say to me. An apology, perhaps, for not coming to my rescue that night on His mountain.

I open up my cloth sachet and pour out my sticks. I lay them facedown as Sesay had done, then choose the first ones to form my base. I notice that I am the only student to have such chunky sticks. I catch a few chuckles cast in my direction. DEFTING TRAINERS, I see embroidered up the side of my sachet. AGES 5–12. I frown. I bought toys. No wonder they were so much cheaper than the others. Still, I try not to let it bother me as I set the first sticks vertical. They stand for less than a second before falling. I try again. And again, with no more success.

"Perhaps Grace has nothing to say to you," Sesay says through the windows of her new tower.

"I bought the wrong sticks," I say, sweeping them back into a neat pile. "Sorry if I don't come from the kind of family that can afford bone and gold like yours."

Sesay laughs. "My family is from Lesser Poloko. I earned these by working evenings sweeping up slaughterhouse floors with my mother for a year straight."

I'm surprised to hear Sesay is comfy stock. Maybe a little more rural than ours, on the other end of Grace Mountain, but she is more like me and Kasim than any other student in this room.

"Lesser Bezile," I say with a nod. We connect in the briefest of glances, if only for a slight moment and in a completely artificial way. Then I remember the felled sticks before me.

There is a hard knock at the classroom door. All eyes fall onto Sesay. She gives a humble shrug as Msr. Bankole answers. Ey falls to eir knees immediately, and the students all follow suit. Even Kasim and I have managed to catch on.

"I am humbled," comes Gueye Okahim's voice. "Please, return to how you were. I am told that this class possesses a student who is extremely deft at divining the words of Grace. I was hoping that I might have a demonstration."

"We were about to start our incantations, Amawusiakaraseiya," Msr. Bankole gushes, arms moving like ey's not sure what to do with emself. "We would be extremely grateful if you could lead us."

"It would be my pleasure." Gueye Okahim clears his

throat, inhales deeply through his nose, then makes the most beautiful sound I've ever heard come from a human— something like a bird call in a high falsetto, interspersed with moaned words in what I can only assume is Sylla. The class calls back in response, the same words and trills. The incantation goes on, back and forth, for a whole minute, followed by absolute silence. After several seconds, the students begin to build. I fiddle with my sticks, pretending as best as I can. Most students' towers top off at three stories, then they watch Sesay as she begins her fifth. Her structure is more aggressive than her first attempt, less support at the base to allow for greater height.

"The fifth suite is usually reserved for our advanced classes," I hear Msr. Bankole whisper to Gueye Okahim. "Sesay is extremely gifted."

Sesay sets her last stick, then exhales slowly. She makes it look so easy, but a bead of sweat on her forehead belies her effortless grace.

But not every student has taken note of her deftness. I look over to Kasim's group and see him building with borrowed sticks, and not our cheap child's things. He has completed his fourth suite and is about to embark on the fifth with a half dozen more sticks still lying on their sides.

"No," Sesay whispers, wind knocked out of her sails. She bites her trembling lip, and her eyes go cross. I feel for the girl. Maybe she thought she was something special, but clearly Kasim is the real prodigy, and my heart bends out of shape from the pride I have for him.

He starts the fifth suite—three sticks come together in a point. He stacks the sixth suite, a single vertical stick from their index.

"Six suites, two holdovers," Msr. Bankole announces to the class. "From . . . from . . ." Ey has forgotten Kasim's name.

"Kasim, right?" Gueye Okahim offers. "Glad to see that your defting far outshines your grasp of Sylla. The Slight Traore Build is a suite removed from perfection. I've seen even seasoned Men of Virtue struggle with it."

Kasim doesn't respond. At first I think he's being rude, but he's still examining his stack, second to last stick in hand. He's going for another suite. His hand rises to place a vertical stick, end to end, upon the last. As he nears, his movements slow to a near pause. He sets it, finds his balance. Removes his hand. It stays.

"Perfection," Gueye Okahim exhales. "Seven perfect suites. Please, do tell us what words Grace has bestowed upon you."

Still no response. Kasim takes the last remaining stick. Sets it impossibly balanced upon the last. Sits back on his haunches. "Msr. Bankole," Kasim says.

"Yes, Kasim?" Ey says the name like ey will never in eir life forget it again.

"Would it be okay if my brother and I take this class period as open study?"

"Oh, um. I don't have the authority to make such a decision. I'm afraid Elementary Defting is a prerequisite, despite your level of skill. I am thoroughly impressed with your build. If you care, you can share your message with your cohort if you deem it appropriate." Seeing how Gueye had already made such a request, there was a pleading in eir eyes when ey asked Kasim.

The class and I sit awestruck as Kasim takes his scratchboard and chalk, observes the letter pairings at the defting stick indices, then scribbles down the message. I try to catch his gaze, to get some hint at what he's up to. He sits back and his eyes finally stick to mine, one brow arched, thin smile hidden behind drawn lips. I know every single one of Kasim's expressions. This is not one of them.

"Msr. Bankole, would it be okay if my brother and I take this class period as open study?" Kasim says again.

"Kasim, I told you that—"

Kasim holds his scratchboard up to Msr. Bankole. Eir lips go pale and fumble for words. Ey takes the scratchboard and compares it carefully to the structure. "Impossible," ey says. Msr. Bankole shows Grace's words to Gueye Okahim whose brows rise up to the holy brand upon his forehead.

Gueye Okahim clears his throat and reads from the scratchboard, "'Msr. Bankole, would it be okay if my brother and I take this class period as open study?'"

"Yes, Kasim," Msr. Bankole stammers. "I think that it will be fine."

The remainder of our day passes much less spectacularly, though Kasim has gathered a small audience of curious on-lookers determined to witness his next live performance. He leaves them disappointed as we finally retire for the evening to Soyinka House, a building conveniently located close to absolutely nothing. It's practically in the wilderness—the front lawn an outcropping of manicured weeds surrounded by knee-high fine bush, medicinal varieties mostly that give the air a musky, astringent bite. The rotunda itself is cold gray stone with tall thin windows built before fire regulations existed. As we near, we hear the disturbing sounds of teenaged ruckus and roughhousing within.

Inside, Soyinka House is one overturned couch away from being declared a national disaster. The few pieces of upright furniture in the foyer are threadbare and/or broken. The large SOYINKA HOUSE banner hangs from the wall, completely skewed, with a cluster of odd stains near the bottom which I'm pretty sure are urine. In a collective effort to keep the place tidy, nearly all of the spent beer cans have landed within five feet of the trash bin. These are the most endearing things about this place.

"Mtuze boys! Welcome to Soyinka House!" a student breathes into our faces, the sting of alcohol grossly apparent. "Here. We want you to feel at home." The kid sticks dented cans of tinibru into our hands. I am so relieved to see something familiar here that it takes a long moment for the offense to sink in. A small group of boys and andies snicker into their hands, pointing at us and our comfy ale. For the first time today, the true brunt of my anger brews within me.

"No, thanks," I hiss at the jerk—the bottom of the barrel, as far as Gabadamosi students go, and yet still, his favored status would allow him to stroll through life without a hitch, without a slipup or a step gone afoul. Spite roils within me, and I squeeze the can tight in my hand, squeeze so hard that foam starts to gurgle out of the seams at the top. Kasim lays his hand on my shoulder, and takes the can from me, then lets it drop at our feet. As we take our leave down the curved hallway, I loosen the muscles I've been so mindful of, channeling the cold to the tips of my fingers. I touch a wall as we pull away from the laughter and mocking behind us. Tendrils of ice creep along the old brick, down to the packed dirt floor, and the thinnest sheet of ice forms beneath the toes of our tormentors. Seconds later, the laughs become a chorus of "Oh, shit!" and "What in Grace's name . . . ?" Seven thuds follow, the sounds of their thick skulls striking the ground, and I allow myself a brief laugh with Icy Blue before tightening the reins. His brusk laugh continues, though, and I have a sinking suspicion that it's directed at me.

Kasim's eyes are focused on the room numbers, which are ascending and not descending like we need them to. A quick chat with a guy on the way to the showers points us in the direction of "supplemental housing," which we learn is a polite term for the basement dungeon.

Our "room" is spacious and damp, with a horrid draft. Sparse furnishings consist of four empty bunks pushed along one wall, two ratty couches that make the ones upstairs look like they are fit for nobility, and a circular coffee table that takes up the rest of the space. An ominous red light seeps from under a locked door labeled BOILER ROOM, only adding to the room's natural ambiance.

"Welcome home, Auben," Kasim says to me, trying hard to find some sideways truth that will make me feel better. He fails and the silence stretches thin between us, punctuated by groans and knocks from the boiler and the squeal of water running through cold pipes. He picks the closest bunk and slings his satchel up on top.

I take the bottom, sitting upon a brown blanket purposely engineered to be the roughest, scratchiest material in the entire existence of man. I unpack my few belongings and scatter them about, trying to forget where we are and why we are here. It doesn't come close to working.

"How'd you do it, Kasim?" I ask, late into the night when it becomes obvious that neither of us is going to get any sleep.

"The thing with the defting sticks?" he says. "I can't

even say. I was in a trance, like I was only an observer in my own mind. You ever get that?"

I think of my time backstage with Ruda, and the room's temperature drops a few degrees. "Yeah. I didn't like it at all."

"Me neither. But at least we have a dedicated two hours to spend in the library each day." His voice trembles against the cold. I pull the scratchy blanket from the bunk next to us and toss it up.

"Thanks," he says. He's always hated the cold. When we were small, and the coke piles in our furnace were smaller, Kasim would come down from his bunk and we'd huddle under my covers, face-to-face, our breath keeping the other's nose warm. I miss that.

I touch underneath the top bunk with all five fingers. The queasiness swells within my gut. Pressure builds until I go icy cold all over, and can no longer stand to hold back the reins. I release, fully. Completely. My fingertips go blue, and frozen crystals arc out across the spring support in the most beautiful pattern and then creep up into the mattress.

"Auben?" comes Kasim's pained voice.

"Yeah?"

"Do you think I could come down there with you?" Kasim asks, his voice ripe with sentimentality. "You know. Like when we were kids."

I bite back my smile. "Yeah, sure. I guess."

Face-to-face, he cringes at the chill on my breath, but smiles a content smile nevertheless. My heart warms over.

"Do you think we made a mistake coming here?" I ask him.

"I . . . I don't know," he says through chattering teeth. "Ask me again in the morning, after I've had a chance to thaw out."

I watch him after he drifts off. His body flinches and jerks. He mumbles incoherently, but the worst are the stifled screams. I wonder about the demon inside him. What is it saying to him that brings so much pain?

I realize that in my eagerness to draw Kasim into my bed, I've forgotten to put Icy Blue back in his. I make a mental move to contain him, but his presence has already spread like an infection. I feel him at the points of my teeth, and behind my eyes—staring out like they're drafty windowpanes. I feel him in the soft press of my lips against Kasim's forehead.

Kasim's nightmares recede. He trembles once more before going as still as a corpse.

We have work to do, Icy Blue bids me.

As much as I wish to deny him, in my bones I know that blood must be spilled tonight. It was foolish of me to wrap myself in the cloak of the devil before first checking the price tag. The cost for wielding my powers is steep, and now it is Icy Blue who wears my skin like an animal's pelt, ill-fitting and unforgiving. My limbs move all the wrong ways within my own body. It's like my legs have too few joints, my hands too many fingers, my jaws too tight for the cram of fangs, but Icy Blue is adaptable if nothing else. Up on the main floor, my hand touches upon every knob I pass. A silent twist. I pray with all my might that each is locked. I smell them all—the sweetness of their breath, the raw stink from the pits of their arms and the crux of their thighs, the tang of iron seeping from their pores. My mouth waters at the thought of warm flesh slipping down my throat.

Finally, a knob turns. Two occupied bunks. Heavy snoring. The most wicked arousal whips through me, and I go hard and heavy as Icy Blue plots which he'll have first.

With all the good I have left within me, I drive my hand into my pocket, break my mirror, crunch glass against my palm until it's a bloody pulp, but the pain is no longer enough, and while my mind panics, my other hand tugs at the scratchy covers of the bottom bunk, eager like a child tearing away the foil wrapper of a proper chocolate. My cravings both repulse and implore me. Gooseflesh rises upon the student's long, lean legs. Up his thighs. Nipples pucker through the fabric of his sleep gown. His throat bobs as he swallows.

There. The throat. Vulnerable, exposed. I get closer. So close, I can already taste him. I try to close my eyes to the ensuing massacre at least, but they remain peeled.

"Don't do this," I strain against my vocal cords. If I cannot stop Icy Blue by force, perhaps I can reason with him. "If you leave him be, tonight is all yours. Do whatever you want with me. I swear I won't resist."

I'd like to see you attempt to resist me. My index finger runs along the student's neck, my nail leaving behind the thinnest scratch.

"Tonight and tomorrow night then."

The scratch deepens, draws blood. The scent of it hits me harder than a brick to the face. My will to resist is waning. I have to bargain with everything I've got. Now or never.

"Midnight to sunup. Tonight, tomorrow night, and every night. No restraints. No restrictions. But you can't harm him, or any of the other students at Gabadamosi."

The finger lifts.

Deal, Icy Blue says coolly, coyly across my lips. I realize in my desperation I have given him too much leash. The conditions of our arrangement are set, but I hope Icy Blue takes pity on me and is open to make one amendment.

"Can I ask that I not witness any of it?"

At my words, I recede into a small cage held in the space an inch behind my navel. Icy Blue locks me away for the night, and the last thing I remember is the breaking of a narrow glass window.

I awake in bed the next morning, body sore and satisfied, Kasim's breath still in my face . . . and a mouthful of soured blood pressing at my lips. I run upstairs to the restroom and puke my guts into the toilet. It's like a massacre in the bowl, but I am careful and neat, and it all slides away with a single flush. When I stand up, I feel like myself. My old self. I know that it is only because Icy Blue is in a limbless stupor, sleeping off his binge, but I allow myself one happy moment of normalcy before my panicked thoughts come crashing down around me. Coming to Gabadamosi to control these demons was a mistake. They're getting stronger by the day, and I doubt even a decade studying here would give us the means to tame their meddling. If there's ever been a time for drastic measures, it's now.

"We need to go to the Sanctuary and beg them to exorcise us," I say to Kasim as I shake him from the grips of sleep with one hand and pull my uniform on with the other. "Gueye Okahim can do it himself, I don't care."

"What time is it?" he groans.

"A quarter to six, and we're already wasting daylight." I yank the covers off him, and he crunches into a pitiful shivering ball.

"Please. Just ten more minutes. I slept awful last night."

"Voices?" I dare to ask.

He shakes his head. "Nightmares for a change. It was gruesome." Kasim winces. "On second thought, maybe more sleep is the last thing I need." He rolls out of bed, stretches tall, then rubs his abdomen as if he's sore from a proximity break. "How'd you sleep?"

"About as well as can be expected with a demon clawing about inside. Come on, let's go. Munashe will know how we can get in to see him."

"See who?" Kasim yawns.

I growl at my brother, throwing his school ciki at him, and stare him down until he's fully dressed.

Besides the broken window and the expense of replacing two-hundred-year-old glass, it seems like business as usual on campus. Whatever Icy Blue's dealings were last night, they took place far enough from here. Still, I can't stand the guilt of knowing I'd killed. It is my only hope that it'd been animal blood, like those hogs from the library book—and not like what came after. Whatever else happens, we can't let another midnight pass. We need to perform the exorcism before midnight.

When we enter the administration building this time, the air is much sweeter and the smiles much more genuine. "How may I help you, Mr. Mtuze?" the fem kigen at the reception desk offers, speaking directly past me and looking dreamily into Kasim's eyes.

"We're here to see Munashe," I say, waving eir attention back my way. "Is she in?"

"Sure, she's in her office. I'll tell her you're here. Can I get you any water while you wait?"

My tongue is still tacky from the night's diversions. "I'll

have some, thanks," I say into eyes that have failed to acknowledge my existence.

"Water would be wonderful," Kasim says. The receptionist perks, eagerly jumping from eir seat. "Two glasses," Kasim specifies sheepishly. Better to be clear now, than to deal with the embarrassment later when ey shows up with one.

Whispers and stares come soon after, and the whole business of the office grinds to a halt. We are told repeatedly that never in the two hundred sixty years of Gabadamosi's history has a student made eight defting suites. It has been rumored over the centuries that Men of Virtue have accomplished such a feat, but even those were few and far between.

Finally, Munashe's little door opens. She exits quickly, though a broom handle escapes with her, and she shoves it back in. "Kasim, Auben . . ." she says, standing taller than our first encounter. Yesterday she'd drawn the short stick and had gotten stuck with the job of orienting a couple of comfy rats. Today she is the envy of the entire office as she advises the young defting prodigy that had impressed their beloved Amawusiakaraseiya . . . and his tagalong brother. "I am so glad to see you this morning. How can I be of assistance?"

"We were hoping to get access to the Sanctuary," I say. "We need to see Gueye Okahim."

"Sure," Munashe says, trying her best not to laugh. "You and everyone else."

My face falls.

"Oh . . . you're serious. Well, there's an eighteen-month waiting list."

Eighteen months? We don't even have eighteen hours. "Well, will he make an exception? It's sort of urgent." I bite my tongue so I won't seem completely desperate. I can't risk going into details, not with the way the entire office is watching us. I'm not even sure I want Munashe to know the whole truth.

"Well," Munashe says, fingers rubbing absentmindedly at her chunky kola nut necklace. "I guess you could try to catch him after services next Tiodoti. The only other option would be to get him to take you into his confidence for a possible apprenticeship." Munashe avoids playing favorites, but I can't help but notice that she looks directly at Kasim when she says this.

"We're not that desperate. We've just got questions," he says in a half yawn, not understanding how serious things have gotten. "Religious questions."

"Well, if you've got questions about faith, I know how you can get answers. All you need is a *library badge*." They're simple words, but when Munashe says them, it's like she's wielding a sword. Maybe all we were lacking was diligence the first time. Lacking proper motivation. I smack my lips again, the receptionist delivering a cool cup of water into my hand at just the right time. "Anything you could possibly need, you'll find there."

"Anything?" I ask. I take a sip.

"Anything," she says with confidence.

Kasim raises a brow to me. I grimace. If this is our only option, we'll have to make it work. "Okay. We'll try the library."

Munashe snaps her fingers, and the eavesdropping receptionist drops the paperwork ey'd been pretending to be shuffling, and rushes to the back of the office to dig through drawers. Ey brings back two forms attached to clipboards.

We fill the forms out and sign them and pass them back to Munashe. She looks down at mine. "Auben, your writing is beautiful. I wish I had script like that."

Half a life spent practicing at signature forgeries has turned it into an art form. "I've got an interest in calligraphy, I guess." I shrug.

Munashe passes the clipboards back to the receptionist, and ey disappears into a room at the back of the office. "So is there anything else I can get you besides library badges?"

"Our accommodations are a bit lacking," I say. Might as well shoot for the stars while I've got the chance. "We were hoping that we could get a room on the main floor. The cold was nearly the death of us in that basement."

"I am so sorry, Auben," Munashe says, directly to me. She doesn't consult Kasim for confirmation. "Housing is always a challenge at the beginning of the quarter, but I'll double-check to see if something more suitable hasn't become available." She touches my arm, down near my elbow. She startles as she feels the keloid scar beneath my sleeve. "Auben!" she says. "How are you two tempered?"

"Six and one," I mutter, fully ashamed of the part of me I used to be so proud of. In my old life, my bad boy persona got me what I wanted, who I wanted, when I wanted. People loved me for my vices. People hated me for them. But here, they make me worse than hated. They make me invisible.

I expect Munashe to fawn over Kasim like everyone else, but she doesn't. Instead she asks me with an inquisitive brow, "Can I see them? Administration doesn't send many six-and-ones my way."

I roll up my sleeve to my shoulder. She traces a finger along each of my vices. Beyond being inappropriate, her reaction throws me completely off. Greater twins are usually repulsed, lesser ones impressed. But Munashe is neither of these. She seems impartial. She observes and takes note without judgment. "You know," I say. "I've shown you mine. It's only fair that you show me yours."

"Auben!" Kasim nudges me.

"Sorry," I say. I've said that line so many times, it's impossible for me not to.

"It's fine," Munashe says. "And you're right. It's only fair." She rolls her sleeve up. Her arm is completely bare. No vices. Six-and-one is rare enough. There's no way she's a seven-and-none. That's impossible. No one is viceless, except Grace. And no one escapes Discernment and goes on to tell about it. That leaves only one other option. "You're a loner?"

"Auben!" Kasim says, a harder nudge this time.

"I was born a singleton, yes," Munashe says, not taking offense.

"Sorry. That's what I meant." No wonder she was a pariah in the office. It has been many decades since singletons were drowned at birth, and though there has been progress toward equality, the prejudice against them is still very real. I can't deny having bullied a few over the years. Not that they didn't usually deserve it. Loners were all rough edges, unpredictable, emotions all over the place, and popular only as villains in storybooks. They were exhausting to be around, and usually ended up in whackhouses well before their eighteenth birthdays. It's been years since I've seen one in school. I catch myself staring.

"It's okay," Munashe says. "I know it's odd. The stuff you're going through, trying to fit in—I know what it's like when you're different. It's tough. That's why I don't hide it from my students. It's also why I ask to advise our more non-traditional students. Seriously, you two, you can come to me with anything. I'll help however I can."

My mind churns over what it must be like to be an only. She could go anywhere she wanted, whenever she wanted without having to consult another person. She wasn't tied down, no bickering, no jealousy, no vying for parental attention. She didn't have to worry about snapping off. In a way, she had absolute freedom, and yet when I think of life without Kasim, I feel a crippling of my legs. Our whole world had once been the confines of Mother's womb, and during the first stretch of our lives, his face is all that I knew and loved. Our worlds have grown wider, and we have drifted apart, but what was forged in our hearts has not changed, will not change. He is mine, and I am his. It deeply pains me that Munashe will never experience this.

"I appreciate your offer," I say to her. "And I'm sorry you have to live this way." Kasim and I are shoulder to shoulder again. I glance at him, the sorrow heavy on his brow as well, but he has the grace not to make himself look like a complete comfy bumpkin.

"No reason to be sorry. It's just the way I am. I don't know any differently."

And that is exactly why I am sorry for her.

On our way to Sylla class, we take a shortcut through the statuary garden, or the *quad* as we've found it's commonly called. The place makes the hairs on my neck rise, but if we went around, we'd lose a whole ten minutes and be late for Sylla again, and I'd really like to avoid any unnecessary drama on our second day of school. The morning sun has taken the chill out of the air, and finally it's warm enough for students to go around in short cikis. They laze among the grotesque stained-glass statuaries, books splayed, fingers running through the soft carpet of grass. Eyes gaze at the slow waterfall of clouds rolling over the top of Grace Mountain. Laughter drifts around us as welshing balls are tossed, risqué jokes are whispered, flirtatious fingers are slapped away. All the while, these mythological glass creatures loom, watching hungrily with chimeral fangs and talons and scaled wings on edge.

"Heads up!" calls a boy.

Kasim stops me short, and a pair of brass welshing balls shoot past us and thud against the ground.

"Sorry, sal," the boy says as he hobbles past us to retrieve them with the most wicked limp, but slows and backs up, carefully approaching us like we're feral dogs. "You," he says, pointing to Kasim. "You're that new kid, right? The defting prodigy? The one Gueye Okahim has gone rabid for?"

"Um, I guess?" Kasim says, giving the boy his patented humble-as-shit-pie smile. "Kasim," he says, extending his hand. The boy eagerly takes it in both of his, and just about shakes Kasim's arm loose from his shoulder.

"Phila," the boy says, all teeth and gums. "Phila Kumalo. Third year. Co-vice president of the Gabadamosi Welshing Club. Do you play?"

"No, never had the chance," Kasim says.

"Never? Not even once? Man, you've missed out. Athleticism, strategy, precision." Phila attempts a couple of stiff-legged welshing moves.

"It's not exactly an accessible sport where I grew up."

Phila's eyes go wide and he nods knowingly, almost embarrassed. "Full of snobs, you're saying. Yeah, yeah. I get that. But the club isn't pretentious. We're really laid back. You should try it at least."

"I'm Auben, by the way," I say, extending my hand.

Phila lifts his chin at me. "Yeah, hey, sal. Good to meet ya." His eyes whip back to Kasim. "We practice three times a week, two games a week—one home and one away, and we usually do a tournament per quarter. There are fees for those, and the uniforms and equipment can be pricey, but we've got wealthy old donors out the dungpipe. We have a yearly exhibition for alums. Let them relive their glory days on the course, and the djang rolls—"

"Phila!" calls a guy across the quad, neck to knees in pads and a mask over his face. "Any day now!"

"Hold your oryx, bait breath. I'm talking to that new kid from the comfy."

"The one that made a deft tower ten suites high?" Bait Breath calls. "The one that called Gueye Okahim a false prophet, and then had Gueye begging him to be his apprentice?"

"Of course. How many other new kids from the comfy do you know of?"

I grit my teeth. "We're actually on our way to class, so if you'll excuse us." I push past Phila, surprised I didn't glide through him like the apparition I seem to be.

"Yeah, we've really got to get going. It was nice to meet you," Kasim says.

"You'll come check out one of our games, right? There's one tomorrow evening at seven. Welshing course B."

"Sorry. That's just not my thing," Kasim says with a shrug. "But good luck. Hope you win."

"Yeah, yeah. It's not really my thing either. Just doing it because it looks good on the transcript, you know." Phila runs over to the balls, noticeably less stiff and gimpy. He tosses the balls back to Bait Breath, and they land wide right. "You can move your feet, you know!" he yells at his buddy, then smiles at Kasim. "See ya around, then." He trots off, a couple of tender skip-steps before easing into a flawless gait.

I glare at Kasim. "You healed him, didn't you?"

"I didn't mean to," he says with a shrug. "It slipped out of me, like I had no control. By the time I realized what I was doing, it was too late to stop it. It was a minor sprain anyway. Would have healed itself in a couple days."

No control. I know all too well what that's like. Fourteen more hours until midnight.

In Sylla class, I become a sponge, absorbing every symbol, every inflection I can. Nearly half of the books in the library were written in Sylla, so that means there's a fifty-fifty chance that the book we need will be, too. I drill Kasim on vowels, on consonants. Pages flip as I cram a week's worth of vocabulary into each of our five-minute partnered exercises. Halfway through class, Kasim clenches his temples.

"Headache?" I ask.

"Yeah," he says through gritted teeth.

"The voices?" I say, whispering this time.

"Your voice. Does that count?" Kasim manages a half smile. "You're pushing me too hard. Everything is going in one ear and out the other. What's the rush, anyway?"

The classroom goes silent, and suddenly Jomealah Aguda is upon us. I expect him to fawn over Kasim like everyone else is, but instead his ruler snaps Kasim's knuckles. *"Nagi gei Sylla biko,* Jomealah Mtuze!" he says. "You may be getting an A in Elementary Defting, but you aren't guaranteed one in here." He speaks so dismissively to Kasim, like it's been raining defting prodigies for the past two weeks. "Sylla, class. Sylla is now your mother tongue." Jomealah Aguda slaps his ruler on Kasim's desk. Kasim flushes so hard, his ears go red. Wouldn't faze me, but Kasim, I don't think he's ever been reprimanded like that. The other students snap to attention, and a tidal wave of perfectly enunciated foreign words fills the air.

I bite back my grin. I hate Jomealah Aguda for embarrassing Kasim, but it's good to know there are a few people on campus who aren't swooning over him for yesterday's antics. I push Kasim harder, making him rattle off irregular verb conjugations, one after another.

What's the rush? Icy Blue says with a satisfied yawn. His sleep was deep, but short.

"Again," I demand of Kasim, in Sylla. "Faster."

As we file out of Sylla class, I give Kasim absolute proximity. I rub his back, hang my arm over his shoulder, but nothing soothes his nerves. He walks in a trance, book satchel clenched to his chest. He doesn't acknowledge the world until cute little Sesay comes scampering around us and gives Kasim a big hug, her head barely coming up to his chest.

"You looked like you needed that," Sesay says. "And if it makes you feel any better, Jomealah Aguda made me cry my first day. He made me feel like a complete idiot, and my mother was a Nri Scholar with a concentration in Sylla, and she's spoken it to me since the day I was born." She purses her lips, looks at Kasim like she's sizing him up, then pulls an enormous leather-bound binder from her satchel and flips through hundreds of pages until her finger lands on a sheet crammed with diagrams, a map, an impressively detailed family tree, and the tiniest, neatest handwriting I've ever seen. "So I dug into his life story. He's seven-eighths Rashtrakutan. Only his great-grandmother was born here, and she was stolen off by Rashtra traders. She was their plaything. Birthed twin sons on board their ship and died a few months later from the pains of the proximity break. The kids were dropped off on a Rashtra port, and raised there. 'Jomealah Aguda' didn't even step foot onto Mzansi soil until ten years ago. Aguda isn't even his real last name. It's Khan."

She proudly pushes the binder into our faces, her finger tapping at a newspaper clipping taped next to a copy of our teacher's birth certificate. She slams the binder shut, and the tension eases off Kasim's face.

"So he's a fraud?" I say. "I knew it."

"Not a fraud. Just an impassioned guy. Very intelligent. You just need to know how to handle him." Sesay nods back at her patiently waiting crew, her finger twirling the thin gold chain around her neck like she's a smitten kitten. "Anyway, a few of us are about to grab lunch. Would you like to join us?"

All of a sudden, Kasim looks a whole lot less pathetic— which is a bit pathetic in its own right. He loosens his grip on his satchel and swings it over his shoulder. Then he looks at me, brows raised. My brow drops. Our eyes connect, and in the silent language of twins, I tell him we don't have time to waste. We need to get to the library. This is important. This is life or death.

Kasim nods, transmission received. "Sure, I'd love to join you," he says to Sesay.

My mouth gapes.

What?

Sesay turns to me. "You're welcome, too, Auben," she says, but for all the grace running through her veins, she cannot hide the fear in her eyes that I will accept. I do not. I make up an excuse about needing to get to the library, which is of course not actually an excuse, but a necessity.

"I'll meet you there after lunch," Kasim says. "I promise I'll give you my full attention. I just need a little mental break right now."

A mental break. That's exactly what I need, too—a break from the demon in my mind. I shake my head in disbelief as I watch them walk off toward the cafeteria in their tight little group, Kasim two heads taller than the others, hunching over and laughing at their jokes. He looks back at me, nods almost imperceptibly with what looks like absolute joy upon his face. I cannot blame him. I don't care how many virtues you have, being wanted feels damned good.

Unfortunately, I'm feeling the exact opposite.

A hand lays itself upon my shoulder. "Twinemies, am I right?" It's Daki, Sesay's twin. Same cute face, but fuller and wiser. Nearly as bad at defting as I am. "Can't live with them, can't live without them."

Twinemies. I've heard the term, but never thought it

would apply to Kasim and me. I push the possibility from my mind. "Kasim and I aren't like that," I say. "He's just hanging out with some new friends."

"That's how it starts. A lunch date here and there. Then come the excuses to why he forgot to show up to that thing you were supposed to do together. Then come the offhand comments that make you feel less than. Then the bickering. Then the avoidance. Don't feel bad. It's the natural progress of things. Especially for twins like us." Daki raises her sleeve to reveal all six of her vice scars.

I gawk. I cannot keep my fingers from touching them without asking, even after a lifetime of giving people the hairy eyeball for doing the same to me. They are smooth to the touch, and give easily when I press upon them. They shimmer in the sun, like fish scales. Finally, I meet another person in this wicked world with six vices. I let loose a long sigh. She's just like me.

She is nothing like you, Icy Blue growls. *She is not destined for greatness.*

"You're welcome to come have lunch with us." Daki juts her chin in the direction of three other students, their faces familiar from class. I wince at how they're all clumped together like the fermented sludge at the bottom of a can of tinibru . . . the stuff nobody wants to drink.

Icy Blue is right. Six vices or no, she is not like me, and is far from being worthy of my friendship. I don't know what it means to agree with Icy Blue, but it can't possibly be a good thing. "Thanks, but no thanks," I say, not bothering to mask the revulsion in my words. Seeing the hurt upon Daki's face gives me an odd pleasure. I feel Icy Blue's grin upon my lips as I walk off.

"This doesn't make us friends either," I say aloud to Icy Blue without a single care to who might overhear.

Oh, we're more than friends, Auben. Much more.

I shudder, and hasten my pace to the library.

Still no luck finding a book on exorcism, but after an hour, I narrow things down to a section on demons. I find Icy Blue among the pages of a dusty tome and trace my fingers along his varied forms. The caracal is the most common sighting attributed to him, and the most well-known, but he is said to take on other shapes—baboons, snakes, and oddly, penguins—but I guess they do enjoy the cold. He has also been known to take on the form of humans.

I think of what happened last night in the dorm room, the smashing of glass as Icy Blue slipped us out of that window far too narrow for my torso to fit through. He had to have shifted into another form. And if he could shift my body, was it possible for me to do the same? It's not safe to entertain such thoughts, but Kasim is already ten minutes late. With every second that ticks by, Daki's words rile my temper. Twinemies. Not us. Not ever. As a desperate distraction, I look at my fingers, imagining them as caracal claws. Something knocks in my gut, followed by a sound like nails dragged along the surface of a scratchboard—only the sound is coming from inside me. I wince against the irritation as my fingertips lengthen and narrow into three-inch claws. Dried blood sits at their nail beds. My heart wrenches into a knot, and for a long moment, I forget how to breathe.

"There he is," I hear Kasim's sharp whisper from the end of the stack.

I shake my hands hard, and when I look again, they are my own. My lungs scream at me to take a breath, and I'm still panting when Kasim—and *Sesay*—reach me.

"I haven't seen someone flush this hard since I caught my baba reading a vice mag," Sesay says to me with a smile. She's trying to be coy and charming, but now isn't a time for schoolyard antics, so she might as well go do it somewhere else.

Kasim laughs so loud he gets shushed by an acrobatic librarian passing twenty feet above us. "Sorry we're late," he says earnestly. "Sesay and I got to chatting about comfy life, and lunch dragged on." He's doing it already. He's making up excuses.

"I'm surprised you didn't bring me a doggie bag. I'm starting to get used to lapping up your seconds," I say, burying myself back into my book. Perhaps I can figure out how to transform myself into a giant clue, so Kasim can take it.

"What's that supposed to mean?" Kasim asks.

"It means that if we make plans to do something important, you show up on time, not twenty minutes late. And not with her . . ."

"I just remembered," Sesay says quietly, "that I hate being in the middle of awkward situations. Lunch tomorrow, Kasim?"

"Yeah, sure," he says, smile lit up like a bush during the narrow season. It fades the moment she turns the corner. "Seriously, Auben, it's just like you to make a mountain out of a molehill. Maybe for once you can make an effort to care about something on this side of the mirror."

And here come the offhand comments. This can't be happening. Not right now. "Are you throwing my vainglory in my face? Sorry I'm so self-obsessed about ridding myself of the demon holed up inside me—and you!"

"That's why I brought Sesay here. She had an idea of where we might look for books. But now she's gone, thanks to you."

We're definitely bickering. I grit my teeth. "You told her about us?"

"Relax. I didn't *tell her* tell her. I told her it was for a personal research project, which is kind of true. She's nice, Auben. You should give her a chance. She says she'll help us however she can." Kasim blushes. "I think she's crushing on me."

"Everyone on this whole damned campus is crushing on you, or haven't you noticed?"

"Shhhhhhh . . ." comes a cacophony of hushes from above.

"You're being ridiculous." Kasim averts his eyes. Avoidance. Just like Daki said. "People have taken an interest in me for a change. So what? I can't control anyone but myself, Auben. I suggest you learn how to do the same. If you need me, I'll be over here." We've fought hundreds of times before, and a lot worse than this, but the resignation in his voice chills me deeper than Icy Blue ever could.

"Fine," I rasp.

"Fine."

What nerve. A rhythmic *swak snick swak snick* distracts me from my brooding, like the sound of a switchblade opening and closing. It takes me a moment to realize that I'm flexing my claws, in and out, in and out like it's second nature. Or first nature. I sigh. Maybe I ought to be making the most of a bad situation. I've got a couple of cool powers.

Enough to make myself into someone that could rival Kasim's popularity on campus. I could grow a few inches taller, if I wanted. I could change my eyes, my hair, my chimeral stripes, my scars. Whatever I wanted to see in the mirror, I could be. Yes, the price is dear, but with popularity, I would gain the power needed to mold this world into one that gives everyone a fair shake. I could bring the whole system of lesser twinhood down, and see to it that all people—male, female, and kigen, vice and virtue heavy, singleton and twin—are treated as equals, socially and economically. Except me of course. I would be treated as a god. My mind starts down an endless spiral of plotting. I'm three decades deep when Kasim taps me on my shoulder.

"I think I've found something," he says, holding a book open to a detailed diagram. He sits down beside me and explains the exorcism process. The supplies we'll need seem simple enough to come by. The celestial alignments are in our favor. The incantations are difficult, but we're both quick learners. But there's one last hitch.

"We'll need a third person," Kasim tells me. "I think it should be Sesay. She already knows the Sylla, so that's one less thing we have to worry about. She really is good people, Auben."

"She's hiding something," I say, shaking my head. I can't quite put my finger on it, but something about her doesn't add up, and it's not just my jealousy clouding up my thoughts. "She may seem polished and poised with all those virtues dangling from her gold chain, but she's got comfy wiles in her eyes. When you did that thing with the defting sticks, you should have seen the look on her face. She was the prodigy on campus before you came along. She's worked a slaughterhouse floor, Kasim. Sesay's not afraid of blood, and she could be coming after you."

Kasim swallows back a laugh. "I highly doubt it."

I nod. "That's her vice, you know. Doubt. It's the worst one."

"Really? Worse than temper?"

"Tempers flare. Maybe there's some cussing. Maybe even a fight. But tempers fade eventually. Doubt lingers. Burrows through your heart, steals away your happiness. Slowly consumes you from within."

"Okay, Auben," Kasim says with an exasperated sigh. "Who do you have in mind for a third?"

I chew my lip, and one name springs immediately to mind. "Munashe."

"Right. Let's bring school staff into this. Then we'll have expulsions on our records as well as demons in our heads."

"Munashe wouldn't turn us in," I say. "She said we could trust her with anything."

"I think she meant more like getting an extra copy of our transcripts or finding a good math tutor." Kasim gets up and begins to pace the aisle like a caged animal. I stand in his tracks, ready to defend my selection. I have to be convincing, or risk putting our fates in Sesay's conniving little hands.

"She said *anything*," I growl.

"You're sure about this?" he asks. "Because there's no going back once the caracal is out of the bag."

"We can trust her. We can do this. The three of us," I declare, hoping to infect him with my conviction.

Kasim stares at me. Looking for what? Signs of weakness? I won't back down. Not on something this important. "Okay," he finally says. Then his brows cinch. His mouth screws up into a sour twist. "Have you grown?"

"I'm not quite sure I understand what you're asking of me," Munashe says later that afternoon, inside the privacy of her office/broom closet.

It smells of bleach and old mop water in here, but she's gone through lengths to make it cozy. Kasim sits in an undersized leather chair and Munashe sits behind an antique desk lopped off on one end to make it fit inside the room. A faux window featuring an expertly painted campus scene keeps the place from being completely claustrophobic, and next to it she displays her Gabadamosi certificate. She graduated only a few years ago, and yet in that time, piles upon piles of embossed folders have accumulated haphazardly on every flat surface. I stand near the door, next to the cleaning supplies, since there is nowhere else left for me to fit.

Munashe tips the lid of the miniature smokestack sitting on her desk, pushes around the pile of half-djang coins, then frowns at the rather phallic-looking candle. "You know that it's against regulations to burn this on campus?" she says, picking the candle up, turning it around, probably trying to convince herself that it's an oddly shaped mushroom, but no. It's a wax dick with a wick. Cinnamon scented. She flushes with embarrassment as she sets it down.

"We know," I say, testing the waters. "That's why we came to you. We were hoping that you could help us bend a few rules. The candles are a part of an experiment my brother and I are conducting. We were hoping that if you oversaw their use, we could trust you to keep this little secret of ours."

"Okay," Munashe says without hesitation. "If it's really that important to you." She touches the head of the candle with her index finger, then as she assesses the seemingly random collection of objects, something clicks. "These represent vices, don't they? Like in Discernment? The candle for lechery. The mirror for vainglory. The coins for greed. A false eye for envy." She leans over the glass jar, eye bobbing in fluid—brown iris, with flecks of green. "Please tell me this is a *false* eye."

Kasim looks back at me. The lie is mine to tell. Agreeing to break a minor policy is one thing, but this is where we will know if Munashe is truly on our side. "We got it from the mortuary down the road."

Munashe gasps. "Buying human body parts is against the law!"

"Well, I guess it's a good thing we stole it," I say.

"Boys!" Munashe looks at us, exasperated.

"We'll return it when we're done," Kasim offers. "Nobody's going to miss it."

"We came to you, Munashe, because we're desperate for your help. This is a lot to ask, and we know that. We won't blame you if you want to turn us in. But you said we could come to you for anything. This is our anything. It's big. Bigger than stolen eyes even. And it's incredibly important to us." Truer words have never fallen from my lips, and I think Munashe hears that in the cadence of my pleas. At least I hope she does. I pass Munashe a roll of aged parchment. She opens it, and sees the diagram torn from the book. She slowly rolls it back up, and looks at us.

"Which one of you is possessed?" she says quietly, flatly.

"The both of us," Kasim says. He looks so damned pitiful right now.

"This is way above my pay grade, but it's always been my goal to help nontraditional students." Munashe pulls a smile through the sheer terror on her face. "I think you guys certainly fall under that category."

"Thank you so much, Munashe," I say. "If there was room, I'd go over there and hug you right now."

"Your gratitude is enough," she says.

Kasim and I beam at each other. "Perfect," he says. "So we'll meet up tomorrow night and—"

"Tomorrow?" I say. I can't go another night with Icy Blue inside me. I can still taste the blood in the back of my throat. "Can't we do it now?"

"It has to be by the light of the full moon. The full moon is tomorrow night."

I feel my eyes running down the curves of Munashe's body.

Mmm. It's been so long since I've tasted the flesh of a singleton.

You promised to leave Gabadamosi alone. Find your prey elsewhere.

I promised to leave the students of Gabadamosi alone.

"You know that's not what I meant!" I yell. Munashe and Kasim stare at me blankly.

"What did you mean?" Kasim asks. "Are you okay?"

I give him a look that I am definitely not okay. I have to tell him about Icy Blue and what happened last night. He can tie me up, lock me in a closet so the world would be safe from me for one more night.

Excellent idea, Icy Blue says hungrily.

What am I thinking? He'd just transform us into a long, slithering snake and crawl us right out the crack at the bottom of the door.

We could always make another deal . . . Icy Blue tempts me.

That would only make things worse. I think carefully around the promise . . . that Icy Blue would not harm any of the students at Gabadamosi. Then I look at the chicken scratch notes covering the writing pad on Munashe's desk.

"I'm fine," I say. "Tomorrow night is fine. Say, Munashe, remember how you told us that you always wanted to learn calligraphy?"

"I said that?"

"Well, you said you admired my writing. Why don't I teach you? It's easy really, just takes a bit of practice. We could start right now, in fact. I'd bet you'd be a good student."

"I don't know, Auben. I'm still trying to wrap my head around the possession thing."

"It won't take long. A few minutes today, a few minutes tomorrow . . ." And so on until I can get this demon out of me. I force my way across the room, knocking over empty mop buckets and a wet floor sign. She stiffens as I squeeze next to her, but I stick a pen into her hand anyway, and press mine around it as we draw a letter, slowly and legibly on one of the few spots on her notepad that isn't covered in illegible scratch. "There. That was your first lesson."

My stomach quakes with Icy's growl. *She is not a Gabadamosi student.*

But I didn't say Gabadamosi students. I said students at Gabadamosi. She's my student now. And she's at Gabadamosi.

This is going to cost you, Icy Blue says before sulking off into silence.

Like it hasn't cost me enough already.

I study the Sylla incantations deep into the night, then wake up with a dozen hearts upon my pillow, arranged like a bouquet of roses. My sheets are saturated with blood, and as I tug those off, I see that my mattress is as well. I keep my heart stone cold as I somehow flip the mattress without screaming, then strip down out of my sleep clothes and bundle the whole gory mess into a tight ball. They could be pig hearts, for all I know . . . yet somehow I know they're not. I press a finger to the lock of the boiler room and concentrate on extending a claw. With a nerve-curling *screeeech*, metal stretches, then snaps, and the lock falls to the floor. I step inside, and place the evidence in a dark corner in the back of the room. It's a joke, that's all. Icy Blue's twisted sense of humor.

But soon after the first class period, the rumors are running wild. There'd been killings, twelve of them, in the comfy down the road from Gabadamosi. Streetwalkers mostly, three wu mystics, and two homeless men. Their hearts were ripped out of their chests while they were still alive. Evidence points to a large prey animal—fang and claw marks—but the sophisticated nature of the attacks points to something more human. They are searching for more victims, but I suspect they won't find any.

Kasim and I pay special attention in Sylla class, and when it comes time for our partnered exercises, we continue to speak our incantations to each other. He looks at me differently and has canceled lunch with Sesay so that we can practice. He knows. Or at least he suspects. I will not confirm it, though. It pains him so to hold back truths, and if the truth got out, any punishment would affect him, too. There is only one way out of this, and it's happening tonight.

We make the climb up Grace Mountain while there is still daylight. This gives us the illusion that what we're doing isn't completely suicidal. Civilization recedes the higher we climb, and soon the city bowl stretches out below us—so distant, it seems more like an insect colony than home. Tiny commuters navigate a weave of streets thin as twigs, rounding stoic buildings no more significant than pebbles. For a moment, my problems seem insignificant, too. It's so peaceful up here, watching the sun set into the ocean, billowy clouds turning shades of pink and red and orange against the too-wide, too-blue sky. A fire keeps the remnants of the narrow season at bay, as we await the moon's rise. I pull my attention away from the beauty to see if my companions are as in awe as I am.

Munashe is nervous and quiet, concentrating all her effort on scraping her knife along the walking stick she'd found during the last part of our climb. She claims she'd brought the knife for whittling as a way to pass the time, but Kasim and I know it is for protection, and we all know that it will not be enough if things go wrong. With each scrape of her blade, I feel her mind churning. She starts at the scurry of dassie rats in the underbrush, at the call of wild dogs in the distance, the melodic screech of a bird of prey overhead. Her edginess is getting worse, not better, and I'm afraid she's going to back out and leave us up here alone.

Kasim's busy mumbling incantations, rocking back and forth with his arms hugged around his knees. It's not helping matters any. When he screams the final words of the chant, Munashe jumps, her knife making a jagged gouge in her stick. I'm struck to full alertness with the smell of life. Munashe hadn't made so much as a whimper, but her knife had taken a lick at her thumb as well. She wraps her other hand around it as blood runs down her arm. She trembles.

"Kasim!" I say sharply, and once more until I break him from his trance. "*Help* her."

Kasim nods, and rips a strip of fabric from the bottom of his ciki. The cloth is saturated in seconds. He tosses it, then applies another. This one stays pristine, and when he removes it, there's nothing but an inflamed paper cut an inch long.

Munashe looks at this. I expect her to be awed like I was, but she starts shaking her head. "Impossible," she says. "I saw that cut. It was deep. Too deep." Her head keeps shaking. We're going to lose her.

I need to do something. Before I can hatch a plan, I notice I've picked up the discarded, bloodied cloth. My mouth waters after it like a piece of ripe fruit.

Take a taste. You won't be able to stop at one.

I feel Icy Blue at the back of my teeth. No one is looking. No one will notice. I slip one end into my mouth, suck lightly at the fabric. The blood is like a rich, thick icing upon my tongue, both savory and sweet. There are high notes that linger on my taste buds, like overripe tropical fruit, and dense, earthy low notes that work their way into my olfactories, digging themselves a place in my mind to establish a permanent craving.

Quickly and discreetly, I suck the cloth scrap dry, then toss the remnants into the fire. I have to force my gaze away from the beat of Munashe's jugular. Icy Blue is desperate and will not go quietly. He will not go at all if Munashe abandons us. I focus my attention on the vice talismans Kasim has laid out so perfectly. A quick swipe when no one is looking, and then I call out. "Oh, shit. The penis candle! Did anyone see where I stuck my penis?"

Munashe and Kasim look at me like I've gone mad. It's better than the terror that was on both of their faces a moment ago.

"I can't find my penis anywhere. Come on. It has to be here somewhere." With raised eyebrows, I bid Kasim to join in on my folly, but he stares blankly. "Come on, guys. Help me look for it. Don't give me the shaft."

This raises the slightest giggle out of Munashe. Kasim finally realizes how much this situation could use some comic relief and jumps in.

"He's right. We can't leave him hanging," Kasim says with a smooth grin.

"Thanks. We need to find it before moonrise, when this whole thing comes to a head." I look at Munashe, still tense and uncertain. There's a hint of a smirk on her face, but I'm not sure it'll be enough.

"I'll help," she says, after a long stretch of silence. "Maybe we should spread out our search. You go north, I go south, you take east. You know. Each of us can look in a different erection."

Kasim and I groan.

"Okay, I'll admit it," Munashe says. "That one was limp."

We all laugh, watching the last bits of sunset, and it's not all that bad. Kasim busts open a few packets of Jak & Dee's. The "meaty" flavor packets are awful, but the dried samp and beans aren't so bad if you let them moisten long enough on your tongue.

If nothing else, it helps distract from the flavor of blood.

"Thanks for trusting me," Munashe says, voice growing more confident even as the night settles in. "I know single-tons don't exactly have a reputation for being trustworthy."

"We don't buy into those stereotypes," I say, licking samp and bean dust from my lips. I smile at Munashe with Jak's big-tooth grin and semi-offensive comfy rat shoulder shrug he sports on the packaging.

She laughs, and warms her hands over the fire. "Maybe if more people were like you . . ." She hesitates, no longer smiling. Flames lick too close to her fingers, but she doesn't seem to notice. ". . . then maybe Tiwa. She was a girl I met when I was little. She was a . . ." The word won't come out, but with the look Munashe gives me, I know. A singleton. It's not a derogatory term, but it makes me squirm just the same. "She was like me. We used to pretend we were twins. Marked our arms up with fake scars and everything. Not at school of course, because everyone knew, but outside the neighborhood, we got away with it."

Kasim and I look at each other uncomfortably. I want so badly to change the subject, but we owe it to Munashe to listen. "You two looked alike?" I dare ask.

"Ha, nothing alike. But people believed us. Why wouldn't they? It was a lot more palatable than the truth. We made friends with twin sisters. Best friends. Tiwa and Sayde, they probably would have gone on to be something more serious, but . . ." Munashe's voice catches. She swats away flies. Or tears. I'm too busy nursing my twin guilt to tell which. "I wanted to come clean. Tiwa didn't, but the four of us, we told each other everything. I convinced her that they would understand. And they did! But a couple months later, Sayde let the truth slip to her parents, and well . . ." Munashe unwraps the bulky kola nut choker from around her neck, revealing a garish scar across her throat. "They took it upon themselves to free our spirits from our bodies so that we could be reunited with our unborn twin." She swats away more flies. "They didn't cut me quite deeply enough, but I'd like to think that Tiwa found hers."

"Munashe, I'm so sorry," Kasim says.

She shrugs. "You trusted me with your biggest secret. Now you know mine."

I stay quiet. One part of me can't help but think about how they kind of deserved it for lying like that, and the other part is aroused by the thought of all that blood. I don't know which part I'm more ashamed of. Either way, the moon cannot rise fast enough. As soon as it is fully over the horizon, I stand and stretch, then move my pelvis around suggestively.

"Well, I declare," Kasim says, breaking the awkward silence with an exaggerated twang. "Auben Mtuze, is that a wax penis in your pocket, or are you just happy to get this exorcism started?"

"Why this little ol' thing?" I retrieve the candle. It is definitely not what I would describe as little. As I set it down in the proper position, my hand trembles at the lurid smell of Munashe blushing in the darkness.

A promise is a promise.

No harm will come to Munashe by Icy Blue's hands, but

what can I say of my own? I volunteer to go first, and Kasim does not object. I stand precisely at the middle of the circle. The process seems simple enough. Kasim will chant a few words while Munashe tends to the talismans, keeping them upright and in place. Why they are susceptible to falling over, the incantations do not say.

Kasim clears his throat, then begins to call out his practiced words, his mouth rolling slowly over the drawn vowels. He reads carefully, enunciating each syllable of the incantation, something about returning me to my rightful form, or so we pieced together from our first-year Sylla glossary.

The penis candle falls over, but it is only the wind. Munashe skitters over to upright it, and relights it. My mouth waters as her blood stirs and heat settles upon her cheeks.

Kasim continues, the primary incantation taking a full five minutes. When he is done we all look at each other. Nothing is happening. "Maybe we should try again," he offers. "Maybe I messed some of the words up."

"No," I say, pointing to a stir of dust whirling up around the eye jar. A dirt devil. Appropriate. I immediately know that it is not simply one of those signs someone sees when they're looking for signs. There's something screaming inside the dirt devil. Tiny, tiny screams that haunt me nonetheless. I kneel down next to it, carefully scoop the dirt devil into my palm and look closely. I see demons, dozens and dozens of them, their miniature faces pressing in and out of the whirling dust. Icy Blue shifts within me, like churning tendrils of ice. Maybe he's nervous. Maybe he knows that I'll soon be free of his nightly reign. He laughs at my thoughts, then goes uncomfortably still. I shake my head. I will not be intimidated. This *will* work. "We're ready for the secondary incantation," I say.

I steady my nerves as Kasim starts to read again. This time a prayer, to give me the strength to survive the process. Personal accounts of the exorcisms are mostly from observers. They say it will not be pleasant, but I will not remember much of the experience, if anything. I just need to get through these next few minutes.

Kasim shouts the next set of phrases, beating the words out with angry clicks of his tongue, and the snapping of his teeth. The dirt devil grows. It startles me and I drop it. It circles around me, nearly up to my knees. The miniature smokestack blows its top, like a temper gone unchecked. Munashe retrieves the lid and replaces it in time to chase after the half-djang coins that have flipped up onto their sides and rolled away. Munashe diligently presses them back into the dirt. I feel a tug deep within me, then a sudden release like I've started unraveling. My neck arches so far back that I feel like my spine is about to give way. I think I'm about to fall, but I no longer feel the ground beneath my feet. Thin wisps of my iced-over breath rise from my mouth and entwine themselves in the dirt devil. It grows larger, larger, until it is as tall as I am.

The demons within the dust are the size of dogs now, their screams no longer tiny. They bay at me, at the moon, gnash at each other, around and around. I feel something letting from me, like an oozing wound. A new shadow forms within the twister. It worked. My toes tip upon the earth. I feel like myself. Normal.

Kasim stops reading, and backs up. Munashe does likewise.

"What?" I say, the voice not mine, but familiar enough. I put my hands around my throat. They are not hands, but tawny paws with scythe-like claws. My face is a muzzle with fangs. My short tail swishes with aggravation. My ears prick at the quick beat of Munashe's heart. My nose fills with the wonderful bouquet of fear and desperation and vulnerability. It is like I've been walking around with a burlap sack over my head all my life, muting my senses, and it's finally been pulled off.

"This isn't right," Kasim says. "I did everything as instructed. You should be back to your true form."

My mind tells me that Kasim messed up and got this all wrong, but there's no doubt in my heart that he has gotten it right. And that scares the hell out of me. At least I wish it would.

"Try it again," I say with a bloodthirsty growl.

LECHERY

Kasim fumbles back to the first page of the incantation. He reads especially carefully this time, so slowly that my mind wanders between words, my thoughts gruesomely specific as I recall last night's killings. The crunch of bone, the delicate scent of fear, and the warmth of a heart clenched in my paw as it takes one final beat. The sensations converge upon my moistened tongue. I should be repulsed by these things, but arousal grips me hard.

Dusty winds lap at my skin, as Kasim reads the incantations with more conviction. The winds escalate until they tower over me like a tornado. Kasim's screams are lost in the oppressive howl. I brace myself, but the tornado snatches me from the ground, and sucks me within. It's trying to unravel me, to separate me from Icy Blue, but there is nothing to separate. Instead, the winds rake at me, siphoning my soul from my breath, ripping me apart nerve by nerve.

I bay at the moon, beg the stars, cuss Kasim, wail into the winds. The tornado constricts, hundreds of pairs of vengeful demon claws dragging me down with them. If I screamed any louder, I'd shatter the sky and send all the stars crashing down upon us.

"You're killing him," comes Munashe's voice, now booming over me like that of a giant.

"You saw what he is. We have to do this. You don't know what he's capable of."

"He's your twin! You have to stand by him no matter what." There's so much longing in her voice. Maybe she understands what she is missing after all. "We have to find another way."

Kasim reads a few more lines, but the conviction is gone. He snatches Munashe's walking stick, braces himself against the storm, and swings. The stick shatters the glass containing the eyeball, and the whole mess of foul liquid goes careening off the cliff face. The winds shift off-center. The pain recedes, if only enough to allow room for my temper to build. My own brother would see me dead?

He knocks away the candle, the coins, the other talismans. The winds release me, setting me down lightly, like there's no harm, no foul. But there was definitely a foul.

Munashe approaches, timidly, yet with genuine concern. "Auben?"

I blink away the lingering dizziness, then focus on her eyes, tuning out the enticing gallop of her heart. "Yes." The voice is mine now, though Icy Blue's growl clings around the edges.

Munashe takes my hand—scantily furred and heavily clawed—into hers. "We're going to fix this, okay?" She casts a firm stare at my brother, the betrayer. "Aren't we, Kasim?"

"Of course," he says. His eyes trace along my demon form, not quite man, not quite beast.

"Good," Munashe says. "I think we should rest up tonight and descend after sunrise. We've all been through too much to try to go down tonight."

"You're not afraid of me?" I ask.

"If you wanted to harm me, you would have done so already. And listen . . ." My ears swivel. Other than the sound of our beating hearts and the panting of our breath, there is nothing. No skittering of dassie rats across the rock face, no chirping of crickets, no hooting of owls, no prowling of lesser predators. "We're safe up here. Nothing is coming within a mile of this place."

Her fingers squeeze my hand in reassurance, but all I feel is the touch of five little sausages, eager for me to pry them from their casings. I think I'll save those for last.

Kasim steps between us as if he can read my thoughts. "She's right. Leaving now would be a death sentence. At least for those of us without the advantage of claws and a counterbalance."

I take his meaning, but not to heart. Though he is a traitor, he is right about this. I cannot stay up here tonight. The strain on our proximity will hurt, but it doesn't compare to the pain of denying myself what I crave most. "I'll be back after sunrise," I say, whipping my tail. "And we'll all leave together. Safely."

"Where are you going?" Munashe asks.

"Hunting," I say flatly. I leave the details loose, and bound off into the night.

The zest of desperation hits me well before the swampy sweet stench of old sex. The night is stretching long and the chance of one last customer tonight grows slim for the streetwalker—a slender andy kigen, couldn't be any older than myself. Eir hair is buzzed, and although ey dresses and projects male, eir features are soft and feminine. The kigen's twin runs deeply in this one's blood, and I smell the dueling aromatic notes split almost evenly. The male. The female. And that third essence that's a note all its own. On top of that, ey will menstruate soon—for a sterile kigen, the blood of futility, but for me, a delicacy too tempting to resist.

Ey starts when ey sees me emerge from the shadows, then smiles and primps. Brows bob and lips are licked. The beat of eir heart quickens. "I'm yours tonight for fifty djang." The streetwalker's voice trembles slightly, like ey is still new at this.

I still wear the cloak of a predator, but now it is better suited for the prey at hand. I tug at the silken trim of my tailored business-style ciki—the type of quality worn by someone who wouldn't flinch at the going rate for flesh. I nod, trying not to look em in the eyes, trying not to see the person beneath the muscle, tendons, and veins begging to be eviscerated. Fangs crowd my mouth, slick with saliva, and my whole body trembles with hesitation. And anticipation.

"You don't have to be nervous," ey says.

No . . . but maybe ey should be.

Ey takes my hand—eirs cold and moist, even compared

to mine—and leads me to an adjacent tenement house. The stairwells and hallways are sparsely lit, but it is of no matter. Sight is no longer my dominant sense. In fact, it doesn't even rate in the top three. The building comes to life through my nose. I can identify the sex and approximate age of everyone on this floor, and the one above and below. I know what they had for dinner, when they last bathed, last fucked, last cried. We pass a door, and I taste the milk of a lactating mother on my tongue, laced with the scent of tobacco and sanjo that permeates throughout this place. From somewhere above, I hear the pleas of a woman begging someone not to hit her, shortly followed by the sound of flesh impacting flesh. From below, the bickering of half-starved siblings. Drugs baking, lovemaking, Grace forsaking. If there is anything but ill repute in this place, I cannot find it. I'm not sure I would want to.

The andy leads me to eir hovel, not room for much more than a filthy mattress on the floor and a rickety nightstand on which to leave my fifty djang. Ey unbuttons eir shirt and reveals skin so taut, I imagine the sound it will make as my claws drag through it. Ey slips out of eir trousers just as quickly, eager to render services so that money can be paid.

I've seen naked kigens before, of course, in locker rooms, bathrooms, and even a bedroom or two, but still, I catch myself staring. Intensely. Not at eir genitalia, nor breasts, but at the throb of the life force running through eir body. I marvel at the beauty and vulnerability of what lies within, the delicacy of Grace's handiwork. I am embarrassed, disgusted by my desire to wreck it all, but I can't bring myself to look away.

"You're the kind that likes to watch," the streetwalker says confidently. Maybe ey's been at this longer than I thought. Ey grips emself, but my eyes do not wander there. I am lost in the maze of veins running beneath eir skin, and the supple meatiness of those thighs. A bit of drool slips over my lip as my craving becomes impossible to deny. "No, you want something more," ey says, eyes narrowing and assessing me. "You *need* something more."

Ey turns eir back to me and digs through a drawer in the nightstand. I open my mouth, bare my fangs, flex my claws. Now. It will be easiest when ey's not looking. I prickle all over, ready and willing. I settle on my entry point. The flank, long and lean. As I inch closer, the gleam of something metal catches my attention. The streetwalker holds a machination in eir hands, a metal ball like the one I'd found in Mother's closet. I fumble my lips over my teeth and hide my hands beneath my back as ey turns. We are nose to nose.

"Oh," ey says, forcing a smile.

"Where . . ." I say carefully over my teeth in a failed attempt to conceal them. The streetwalker scrambles backward on the bed until eir back hits the wall.

"What are you?" ey says, knees drawn to eir chest. "You . . . you're the one who killed all those people!"

"Where did you get this?" I ask, picking up the machination. Nearly identical to my mother's. I hold it by the chain.

"I—I—I—I . . ." the streetwalker stutters.

"Tell me where you got it and what it's for, and I'll leave you unharmed."

With trembling hands, ey reaches into the drawer and pulls out a sanjo pipe and match. Ey lights it, takes two drags, then sets it down, noticeably less unnerved. Ey takes the machination from me, and carefully twists it. It hums aggressively, vibrating in the palm of eir hand.

I jump back like the thing is betwixt by the devil. Why would my mother possess such a thing? To what purpose would she risk imprisonment or worse?

"There's a subsecular group that meets across the hall. They gave me this and two hundred djang in return for my silence. And what it's for . . ." Ey guides the vibrating sphere beneath a flat nipple, and it instantly puckers to the size of a small berry. Then ey moves it down, down, down until ey shudders with pleasure, once, twice, again. Drowsy, desperate eyes meet mine. "I'm yours tonight for a hundred djang."

I kill tonight, for the first time—a mangy street dog rummaging through trash. With every gristly bite, I imagine it is the streetwalker's flesh that fills my mouth. The blood is far from icing sweet, but it satisfies my need well enough. For now.

I sleep like the dead until sunlight warms my skin. I lift my groggy eyelids to see Munashe on the far side of our smoldering fire, snoring. I smell nothing other than smoky ash and the sourness of my own breath. My mouth is full of nice, blunted teeth. The details of last night's escapade congeal, no longer muddied by my blood cravings. All I can think about is that machination, just like the one Mother had tucked away in her box of dirty little secrets. I try to deny the obvious, but after all of her duplicity, is it so hard to believe she'd once sold her body? A pretty, lithe lesser twin, broke and out of options? No, not Mother. I clench my eyes, willing my senses back on edge. I'd rather deal with the blood cravings.

I toss and turn, but the only smell to strike me is that of new leather and foot sweat. I open my eyes and find my face directly upon Kasim's shoe. He's staring down at me, frown stitched upon his brow.

"I'm fine," I say. "You don't need to watch me."

"Don't I?" He touches his left cheek. "You've got a little something . . ."

I press a finger to my cheek and pull back tacky blood. I wipe it into the dirt.

"You killed again."

"Just dogs," I say. No need to admit that it had been twenty-seven of them. My joints creak and pop as I stand, like they're offended by my human form.

"And before?"

"Before it wasn't me who was in control." I clear my throat, trying not to think about what would have happened if the streetwalker hadn't pulled out that machination when ey did. My brow tightens. "While we're throwing accusations around, *you* nearly killed me last night. What if your little lackey, Sesay, had been here instead of Munashe? Would she have talked you down?"

"I—I don't—" Kasim stutters.

"I'd be dead, now. Worse than dead. And you would be all alone."

"I wouldn't have been alone," Kasim says. "The incantation—I don't think it was meant to be spoken by someone like me. It was devouring me, too. And I was going to let it. Maybe it wasn't the right answer, but it was *an* answer. I just can't shake the feeling that I don't belong here." Kasim stares at me from beneath heavy, mournful lids. "You were right about the doubt. It really is the worst."

I can't have him talking like that. If we're going to get through this, one of us needs to keep it together. I lay a hand on Kasim's shoulder. We connect, and the world melts away. It's like we are back in the womb, black and infinite, floating in the emptiness of space. There is me, and there is him, and there is us.

It is a short reprieve from the world, but we've steadied ourselves enough to take it on.

"The answer is out there," Kasim says. "But I doubt we're going to find it among dusty books."

"So what's our next step?" I ask.

"It depends how long you think you can stick to killing dogs," Kasim says, eyes beseeching.

Indefinitely, I want to say. *For a few months.* But if there was ever a time not to lie to my brother, it is now. So how long can I allow myself to starve? How long can I deny myself these urges that tug at my entire being? "I can guarantee you a week, and I'll let you know as soon as anything changes." A week will be torture. I am ashamed to admit the depth of my depravity, but my brother rewards my honesty with an embrace.

"Then we've got a week," Kasim says into my ear, "to impress the hell out of Gueye Okahim."

Together we hatch our plan, huddled under blankets on my bunk to brace ourselves from the basement's chill. Between us sits a model of Gabadamosi. Mounds of coconut husks represent important buildings, limp steamed broccoli for wilderness patches, and half-sucked glass candies for the quad's statuaries. Kasim and I moisten the last candy pieces in our mouths, and when they are sharp and sticky, we press them into place.

"There," he says with bright purple lips and tongue. "So this is what we have to work with."

"The entire campus is our canvas," I say in giddy agreement, sugar high itching at my mind. Twitchy fingers walk themselves along the lawn, around the statues of the Seven Ladies of Virtue, up the path to the school sanctuary and jump atop the domed roof. "What about here? You could fly off the roof and land over here . . ." My fingers touch down in the middle of the quad for everyone to see. "Ta-da!" I say, as if the feat were applause worthy.

"I think we're going for something subtler. We want Gueye Okahim to take me into his confidence, not have us expelled for witchery. Besides, I can't fly. Just hover."

"Oh, right. Ooo!" My fingers suddenly lose their footing, and tumble dramatically down the library's stick gum stairs. "I could put a slick of ice under his feet, and he could take an awful tumble, break a leg and a few ribs. You'd be waiting there at the bottom step to heal him up."

Kasim grimaces. "Too morbid."

"Walk across the surface of the turtle pond?"

"Too cliché." Kasim scratches at his chin. "What if we do the whole caracal thing? Everyone's already on edge. You could wander onto campus, attack Gueye Okahim, and I'd be there to turn you away."

"With mystic mumbo jumbo? Like you can speak to the animals?" My brows bob.

"Sure, I guess." Kasim tugs me out of bed. "Here, let's see your best caracal."

I stretch my muscles to warm them, not that I need to, but I enjoy putting on a show for Kasim. I pop my knuckles, and twist my neck from side to side. Take a few standing jumps. "Okay. Caracal." My skin prickles and my bones go to dust as my body slips into the form, like pouring myself into an old familiar boot. I cock my head, the caracal's mischievous smile tucked on my face.

"Can you look a little less like a house cat?" Kasim says, unimpressed.

I make myself bigger, broader. My long ears go from cute and perky to scraggly and sinister. Paws grow to accommodate intimidating claws. I open my mouth to reveal fangs.

"Bigger," Kasim commands.

My teeth transform into the weapons I have used to sever a dog's head from the rest of it. Something within me shifts, and my hunger resurfaces.

"Perfect," Kasim says. He scratches between my ears, and I'm ashamed at how good it feels. I purr involuntarily and he pulls his hand away. As quickly as I can, I shake away the fur and rein in my muscles, until I'm standing shoulder to shoulder with Kasim. Human shoulders. At least human enough. With relief in his eyes, Kasim says, "Now we need to find a way to get Gueye Okahim on campus."

We both stare at the Gabadamosi model, flummoxed. My eyes travel up the pile of steamed broccoli that represents Grace Mountain, right at the ridge where the Sanctuary sits. "We don't have to get Gueye Okahim here. We can go to him. Tiodoti is tomorrow."

Kasim winces. Tiodoti, the day of dirt, was practically a cuss in our house, and we were guaranteed a soapy mouth if Mother ever heard us utter the word. My uncle-father tried to get us to attend Tiodoti once when we were kids. The Sanctuary's distance away from the city and the duration of the services meant pretty much everyone needed to bring their twin with them to maintain proximity. I can't help but wonder if that was by design, to keep families connected whether they wanted to be or not. In any case, all of us shoved into a single carriage in the heat of summer got old real quick. Mother gave us ink puzzles to keep our minds busy and our mouths quiet on the ride up. The cousins entertained themselves with a new game they'd learned at school called "pull my finger" and Uncle Pabio insisted that Grace wasn't real, and they all might as well be praying to a puppet . . . which he conveniently had brought with him: an unwashed sock with button eyes and a mound of human hair that looked like it'd been culled from the shower drain at the gym. Anyway, after an impressive bout of flatulency, blasphemy, and a hand-shaped ink stain on a several-thousand-djang designer ciki, we all decided it would be best to just turn the carriage around and go back home.

Life was always chaotic with our family, and oftentimes painful, and yet I manage to look back fondly on these moments we'd shared, however imperfect. To keep the tradition going, I'm sure my first Tiodoti with Kasim will prove to be just as excruciating.

"You really think we could pull this off on his turf?" Kasim asks.

"By His Hallowed Hands—" I say, remembering how loud Yeboah had screamed when my ink-black hand came down upon his hand-spun linen "—we can pull off anything."

I'd gone barefoot much of my childhood, mostly out of necessity, so I thought I'd be used to the feel of dirt between my toes. But the dirt up on Grace Mountain is not the same sort found on the gritty streets of the comfy. Here it is cool and damp and red, and it sticks to your soles. I think it's supposed to make us feel like we are connected to the mud clay from which Grace formed our bones, but it makes me feel like I need a shower. As Kasim and I push our way through the horde of parishioners, I notice that feet are the only body parts being bared. Everyone is conservatively clothed, and the body odor itself is enough to thank Mother a thousand times for never subjecting us to this. Babies are crying, the elderly are cooling themselves with decorative paper fans, and people of all ages are looking hot and miserable and anxious—clamoring to be one of the lucky seven thousand to get inside the great dome of the Sanctuary.

The Sanctuary beckons us forth, a wave of sleek sea blue stained glass on one side, gracefully overtaking the pitted limestone on the other. Within the stained glass, the seven virtues are represented in glorious detail. Within the recesses of the limestone, grotesque stone creatures frolic in stillness, representing the seven vices without a lick of modesty.

And not a rock's throw away from the quartet of stone beasts caught in the graphic throes of passion, guards wind their way through the masses looking for parishioners in violation of dress code. A fem kigen is pulled out of line for a skirt that shows the slightest hint of shin. Ey tugs against the hem, argues with the guard, but in the end is turned away. The look ey gets from the parishioners is one of disgust. They pull away from the kigen as ey walks past, dejectedly, all the embarrassment of the world upon eir face.

"We should have gotten here earlier," Kasim says, disappointment thick on his brow. "We'll never get in, and even if we do, we'll be nowhere near Gueye Okahim."

"Ah, dear brother. Where has your diligence gone?" I tap the shoulder of the woman ahead of me, my mouth moist with the possibilities of duplicity. I can think of a hundred lies that would get us to the front of this line. I open my senses, assessing which might work the best on her. I catch the bouquet of hospice care beneath the mask of her perfume. Stale urine, concentrated bleach, boiled vegetables, tears of regret. "Pardon, miss, our uncle is on his deathbed, and he would like nothing more than to hear us tell of one last sermon from Gueye Okahim. Could we please move ahead?"

"Sure, you can pass ahead," the woman grunts, "if you're keen on having your uncle outlive you."

Another woman gets called out by a guard. Her ankles and elbows are fine, but a scant amount of cleavage is deemed inappropriate. "Okay," I say under my breath. "Lechery is one thing, but even Grace can't be above appreciating a little mammary action. Especially with the view He's got." I look up into the clouds, and tug down the collar of my ciki to give Him a show.

Kasim slugs me in the shoulder. "You're going to get us kicked out, and then our slim-to-none chances of getting in will be none-to-none."

"It's stupid is all I'm saying. Why are people so afraid of skin?" The bells toll. The sermon will soon begin. We're running out of options and fast. I could turn into one of the guards and wedge my way to the front. People part for them, no problem. But last night, when we'd rehearsed, I'd felt my cravings for blood deepen with each transformation. I only think I've got a couple left within me before I need to feed again.

Cleavage girl passes by us, and everyone gives her wide

berth, as if her breasts had been slapped onto her chest by Icy Blue himself. Exactly the same kind of berth we could use to get ahead in line. "I've got it," I say to Kasim. "All we need to do to get to the front is show a bit of skin."

"What do you mean? Take our cikis off?"

"Take our everythings off."

"I'm not going nude. Especially not here!"

"These people are ridiculous. You can't tell me that Grace spent so much time sculpting our bodies, beautiful bodies, just for us to keep them hidden. Would you buy a million-djang piece of artwork and then hang it in the broom closet so that no one would see it?"

"I don't have a million djang, so it's impossible for me to say either way," Kasim says with intentional bite. I've got the feeling that convincing Kasim to part with his clothes is going to be a lot more difficult than convincing him to part with our uncle-father's money.

I wave to the statues inset into the limestone. "What about those? What if they kept them locked away in the back of the Sanctuary's vault, and we could not marvel at the fine detail that went into them? And what if Biobaku had decided to keep his plays bound up tight in a foot locker for all eternity?"

Kasim's eyes narrow at the mention of Biobaku. I'm hitting all the wrong nerves, reminding him of how my unyielding duplicity has led us into darker and more desperate situations—the comfy tour with Ruda and Nkosazana, the secrets in the back of Mother's closet, the grand ruse to get the truth from our father . . .

"Okay, so maybe I've come up with some bad ideas," I say. "But at least I'm coming up with ideas. Where would we be if we hadn't discovered who our father is? If we hadn't confronted him? If we hadn't gone to Gabadamosi? We'd still be at home with demons holed up inside us. And we'd be no closer to getting them out. Come on, Kasim. We have to do this. Yes, it's a bad idea, but it's the only idea I've got. So unless you can come up with another one in about thirty seconds . . ."

Kasim spends a whole twenty-five seconds in disgruntled silence, then starts looking around. "What if someone recognizes us?"

"Keep your head down. Run fast, and stay close." I heave a sour laugh. "Trust me. No one's going to be looking at our faces."

Kasim opens his mouth to say something, but I'm out of my clothes, buck naked before he gets the chance. A woman screams, and the crowd parts, shrinking away from me like oil from water. I run. Kasim follows, undressing as quickly as he can along the way, then clutching his ball of clothes to his crotch. We cut through the crowd, all eyes upon us. Au natural, the way Grace intended. No worry, no shame. It's hard to explain, but in this moment, I feel I've made a cosmic connection with Him.

"Yeow-hoo!" Kasim exclaims from behind as we near the threshold.

"Yeow-hoooo!" I concur. Two elderly women faint. Several guards are upon our heels, but it is too late for them.

We step through the doors, seep into the shadowed crevices and into anonymity. Kasim and I grin at each other, eyes wide and full of mischief, then he dresses as I stand watch, and then vice versa. Clothes back in place, we sneak around, trying to look like we fit in. Like we aren't completely blown over by the sheer vastness of the Sanctuary's interior. Domes gilded and glassed to rival the sky's beauty, archways lousy with painstakingly carved statues of men, women, kigen, beasts, birds, and everything in between. Sunlight trickles down, and thin windows stand open, giving the place an impression that air is in fact circulating, and not stagnating to the point of everyone suffocating, which is exactly how it feels.

"Mom! Mom!" I whisper harshly as we push our way toward the center aisle—one of many aisles, but the only with an unobstructed view of the pulpit. Thankfully, we're not too late. There are several hundred empty spots remaining, but we still need to get through the thick of the crowd to get to them. I wave to an imaginary woman. "Mom, I found him!" I point back at Kasim. People look at us dubiously, but part anyway. "Mom! He's okay. You can stop worrying now. I found him!" As we wedge through, I feel the brush of quality fabrics against my skin. I notice the stitching of coats, tags of designers I will never be able to afford. The farther we get, the more inadequate I feel in my school-issued pants and ciki. I know that all these people cannot be wealthy, and I can see the comfy blight on many faces, but despite that, they have come dressed to impress. I can only imagine how long they'd scrimped and saved and cut corners to pay Grace service in style.

Halfway up the center aisle, Kasim lays a hand on the rope railing. "Here," he says. "I think this is as close as we're going to get." He looks back at me. "Are you ready to—" He looks me up and down. "Auben, what did you do?" he whispers.

"Huh?" I look down at myself, thinking I forgot to fasten

my fly, but I am no longer wearing my ruddy Gabadamosi uniform. Instead, a rich, luxurious lap coat, a deep shade of purple, adorns my body with gold grommets and a wide, pretentious lapel. I run my fingers along wool so fine it makes me shiver. "What?" I say with a defensive shrug. "This entire building is one giant display of vainglory." I flex my powers, and add a bit of fringed lace to my cuffs.

"Whatever. We'll wait for prayers, and when everyone's eyes are closed, you slip out. Wait ten minutes, then come back in with—" Kasim swipes nonexistent claws at me. "You know . . ." He tugs self-consciously at his Gabadamosi garb, then attempts to press himself into the two vacant spots in the row.

A man presses back. "Taken," he grumbles.

We look around for another option, but within the span of seconds, the few spots left in the Sanctuary are gone. The crowd mills around, hoping to get lucky, but the place is filled to capacity. The stream of destitute worshipers empties from the Sanctuary like dirty dishwater down the sink drain. Kasim and I are left in the aisle, clinging to hope where there is none left. In a fit of thoughtless desperation, I close my eyes and rattle away a little prayer.

Grace, if you're listening. Help us out here.

"Pssst. Kasim!" comes a giddy whisper. I open my eyes and see Sesay waving us over, a few rows up.

I grit my teeth. I couldn't be any unluckier.

"We couldn't be luckier!" Kasim says to me. He trots over to Sesay, wedges his way into the overcrowded row. When I arrive, it's clear there is no more room left for me, and not just physically. Sesay smiles brightly. "Hey, Auben. Sorry. We're pretty pressed in here. But you should get a great spot outside, right up next to the Vice Cardinal. His sermons are nearly on par with Amawusiakaraseiya's. I think Daki and her crew are out there, too. You should look for them."

"If Kasim stays, I stay," I say, staring into her too-big, too-bright eyes.

Kasim smiles and leans down into Sesay's ear. He whispers and Sesay nods.

"Don't I know it," she says. "Okay, Farai, you're out. Auben, you're in . . . *if* you apologize for the way you treated me in the library."

"Kasim," I say through clenched teeth, my eyes demanding a sidebar.

Kasim steps away with me.

"There's no way we can do this with her hawk eyes on us," I rasp.

"We don't have a choice, unless you think you can wait it out until next Tiodoti." Kasim glares at me, knowing that I'll be lucky to make it to the end of the day without killing. "I'll take care of Sesay. You take care of the apology. And act like you mean it."

Intense organ music fills the Sanctuary's dome, echoing to the point of rattling my teeth. We make our way back to our spots. I utter sweet untruths, and Farai sulks her way back up the aisle, toward the exit. I squeeze into her spot.

A grand procession files in, young children carrying spicy incense flames, a parade of teens—each carrying an eight-foot-tall defting stick, adults carrying one of the Seven Books of Grace. The books are each laid in their cradles as the teens carefully assemble the sticks around the pulpit. Despite their size, they seem easily maneuverable, and are notched so that they stand securely—not the precarious things that defy me so. Incense is swung around diligently and officially, most likely in an attempt to mask the body odor of the masses.

The organ music settles, and is replaced by that of barely audible chimes. There is a collective gasp as Gueye Okahim enters, looking like a peacock who'd taken a bath in a vat of sequins and gemstones. Layered in three sets of heavily embellished robes, there isn't a square inch of him that doesn't scream *spectacle*. A wave of voices saying "Blessed Amawusiakaraseiya" moves through the crowd. And then there is a vastness of silence. His footsteps fall, one after another, as he struts his way to the pulpit, then takes a dramatic bow. He puts on a good show, I'll give him that, thoughtfully examining the defting sticks from all angles. Then he reads them in perfectly enunciated Sylla, and translates for the rest of us.

"My eyes are cast upon you, in shadow and light alike," he proclaims with ample flourish and hand-wavery. "And so are spoken the words of Grace."

"May His Hallowed Hands guide me from vice," the congregation intones.

"On this day of dirt, Grace's message will come from the book of Chastity." Gueye pauses to let the appropriate book be placed on the cradle in front of him. With both hands, he opens the tome, turns delicate pages, then raises his hands. "First, let us pray." Hands are raised all around us. Kasim and I play the part and raise ours, too.

I clench my eyes shut. Gueye's voice is soothing, almost like an instrument in itself. His pitch rises and falls, his words are spoken with deliberate cadence. I almost get caught in them, but then remember what we are here for. I open my eyes. Seven thousand heads are bowed. I stare at

Sesay for a long moment, sure one of those big brown eyes is going to pop open and catch me, but she's deep in prayer. Kasim's deep, too. His hands are no longer up, but pressed at his temples. His brow is bunched in obvious pain. I nudge him, and an eye opens and falls upon me. A tear has budded in its corner.

Are you okay? I mouth.

Kasim shakes his head. His lips tremble like he's holding back sick.

Do you want me to stay?

He shakes his head again. Closes his eye.

The voices are plaguing him. It's getting more frequent, more intense, but Kasim is too humble to let me know how much he's hurting inside. We have to get this right.

I duck under the rope railing, and walk quickly to the back, and then slink sideways when I see how many guards are now posted at the main doors. Just my luck. Or maybe it has something to do with the pair of naked boys who'd gotten inside. I bite my lip. Stupid. Stupid. After a bit of searching, I find a side exit with only two guards and excuse myself, hunched over and complaining of stomach pains. I find a quiet spot outside, lean up against a statue of some mythological beast overlooking the city bowl and the ocean beyond. The caracal won't work. No beast would be mighty enough to burst through those heavily guarded doors. At least not without taking blood. I flex my claws in and out, searching for ideas.

Then one shits on me.

"Coooo," says the pigeon from above, perched on the statue's beak.

I wipe the warm, white spackle from my forehead and

move back in time to avoid the splat from a second release. I chuck a rock at the bird. It flaps its wings, then settles again in one of the Sanctuary's high, thin windows. Unguarded windows.

My eyes fall on the statue before me, a frightening mix of a lion-maned rhinoceros, with vulture's wings. This. This is what I need. Spectacle to match Gueye Okahim's. Wings. I concentrate, willing my bones to dust, then forcing them into the massive, bulging mold my mind has mapped. My hands and feet puff out into formidable hooves. My skin goes gray and stiff, and bristly hairs erupt, causing me to itch all over. When I shake my head, the luxurious frock of my golden-red mane sweeps across my shoulders and back. Finally, I press my shoulder blades back, expecting to sprout equally impressive wings . . . but they're two pathetic things, like those on a plucked chicken.

They flap futilely, nowhere near what I need to get my girth off the ground. I press harder, and the action comes easier this time. Wings unfurl, large and luminous, and slowly they bloom with iridescent plumage. I stomp my hooves, and wave my horn too enthusiastically, nicking my stone counterpart and causing the left side of its face to crumble. Yes. This. Scary as all hell. But the real question is, can I fly?

I take several swooping flaps. Nothing. I hollow out my bones, and double my wingspan. With quite a bit of effort, my front hooves finally leave the ground. My rear hooves follow. It's working. Hard work, not the natural fit of the caracal. But I'm doing it. With focused deliberation, I maneuver to the front of the Sanctuary. The maddening crush of people below roils like a wave as they see me, theirs screams as discordant as they are penetrating, like a choir without a conductor. I'm too busy fixing on my target to pay them much attention, the open window ahead just wide enough to accommodate this form. Nothing stands in my way, but I've failed to take into account the way the wind wraps briskly around the building up here, and I find myself thrown off by a sudden gust. I try to course correct, splaying my flight feathers, but nothing stops me from careening toward the image of Chastity set beautifully in stained glass, her modest robes made of shards of every single shade of blue. The centuries-old window smashes, and my momentum sends me tumbling, tumbling, tumbling down the wide center aisle of the Sanctuary.

There are screams, but mostly there's stunned silence. I stand up on all four hooves, trying to reclaim a smidgen of pride, and let loose a ferocious roar in Gueye Okahim's direction.

Ruckus. Mayhem. I smile my rhino's smile, then bare lion's fangs—my own touch.

"G-get back, b-beast!" Gueye Okahim says, words a-stutter and feeble compared to his usual intonations.

Kasim, our brave hero, squeezes his way between Gueye Okahim and me. We play out our rehearsal mostly to plan. Kasim waves his arms, chants nonsensical throaty words that seem real enough to convince me of ancient mystical powers, so I know the crowd will fall for them as well. I feign fright, back up on trembling hooves, let loose a pained roar, and even with me being several times larger than agreed upon, our concessions make our spar seem plausible. Finally, Kasim says the words to cast me away. I flap my wings to make my retreat, but I am drained, both physically and metaphysically. There's no way I'll make it back up to the windows . . . and no way I can go back up the aisle without killing dozens. Unintentionally, and intentionally. I catch a whiff of Gueye Okahim's fear, taste its richness upon my tongue, like fresh buttered biscuits. Hunger shoves our dutifully laid plan back into the recesses of my mind, and instead of focusing on retreating, I take a step closer. Then another. The great Amawusiakaraseiya cowers and shivers like a newborn pup. My tongue wets my ravenous maw.

Kasim knocks me across my snout, and shouts the words at me again. Shifting again will put my cravings over the edge, but I can't risk staying in this form either. I release my concentration. My wings revert to chicken wings, and the rest of me goes a-fowl as well. I'm small. Agile. Nonlethal. Then I run, for lack of a better phrase, like a chicken with its head cut off. Daring hands try to grab me as I navigate between legs, around shins, over shoes, but I squawk and peck them away. Feathers fly. I still manage to draw sweet blood, but nothing anyone will die over. Finally, I see my salvation in one of the narrow windows. I jump once. Twice. And I'm on the sill, looking back at the disaster I've left in my wake. But there's something good, too. Kasim and Gueye Okahim are talking. And through the fear still lingering on his face, I can see our Blessed Amawusiakaraseiya is definitely impressed.

"A caracal," Kasim says to me, as we stroll across campus back to our basement dorm room later that evening after things have finally calmed down. His voice is hoarse from answering a million and one questions, from defending himself against the accusations of witchcraft, from hooting and hollering during the following spontaneous vice parade celebrating the miracle with a loosening of morals, and the subsequent three-hour circle chant to call Grace back into everyone's hearts. "I asked for a caracal, and you give me a—what did Gueye Okahim call it?"

"Zekwenusi," I say with a firm smile that I cannot shake from my face. Yes, it was Kasim they were celebrating, but he would be nothing without my ingenious improvisation.

"I asked for a caracal, and you give me a zekwenusi!"

"I'm not hearing a thank-you in your voice."

"*Thank* you? Have you even noticed how everyone is looking at me now?"

"Um . . . like you're the most amazing thing to ever step foot on this campus?"

"They're looking at me like I'm a freak. Like a magical misfit who could pull a rabid penguin out of his ass at any moment. Gueye Okahim confided in me that was the first act of Grace he's seen in eighteen years. That *anyone* has seen." Kasim stops, and grabs me by the shoulders. Pulls me in close. "He thought Grace had abandoned us," he whispers. "Or worse, that He was dead."

"Cry me a river, Kasim. Maybe people are looking at you like a freak, but at least they're looking at you. You can't even imagine how much that stunt took out of me, when all you had to do was stand there and say a few words! And now you're blaming me for something that got us exactly what we were trying to accomplish. Gueye Okahim took you into his confidence, did he not?"

"He did."

"And until today, exactly how many secular-raised comfy boys has he taken into his confidence?"

"None."

"We went big, Kasim. And together we did the impossible."

"We did," Kasim says, rolling his eyes. "Thanks for that."

"Sarcasm, but I'll take it."

We continue to make our way to the dorm, and Kasim is right. People are staring at us. At him. It's eerie as hell. Just when I think we've hit the privacy of our own dorm, we're intercepted at the entrance by a small group of students. One of them is Chiso. The two others hold duffel bags. Our duffel bags.

"Cousins!" Chiso says, pulling Kasim and me into a warm embrace. "I am so glad to see you both." Chiso being cordial? This is the second miracle we've seen today.

"Chiso. I'm glad you are well," Kasim says with a grumble. "Six days on campus now, and I was beginning to think you were going out of your way to avoid us."

"Nonsense! Why would I ignore my much-favored cousins? I'm so sorry I haven't had the chance to welcome you, but I've been so busy trying to get things set up for you two. I have good news. We've found room for you in Kalukenzua House!"

"K-House!" call the hulking guys carrying our duffels. They grunt, slap their elbows, and stomp a foot in unison.

If there's anything worse than living in a cold, damp, dank basement, it's living under the same roof as Chiso. "We already have a House," I say. "Right, Kasim?"

Kasim nods. "We already have a House."

Chiso lifts his nose to Soyinka House. "This hovel? The only reason they haven't demolished it is because of its historical value, and even that is debatable. Kalukenzua House—"

"K-House!"

"—doesn't even compare," Chiso continues without missing a beat. "Full-size beds with plush mattresses. Private baths. Maid service. On-call tutors. Quiet rooms—"

"Quiet rooms?" Kasim says.

"Dead quiet. Surrounded by eighteen inches of concrete on all sides."

"Can we have a moment, dear cousin?" Kasim says to Chiso.

The K-House crew shuffles off, leaving Kasim and me alone on the stoop of Soyinka House. "I know we've got our pride, Auben, but this sounds too good to pass up. Besides, it's not like we'll be actually rooming with Chiso. I'm sure we'll barely even see em."

"Munashe is still working on getting us a real room. Just give her a couple more days. You know we can't trust Chiso. Since when has ey done something for our own good?"

"Maybe ey's turning over a new leaf. I don't know. What I do know is that my headaches are getting worse. Today, during the prayer, I heard voices."

"That's not exactly news."

"Thousands of them, all talking over one another. It's better when I isolate myself. I just need my quiet, and I'm afraid this is the only chance I'll get to find it."

"It can be quiet here," I say.

The House's worn and splintered doors burst open, and a few dozen Soyinka residents spill out onto the weedy lawn. They each hold two enormous mugs of golden ale.

"Soldiers of Soyinka House, are you ready for battle?" someone calls out, that same jerk who'd offered us the tinibru. The Soyinka residents bark back in affirmation. Drinks are mightily guzzled, and surprisingly, or maybe not so surprisingly, despite all of the sloshing, very few drops of ale fall to the ground. Eyes go wide and glassy. Smiles go rabid with foam. "Body shots and you're out for three minutes. Head shots and you're out for the rest of the round. Soldiers, ready your weapons!" Zippers are downed. "The Seventy-fifth Annual Piss Wars will commence in ten . . . nine . . . eight . . ."

"Yeah, we need to get out of here," I say to Kasim.

Kalukenzua House is restrained luxury. Not ornate or showy, but judiciously well taken care of. Not a scuff to be found on the floors, not a single notch in the woodwork, and brass doorknobs polished to a high shine. Windows are wide, hallways are ample, lighting is sufficient enough to ensure that no corner goes unlit, but dim enough not to break the studious mood.

Chiso leads us into the foyer. I pass my hands over the backs of one of the maroon leather chairs arranged in a circle, the grain like a cool whisper across my fingertips. Each is branded with a scripted *K*, and looks capable of lulling even the most high-strung students into a state of peaceful bliss. The air is crisp and sweet, the smiles wide and genuine—which is why I stay guarded, waiting for Chiso's promises to start unraveling.

"Kasim! Welcome to K-House," one of the students says, a big bandage covering his forehead. It's that welshing idiot who'd almost brained us with his brass balls.

"Phila, right?" Kasim says. He nods at the bandage. "Welshing accident?"

"This? No, no. I'm not in the welshing club anymore.

Bunch of high-class snobs, if you ask me. But I've taken up a couple of new hobbies." He picks at the end of the bandage, slowly peels it up to reveal a puffy mess of blue-black ink and inflamed skin. "It's a *K*, can you see it?"

I knew Chiso was up to something wicked. I gnash my teeth and grab eir arm. "What is this, some kind of sick K-House initiation? If you think we're next, then——"

"I've never seen anything like this, honest," Chiso says, pulling from my grip. The meat-men carrying our satchels rile, but Chiso settles them with a half shake of eir head.

"No, no!" Phila says, eyes wide and rabid. "It's not a *K* for *Kalukenzua House*——"

"K-House!" comes a chorus from every study nook surrounding us.

"It's a *K* for *Kasim*." Phila flinches as he finishes pulling off the bandage. A swatch of yellowed skin comes off along with it. "I did it myself. In the mirror."

Chiso pushes Phila out of our way. "Sorry about this, Kasim. Please, don't let this be your first impression of K-House."

Kasim and I exchange a heavy look. Judging from the fetor of Phila's forehead, I'd give him forty-eight hours till he's on his deathbed, feverish and delirious. I nod.

"Good seeing you again, Phila," Kasim says, shaking the poor kid's hand. The puffiness recedes, and looks a lot less angry. As for the garish, ass-backward tattoo . . . Kasim can heal a lot of things, but he can't heal stupid.

Phila's eyes brighten. "Yes, yes! Good seeing you, too!"

Just when we start down the hall and think we're free of that whack-hat, Phila scampers around in front of us and throws a handful of pepper in Kasim's face.

"Guys," Chiso grumbles to eir meat-men. The meat-men drop our duffels and pin Phila to the wall. Chiso's voice turns cheery, and gets loud enough to cover up the sounds of a futile struggle as ey leads us on.

Kasim sniffles, eyes tear up. He puts a finger to his nose to hold back a sneeze.

"Come on," Chiso says, tugging Kasim out of the peppery cloud, and ushers us up a back stairwell to a short hallway with several large, intimidating doors. "This is it. Some people say it's so quiet, they can hear their blood pumping through their veins. Watch this. Attention Kalukenzua House!" Chiso shouts at the top of eir lungs. "We have new residents. Come out and greet them!"

Not a single door stirs. Not a single "K-House" is uttered. Kasim's smile goes ravenous. He turns to Chiso. "Can I try one out?"

"Sure thing." Ey leads us to the quiet room at the end of the hall. Kasim steps inside and shuts the door. From the outside, Chiso and I take turns yelling, stomping our feet, making catcalls. Seconds erode into minutes, and the novelty wears thin. Finally, we fall silent.

"Sooo . . ." Chiso says, filling the void. "What do you think of K-House so far?"

"It's nice. But honestly, I'm just waiting for the 'minds.'"

"The minds?"

"You know. 'K-House is a great place to live, if you don't mind having to get up at 5:00 A.M. to catch a warm shower' or 'K-House is a great place to live, if you don't mind having pepper thrown at you . . .'"

Chiso sighs. "Yeah, I'm sorry you had to see that. As you've probably guessed, Phila didn't get into Gabadamosi on his mental aptitude. But the Holy Scrolls say that when Grace sneezes, everyone around Him is blessed with health and long life. Phila's an overzealous jock who thinks Kasim is Grace incarnate. Can you imagine?"

No. No I can't imagine.

"Sure, Kasim has talent," Chiso says, "but honestly he's lucky to be in Gueye Okahim's confidence. No way will a sec-head, no offense, rise up higher than a Vice Cardinal. Six-and-one-tempered twins may be rare in the general population, but Kalukenzua House is lousy with them! Grace? Ridiculous."

"Ridiculous," I say. I wish my voice sounded as sure as Chiso's.

"That'd make you Icy Blue. Ha!"

"Ha!" I manage. Then "Huh?"

"Grace and Icy Blue . . . the first tempered twins? Come on, everyone knows that."

I nod, but Chiso must see the confusion bleeding into my face.

"Seriously, what did they teach you at that comfy school? You know, in the beginning, Grace had all seven virtues. Icy Blue had all seven vices. Then together, they made sets of twins from dirt and clay, their touch leaving their virtues and vices upon us . . ."

"Right," I say with a laugh. I've got charity as a virtue and Kasim has greed as a vice. Close, but not quite. Then the silence goes thick enough that neither one of us has the skill to break it.

Finally, after twenty minutes, Kasim emerges, sloppy smile spread across the width of his face.

"I trust the room is satisfactory?" Chiso asks. "You didn't hear a thing, did you?"

"It was satisfactory," Kasim says. "Did you hear me? I sang a verse of 'True and True.'"

"Then we're all lucky these rooms are soundproofed, cousin." Chiso lays an arm over Kasim's shoulder. "Because I've heard your singing. Here are the keys to your new rooms," Chiso says, handing each of us a key attached to a leather key ring bearing the branded *K*. "Let's get you two settled in, then you can enjoy all of Kalukenzua House's amenities at your leisure."

"Rooms?" I ask pointedly. And there's the mind: K-House is a great place to live, if you don't mind being ripped apart from the person you are closest to in the whole world. "We're not going to room together?"

"Of course not! We find that putting twins together stifles their development and we prefer to let them forge a way on their own. Putting individuals with similar talents together has proven highly successful. Over the past century and a half, better than eighty percent of Gabadamosi students taken into confidence have come from Kalukenzua House."

I shoot Kasim a glare, but he's still too deep in his stupor to notice. "By talents, I take it you mean virtues?" I ask.

"Virtues are a part of the consideration process, yes."

"A large part?"

"If you are so interested in the policies of Kalukenzua House, perhaps you should run for office next year," Chiso says briskly. "Now, if you would, please follow me."

"Actually, I've got somewhere I need to be," I say.

"But your room!" Chiso says to the back of my head.

"I'll find it."

In the library, I swallow my pride and wave down an acrobrarian passing above. Ey eyes me, nods, then jumps from perch to perch, until ey's low enough to climb down the remaining shelves as a ladder.

"Yes," ey rasps. "How can I help you?"

"I'm looking for a book on ancient mythologies."

Ey cocks eir head.

"You know. Stories about Grace and Icy Blue before they were Grace and Icy Blue."

Eyes narrow. Arms cross. Biceps flex. Suddenly I get the feeling I'm about to be tossed out on my ass. I backpedal over my request . . . *mythologies*. I'd basically put eir god on the same level as Nlola, the trickster hare. "I meant mythology in a broader sense . . . religious prehistory? Is that a thing?"

"Up there," ey whispers, pointing to the rafters with a feisty smirk on eir face. "Follow me." I hear a grumble, maybe even a cuss, then the acrobrarian is off. Ey thinks ey can lose me in the climb, clearly not one for the faint of heart. Ey underestimates both my desperation and my determination. I find my first foothold on the bottom shelf. I've climbed mountains, I tell myself. This should be easy. I go slowly at first, but the acrobrarian is almost a speck now, so I hurry things up. I find my footing on the first perch, an outcropping of polished, ageless wood, three feet wide and a foot and a half deep. My tailbone itches, wanting to sprout the natural counterbalance I could use right now, but I can't change, not right here with all these people around. I eye the next perch.

It's far, but humanly possible. I bend my knees, then spring forward, catching myself before I tip over the other side. I jump to another perch, then grab onto a crossbeam and swing myself onto the top of a bookshelf. I make the mistake of looking down. Fifteen feet at least, and I still have twice that distance to go. I run along the top, getting the momentum I need to make the jump across the aisle. I whoop as I land, and at this, the eyes of a dozen acrobrarians cut my way.

"Shhhhh!" they say in unison.

My acrobrarian looks back as well, half annoyed, half impressed that I've made it this far. I smile. Three more jumps, and I'm closing in. We've caught the attention of spectators below. It is a game, now. One that I intend to win. We scale another tier, and somehow the perches seem thinner and spaced farther apart. The books are dustier up here, and it's harder to catch a clean breath, but still I follow. I no longer see the acrobrarian, but I've made it this far, and my familiar friend, vainglory, sets in. I'm good. Good enough to make this last jump. I take a deep breath, hold it, and launch myself. I clench all over as I realize I'll come up way short.

Well, shit.

I've got two choices: eat floor, or fly. I take a breath, and begin to will my bones to dust, about to sprout wings in front of all these people, but before I can ruin everything, a hand stabs through the gap between books and catches mine. I crash face-first into the stacks, decades of dust caked onto my face. I blow it from my lips, and look up to see my acrobrarian. My savior.

"I got the feeling that you didn't much like me," I say.

"I still don't. But I don't want to spend the rest of the

evening cleaning your gut splatter from the spines of price- less books either." Ey pulls me up with an impressive feat of strength. "The section you are looking for is right behind you."

RELIGIOUS PREHISTORY, the section header says. I turn back to thank the acrobrarian, but ey's gone. From up here, I can see every corner of the library. I can see the flaws in the stained glass. I can see the subtle highway of hand- and foot- holds the acrobrarians use to maneuver around. I pull a few books, and leaf through them, legs dangling over the shelf edge while the rest of the world goes on, insignificantly, four stories below.

The first three books begin with Grace's creation of man. The story goes the same in all of them, pretty much as Chiso had told it, but then I come across one book that starts before all that. With the birth of Grace and Icy Blue them- selves. I read so deeply, I catch myself leaning precariously forward, so eager to get to the next page that I forget where I am. I push myself back onto the bookshelf top, then sit squarely in the middle, cross-legged, and continue to read:

The Great Nothingness ended with an immense bang that ruptured time and space, as the Original Twins were birthed into existence. Their afterbirth became the stuff stars and planets are made from. For eons, they huddled together as infants, growing, and learning, and expanding the cosmos around them. They were entertained by the light of newly formed suns. Comets became their playthings. As children, they crashed galaxies into one another, taking joy in the destruction, and sending hot bits of matter farther and farther into space.

As the Original Twins segued into adulthood, these simple games failed to amuse them, and they found delight in each other's flesh. It was pure, and right, and it was good. Stars were birthed and destroyed in the span of their kisses, and the stars' light paled in comparison to that cast by the depths of their love. They were each other's everything.

But what was pure and right and good began to turn in on itself as one twin had the first twinge of Doubt. Vice and Virtue were born in this moment. But the Original Twins were still young, still foolish, and continued their ways, and their love became so dense that it distorted the very light around them. One twin tried to warn the other of the strange happenings, but the concerns were smoothed over by the forked tongue of Duplicity. In the wake of their Lechery, they left a deep void that sucked in stars and destroyed everything that ventured too near.

This new phenomenon rekindled their interest in the cosmos around them. They began to build with purpose. They cracked open stars and used the matter within as their pigments, laying their mark upon the universe in intricately painted nebulas, so bright and vibrant. There was a competition to build the biggest, the most impressive, the most exquisite, and from that sprung Vainglory. Envy ran close behind it. And Greed followed suit.

They hoarded and flaunted galaxies, each one

bigger than the next, until one twin had an idea to go small. Microscopic. He used the dust and clay from a barren planet to mold a tiny creature in his likeness, and with several mighty strokes to his godhood, wished the seeds of life into it. He placed it on the planet, and surrounded it with plants to eat and streams to drink from. And suddenly the Original Twins were no longer alone.

The twin spent much of his time tending to his new creature and improving upon its surroundings. He made it animals to hunt for meat and pelts so it could feed and clothe itself. He talked with it regularly, of the Secrets of Life and of the Nature of Things, but the creature's mind was far too fragile to comprehend. The creature grew lonely and lethargic.

The twin complained to his brother about this, the first words they had spoken to each other in the eons since his new obsession. The brother had also learned of loneliness during the time they'd spent apart. He missed his brother as if a part of his own body had gone missing.

He had a solution to the problem, though. When he thought his twin not to be looking, he smashed the creature beneath his thumb. His brother, however, heard the prayers called out by the scared creature right before death, and came, too late, to its aid.

"What have you done?" the brother said, his voice boiled over with his newborn Temper. His fists balled, he punched down on the planet so hard, a giant piece flew free, and the planet's moon was born.

"I know what this creature feels," the other brother said. "It is lonely. As I have been lonely without you." As he talked, he added in his own equal amount of planet dust and wishing to the mash, and molded two creatures—one as him and one as his twin.

"No one deserves the pain of coming into this world alone," he said to his brother.

They agreed upon this.

And so it was. More creatures were brought to life, two by two by two.

I close the book, my face tight with revulsion. Gods and their flaming incest, and again with the body fluids, wishing semen into dirt and clay to create life on a whim! I smack away the sour taste in my mouth, and flip to the last page, wondering who in their right mind would write such incestuous drivel.

Professor Mane Mbanefo serves as the Chancellor of Arcane Studies at Kadigbo University, and is a leading researcher in the field of prehistoric religion. He is most known for his controversial stances, and eye-opening interpretations.

A portrait of an aged man, decades past his prime, sits above the text. He looks dignified—glasses, neatly trimmed beard, with a haughty little smirk stretched across his face. I slide the book back into its spot, then wipe my hands on my pants, trying to make the icky feeling beneath my skin subside. I glance down at the four-story drop below me, making note of the suitable hand- and footholds, and jump.

———

I prowl the campus deep into the night, eyes wide open. The statues of Grace and Icy Blue seem different to me somehow. I question everything. The statue of them in the quad, the one in blue-and-red glass where they are wrestling—now it seems equally likely that they're caught in the throes of passion, sculpted muscles tensed, faces contorted in sweet agony. Icy Blue's hand is at Grace's neck, but does he like it?

I look away, embarrassed at my thoughts. I can't stay out here. The call of the night is too tempting, but I don't want to go back to my new room, either. My claws flex at the sound of footsteps in the distance. My heightened sense of smell clicks in, and I catch delicate notes of vanilla lavender perfume on a young girl's wrists, the chalky burn of her pressed hair, and the heavy starch in her recently ironed ciki. She's the prim and proper sort. She's also the vulnerable and alone sort.

Her heartbeat quickens as she notices me. I can hold back my fangs between closed lips, and I can hold my claws behind my back, but I cannot hold back my hungry stare. She hastens her step, which ignites the predator within me. The whole of my body feels as if it's made from a thousand mouths, each keen for flesh, and it takes all my will not to spring upon her and tear a hole in her throat.

I *have* to go back to the dorm.

The halls are silent, aside from helpful night staff and a few groggy students lingering about, and I catch sight of all-too-familiar afro-puffs—Sesay, tucked in a study nook with her binder wide open and her nose buried in an old and dusty tome. I grumble, then quickly shuffle through the common area, duck into the hallway, searching for my room. Quietly, I turn the key in the lock and open the door. The lights are low, but on. Chimwe peeks over the edge of eir textbook, then continues reading in bed. I knew ey would end up being my roommate, but there was some part of me that hoped beyond hope that it would be someone else. *Anyone* else.

"You missed curfew," Chimwe says. "You earned our wing three demerits."

I shrug eir words off, briefly allowing myself a smug thought about how many demerits I would have gotten for killing that girl.

"This isn't like Soyinka House," ey scolds me. "You can't come and go whenever you please. This is the High House of Gabadamosi."

"No—Chiso and Kasim are in the High House of Gabadamosi. We're along for the ride."

Chimwe slams eir book closed. "Yeah, well I need this ride, because I'm for sure not going to end up living in Chiso's basement. I'm not wasting this chance like Uncle Pabio did."

"There are worse people to be like," I snap, coming to Uncle Pabio's defense. *People in your own family,* I want to add, but the way Chimwe looks at me, I can see the exposed nerve. I won't be cruel and pluck it, but that doesn't mean I'm going to play nice. "Besides, what do you have to worry about? You'll do a few years at university, then end up taking over your dad's business."

"Chiso's got eir life laid out in front of em. Ey'll take over our father's business, even though I've got the aptitude to run it with both my eyes closed. I've read ahead to university level in economics, accounting, and finance. But then again, I've had to. I need to be twice as good as my sib to earn half the respect. Maybe I'll luck out, and end up with a solid career in midmanagement."

"And you don't see anything wrong with that?"

"Everything is wrong with that! But it's the way things are, and unless you plan on overturning centuries of institutionalized oppression in the next decade, that's the life we're both going to lead. So while you're only here playing around for a few more weeks, I'm here fighting for the rest of my life."

And I know exactly what ey means.

I am quiet. I'd always seen Chiso and Chimwe as one. Yes, they were horrible to us, but I thought they were some united front. The hatred in Chimwe's voice tells another tale. One of suffering and anguish and regrets for a future not yet lived.

It's pathetic. And yet I know exactly how ey feels. The pain of loving someone with all your heart, and hating them to its bloody depths on the very same breath. "It's exhausting." The words slip from my lips.

"It is." Chimwe picks the textbook back up, opens up to the page ey left off on, and continues the late-night cram session.

I wouldn't say that we bonded over this like there's some secret kinship between all lesser twins, but my hatred for Chimwe dims, and Chimwe seems less annoyed at my being here. I retreat to our adjoining bathroom and wash my face with cool water.

Tonight will be the first night that Kasim and I have ever slept apart. I wonder if he's up, awake, thinking of me, or if he's sound asleep, mind swimming with the delights of privilege. I wonder who will comfort him when he has night terrors.

I wonder who will comfort me.

I'm left with nothing but my own fantasies, wondering how things could have been—lamenting about how my *life* could have been—if I were born with six virtues instead of six vices. Would people look at me differently, treat me differently? Would *I* treat people differently? Would I live differently? Would I love differently?

My mind snaps to Ruda. I still feel that breathless moment where there'd been a spark between us, a connection that rose above vice and virtue, rose above rich and poor. But even if Icy Blue hadn't ruined it all, it couldn't have lasted. Better my heart broken now, than years from now, when her father refused us permission to marry. Ha. If she'd even wanted me for anything more than a plaything to begin with. Probably would have gone home and bragged to all of her little posh friends about how she'd fooled around with a comfy boy, and how it made her feel dirty in all the right ways. Then they'd all have a good laugh at my expense, and Ruda would move on with her life. Leaving me. Alone.

Perhaps tonight then, it will be she that comforts me, my plaything. I look in the full-length mirror hanging from the bathroom door. My bones go to dust, and suddenly Ruda stands there in the reflection, smiles at me, looks at me with those bright, innocent eyes she'd had from before Icy Blue . . . before *I'd* stolen that from her. She smacks those big, beautiful, unkissable lips, beckons me closer with a come hither, then peels up her school ciki, baring her deep navel, hints of ribs beneath her fleshy torso, and the ample swells of flesh peeking over her black lace bra. The ciki is discarded and she removes her bra, too. Ruda's breasts fall free to gravity. My sense of self constricts, and the whole of her being envelopes me, and for a brief moment, I become her. Ruda's nipples harden as she caresses herself. She continues to smile all the while, and mouths sweet nothings through the mirror. Then finally, her hand drifts over the slight pooch of her belly, disappears into her trousers.

I snap back to my senses from the momentary panic at what I find there, or rather what I don't find there within my own hand. But the foreign folded flesh eagerly welcomes me just the same. Ruda unbuttons her fly, trousers hit the floor a second later. She explores. Cold tile floor at her back, warm everywhere else, and yet shivers consume her, again and again. Finally, I sit up, groggily. Delighted. Ruda sits up as well, but when I smile at her in the mirror, her reflection does not follow suit. She's looking at me with those eyes I'd given her. Eyes full of mistrust, fear, disillusionment. *I hate you,* she mouths at me. *I hate you for this.*

My mouth puckers tight. She is not alone in that feeling. I hate feeling like this. I hate being like this. I wish for Icy Blue to speak to me. To laugh at how he'd tricked me into performing this violation. To goad me into doing more of his ill will. But he is silent now. His will *is* my will. He *is* me.

I shift, body again my own, and storm out of the bathroom.

"What were you doing in there?" Chimwe asks with a repulsed look. "Where are you going?"

I open the door, and run out into the hall. I hear em yelling something about curfew, but it's inaudible over the rush of blood beating in my ears. Frustration and anger curl my nerves. I kill that night.

Every damned caracal on Grace Mountain.

I knock on Kasim's door the next morning. It is a simple act, but at the same time, completely and absolutely foreign. Chiso answers the door, of course, and greets me with a smile that stops short of eir calculating eyes.

"Good morning, cousin," ey says, then after a second thought, welcomes me in. "Rumor has it that you've cost your wing a total of six demerits. And you haven't even been here a whole day. Perhaps it was my fault. I should have been clearer about the expectations at Kalukenzua House." Chiso's voice reminds me so much of our father's, terse and condescending with a hint of self-satisfaction. "Curfew is at 10:30. No exceptions."

I can't afford to make enemies right now. I bite back my pride, and offer an apologetic smile. "I'm sorry. I'll be more careful from now on." More careful to slip out unnoticed.

"Your wing is who you should be apologizing to." Ey looks me up and down. "And I probably need to mention this also, but Kalukenzua House is a place of chastity. As a mixgen house, it is something we take very seriously. Any act of sexual advance is grounds for expulsion."

"Of course," I say. It's true there was a time, not long ago, when my lecherous side would have reveled in the temptations under this roof, but right now, my eyes desire nothing more than to stare at the beat of Chiso's jugular. *Thump thump. Thump thump.* A song, sweeter than any serenade. My nerves twitch. The killings last night . . . they were not enough. The blood went down like water. Tasteless, flavor-less. I am still hungry, and despite my anger at my brother, I promised to tell him if something changed within me. "I need to speak with Kasim. Is he around?"

"Up in a quiet room, where he's been all night."

"Which one?"

"The last room on the right. He's pretty much set up camp in there, so I wouldn't bother. I think he disabled the doorbell. You know how he gets when he doesn't want to be disturbed." Ey shrugs, speaking to me like ey knows my own brother better than I do. Chiso packs books into eir satchel, including the same one Chimwe was up all night with.

"Sorry for bothering you. I'll let you get off to your test."

"Test?" Chiso says.

"You and Chimwe are in the same class, aren't you?" I squint at the title across the room. *"Prehistoric Religion?* Chimwe was cramming all night."

"We don't have a test. Chimwe's just a bit . . . diligent with eir studies."

Something else catches my attention. The author's name, the same skeevy old bastard who wrote that prehistory book in the library. "Mane Mbanefo. Your professor actually lets you read that crap?"

"My professor wrote this 'crap.' Mbanefo is the most sought-after teacher at Gabadamosi. His knowledge of religion is second only to Gueye Okahim himself. In fact, he taught Gueye Okahim." Chiso's temper flares below the surface. Ey takes a moment to calm, then adds, "He knows everything, from Grace to Icy Blue and everything in between, so I'd ap-preciate it if you gave him the respect he deserves."

Chiso doesn't shut the door in my face, not literally, at

least. But ey turns eir back and refuses to acknowledge me further. I take my leave, my feet leading me to Munashe's office. If Chiso is right, and Mbanefo knows what he's supposed to, perhaps he'll be able to help. Munashe greets me with a guarded smile and mint tea on her breath. The whole of her office smells of tropical fruit compote drizzled in warm syrup with a hint of disinfectant. My body buckles with hunger, and I grab the doorframe for support. As glad as I am to see her, I'll have to make this visit quick.

"I was wondering if you could adjust my schedule so that I have Professor Mbanefo for Prehistoric Religions class?" I spurt out.

"Hello to you, too." Munashe puts a hand on my arm and guides me to the chair in front of her desk. "Have a seat." She then closes the door, and the sweet scent of her blood intensifies. I close my eyes, trying to dull my cravings, but behind my lids, my imagination surges forth, and images of her disemboweled body plague my thoughts. "I've been thinking about you," she says. "Worrying. How is *everything*?"

I open my eyes, force a smile. "Could be better," I squeak out through a mouthful of soured saliva. My sleeve catches the bits that escape past the corners of my mouth. "I think Professor Mbanefo might be able to help. Can you get me into his class? Please?"

"Prehistoric Religions. Let's see . . ." Munashe shivers and takes a long moment to warm her hand on the sides of her Gabadamosi mug. The seconds creep by like eons, but finally she turns her back to me, and rustles through filed papers. Munashe then steps over to the map of campus hanging from her wall. She does a set of calculations with some sort of sliding ruler, then shakes her head. "Just as I feared.

It'd put you on opposite sides of campus from Kasim, and you'd be out of proximity. Unless you'd both like to change schedules, then I could—"

"No," I say from beside her. I'm so close she stumbles and drops her ruler. The pounding of her heart is too much for me. I grab her arm. My claws do not puncture flesh, but they come damned close.

"Auben," Munashe says, voice quiet but firm. "I can see you are struggling, and I'm here to help. I've done some reading of my own. You need blood. Human blood?"

"You would let me feed upon you?" the voice from my throat is salty and deep. The pulse of her veins becomes a song in my mind, the lyrics simple. *Feast, feast, feast . . .*

Munashe snatches her arm from me. "Of course not!" Her sudden movement leaves scratches upon her skin. She swats me across my nose, which has apparently become muzzle. In those few moments of confusion between the blood blooming on her skin and me sinking my teeth into her flesh, she sets a lidded box in front of me and opens it.

The scent is so pungent, my vision goes white. By the time it's cleared, she's set four bags of blood in front of me. "You're not the only one who can sneak into a morgue," she says with a smirk. "Would you like some privacy?"

"Please," I say, my voice trembling. "And thank you."

She shuts the door behind her, locks it. It's then I notice the changes to her office. The deep red rug on her floor. The stack of school uniforms on a shelf behind her desk, just my size. All of the paperwork and folders usually sprawled across her desk are neatly filed away. It's like she expects to come back to a bloodbath. Like she thinks I'm some kind of beast. Well, I *am* some kind of beast, and worse than that even, but still it bites at my pride. She means well. And she's the only one that understands me, and accepts me for who I am. I rifle through her desk drawer, find a pair of scissors and cut the edge from one of the bags. I dump Munashe's tea into a mop bucket, then pour the contents of the bag into her mug, and sip.

Cold. Acrid. Foul. It tastes worse than the salted stew I'd sabotaged for Kasim, but it nourishes me, and anything is better than starving. Better than killing. Bit by bit, I am able to drink two and a half bags' worth before my stomach starts to churn. I pack the remainders away in my satchel, right as there's a soft knock at the door.

"It's me," Munashe says.

"Come in," I say.

She surveys her office and looks relieved it is in the same condition as she left it. "Good?"

"Good enough," I say. The pulsing of her blood now ranks third or fourth among my most pressing thoughts. She's safe from me, for now.

"I was able to get you in Mbanefo's Curiosities of Nature class. I know it isn't exactly what you were looking for, but I hope it's close enough." She hands me a slip. Class starts in fifteen minutes.

"Thanks!" I snatch the paper from her, and kiss her on the cheek—an action that catches us both by surprise. Between her flushing and the taste of salt upon my lips, I need to put some serious distance between us. Now.

I cross the quad in a hurry, trying not to notice all the lean, tender bodies scampering around me like an oblivious herd of antelope.

"There he is!" someone shouts. Three students come running. They assemble in front of me, eyes wide. Breath short. Fresh scripted letters are tattooed onto their foreheads. ASS reads the three of them all together.

The middle *S* whistles, and three more come running: Phila, the backward *K*, the *M*, and Sesay, the *I,* carrying her stupid binder that must be half her weight. They're multiplying. Despite their obvious fanaticism to my brother, they make little effort to arrange themselves in the proper order, and instead form the word *KISSAM*.

"You know *Kasim* is spelled with one *S,*" I say, shaking my head.

"We know that—" Phila says "—now. We've been looking for you everywhere."

"You mean you've been looking for Kasim everywhere," I say, trying to hurry things up. Five minutes until class.

"No, no. We know where Kasim is," Phila says. "We *always* know where Kasim is. It's you we're looking for, Auben. We want to know everything. Start from the very beginning. What was it like having Kasim as your brother growing up? Was he always so amazing? So perfect? When did you realize he was special? How hard was it being raised in his perfect shadow? Did it make you want to be a better person? Did you ever wish you were just like him? Or did it make you realize your failures that much more? You are so blessed to have had him all this time. All to yourself. Don't you feel blessed?"

"Very," I mumble, with what I assume is the biggest eye roll in all of history. I brush past them, but they swarm behind me, sticking close like flies on shit.

"Is it true he can speak directly to Grace? It's true,

isn't it? I heard about the defting sticks. Tell us everything, slowly, so Sesay can write it all down. And the incident at the Sanctuary? You were there, weren't you? How big was the beast? What did it smell like? Was Kasim scared at all, or did he feel powerful and confident? What made him decide to take the risk to protect Gueye Okahim? Was he called into action by Grace?"

"What if he's the embodiment of Grace Himself?" asks Sesay. She doesn't look up from her frantic scribblings as all eyes turn on her in stunned silence.

"Sesay!" Phila says. "What if we're wrong?"

"We're not wrong." She points to her tattooed forehead. "I wouldn't have gotten this if there was even the smallest chance that we might be. I was there for the defting sticks. I was there at the Sanctuary. I felt that beast's cold breath at the back of my neck. It was the breath of Icy Blue for sure, and only Grace would be able to best him, and make him look like a complete fool." Her eyes rise and stick to me like she's keen on the details of our Sanctuary performance.

"Kasim is not perfect. He is not Grace," I say. "He's got vices just like everyone else."

"He's got *a* vice. And I'm not sure it's even his." Sesay's eyes narrow. "Tell us about your Discernment. Was it done by federal officers, or private?"

"Maybe it was done by your *mom*," I jest. Yet even as I say it, I strain back, trying to remember the details of the day our vices and virtues were doled out to us. We were only five, so the memories are sparse and hazy as it is, but Mother had given us each a long sip of spirits to dull the pain, and I can only dredge up images of my small trembling hands reaching out for vice talisman after vice talisman.

Sesay flips the pages of her binder and retrieves a thin folder embossed with the Gabadamosi seal, like the ones in Munashe's office. She pulls out a stack of papers. "Private," she says, reading from official-looking documents. "No federal officer would have dared with twins so young. Your test was conducted by Sall Iweala."

"So?" I snap back.

"So, Iweala is a master wu mystic, imprisoned for falsifying test results fourteen years ago. Lesser twins, well-aware of the privilege/discrimination gap, would hire him to give their five-and-two children a four-and-three tempering, hoping that they'd be treated closer to equal."

"Kasim and I are six-and-one, so that doesn't even—" I blink. Unless we weren't.

"His practice was expensive, costing thousands of djang. It was also imperfect, and the swapping of vice and virtue was incomplete, but not enough to raise suspicions. So you have a few charitable bones in your body. Kasim has been marred by your greed."

"This is ridiculous," I say. "Our mother was way too poor to afford anything like that!"

"And yet here you are at the most prestigious and expensive school in the Cape. If it was important to her, she would have found a way." Sesay steps up to me. Challenging me. Tempting me. "I noticed you slipped out of the Sanctuary during prayer, Auben." She says my name like it's a question.

"Then maybe you should have been praying harder," I snap back.

"What lies behind those eyes?" She cocks her neck so that the throb of her jugular falls into my view. "What cold darkness stirs in your heart?" Her blood calls to me, a whisper, a song, a symphony slightly off-key. There's something about her blood that's not quite right, but not wrong enough to stop my desire to spill it on the ground between us.

I ball my fists tight to keep my claws from erupting. It works, mostly. But it does nothing to quell the hate for her, and the hate of what I've become.

I grab Sesay's binder, snap the thick spine in two. She'll never know how close I'd been to snapping her spine instead. But not here, not now. Not when I'm so close to getting the answers I need. "There's some charity for you," I hiss, throwing her binder to the ground. And in her wan smile, I can see she understands exactly what I mean.

I'm shivering when I take my seat in Professor Mane Mbanefo's class. Was Sesay right? If wu potions could swap vices and virtues temporarily, maybe it was possible that more powerful wu could switch them permanently. What if Icy Blue had always been within me, lying dormant, waiting patiently for puberty to turn my body into a vessel worth steering? What if Kasim had been born perfect, free of vice, and I'd polluted him?

"Mr. Mtuze," Professor Mbanefo demands, voice strong and virulent despite his hunched-over body. He was old on the back cover of his book, but he is ancient now, long rows of coarse gray hair plaited intricately down his head, his generous beard given the same treatment. "I assume you asked to be placed into my class this late in the quarter because you want to be here. Please pay attention." His pointer snaps against a detailed painting of a pair of broad backs, chimeral stripes prominent—one with tan on dark brown skin, like my own. The other dark brown stripes on tan skin. Had the dark-skinned twin a couple more keloid scars on his arm, I would have sworn it was Kasim and me. "In this illustration, we clearly see the marks left by our makers, Grace, and yes, Icy Blue, too. All of you bear these marks, though it is easier to see on some than others. But . . ." Professor Mbanefo draws black curtains and dims all but a couple of the classroom's lamps. Giggles fill the room as we're plunged into near darkness. He then holds up a lantern with violet panes. "Can I have a volunteer?"

An andy kigen raises eir hand. I recognize em from my wing of Kalukenzua House, slightly built with skin darker than mine, and intense, widely set eyes that never lift from the floor.

"Yes, Ezek, you'll do nicely. Please, class, mind your curiosity." Professor Mbanefo places a hand on Ezek's shoulder. "I'm going to lift your ciki in the back, okay?" Ezek nods quickly, then crosses eir arms as the shirt rises revealing black skin, perfectly smooth and uniform. Professor Mbanefo is disturbingly gentle, finger catching the bottom edge of Ezek's chest wrap, and lifting it discreetly out of view. Still, a few students notice, and giggles erupt once again. "Class, I will not warn you again. Now, what do you observe? Yes?" Professor Mbanefo nods to a studious fem kigen sitting up front.

"No stripes," ey says.

"No stripes. For most of us, it is easy to forget that our bodies were forged from heavenly blood and seed of both Grace and Icy Blue. But look here . . ." Professor Mbanefo raises the lantern to Ezek's back. The entire class gasps as beautiful stripes are revealed under the pale violet light.

Ezek's neck snaps back, trying to see over eir shoulder. "We owe our lives to both of them, and yet we worship one and vilify the other."

"You're suggesting that we worship Icy Blue?" the fem kigen says with derision.

"Of course not," Professor Mbanefo's face puckers sour. "But we should pity him, have mercy. He is compelled by vices to do his evil, just as we are."

My temper swells, and the surface of my desk ices over. I do not need these people's pity. I calm myself with the biology I learned at my old school. "It's not Grace and Icy Blue," I shout.

"Mr. Mtuze?"

"It's not gods that make the stripes. It's biology. Genetic material is swapped in utero between twins. You can see evidence of that in the striping as you described. The darker twin got his light stripes from his twin, and vice versa."

"Mind your curiosity, Mr. Mtuze! This classroom is not a place for your mental masturbations!"

"It's science, Professor Mbanefo. It's why Ezek has breasts and a penis, and whatever else ey has going on down there. Eir sibling contributed male genes, and ey contributed female genes and everything mixed together. It's why half the population is chimeral gendered!"

"Enough, Mr. Mtuze," Professor Mbanefo grates, his heated eyes drilling into mine, until I'm forced to look away.

When I do, I catch the sour look on Ezek's face, and I give em one right back. Yeah, I feel shitty, but sometimes it's easier to tear people down than to waste time trying to build up all the broken pieces inside me. I spend the rest of the class biting my lip, listening to this nonsense pseudoscience: leaves drop right before the narrow season because they are vulnerable to Icy Blue's breath, and would cause the tree to die if they didn't; meteor showers are Grace crying for joy over the devotion of his followers while the twin islands to the south of the Cape erupt with the molten blood of the gods from wounds caused by the failings of nonbelievers. I look around and everyone is wide-eyed, eating this all up. Bunch of gullible pricks.

And they have the audacity to pity me?

A rigid chill whips through the room, and the entire class braces against it in unison. The bells toll, and class is concluded.

"A word, please, Mr. Mtuze," Professor Mbanefo says as I hastily pack my belongings.

Great. I make my way to Professor Mbanefo's desk. I wait for him to reprimand me for my tirade about kigens, but he just looks me up and down, eyes sticking to the angles and curves of my body.

"Mmm," is his only comment.

"What?"

He fondles the length of one of his beard plaits. "Your mind is so nimble, yet your heart is so unyielding. Amazing. You've spent your whole life learning to draw a line between science and religion. Everyone has, religious and secular alike. The truth is, there is no line. They sit on top of one another, two sides of the same coin."

"That type of talk could get you excommunicated. Or is that why you're a teacher here now instead of chancellor at one of your Prim universities?"

"My resignation was my choice. By college, it is too late to mold minds that have already been set. Your brains are younger, suppler." His index finger meets my chin, tilts my head from side to side like I am cattle and he is assessing my worth. I may be young, but I am not vulnerable. My claws itch beneath my nail beds. "Mmm," he says again. "So much like your mother. In mind and in spirit."

His words snap me from my brewing temper. "You know my mother?"

"I do."

"What, did she clean your house or something?"

"Or something," Professor Mbanefo says with a lecherous grin.

My mind snaps back to the machination I'd found in Mother's closet, like the one the streetwalker had turned emself out on. I can't even imagine what Mother had been thinking all those years ago, so proud, yet so desperate. She knew all too well what life would be like for her young sons who would certainly test lopsided on Discernment. She saw the way her and her sister's lives had diverged, based solely on their own virtues and vices. She would do anything to ensure Kasim and I had a better life. Maybe even sell her own body for the money to pay a mystic to tamper with the results.

I shudder at the thought. And the next thought knocks me back altogether. I grab the desk behind me for support.

What if she hadn't stopped?

I think of all the sacrifices she's made to put us through a private secular school. Cleaning houses in the morning, businesses at night. Or so she said. For all her grace and diligence, duplicity runs strong within her. Could she have been just as easily sneaking away to see her regulars, legs spreading as quickly as her smile? And was this pervert . . . Mane Mbanefo, one of them?

"Oh, Mother . . ." I eke out before flipping the desk so hard it hits the far wall before clanging against the floor.

"Mr. Mtuze!" Mbanefo yells after me as I storm out of his classroom. I do not turn to engage him, for if I did, there would be nothing of him left.

That evening, I scurry about our childhood home, along the floorboards, underneath furniture, around cheese-baited traps, silently following her. From my vantage, the meekest of mice, my mother is as tall as a giant, though I suppose she has always seemed so grand, so formidable. She wears loose slacks and a boxy button-down shirt. Comfortable shoes. Her smell is hers, but with my new senses, it is a hundred times more potent—citrus blossoms, polished and powerful, doing their best to cover up the ground-in scent of industrial cleaning solvents. Her breath smells faintly of tinibru, just a few sips to take the edge off. Nothing about her smells like that streetwalker had.

She quickly brushes her fro into a large puff, perfectly balanced upon her head, pomades the edges, and checks herself over in the mirror. Her vainglory is in full force. She practices a lackluster smile, clips her work badge to her breast pocket, then gathers a light jacket and a large lunch bag.

I chide myself for leaping to such farfetched conclusions. She's not hiding anything. My mother works her ass off for us. No more, no less. I shout out an apology, but my squeaky voice gets lost in a jungle of cobwebs and dust bunnies beneath the couch.

Before she leaves, she touches the clay heart sitting upon her writing desk. Kasim's and my five-year-old handprints fill the center of it, our thumbs overlapping. I smell the tears budding in her eyes. She'd been so angry when Kasim and I told her we were going to Gabadamosi. Didn't help us pack. Didn't see us off. My heart is heavy, seeing her like this, tracing each of our fingers set so long ago in clay. Then she twists it upside down, and something clicks.

There is silence for several seconds, then gears churn. The top of her desk rises on well-oiled hinges, but I am too low to the ground to see what is inside. I forget my stealth and claw my way up the back of the couch, and perch on the high cushion. I catch a glimpse of metal, but still I need to get higher, closer. I run along the back of the couch, down the arm, make a risky leap to the glass-top end table, skitter around her still-cold can of tinibru, across a dozen water rings, and another jump onto the high-back recliner, just a few feet away from my mother. From up here, I see it all. The left half brims with tools baring sleek, wooden shafts ending in every combination of steel tips. Hammers, screwdrivers in ever-diminishing sizes, and a dozen objects I have no words for, capable of measuring things I have no concept of. The other half of the desk, the right half—it steals the breath out of my little mouse lungs. Brassy machinations inset carefully into red felt-lined divots. Mother sets a small leather satchel in the middle of the desk, picks and chooses several tools— sharp, precise things, as well as a set of reticulating lenses. Her hand brushes one of the machinations as she sets the lenses into her satchel, a brass ball, like the one I'd found in her closet. It hums for a moment, then six spider legs ratchet out from its sides. It lifts itself out of the divot and makes a rush at Mother's arms. She tsks it, shooing it away as if it were a fly, and not an abomination that could get her locked away for the rest of her life. It skitters around for a moment, as if confused, before settling back into its divot. Legs retract.

My heart retracts.

Mother, *my mother,* is making these machinations?

She carefully ties up the tool satchel and places it into a lunch container, and her lunch container into her lunch bag, and stacks an oily sack of samosas, a bunch of plump grapes, and an orange on top.

She checks herself in the mirror once more. She is not overcome with vainglory. It is the opposite. She is making sure she blends in. If she is caught in public with such tools, she would be detained, questioned, searched. It probably wouldn't be enough to have her imprisoned, but eyes would be upon her every movement.

"Mother, no!" I squeak out as her hand touches the doorknob.

Her head whips back, and she sees me. She is not startled, but exasperated. Mice have never been an uncommon sight in our home. She takes a pair of balled socks from Kasim's old loafers still sitting at the door, and chucks them at me, all in one smooth motion. They hit me dead on, knock me back and onto the floor.

I lie in the dark, dazed. Confused. Mother is sneaking out at night with lecherous intent, only it's a lechery of a different sort. A more dangerous sort. Masturbations of the mind. Science. She's hiding machinations in her closet, hiding mechanical sketches in posh magazines, and hiding these skittering automatons in her desk. For as long as I can remember, she'd left Kasim and me to fend for ourselves in the evenings several times a week so she could "clean office buildings," well into the night.

238 / NICKY DRAYDEN

A pair of long, rough whiskers brush against mine as something climbs upon my back. Buck teeth nibble at my ear, and side by side, a beaded red eye stares me down. Big rat balls lie heavily upon my tail.

"SQUEAK," the rat says to me, aggressively, and so sure of himself. I'm pretty certain he's told me that I am about to become his bitch.

I turn back on him, stretch my jaws wide to show a pair of sharp fangs, like those of a snake. He tries to scurry away, but I catch him with mouse claws that aren't quite so little anymore. I sink my fangs into the back of his neck, swallow, moving him slowly through my throat. His legs still wiggle and fight, and scratch at the inside of my mouth until they are swallowed, too. I make sure not to kill him. I'll let that happen in the acidic hell of my stomach.

By the time he's fully inside me, my little mouse belly is so swollen that my paws can no longer reach the floor. I shift into my old friend the caracal, and pounce through an open window, sprouting wings. I catch my mother's scent on the breeze. I soar toward her, not caring who else sees me. I land a block behind her, crouch and stick to the shadows as I follow her to an office building. She shows her badge to the door attendant, who acknowledges her with a heavy nod as ey lets her in.

It's obviously a front. My mind snaps back to Msr. Ademola's class and the fifth of the Seven Holy Wars—The War of Masturbations, 836, the year of the Benevolent Fishmonger. A bloodless war, compared to the others. Knowledge was the primary casualty. One hundred and twelve Mzansi scientists were imprisoned right here, on a small island off the Cape's coast. Religious zealots claimed that their work was born of self-satisfaction, and that their mental masturbations were driving Grace from the hearts of the people. Science was deemed a form of lechery. After some twenty-something years of protest, the prisoners were released. The direct references to science being lecherous were begrudgingly removed from the Holy Scrolls, but the subtext remained. Science became something you did alone in shame, under the covers of night, maybe with a few close and trusted partners if you yearned to share your titillating theories of chemistry, biology, astronomy. And, if you were feeling particularly dirty, you might partake in mechanics as well.

There's an open window up a few floors, but I get the feeling that this is the kind of place where everyone knows everyone, and I won't get any real answers scurrying about at people's feet.

I hear footsteps, smell the sweat of anticipation upon the breeze. A heartbeat, quick but steady. An andy kigen emerges from the shadows—big, burly, and awkward, wearing the same getup as my mother, buttons on eir shirt straining across the chest. Not my first choice for blending in, but I can't take a chance that another will come along.

I crouch, swish my caracal tail, then spring upon em, my claws half-extended, bracing against my instincts to kill. I have the element of surprise, ready to knock em unconscious and hide eir body in the shadows. Eir eyes snap to me, quick as lightning, and there's not a lick of fear to be found in them. Instead of me catching em by surprise, I'm caught by the neck. Several snapped vertebrae later, the kigen lets me fall to the ground with little note, as if ey'd swatted a fly.

I lie there in the streets, dead, but not dead. Angry. Embarrassed. I shift, though my body is slow and stubborn to respond. I flop over like a fish out of water, so I can stare up at the stars in the night sky. I reach down, deep into the pit of my stomach, futilely stoking an oven that almost certainly has no fuel left to burn. But there's something, just enough smoldering embers to shift one last time. As soon as I'm done, the desperate need to feed overwhelms me, so intense, I feel like I'm gasping for air.

"Oy!" I call out to the kigen. Ey turns, and eyes go wide as ey sees me wearing the bulky suit of armor that is eir body. There's the fear I was expecting. The kigen runs and is surprisingly fast, but not fast enough. I am upon em. My girth matches the kigen's, muscle for muscle. We are one and the same person.

"What kind of evil is this?" ey asks, voice deep and quavering. I tune it out. This is a kill just like any of the others. I run my claw neck to pubis, cutting through clothes and skin all in one swipe.

Ey screams, but they all scream, and it does not deter me. I lap greedily, blood both overwhelmingly savory and sweet. "Grace help me!" ey whispers—the very last words I expect to hear from a subsecular scientist. All the same, the kigen's warm blood goes chill and sour in my mouth. I spit it out, and back away, but the aftertaste sticks with me like a curse upon my tongue. I brood over what could have caused this abomination, and then, for just an instant, I swear I see Kasim's reflection in eir eyes.

I divert my gaze to eir badge, snatch it, and run. I shift again to rid my clothes of bloodstains, and clip the badge to my pocket. It is cruel to leave em to bleed out like that. Those few weak strings of charity tug at my heart. I should turn back, put em out of misery at least. I ignore the thought. According to Sesay, it isn't my charity in the first place. Let Kasim do so if he sees fit.

I hold my badge up to the door attendant.

"Rabe," the attendant says with the same heavy nod ey gave my mother. "How are the kids?"

"Fine," I say over the sick bulge in my throat. Figures I'd killed one of the few kigens who managed to procreate. Never has my conscience weighed so heavily. I have to do something to help the real Rabe. Anything. I turn back, but the attendant shoves me through the door. "You're the last one. They're waiting on you," ey says, eyes drilling into mine. Ey nods me in the direction of a mop and bucket, but I get the overwhelming feeling that I'm definitely not here to clean.

Forty scientists fill a hot cramped room on the fifth floor of the building. Small groups huddle around demonstrations, motors humming, test tubes bubbling, and gears churning. Thanks to Rabe's stature, I can see over everyone's shoulders. There is a small mechanical coach, one that moves on its own under the power of magnets. I marvel as it does lazy laps across the tabletop. At the window, several people huddle around another machination. They argue over it, each spurting out numbers and nonsense names and pointing up at the star-filled sky. The word *astrolabe* is tossed around, and I edge my way closer. It is some sort of tool for measuring the stars. I listen intently as they blabber on about focal lengths and lenses and apertures. I even snag a look through the small handheld telescope everyone is bickering over. For a handful of seconds, I become one with the stars, hanging so close in my view, I swear I could touch them. Then the scope is gone, snatched out of my hands.

At another demonstration, a machinist pulls a cold can of tinibru out of an icebox. I am not impressed until he tips the box forward to show there is no ice block tucked inside, and says it is cooled by a machination called a condenser. On another table sits a teenaged girl, warm brown skin, oversized spectacles, hair dangling in greased twists. Or so it seems, until I take a closer look. Her head cocks, glassy eyes make contact with mine, rouged lips spread into a stiff, unnerving smile. Behind every movement, there is the whisper of gears. "You've been a naughty boy," she says to me. Her hand rises to her mouth with a clunky stutter-stop, then she blows me a kiss.

The room fills with the deep laughter of men and the sharp scent of arousal. The women suck their teeth like an orchestrated chorus, and the kigens exchange quick, irritated looks as they scrawl lecherous equations upon a tattered chalkboard. The ruckus stops cold when a silhouette dressed in ruddy brown robes enters the room and steps upon a makeshift stage. The twitchy light of electric lanterns touches the graceful features beneath a hood. Familiar features. The piercing eyes, the smooth skin impervious to the effects of serving innumerous scowls, the false calm upon her lips . . .

I go chill all over. All my life, I've fantasized about a parent with a supersecretive life. Turns out I'd picked the wrong one.

"Omehea!" Mother smolders.

The clockwork girl's master shuts her off with a flick of a switch. Her smile fades, and she slumps forward slightly.

My mother sucks her teeth in that way I've come to identify as her utmost disappointment. "It's enough that they accuse us of mental masturbation. Do we really need to give them more ammunition?"

Omehea flushes. "She is not meant for dalliance, Enna Zeogwu. I was just having a little joke, I swear. All my energies are spent for the cause!"

"This isn't a time for jokes." Mother's browline goes razor sharp. I find myself cringing, even though it is not directed at me. "With the incident at the Sanctuary, faith has wedged its way back into the hearts of those who had forgotten. It won't be long before secular teachings again come under attack."

"Maybe we should be the ones to attack," someone says from behind me. "Between all of the sects in Mzansi, we've got sufficient numbers now. We should go on the offensive."

"And cause an eighth Holy War?" grates my mother. "Times have changed since The War of Masturbations. We've gained a solid foothold, and you're right, we cannot allow ourselves to fall back into the debts of gods. But we've got our own schools, and we're changing people's way of thinking. There are plenty of nonviolent options. We should pursue those first."

"With all due respect, Enna Zeogwu, I think you've gone soft. These are not the words of the Enna we elected twenty years ago. Certainly, not the Enna who broke bottles on the heads of law officers and Men of Virtue!"

My mother steps down from her stage, crosses the floor as if she's floating upon it, and bears down on that poor sap who'd misspoken. Of all the things my mother is, soft is definitely not one of them. "You doubt my temper?" she asks the andy kigen, fingers wrapped at eir neck. "I'd kill a hundred times over, if that is what we decide to do. I have no qualms about killing." She releases eir neck, and the andy kigen coughs something fierce. She waits for em to subside. "All I'm saying is just because we *can* attack the Sanctuary, doesn't mean we *should*."

"And what would you say if it weren't your boy that Gueye Okahim has taken under his wing?"

"That does not factor into my decision. I will not hesitate to do whatever it takes to preserve the pursuit of knowledge. You don't need to worry yourself about my—"

The door flies open, and in stumbles a massive figure. Ey steps into the lantern light and everyone gasps. It is Rabe. "Icy Blue . . ." ey says with a wet gurgle, clenching entrails to eir splayed stomach. "He's here."

All eyes fall wide and hot upon me, the imposter, though Mother's are the only ones filled with disappointment instead of fright. She knows. Mothers always know.

I take a deep breath, assess the scene. My first instinct is to flee, but then I see Rabe there, slumped and bleeding. So. Much. Blood. My mouth waters, my mind becomes a flurry. I shudder, fighting against my nature. Despite myself, my claws unseat themselves, palms become padded paws. A billion pricks against my skin become tawny fur. Erupting fangs scrape through the bone of my jaws.

I am upon em. My arms surround em. Rabe struggles, but in this state, ey cannot fight me off. I hunch forward, membranous wings unfurl from my shoulder blades. I flap them, and in the next second, I'm crashing through the glass of the closest window, catching myself on the breeze.

I hold my bounty tightly, get my bearing, and cross the

city until I see what I am after. The hospital. I alight in the shadows, shift to my normal self. My normal human self. Rabe's arm drapes heavily over me, so out of it now, mumbling about eir numerous sins, praying they are forgiven. Ey doesn't pray to me, but Rabe is just as much mine as ey is Kasim's. I understand Rabe's vices, perhaps even more so than my brother. I am the root of Rabe's vice.

"Your sins are forgiven, but you aren't going to die," I whisper to em, as his eyes go dim, his body goes slack. "I can't let you die."

I'm powerful, but apparently not powerful enough.

"You've earned us three more demerits," Chimwe says into my ear.

My eyes are too heavy to lift, and the depths of my tear-stained pillow are too comforting to part from. "Well, you don't have to worry about my getting any more," I say, my voice like a rake through gravel. "Because I'm not moving from this bed ever again."

"I'm sure that will look great on your transcript."

"I'm serious. I'm not going to class. Not to the cafeteria. Not the library. Not home." Especially not home. How can I face my mother? What could I tell her? I've killed now. Rabe's blood is on my hands. Eir children have lost a parent. How can I right that? Even if I tried, I'd only end up making things worse. "I'm no good to anyone out there. It's better if I lie low. Keep quiet. Do nothing."

"Great, so now you'll just be no good to me." My mattress gives as Chimwe takes a seat. I roll away from em, toward the cold cement wall. "You're really a mess up there, aren't you?"

Eir knuckles rap softly against my temple. "You need me to hail your mother?"

"No!" I shout, sitting bolt upright. "I'm fine. At least I will be."

"You wanna talk about it?" Ey seems sincere. And it's not like I've got anyone else to turn to.

"Everything I touch turns to shit," I say. "That in and of itself is bad enough, but then I start comparing myself to Kasim . . . even the stuff he shits on comes out smelling like roses."

"Classic lesser twin syndrome," Chimwe says with a nod. "You can't fall victim to that. It'll eat you up inside. Remember, Kasim's human, just like the rest of us. He's prone to vice, too. Everyone has their weaknesses. Even Chiso." There's something sinister brewing in Chimwe's voice, and I like it quite a bit.

"Go on . . ."

Chimwe leans in with a grin. "So our first year at Gabadamosi, Chiso and I had Mzansi History together. You know how smart Chiso is, but eir brilliance is only rivaled by eir laziness. Ey'd wait to the last minute to do every assignment, then pull an all-nighter and come up with the best damned papers probably anyone has ever written. You could see it in Prof. Orji's eyes, leaning forward on the edge of her seat during Chiso's oral presentations. It was disgusting. Meanwhile, I spend weeks researching and fact-checking, my ass glued to a library chair every spare moment of my life, and Prof. Orji won't even bother to look up from her desk to acknowledge me. It hurt knowing that no matter how hard I tried, I would never be seen as more than Chiso's shadow. It hurt even more when Chiso waved eir perfect papers in my face, consoling me that maybe if I tried a little harder, I could be more like em . . ."

"They don't understand," I say. "It's like we're on the same planet, surrounded by the same people, but we're living in two totally different worlds."

"Exactly." Chimwe grabs my shoulders and stares me down, like I've tapped directly into eir mind. I see Uncle Pabio's eccentricity peeking from behind those eyes. "I got fed up with Chiso and all eir holier than thou bullshit. So I decided to do something about it. We got our assignments for our final papers midway through the quarter, but like always, Chiso waited until the last minute to start it. Ey had to write a paper on Kalu Fagbare."

"The explorer."

"Yeah. Everyone knows the basics . . . sailed from Nri to Mzansi, established contact with the people here. The first celebration feast, the spreading of religion and writings, the introduction of the tonic that became tinibru, blah blah. Well, as soon as I saw Chiso's assignment, I knew what I had to do. Each morning, as soon as the sun cracked, I was at the library on their typesetter, creating a detailed booklet on the secret life of Kalu Fagbare, penned by noted historian Igwe Jakande himself, to add authenticity. It was painstaking. It took me well over three hours to set the text for each page, and there were forty-eight pages altogether. My fingers were cramped and bloodied, and my grades suffered, but I pushed on, until two days before our presentations. I checked out every book in the library that even mentioned Kalu Fagbare, and left my creation in their place."

Chimwe stands. Ey has both my mother's diligence and her grace. Perhaps that's why I've always hated em a little less than Chiso. Ey goes to eir desk, pulls out a drawer, and retrieves a small locked box. Inside, the book, *The Secret Life of Kalu Fagbare.* Ey places it into my hands. If I hadn't known any better, I would have thought it to be the real thing. Worn leather binding, yellowed pages. Illustrations even. Beautifully inked.

"Did you draw these?" I ask. "They're amazing."

Chimwe smiles.

I flip to the middle and read a passage, detailing Fagbare's involvement in losing both his ship and his mother to drunken Rashtra pirates in a wager gone wrong, his outlawing farting in public—a crime punishable by death—funding a brothel staffed by tamed apes, coordinating child fighting rings, burning books written by kigens, burning kigens, denouncing Grace and forcing everyone to pray to a sentient yam that he claimed lived in the crotch of his pants. People rubbed upon it during their prayers. There is an illustration of this, unfit for anyone to gaze upon. "You didn't."

"I did."

"Ey didn't."

"Mmm-hmmm. Chiso's paper was brilliantly written, as always. But the silence that fell upon the class after ey read it, it was so thick, I thought I might have drowned. Prof. Orji . . . her jaw was hanging so low, it nearly hit her desk. How I managed to contain my laughter, I will never know."

I'm rocking back and forth, unable to contain my awe for Chimwe's flawless execution of this duplicitous deed. I can't help but wonder what kind of mischief we could have gotten into if we'd teamed up as kids. "So what happened next?"

"Chiso failed the assignment, of course. Nearly failed

the class. Probably would have gotten expelled if ey'd been one of us, but you know how that goes. Ey was outraged. Eir temper swelled like I've never seen. Chiso dragged both Prof. Orji and the headmistress to the library to point out the book, but of course by that time, it was long gone." Chimwe takes the book back, locks it under key. Returns it to its resting spot deep in the drawer. "Chiso still has no idea it was me. And you're the first person I've ever told."

"Wow. Now that's wicked. And genius." I thump my duplicity brand twice with my fist, and Chimwe does the same to eirs in an unspoken sign of solidarity. "Sooo . . . you trust me with such a secret?" I ask.

"Sure. We're roommates now. It's us against our siblings. Besides, now you know what I'm capable of, so crossing me probably wouldn't be in your best interest."

I laugh inside. If only Chimwe knew what I was capable of . . .

Still, I revel in the moment. It feels so normal. Just two students, two cousins, hell, two *friends* chatting it up before class. Nobody killed anybody. Nobody's the reincarnation of the devil. Nobody's got a mother with a secret agenda or Grace for a brother. "Yeah, roommates. It won't be so bad, right?"

Chimwe shrugs. "It'll probably be tedious and full of disappointment. Life's hard, but it beats the alternative, right?"

"Death." The word slips coolly over my lips. My eyes twinge. I taste Rabe's blood in my mouth, coarse and peppery, with vanilla undertones.

"Shit, I'm sorry. I shouldn't have said that. You were close to her, weren't you? That counselor?"

"The what, huh?"

"The one that died yesterday. You didn't hear? They found her in her office. Cold as stone. Mushea, Munane, Manusa, or something."

"Munashe?" The name scrapes over my lips. Not her.

"That's the one. I hear it was weird. She was still sitting at her desk, pen in hand."

I get light-headed, lose focus. I notice a patch of fur on the back of my hand and rub it away. There's a knock at the door, but it feels so far away. Chimwe gives me a soft punch in the shoulder, then goes to answer it.

I'd sworn I wouldn't hurt her. I did everything in my power to protect her from my wrath, but I'd forgotten to protect her from the perils of my affection.

. . . And if your heart stops cold,
Then you've been kissed by Icy Blue.

The childhood songs were true. My kiss, just a simple peck on the cheek. My kiss had killed her.

"Auben?" comes my brother's pained voice. Instantly, I am at the door's threshold and upon him. My arms are wrapped as tightly around Kasim, as his are around me.

"It's true, isn't it? About Munashe? I'm not dreaming?" I shudder and weep upon his shoulder.

"There's going to be a prayer vigil today." He pulls back, suddenly a pained look on his face. His eyes move to his shoulder. Small holes dot his ciki where my tears had fallen. I dust at them futilely, trying my best not to fall completely apart. "It's fine, it's fine," he says to me. "Just be at the school sanctuary this evening. I'm going to say a few things. I hope you do, too."

"I can't," I say, shaking my head.

"Chimwe, can we get a moment alone?" Kasim asks.

"You can pretend I'm not here, if you'd like. But this is my room, and I'm not going anywhere." Chimwe rolls eir eyes, sits on eir bed, and takes to a textbook.

"I heard you were out past curfew last night," Kasim says to me, but there is oh so much more context within the depths of his glassy eyes. He saw. I'm not sure how, but those same eyes had filled Rabe's soul when Grace was called upon.

"I was." I do not offer explanation. There is no need. "It won't happen again, because I'm not leaving this room." Memory of Munashe's coy smile wrenches my heart. If this is what happens to the people I care most about, then what hope is there for the rest of the world?

"It was a mistake. We all make mistakes." Kasim's hand touches my arm, and twists so my vice brands come into view. "Remember, you are not your vices. They do not control you. You are the one in control of your life."

I nod my head like an impish child.

"Urges come and go, but you don't have to give in to them. I'm not expecting perfection, but you could try a little harder. Be a little more like me," Kasim adds.

Chimwe clears eir throat and noisily flips a page. I shake my head. Kasim is not like Chiso. He says things, sure, but they aren't meant to make me feel less than. He just doesn't know what it's like to walk a mile in my vice-trodden shoes. It's not like he's looking down on me. Except that he *is* looking down at me. Literally.

"Kasim . . ." I utter through clenched teeth, nod at his feet. He's hovering six inches above the ground.

Kasim starts, looks embarrassed, then steps back down onto solid ground. We both turn and look to Chimwe, mouth as wide as the textbook that's fallen out of eir lap.

"Whoa," Chimwe mutters in a daze.

The lies fall on me. They always have. My mind spins, and the falsehoods fly from my mouth. "Cool trick, huh? You remember how we used to play 'levitate' as kids. It's all angles and point of view."

"Yeah, but he was a foot off the ground. I could see all the way underneath. You can't fake that. You *can't*."

Kasim's hand presses at my chest, and he pushes past me into the room. "You didn't see anything out of the ordinary. Your eyes are tired from reading, that's all."

Something fades behind Chimwe's eyes, like a lantern gone dim. "I didn't see anything out of the ordinary," ey says. "My eyes are tired from reading, that's all."

Kasim turns back to me. His face has gone queasy.

"What did you do to em?" I whisper.

"New trick."

Deep inside, my hackles rise at how easily he'd performed this ultimate act of deception on our own cousin. On our own *sibling*. "Have you used it on me?"

"Of course not."

"Have you tried?"

"It only works on the weak-willed," Kasim says. "Plus I hate using it. Gueye Okahim says that free will is the foundation of religion. Without free will, faith is meaningless."

"You're quoting Gueye Okahim now?"

"I have questions. He has answers. His teachings help my mind to focus. He helps me to feel like I'm not coming completely unraveled through all of this." His voice catches in his throat, which catches me by surprise.

Kasim does seem different. Less manic, more confident, and I no longer get that feeling that he's putting on a good face while falling apart at the seams. I guess it makes sense. While I've been entertaining my vices to get through these lengthy separations, Kasim has been strengthening his virtues. Sometimes that's just the way it happens, bonds stretch, and stretch, and stretch until twins are leading completely separated lives, punctuated by an obligatory dinner once or twice a week to reconnect. But that's not the only way to do it. If Gueye Okahim is helping Kasim to focus, then perhaps he can help me, too. If I try a little harder. If I follow a little more closely in Kasim's footsteps. If I stop acting like an asshole jerk brother, pushing Kasim away out of fear of rejection, then we could work together to overcome these forces that have wedged their way between us. The past of the Original Twins may already be written, but no one has control over our future. It can be anything we want it to be.

"I want to come with you next time you go see Gueye Okahim," I say. This feeling I feel right now, I don't ever want to feel it again. And though the thought of leaving this room terrifies me, I know I could do it with Kasim by my side. "I want to learn everything I can. Whatever we're going through, it's happening to the both of us." I reach out, grab his arm. "Remember that time I got real sick with the pox, and you crawled into bed and refused to leave me, even for a second?"

Kasim's lips spread into a grin as he reminisces. "I'd never seen so much snot come out of one nose. Ugh, and those blisters."

"Then you caught it a few days later, and I tended to you the best I could."

"We were both a mess then. Covered head to toe in salve. Oh, that stuff smelled so foul."

"We're still a mess," I say. "I miss you, Kasim. I miss how we used to be. I think we can get there again if we work together, stick side by side. I'll go to the Sanctuary with you, every Tiodoti. Every day, if that's what it takes."

Kasim's grin shifts, like he's forcing it now. "I appreciate the sentiment, Auben. I really do. But I think it's best if we continue to keep our distance when we're out in public. You've been getting these *demerits* . . ." He lets the word hang, so I know that my demerits are the least of his concerns. "And I need to keep my nose clean if I want to stay in contention for Gueye Okahim's apprenticeship."

My heartbeat goes hollow. "Yeah," I say. "You're too busy playing Grace to bother with the lowly likes of me."

Kasim shivers against the sudden cold. "I haven't upset you, have I? Because we can still hang out, just not—"

"Publicly. Got it." My temper swells, and envy and doubt are close behind. Kasim acts like he hadn't intended offense, like I'm to blame for overreacting. Here he is treating me like shit on the worst day of my life, and somehow I feel like it's all my fault. *Classic lesser twin syndrome,* Chimwe would say if the lights weren't still half-dimmed inside em. Kasim can play Grace all he wants, but he's not immune to vice, and no one knows his weaknesses better than me.

Ruda struts across the Gabadamosi quad in thigh-high leather boots, a tight white blouse, and a fitted skirt that leaves little to the imagination. And with her loose, fire red afro-puff perched atop her head, she sets all of campus ablaze. She draws stares from guys, gals, kigens, teachers—her ample figure putting those of the two-hundred-year-old glass masterpieces surrounding her to shame. She sets her sights on one of the few students daring enough to meet her gaze.

"You," she says, finger pressed against his chest, her jaw smacking hard upon a rubbery wad of neon green gum. She peers at him over the rims of her thick black frames. "Where can I find Kasim Mtuze?"

He points to Kalukenzua House, visibly shaking.

She finds Kasim sitting in the foyer, surrounded by his following, foreheads tattooed, their numbers in the thirties. Their devout eyes do not lift from Kasim as she enters the room, but Kasim's snap to her like she's reawakened something within him that he'd forgotten all about. "Ruda!" he says, tripping over his own feet as he rushes to greet her. "What are you doing here?"

"There's a rumor going around school that you slew some kind of a beast. I came here to see if that was true." She sets her hands on her hips, and the collection of metal bangles on her wrists clang together. She chews her gum, blows a giant bubble. She rounds her lips around it, filling the void of absolute silence with a brash pop and the soothing scent of lime.

"Well, I didn't *exactly* slay him . . ." Which isn't *exactly* a lie.

"So it's true? You've been playing around with some extrastrength wu? That's how you nearly talked me out of my panties on your couch, isn't it?"

"It's not wu!" Kasim shouts. "And what happened that day . . ." Kasim looks around at the dozens of quiet eyes trained upon him. "Mind if we go somewhere private to discuss this?"

Ruda crosses her arms over her chest. "Fine," she says.

She follows Kasim, slipping a small folded piece of paper into the hand of one of Kasim's disciples as she passes em. They make their way through the hallway, up a flight of stairs, and enter a quiet room—the last one on the right. Inside, the walls, ceiling, and door are lined with a patchwork of cork wedges, and a thick carpet absorbs each footstep. It's so quiet, it's almost maddening. Kasim takes a seat at his desk chair. She forgoes the overstuffed chair tucked in the corner and knocks a half-empty carton of dried sap and beans out of the way so she can sit directly upon the desk.

"No bullshitting me, Kasim," Ruda says, legs crossed. Arms crossed. "I want the truth."

"It was one hundred percent us, I swear. I got caught in the moment. I didn't even know I had powers back then. Even if I had, I would never have used them on you." Kasim's voice escapes out of him in a pathetic wheeze. "You believe me, don't you?"

Ruda examines him with a tight brow, then uncrosses her arms. "I guess I believe you." She leans in. "So what kind of powers are we talking about exactly? Can you turn rocks into gold? Bring the dead back to life?"

"No, nothing like that. Just some small tricks. I can levitate for a minute or so. Heal a minor wound. Bend someone's will."

Ruda's brow rises as she pops open the top button on her blouse. "Really? Could you show me?"

Kasim nods at her open blouse, a hint of flesh spilling from overtop her bra. Ruda recoils, covers herself. "How did you do that?"

"I can only bend will, not break it. If it's something you were thinking about doing already, it's pretty easy."

"Are you accusing me of lecherous thoughts, Kasim Mtuze?"

He grins and looks away. "It's good to see you again. It's nice to have a reminder of home. Things here are moving so fast and in so many directions, it's easy to lose your bearings. Too easy to forget what's really important."

"Yeah, well, school hasn't been the same without you. It's good to see you again, too." She looks down at her blouse, unfastens a second button. "That was all me that time," she says, voice huffy and certain. "Wasn't it?"

"It was. And I'm flattered. But I'm chaste now. I mean, I always was, but I am especially now." Kasim stumbles over his words, then nods decisively as if to shake the doubt from his head. "I have to set an example. I have to hold myself to a higher standard."

"I get it. You can't give in to the temptations of the flesh." A third button pops free. And a fourth. The last. Ruda's blouse falls open, revealing the entirety of a black lace bra. "But what good is flesh if you can't appease it on occasion?"

"Believe me, I'm wondering that same thing right now." After a long deliberate breath, he goes to the door, opens it, and peers out into the hallway. He closes it and turns the lock on the knob. Then he's next to her, a finger running across the sharp edge of her collarbone.

"You're shivering," Ruda says with a sly grin. "You don't have to be nervous about this."

"I'm a little cold, that's all. Aren't you cold?" His eyes drift down to her nipples puckering hard against lace. Kasim bites his lip.

"Perhaps we can think of a way to warm each other up." She shrugs off her blouse, and slings it into the corner.

"I'm chaste now."

"So you said. And I suppose that's why your hand is between my thighs?"

Kasim tries to retract, but Ruda's knees knock together as she locks him in tight. He mutters under his breath, some sort of prayer.

"You don't have to be afraid, Kasim. You might like it."

"That's exactly what I'm afraid of." He leans in, mouth open, but pulls back a fraction of a second before their lips touch. "Weren't you chewing gum?"

"I got rid of it," Ruda says, bobs her brows.

"Good. Gabadamosi's got a policy against chewing gum on campus. Devil's habit and all that." Kasim presses his nose to her neck and breathes her in. "Good Grace it's been so long," he mutters, then runs his hand up Ruda's arm. Looks her in the eyes. Smiles. A large wad of neon green gum sits between his front teeth. He chews it with devious intention. "Still has some flavor. I found it crammed into the door's lock plate. That's a funny place to lose your gum, isn't it?"

Ruda's eyes go wide. She looks over at the doorknob. It turns once, twice. There's a muffled knock from the other side. Another. Kasim's disciples had read the note, and they're right on time, but everything is going so wrong. The doorknob twists again futilely, and then there's silence.

"You weren't expecting anyone, were you? It'd be unfortunate if someone walked on in here and caught me in an unsavory act, wouldn't it? Like chewing gum, for instance?" He smacks hard, blows a bubble slightly larger than his mouth, then rounds his lips over it and swallows it whole.

"Kasim, I can explain . . ."

Kasim leans upon her, her back pressed to the wall. He

shushes her, finger to her lips. "Look who the nervous one is now, Ruda."

"But I'm not really—"

His lips are upon hers. He kisses her like he means it, and the entire world melts away. Their bodies cease to exist. Instead there is a oneness that is whole and good and filling and wrong and perverse and lecherous. It is all that—it is every possible thing beneath these star-filled heavens. Suns are born. Galaxies die. Then Kasim pulls back. The stars in his eyes fade first, then his lips ashen over. "You're not Ruda," he says with a pained exhale, then falls heavily upon her, his skin drying up and cracking over like the desert floor. Kasim cries out, and even the soundproof room is not enough to contain him. The window overlooking the quad shatters, and beyond that, the sound of broken glass echoes on and on.

For a long moment, he is dead. But then, from deep within his desiccated body, a soft yellow light emanates through the cracks. His skin smooths over, and becomes supple once again. Distant galaxies spin lazily upon the glassiness of his eyes. Finally, Kasim sucks in a ragged, desperate breath, and then with lips full and flush, he whistles the last stanza of "Kissed by Icy Blue."

CHARITY

An old man with a failing liver. A young kigen suffering needlessly from a severe case of the pox. A comatose business exec cut down by a runaway oryx. They were all dying slow, lonely deaths in their hospital beds. I did them a favor. I killed them out of charity. The tang of their blood still lines my palate, ranging from tart and crisp to smooth and sweet, like the flesh of a deep red plum. I use those unique signatures to hunt down their twins. The stressed teacher running errands after school, the bitter grocer who'd stayed behind to lock up the store, then the old baker two streets down—dragging himself into work hours before dawn. I saved them all the agony I now feel—my broken proximity raking my gut like it's full of glass shards, the pain only relenting when I appease my lone virtue.

My rough cat tongue licks flecks of marrow and raw

sourdough from my tawny coat. Nothing but the skull has gone to waste, and yet my stomach still rings empty, as hollow as my heart. There is a knock at the baker's door. I look up from my preening, and see a lanky young boy, hands cupped against the glass storefront, peeking in. The sun is already a sliver on the horizon. My body whips to human form, my skull taking on the shape of the one tucked neatly under the display of day-old breads. I arrange the features on my face the best I can remember, then open the door.

"Mr. Ntombela?" the boy asks with a tremble.

"Yes?" I say briskly. All I remember of the baker's voice is from his screams.

"Nothing is ready," he says, looking around. "The ovens are still cold. Are you feeling okay? You look—" his eyes stick to the odd contours of my face "—sick." It is not the word he wishes to use, I can tell that.

"I feel sick. Come closer. Check if I have a fever."

The boy thinks twice of it, but steps nearer anyway. His hand presses against my forehead. "No fever, but you feel cold. Ice cold." He buries his hand in his jacket pocket. This narrow season has been cooler, crueler than most. "You should get back home. I can run the store for you."

"Perhaps I can trouble you for something warm before I go?" Fangs crowd my mouth.

The boy shrugs off his jacket and hands it to me. The gooseflesh is quick to rise upon his exposed arms.

"Warm and wet, I mean."

"I can make soup." He looks at me for a long while. "It isn't soup you're talking about, is it?"

I shake my head, bare my teeth. The boy doesn't cower like the teacher. Doesn't run like the grocer. Doesn't shriek bloody murder like the baker. He stands his ground. "You're not scared?" I ask him.

"No, sir," he says, then mutters something under his breath. A prayer?

"Grace won't save you," I tell him.

"I don't believe in Grace. My mother raised us secular." He laughs as I circle around him, calculating where I'll take my first bite. Nervous laughter, but still.

"What's so funny?" I ask him.

"It's a bit like the religioners not believing in science. Believe what you want, but it won't stop gravity from busting your skull when you dive off the top of your tenement building, right?" He laughs again, then scratches at his navel. I smell the salt from his tear ducts, but the tears themselves never make it to his cheeks.

I recognize the distance behind his eyes, the same distance that's filled my soul these last forty-eight hours. He's broken proximity, too. Permanently, though. His twin is dead, and so is something inside him. "How long since you snapped off?" I ask. I have a million questions for him. Does it get better? Does it get worse? The glass in my stomach churns, leaving hot white streaks up and down my soul. I wince. It couldn't possibly get any worse.

"I didn't snap off. Nyambeni died, and that's it. He's gone. I'm still here. Life goes on." He frowns at me. "Until it doesn't."

How can he be so callous? So cruel? How can he deny the longing that bites at me with each breath? I should kill him, put him out of his misery, do my bit of charity and revel in the few seconds I can push Kasim from my mind. I should devour this whole city, but I know that it'll never be enough.

I look at this poor kid, offering up his jacket to the monster about to take his life. Charity has an evil grip on him, too. I realize I'm staring at him with the fear he ought to be showing me. The boy steps closer. I step back.

"I'm not crazy," he says, shaking his head. "People die all the time. Maybe some snap off, but not all of them do. I didn't." His lies are smooth and effortless, just like mine.

"You offered me your jacket. Me of all people." People. I use the term loosely.

He shrugs. "Not like I'm going to need it. Right? I might not be religious, but we've all heard the stories. We've sung the songs. You're hungry. An undeniable hunger that won't go away. I know what that's like. I should have been the one who ate concrete, not Nyambeni. Sometimes I crave it, too." He smiles, his teeth as jagged and sharp as mine. Gums raw and red and pitted. I've seen so much gore, and yet the sight of them turns my stomach until it's tight with greasy knots. "What's wrong?" the boy asks. "Don't you want me?" He tugs down the collar of his shirt and exposes his throat. I could release his blood, and temporarily ease the pain in my gut. Or I could welcome his company, and we could commiserate and face our demons head-on, so to speak.

"Do you drink?" I ask the boy.

"Mr. Ntombela keeps a couple cases in the back for the beer breads. I'm not supposed to know about them." He glances at the bone-white skull beneath the display shelf. "I suppose that's moot now."

We drink together. Reminisce about our twins, chatting about the good memories mostly—the games we played, the trouble we got into, but as we crack open the second case of beer, Tshidino, Tshidi, that's what his friends call him, bares his soul.

"We were up on the roof of our tenement, walking the ledge like we always do." Tshidino's sloppy smile falls from his face. "Always did. This day was different, though. A crowd gathered down below, and we both got the wiles to show off, doing wild leaps and play sparring. Lulama was down there, too, the girl from next door. So sweet, so soft-spoken and kind. Smells really good, like little blue flowers. I didn't like her or anything, but Nyambeni did. And she liked him, only his stupid chastity kept him from building up the nerve to talk to her. I thought I could help him get over his shyness. So I tugged his pants down to his ankles for our whole audience to see. He shouldn't have tripped. Nyambeni had all the grace in the world. But he fell. I kind of suspect he jumped out of embarrassment. Doesn't mat-ter either way, I guess. He still landed face-first. Busted out all his teeth. Busted a lot more than that, but that's what I remember most." Tshidino pulls a handful of gravel bits out of his pocket. Pops them into his mouth like they're nuts. Chews. The grating sound echoes in my skull. My nausea deepens as he smiles at me, his mouth full of blood. "What about you? How'd you and Grace part ways?"

I tell him. Everything. From Icy Blue's first whisper, to Ruda, to our father, to our powers, to the killings, to our mother, to Ruda, to the kiss, and Kasim's lecherous scream that had broken every single pane of glass at Gabadamosi, closing the school indefinitely, and closing my heart indefi-nitely, as well.

"Grace is a twisted bastard," Tshidino slurs, eyes wide and bloodshot. "And he just left you there, like trash?"

Not like trash. More like the trash can, a receptacle for his vices. I don't care what's been branded on his arms, I saw much more than greed in Kasim's eyes as I lay there in the quiet room, glass pressed into my cheek, his sour breath lingering upon mine. "He said the world needed him to be Grace more than I needed him to be my brother."

"He didn't deserve you anyway. Serves him right to be holed up in the Sanctuary with his precious false prophet! How did he say it? How did he say . . . Ama . . ." Tshidino's head is too heavy, and it lands on my shoulder. "Amawu . . . Amawusiekeseiya?"

Tshidi, that's what his friends call him, is midsentence, blubbering away about all of the reasons I'm better off without Kasim, when I make the careful slit. He bleeds out in a matter of seconds, the alcohol sharp and comforting in my silenced gut. I hold his hand tightly until the longing has disappeared from his eyes. Tshidi doesn't thank me. He doesn't have to.

True charity expects no compensation.

I peel myself up from the bakery floor, trying to clear my head of the drunken stupor I've inflicted upon myself. The morning has come and gone. The sun sits high in the sky, and there is something odd afoot. There's too much traffic outside for this time of day. Lunchtime has passed, but the business day is not quite through, and yet hundreds, thousands line the streets. The air smells faintly of musky-sweet smoke.

"What's going on?" I ask, grabbing the arm of a woman striding down the sidewalk.

She takes one look at me and screams. I let her go, and turn to my reflection in the glass front of the bakery. My skin sits oddly upon my face, like a jacket two sizes too big. My jowls hang like an old hunting dog's, pockets of red drooping beneath my eyes exposing flesh and nerves. Deep wrinkles gouge every inch of my face. I look like something beyond ancient. I shake it off, skin goes taut, eyes brighten.

"What's going on?" I ask, grabbing a passing kigen this time.

Ey points my attention to Grace Mountain. "They're burning fine bush at the Sanctuary. Twenty-four hours from now, Gueye Okahim will be making a big announcement."

My gut stirs and my knees go weak. If Kasim has risen as much as I've sunken since our proximity break, then there's only one thing this could be about. "He's announcing his new apprentice?"

"No, not an apprentice. This is something major. Like once-in-a-lifetime major." The kigen pulls away, and stares at me like I've stolen something from em.

I move my hands to my face. My skin feels right, and my teeth are still blunted.

"Pardon, but I've got to go," ey says, voice atremble. "I need to get a good seat for this. I'm probably already too late."

I pry further, but everyone is too harried, too flustered to be bothered. I catch snippets of rumors and speculations. *Gueye Okahim is sick and dying. Gueye Okahim has taken a lover and is stepping away. Gueye Okahim has received a new Covenant from Grace.* But there is nothing concrete.

Gueye Okahim is a false prophet . . .

Kasim's words strike me hard. What if he hadn't mispronounced Gueye Okahim's title? Sylla be damned, if Kasim had said it, it must be the truth. That means a liar has taken Kasim under his wing, to mold him with his duplicitous tongue, and do whatever the hell else. But why should I care? Kasim chose this path, and has forsaken our brotherhood in the process. I turn my back to Grace Mountain, and walk the other way. He no longer holds an obligation over me.

The pain whips back to my stomach. I hunch over, then bite past it, my eyes scanning the crowd for my next act of charity. There, that woman. Old and gray. Graying at least, some around the temples. Debilitated by some affliction that makes her favor one leg over the other, though perhaps it's only the sole of her shoe gone bad. But her scent, her scent is divine. Smooth and sharp, like she's got garlic butter pumping through her veins. I take a step toward her, and her eyes flick to me. Kasim stares out from those too-wide pupils. I back up, set my eyes on another mark. My brother stares back at me yet again.

"Leave me alone, you sick bastard!" I yell at the kigen.

Ey looks at me, concerned. "Sir, you're going the wrong way. Gueye Okahim is making a big announcement." Ey points me in the direction of Grace Mountain.

"Gueye Okahim is a false prophet!" I yell. People brush past me, without hearing, without notice. Here I am, invisible again. My words are powerless. Doubt rolls me over, does a wicked number on me, but from the grisly depths of hopelessness, I see light. Here is my chance to do the ultimate charitable act. I can prove to these people that Gueye Okahim is not who he says, and free them of his mind tricks. I need proof. Solid proof. Then they'll see me. They'll thank me. They'll worship me.

I'll dig. Dig deep. Gueye Okahim, Gabadamosi, Class of '71.

"Get outta here, kid," the maintenance worker scolds me. He sweeps up two-hundred-year-old glass into a large plastic bucket, giving it no more thought than cleaning up spent beer bottles after one of Soyinka House's parties. "You'll slice yourself to pieces standing round here."

"I'm here to retrieve some papers," I say, my tight fake smile threatening to shatter my teeth like every last piece of glass on this campus. I keep my thoughts firm on my goals, getting to the administration building, finding Gueye Okahim's files, and not letting my mind wander to the delectables held behind the worker's orange jumpsuit. "I promise, I'll be careful." Just as I've promised the last twelve maintenance workers. This one will make a baker's dozen.

"No skin off my teeth, then. Don't say I didn't warn ya," says the worker, not bothering to look up at me this time. I flex my claws, then notice the statue of Grace and Icy Blue standing before me—the one where they're wrestling. Or not wrestling. Grace is missing his head. Icy Blue is gone from the chest up. The rest of their entwined bodies is a million shards with a large crack running between them, but still their muscled bodies cling together by the forces of temper and regret.

Carefully, I stoop down to pick up a large sliver that contains Grace's ear and cheekbone. I hold it in my hands, and my whole body goes numb.

"Good Grace, kid!" the worker yells at me, sweat bead-ing on his brow. "Look what you've done. Stand still. Don't panic." With his heavily gloved hands, he plucks the glass from my grip, then tears the sleeve from his jumpsuit. He wraps it tightly around my hand. Blood blooms through quickly, angrily, then begins to eat away at the fabric. "Stay here and keep pressure on that. I'm going to go hail an ambulance." And then he's gone.

The glass at my feet glows molten white where my blood drips upon it. I suppose there's pain, but Kasim's betrayal cuts so much more deeply, it doesn't register.

I've got a straight shot to the administration building. No more questions. No more blood.

Inside, light seeps in through the orifices that used to contain windowpanes. My every step is filled with the crunch of broken glass. My frigid heart stirs when I pass the closed door to Munashe's office. It's like I still feel her presence in there, the quick beat of her pulse in my ear, the warmth of her breath. Guilt piles onto me, but I need my head clear for this. I dampen my senses, concentrating on finding the file I need. I make quick work of the locked cabinets in the back of the room. Thousands of files hang, embossed Gabadamosi folders tucked inside. Alphabetical order. I make my way through the Os . . . Okadigbo, Okafor, Okahim. I pull Gueye's too-thin folder. It's empty. My temper cracks like a whip.

"Shit!" I growl, throaty and deep enough to send the shards of spent glass reverberating upon the floor.

A muffled squeal comes from Munashe's office. I release my senses, and smell her now. The scent so obvious. I wasn't imagining things. I twist the knob on Munashe's door, force it open. I shiver at the sour smell of her corpse, though it has long since left the room.

"Come out," I demand from the door, somehow managing to keep the fear out of my voice. She has to come out, because I'm sure as hell not going in there. There's no delusion deep enough to convince me that Munashe's death involved any sort of charity.

The pulse quickens. Munashe's chair moves back, and a small hand reaches up from under the nook in her desk. A forehead peeks, tattooed with a scripted *I*, and then Sesay's stoic face slowly comes into view. "Auben," she says, holding her ground like a cornered cat. "Or do you prefer Icy Blue?"

"What are you doing here?" I growl.

"Same thing as you, I suspect," she says, nodding to the empty folder I'm carrying.

"You took the files?"

"No, the folder was empty when I looked last night. I'd been compiling my interview notes on Kasim and his exhibitions, but his first interaction with Gueye Okahim stood out against the others. It didn't feel right. I thought about downplaying it, even omitting it altogether to write that bit of embarrassment out of history, but that felt even more wrong. That's when it struck me: Kasim hadn't misspoken when he'd called Gueye Okahim a false prophet. I started digging, and found—" Sesay's eyes, wide and vulnerable, suddenly flick to meet mine, narrow and hungry. "You know, I'm telling you all of this because we're on the same side now. We're both working to reveal that Gueye Okahim is a fraud. I can't do this without you, and you can't do this without me. We're teammates. Friends."

She's a fast talker, but her comfy wiles won't work on me. She's twelve steps ahead of me, though, and she's right that I can't do this without her. "Friends." The word slips coolly between my bared fangs. I offer out a clawed hand to shake on it, but Sesay has conveniently looked away.

"Good," she says. "So I went to the library, dug around, found this . . ." She slips a playbill in front of me. *The Mouse Prince*, it reads, one of Biobaku's plays apparently, starring one Gueye Okahim. "He was in the Theatrics Club here."

"Gabadamosi has a Theatrics Club?"

"It used to. Up until about fifteen years ago."

"That's right around when Gueye Okahim became the Man of Virtues, right?"

"Mmm-hmm. So I couldn't dig up his files, but I figured someone else in the cast might have some insight. I pulled them this morning, did some research. Every single one of them is dead."

"The Class of '71 was quite a while ago."

"Yeah, but the last four surviving actors all died within a month of one another. Fifteen years ago." Sesay raises a brow, gives me a meaningful look. "Nkitidoroane, the previous Man of Virtues, took Gueye Okahim as his apprentice a few months later. And a few months after that, Nkitidoroane passed on. The rumors were that he'd lost contact with Grace a few years prior, and the abandonment had driven him mad. That's eighteen years ago, if you don't want to do the math. Right at the time a certain pair of twins were swimming around in their mother's womb. People were losing faith left and right. Secular groups were gaining a foothold, making their own schools, promoting scientific explanations of twinning, the origins of the universe, and everything. And the sub-seculars were getting bolder as well, setting out to prove Grace was a lie all along. Something had to be done before the whole system came crashing down. If they couldn't find someone who could communicate with Grace, they could at least find someone who could fake it." Sesay clears her throat. "That's my theory, anyway. We need solid proof if we're going to bring Okahim down."

But this is enough proof for me. My claws flex, imagining Gueye Okahim pleading for his life, spilling his truths to his faithful congregation as I spill his guts from the perch of his pulpit.

"Thanks, friend," I say to Sesay, giving her a slick, toothy smile.

"Why are you looking at me like that?" Her voice is sharp and knowing.

I let the silence stir along with the ghosts in this room. The flavors of her fear and desperation commingle, resonating as I sip them in. I'm going to take my time with this one.

"Please, don't do this," she says. It's what they always say. "Don't do this to Daki."

My fangs retract halfway. I think maybe I've heard her wrong, my mind too knotted from the drumming of her heart arousing every nerve in my body. "Daki?" I say.

"She'll be all alone without me. She'll snap off, I just know it. I can't have her go through that pain. I can't—" Sesay starts bawling into her hands. The scent of her tears is delicate, sweet like a rosebud. She is not crying out of fear, but out of love. I take a second whiff to make sure I am not mistaken.

"Maybe you've already broken from each other, though. She says you are twinemies. You abandon her each day to go have lunch with your greater twin friends. I'm sure she's used to you not being there for her."

Sesay shakes her head. "We knew what we were signing up for when we came to Gabadamosi. The finest education comes at a steep price. During the school day we play the parts, but we promised to do whatever it took to keep this place from driving a wedge between us. Every evening, back in our dorm room, I say a million sorries to her, and she forgives me a million times before I utter a single word. It's stupid and I hate it, but in four years, when we both graduate from this place with honors, we'll have the knowledge and power to do something about it." Sesay looks up at me with her pitiful big brown eyes. "At least, that was the plan."

Her comfy wiles nearly crack their way through my heart, but I've caught her in her velvety lie. "Twins aren't allowed to room together at Kalukenzua House." With the next breath, I am at Sesay's throat, the welcoming beat of her jugular strumming against my fangtips.

"It's not allowed," Sesay squeals. "But I dug up some dirt on the housematron. Turns out she was a housematron of a different sort back in the day—the kind of establishment where lechery paid the bills instead of students' tuition. I pointed this out to her, and she found a way for Daki and me to room together."

"You blackmailed her?" I say, a devious smile spreading upon my muzzle.

"It's the best kind of mail," Sesay says, giving a pathetic wheeze of a laugh. "Doesn't even cost a stamp." Her eyes plead, tugging at something buried deeply within me.

Kasim was right. She is so fucking adorable. My bones go to dust, and I put on my Auben cloak. It feels so wrong on me now, itches all over like cheap wool, but Sesay looks less terrified, and I need her. I may be smart, but she's operating on a level I can't even grasp. "So how do we get to Gueye Okahim?"

"With the announcement coming, the Sanctuary is going to be heavily fortified to keep the masses at bay." Sesay smiles, and amazingly, it's not relief in her eyes. It's *knowing*. And that makes me feel like I've made the right choice in not killing her . . . yet. She shrugs, as if recognizing that, and says, "But I've been doing some digging . . ."

Three hundred meters down from the Sanctuary and its fortifications, there's a patch of vegetation, more lush and vibrant than any other spot upon Grace Mountain. The greens of the leaves are rich and deep and unnatural, and in the spring, when all the different species of plants bloom, it's like an intricate stained-glass design unrivaled by what human hands could create. I'd noticed the patch before, of course, but I never knew it had a name. Grace's Kiss, Sesay tells me. I shudder as the undergrowth brushes my shins, trying not to think about the power of life that sits upon Kasim's lips, nor the opposite power of mine.

"There, I see it," says Sesay, pointing up toward the top of the patch, along the border where the plant life again takes on its natural hues. Through a tangle of reeds and vines, there's a metal grating. I pull it, and then peer into the drainpipe. It's narrow. Too narrow for Auben's shoulders—*my* shoulders, I remind myself.

Sesay exhales, sticks her head in, and wriggles back and forth until she's waist deep. "It's tighter than I thought, but it's doable," she calls back to me. She inches forward into the darkness with unwavering resolve. If she has doubt, she keeps it close to her chest.

I shrug off my cloak, and four tawny paws press into

the soft fertile earth. Instantly, the scent overwhelms me—
the sharp and syrupy tang of iron. Blood. Goat blood mostly,
some sheep. My reflexes buck, and I have to restrain myself
from latching onto Sesay's ankles dangling around in front
of me like worms on a fishing line. I wait until they're safely
out of view before following her in.

"What is this place?" I growl at Sesay, hoping she doesn't
notice the wetness of my words.

"Slaughter room runoff," Sesay says, nonchalantly, like
it's an everyday occurrence for a girl and her pet caracal to
be squeezing themselves through blood-soaked drainpipes.
"Oh, shoot. The blood. I didn't . . . Are you—"

"I'm fine," I say. "Just keep talking."

"About what?"

"Anything but blood."

"Can I tell you a secret?" she asks. The echo of her words
helps to drown out the rhythmic sluicing in her veins. Some.
All this blood has got my olfactories in a knot. I could swear
Sesay's scent is laden with masculine signatures. I'm getting
light-headed and disoriented in this long span of dark. If I
can't trust my smell, what can I trust? I rein in my senses as
tightly as I can manage.

"Sure," I say.

"I think I might have made a mistake. Phila talked a
good talk, and got me to believe with all of his fanatic raving. I wanted to believe. I did my research, of course, but
now I'm thinking I didn't do enough." Sesay groans. "And I
have this stupid tattoo on my forehead now."

"You don't think Kasim is Grace?"

"Oh, no. He definitely is. I'm just not sure he's the one
we're supposed to be following . . ." She lets her words hang.

My gruff laugh fills the void around us. "Me, you're thinking?"

"I don't think you're as bad as you think you are."

"You don't know the things I've done." I bite my tongue. Of course she knows. She knows everything about everyone.

"I need food to survive. You need blood. We're really no different when you think about it."

"I told you not to mention blood." My fangs scratch through my skull.

"Well, we can chat about rainbows and kitten farts, if you'd like, but that's not going to get us closer to resolving your issues. So, do you enjoy killing?"

"Of course not!" I say, but that isn't exactly true. I don't want to talk about it, and especially not to her, but Sesay's incessant digging has gotten us this far. Maybe she's the one who's had the answers I've been searching for all along, so I say, "I hate myself for it before. And I hate myself for it after. But in the moment, staring my prey down in the face of uncertainty—my senses open wide, and I savor every scent, every taste and texture, then the split second right before the kill, ice crashes through my veins, and it makes me feel so . . ." I can't find the right words. *Aroused,* maybe. *Intoxicated. Sexually charged, right there on the brink,* but that makes it sound so lecherous, and it's not like that at all.

"Connected?" Sesay offers.

"Yes! Connected to my prey. Connected to the entire world. To everything that ever was, and ever will be." I release a long exhale, and the remnants of blood in the drainpipe go slick with ice.

Ahead of me, somewhere in the dark, Sesay slips. "Oof!"

"Sorry."

"No, this is good. I can't imagine how hard this has been for you. You need to process. So, if you don't mind my asking, what's your number?"

"Huh?"

"How many lives have you taken?"

"I don't know. Maybe three dozen?" But of course I do know exactly. Thirty-eight. I can taste them all on my breath. Their last words echo in my skull. From the scents lingering on their skin, I could tell Sesay the story of each of them— where they lived, the sex and approximate age of their children and partners, their hobbies and vices—but I save myself the torture.

"Okay, so that amounts to two per year, averaged over the seventeen years of your life. That seems about right. For all of documented history, Icy Blue's averaged about three to four lives per year. Some years it's more, and then there's a dry spell. You're bingeing, that's all. I suspect things will level out soon."

"That's *all*? These are people's lives we're talking about!"

"Well, do you know Grace's record for killing? Seven thousand, five hundred and sixty in a single day. Including well over two thousand children. Smote the whole city of Moipone, up the coast, eighty miles north of here, or so it used to be. Distant observers reported over a thousand lightning strikes per hour. Nothing was left living, not a street dog, not an insect, not a single blade of grass."

"*Moipone, Moipone, up in flames. Lightning, thunder, who's to blame? Count the bodies, all the same . . .*" I shudder, remembering how Kasim always loved skipping rope to that rhyme. He never got to 7,560, of course, but he'd broken a hundred easily on several occasions. "I thought that was just a stupid kid's song."

"Nope. Three centuries of digging, and no one's turned up any explanation as to why it happened." Sesay's voice goes soft. "We're getting close. I can see light up ahead." She stops, and the drainpipe fills with the sour sweetness of her fear, only this time the scent doesn't cause me to salivate, but steels my nerves and stirs up the instinct to protect her.

"Maybe I should go up first, check things out . . ." I offer.

"I'm not scared, if that's what you're thinking," Sesay snaps. "I've spent all night reconstructing the layout of the Sanctuary's underbelly. I know what I'm doing."

"Got it," I say, a smile curled quietly upon my muzzle. "It's your drainpipe. I'm just crawling through it."

"Good," Sesay says, then heaves a heavy sigh. "I know you know I'm lying, so go on ahead."

Her body shivers as I slip past her as an elegant black mamba—eighteen feet of abdominal muscles moving, writhing, body covered in sleek dark scales. My forked tongue flicks into the air, bringing back smells rimmed with a metallic aftertaste, but apart from Sesay, none of those smells taste human. I peek my head through the grate. The slaughter room is long and narrow, lined with dank gray stone cobbles from floor to ceiling. On the far wall is an old wooden door, with half a dozen knives hanging on either side, kept at a meticulous shine. Along each of the long walls hang four sets of iron shackles, with matching ones below. For a brief moment, my mind twists over the reasons someone might restrain a goat or a sheep in that manner, but then the truth hits me.

"It wasn't always animals they slaughtered here, was it?" I ask Sesay.

"They say it takes the blood of seven hundred goats to equal the potency of the life force found in a single virgin." Sesay shoves at the grating from below, and once I have hands again, I help her from above. "Thanks," she says, pulling herself up into the slaughter room. Her necklace has come untucked from beneath her collar. I expect to see six virtue charms upon it, but instead there is only the shadowed doubt signet. My eyes narrow, and my own doubts set in. She notices me staring, tucks it back away. "What? Does my vice offend you?" she says with a chuckle. "I'm not ashamed, but if you'd rather I take it off—"

"No, it's fine," I say. I see now how much her doubt fuels her virtues, driving her toward unearthing the truth. Maybe it makes her a bit of a fanatic, but we've all our shortcomings. My cloak begins to itch all over. I scratch like a flea-bitten dog at the base of Auben's neck.

"You know you don't have to wear that thing for my sake," Sesay says with a sympathetic smile. "You look so uncomfortable."

"It's no trouble. I swear I don't mind." My skin sits loose where it should be tight, tight where it should be loose, and feels threadbare all over, like Uncle Pabio's old smoking jacket, the one whose patches had patches, and whose red satin lining had the power to transform me into the duke of the Cape, or a superhero, or a dozen other people who I wasn't. And here I am now, still playing pretend. Still wearing an ill-fitting jacket that isn't my own.

"You know I know you're lying," Sesay says with pursed lips.

"Maybe we're both lying a little," I say. Sesay stiffens.

I look at her. I mean really look at her. The tells are subtle, especially on a kid her age, but there's just something. I take a final sniff to be sure. The scents in this room aren't nearly as tangled as they'd been in the drainpipe, and yet Sesay's scent continues to baffle me. "Your blood . . . it's kigen? *Andy* kigen."

Her eyes widen. "I'm a girl," she practically whimpers. Sesay shakes her head so vehemently, and looks so hurt, that my pride in outing her fizzles into guilt. I could kick myself. Instead I just sigh, and pat myself on the back for not swallowing her whole.

"I know you are. A cute, mouthy, brilliant girl." I shrug my shoulders, letting my skin shift at the seams. Could I really let her see me? She knows what it's like to be constantly holding a shield out to the world. That shield protects us from the cruelty out there, but it can also deflect kindness and deeper connections. Maybe if I throw down my shield, she'll follow suit. "You really don't mind if I slip into something more comfortable? I mean, it's just skin, right? It's what's on the inside that matters."

"I'm pretty sure what's on your inside has wanted to kill me at least twenty times today," Sesay says with a precocious grin. "But yeah, go ahead. Do what feels right."

So I relax, release. I let loose all the tension and energy spent holding this form, but I do not shift into another. My bones simply settle. They become what I am. I've been hiding from my true self for so long that I do not know what that is, but from the fear on Sesay's face, and the thorny scales upon my arms, I know that it is not Auben Mtuze.

My hooves clack on the cobbles as I walk toward the

door, knees bending the wrong direction, the sharp tips of heavy, taloned wings gouging ashy trails through centuries-old stone. I pull a gleaming cleaver down from the wall, and stare balefully at my reflection. "I'm hideous."

"Yeah," Sesay says with a quaver in her voice, not bothering to lie this time. "But it could be worse. You could have this." She tips up on her toes, and looks at her own reflection, rubbing at the ink on her forehead. She groans again, then heaves open the door. "Come on. Gueye Okahim will be meditating and tending the flames at the Overchamber in the hours prior to the big announcement. I'm certain we'll find him there."

Something warm and unfamiliar buds in my heart. It only takes a few seconds for the ice to overwhelm it, but it was there. Humility. Or at least as close to it as I'm going to get. I bolt after Sesay, like her eager lap dog. "Hey, Sesay. Your tattoo . . . maybe it's not the *I* in *Kasim*. Maybe it's the *I* for *Icy Blue*."

Sesay spins around, eyes as wide and bright as they were that first time we'd met. "Yeah," she says. "I'd like that."

I don a cloak, an actual one this time, the same dark robes worn by the dozens of Men of Virtue bustling about the place. There is a hurried madness all about, and one new and mysteriously robed visitor with a mysteriously low-hanging hood, walking with a mysteriously awkward gimp is hardly noticed, much less questioned. Still, we stick to the shadows, to the back hallways, slowly making our way up one flight of stone stairs after another.

When the hallway is clear, I stop. The slit in my robe

parts open enough for Sesay to look out and get her bearings. "Up another fifty feet, make a left at the horny zekwenusi."

The place is lousy with zekwenusi, their fangs bared, creeping all around us like apparitions set in stone. Their chimeral combinations vary in infinite ways—zebra-falcon-rhino, lion-crow-ram, cobra-oryx-vulture. They all have hooves, wings, and horns of some sort or another, but none of them do justice to the horrid mix of flesh that dwells beneath these robes. Sesay's hands grip around my furred leg, ready to continue our slothful journey. I'm about to ask her which of the horned statues, but then I see the lecherous monstrosity ahead of us—a lion's head cocked back in a mighty roar set upon a finely striped zebra's torso sporting a thick, thorny dick jutting out into the hallway—impressively erotic, even though the head has been lopped off. Whether this was done out of a sense of decency or simply to remove a trip hazard, I cannot say. I veer toward it, but then I catch the scent of three men approaching. I tuck my head deeper into my hood, and stick as close to the wall as possible.

"*Orefe rin peileu wan,*" the Men of Virtue say as they near me.

"*Orefe rin peileu wan,*" I repeat, exactly as Sesay had instructed me to.

Their steps slow. I said it right, I know it. Then I see it. My robe has snagged on the jagged edges of the zekwenusi's erection. Sesay is fully exposed.

"Um . . . *Orefe rin peileu wan?*" she says, giving them a full dose of her big brown eyes.

Underneath my robe, my claws turn to daggers. Three. It's just three more lives to add to my tally. That'll make forty-one altogether. It'll be easy, quick, painless. Well, easy

and quick anyway, but I can't do it, not in front of Sesay. I
know it's stupid, but I don't want to take that innocence away
from her. I don't want her to look at me the way Ruda did.

"What is the meaning of this?" asks one of the men. He
tugs Sesay by the scruff of her shirt, then pulls back my
hood. He gasps, his eyes dart down. "I—I'm so sorry," he
says, trembling. "I didn't know it was you, Inegberunako."

I stare back at him with Kasim's frown upon my face.
Wearing Kasim's skin makes Auben's seem like a perfectly
tailored cashmere ciki in comparison. Each second I wear
it makes me want to tear the flesh from my own limbs, so
I hastily pick Sesay up, and pull her in tight. Everyone has
vices, and I've come all too close to knowing Kasim's. "You
have an issue with my taking a turn of dalliance?"

The three men exchange hushed words and worried
glances.

"No, Inegberunako!" Hints of a lecherous grin hit the
corners of the man's mouth, but he swallows it back. "But
there are private passages for that. If you were caught up
here, so close to the Overchamber . . ."

"Noted," I say, and push Sesay around the corner. The
instant we're out of view, my bones settle. I wish I could say
the same for my nerves.

"They've given Kasim a title . . ." Sesay says, walking
with more purpose. "Students taken into confidence don't
get titles. And even Men of Virtue don't get titles like that."

"Like what?"

"*Light of a Thousand Seasons* is the literal translation, but
a more practical one would be *Eternal Light*." Sesay stops in
front of an ornately carved wooden door. "And where there
is light, there must be shadow."

Eternal Light my ass. I know dark things my brother is capable of. But I can't let those thoughts consume me, not when I'm so close to Gueye Okahim.

"I'm going in alone," I tell Sesay. I nod at the dark recess behind the tangle of raised hooves on a pair of fighting ze-kwenusi. "Stay here, out of sight. I won't be long."

"What are you going to do?" she asks.

"Talk to him." It's not exactly a lie. I will talk to him . . . at first. My claws glide through the seal of the door like a let-ter opener through the lip of an envelope. Seven locks slice in half, and I press the door open quietly and step into the domed room. The sharp, medicinal smell of fine bush burn-ing in the room's central smokestack overwhelms me. I blot away the tears in my eyes, and see Gueye Okahim sitting cross-legged, next to the smoking stack. Candles burn on mirrored plates, and short stacks of ancient books line the parameter all around.

"Please, join me, my lord," Gueye Okahim whispers, and yet his voice consumes the space, filling me with a quiet un-ease. He holds something in his lap, strokes it, strokes it.

"I'm not your lord," I say, throat full of gravel.

"Oh, aren't you?" Gueye Okahim stands, goes to the far edge of the room, and stares through a giant pane of stained glass, just clear enough to reveal the silhouettes of the thou-sands of parishioners gathering below to hear his lies. "Their minds are simple. They forget that they are yours, too, Auben. That you are their lord as much as Kasim. They worship the purity of virtue, and forget the lessons of vice." He turns and looks my true form over, as if taking in the visage of a child-hood friend.

Cradled in his arms, he holds the tip of the zekwenusi's

stone penis. He strokes it absentmindedly, like a pet lulled into sleep. My mind reels. What kind of perverse fetishes have these walls witnessed?

"Tell me, Amawusiakaraseiya, what vices have you forgotten? Duplicity, I'm guessing. I know you were in Gabadamosi's Theatrics Club." I look deeply into his eyes. They twinge ever so slightly with the jealousy of a man who's spent half his life pretending to be a god, finally looking back at the real thing. "Envy as well?"

"I set aside my vices when I went through Transcendence." Gueye Okahim dishes me a helping of humility, but I refuse to be swayed.

"You're a magnificent actor, I'll give you that. More craft than you could have learned from a preparatory school. Where'd you study? And how many of your fellow thespians died in the cover-up?"

Gueye Okahim stares me down, doesn't even flinch. "Wars are still being fought in Grace's name. Blood is still being shed. Only the weapons have changed."

"You're not lying about that." I pounce upon him and set a claw at his throat. The penis hits the floor tiles with a thud.

"Do it, and you'll only send them further into Grace's arms. It doesn't matter how I got here. I'm a believer now. My blood will be a testament of that." Behind Gueye Okahim's wide and bright smile, I suddenly feel the weight of his duplicitous tongue. My skin prickles as my eyes dart to the mirrors sitting beneath the candles, over to the smokestack and the wheezing cauldron filled with madly burning fine bush, back to the stone phallus. Mirrors for vainglory. Steam for temper. A penis for lechery.

I look at Gueye Okahim, overcome with the feeling that

he is the cheese. The bait. And I am not the hunter, but the hunted. I scan the room for other talismans I've overlooked, then from the doorway, I hear the ringing of small bells, no—the jingling of coins in a pocket.

"Greed," I exhale. It is so easy to forget about Kasim's lone vice. A vice that has gone unchecked since I've been away. Here I was, thinking that my brother had already taken everything he could from me, but I have one thing left that he covets.

My charity.

Kasim steps into the room, dangling Sesay by the scruff. His own feet don't quite make it all the way down to the floor. "Yes, greed. It pollutes me."

I pull Gueye Okahim closer, holding him between my brother and me as a human shield. "Let her go, or I swear I'll spill his blood."

Kasim laughs. He hovers, a sliver of the brother I knew. Gaunt and sickly, save for his bright smile. He steps closer. His arm raises slowly, hand locked like an open claw. He gives his wrist a sudden and violent twist, and Gueye Okahim's body goes stiff in my grip, his head swiveling in my direction with an awful crack. The light behind his eyes vanishes. "For all the tastes of pure delight." His mouth flaps like a dummy's. "My dear, sweet Delilah, I bid you good-night."

I let go. Gueye Okahim stands there, an empty husk, then crumples into a pile on the floor. Sesay screams. My blood rushes warm all over. The urge to protect her drills its way into my bones, but I do my best to ignore it.

"Final act, final scene, final line from *The Five Curses of Akerele,*" Kasim says. "Did you know he played Akerele for six years in an acting troop in Nri before finding his way back to Grace? Sadly, I have to say I've lost my taste for the-atrics."

"I know you're after my charity," I tell Kasim, backing toward the window. I stretch my wings, smashing the glass with their taloned tips. Screams come from below, and I'm startled by the sheer size of the crowd gathered on the Sanctuary's grounds. They came for Gueye Okahim's announcement, but it seems like I'll be the one giving them something to gossip about. All eyes look up upon my beastly form. Three flaps, and I'll soar right over their heads and be safely out of Kasim's reach. But in the midst of freedom, I keep looking back to Sesay, dangling there. Kasim killed Gueye Okahim so callously, it pains me to think of what he'd do to her. I grit my teeth. What a shitty time to start growing a conscience.

"Let her go," I demand of Kasim. I pull harder upon my instinct not to care, but then I fall into the trap of looking into Sesay's eyes. Damn it. What good is fighting for my charity if I'm not even going to use it? Saving this life won't bring back the ones I've already taken, and it won't prevent me from taking more, but it will make a difference to Sesay. And to her sister, Daki. And, I realize, to me. "Let her go, and I'll give up my charity. Willingly." Before I can get the words out, my voice catches as if a hand is at my throat. My hands rip at the nonexistent fingers pressing against my windpipe.

"Brother, you've gone soft. I thought you were a natural-born killer."

"I kill, but only out of necessity. You, on the other hand . . ." I look down at the body before me.

Gueye Okahim's mouth seizes open. His head lurches, once, twice, with the wet sound of flesh tearing. Then his tongue worms its way over his lips, bloody pulp trailing behind it as it makes its way over to the other talismans. Next, his eyes begin to bulge against partially closed lids. I look away.

"Oh, his death was definitely a necessity. You were right, brother. Duplicity and envy were his vices." Kasim reaches into his pocket, and tosses his coins into the center of the room, then lets Sesay down.

"Run!" I tell her. "Get out of here." My heart pounds, but Sesay doesn't move.

"That just leaves doubt," Kasim says with a grin.

My eyes dart to Sesay's neck, and I hope beyond all hope that I could not have allowed myself to be so blind to the depths of my brother's trickery and deceit. Yet again. Sesay looks up at me, her face etched with sorrow, and untucks her necklace. "Are you sure we're doing the right thing?" she asks Kasim.

"Of course, I'm sure." Kasim rips the chain from her neck. "Go get the book."

Sesay cowers, then retrieves a dusty tome from atop the stack in the corner. She opens to a dog-eared page, and begins to read, her lips moving flawlessly over the Sylla incantations. The invisible fingers at my neck force me down. Kasim takes a seat opposite me. The talismans stretch down the middle, equidistant between us. My mind snaps back twelve years to the first time we'd sat before these talismans. Our Discernment. I still taste the bitterness of the spirits Mother had let us sip upon beforehand to help dull the pain and help the memory of the event to slip away. It had worked on both accounts. But now, sober both in mind and soul, I feel the scraping at my nerves, the twitch of my fingers. My hand reaches out for the mirror. I try to draw my hand back, but something within me has overridden my control. I retrieve the mirror and set it before me, and likewise, Sesay's doubt signet.

The envious eyeballs, the duplicitous tongue—I resist more for those, and am rewarded with my vision going white-hot with shooting pain at my temples. My temper flares, and the boiler along with it, shooting out heavy plumes of smoke. Glowing metal burns my hands as I remove the cast iron boiler from the fire. When I set it next to me upon the tile floor, the smoke doesn't abate, but instead grows thicker. By the time my hands reach for the zekwenusi's stone-cold cock, I am completely drained.

Kasim and I stare at the lone talisman left sitting between us. The coins. His eyes flash, and this time his fingers twitch. He reaches for the stack of gold, winces, probably from the same resistance headache I'd had. "Now," he tells Sesay.

Her incantations change, her words becoming throatier, deeper, and sounding of a language much more ancient than Sylla. My gut twists and goes sour.

"Don't do this," I plead. "You're the one who always told me that we are more than the sum of our virtues and vices."

"I was wrong." Kasim's hands are inches from the coins now. His worried eyes cut at Sesay, who reads faster, her words like projectiles.

Then comes a chill, one so deep, it drives me into a shivering fit. It is as if all this time, I have never really known what it is to be cold at all. My blood turns to crystal ice, scraping its way through my veins, nicking away at my heart. My mind swells to encompass the infinite. I push back upon it, holding away eons' worth of memories. My vision is a kaleidoscope—a hundred Kasims stealing both nothing and everything from my being.

When there is no more to take of me, nothing more to give me—when I am both spent and fully filled—Kasim lowers his hand. A warm yellow-orange aura fills in the gauntness of his limbs, the sunken patches at his cheeks. He looks satiated, eyes brimming with the silver-white of starlight that reflects all the knowledge of the cosmos.

I reach willingly for the coins. They are mine.

"It is done," Sesay whispers with delight. "It is done! Grace walks among us!" she calls out to the onlookers below.

The masses cheer, but Kasim pays them no mind. Instead, he stares directly at me. I'm drawn to him, a beacon of light, and despite my best efforts, I can't look away. "We are together again, one and one, as we should be," he says to me softly. "Now we can start fresh, start anew. Grind these people down to dust, and start again. From the beginning. It'll be fun."

"You would murder the entirety of your followers for a little diversion?" My eyes narrow. *Moipone, Moipone, up in flames* . . . Historians could find no reason why that poor city had been destroyed. And now I know there *was* no reason. Just a selfish god who got his jollies kicking over anthills and watching the aftermath unfold.

"You don't miss it? Having the planets and stars as our playthings?" Kasim raises his hand. A stiff, unnatural wind follows, and the sun arcs across the horizon, and dips below with a brilliant green flash. A moonless night is upon us in the span of seconds. I go dizzy as the world slows beneath my feet, my eyes rejecting what my other senses are telling me. And yet Kasim stands there on firm ground, so bold, so brazen.

"I suppose I am merely your plaything as well?" I yell at him, refusing to give him the pleasure of acknowledging his impressive trick.

"Oh, Auben. We have been among the humans too long. Open your mind to the possibilities. We could play hide-and-seek in nebula clouds, blow stars out like they're dandelion seeds and flick moons like they're marbles. We have the universe and we have each other. It's the way it's always been."

The night is brilliant, the stars hang so close and succulent, as if they are fruits ripe to be plucked. They anger me. My temper swells, and it comes so quickly, it catches me off guard. Kasim notices and steadies me with a hand to my shoulder.

His touch is like a silk scarf—smooth, delicate—and it slips down into my gut to calm my rage, but there is far too much fuel this time. I am done being played with. I gather my true voice, deep and ragged. It trembles all of Grace Mountain. "Don't touch me. Don't ever touch me again."

"You don't mean that, brother."

"I'd rather die than to be yoked to you a second longer."

He looks into my eyes, and sees my truth. And for a moment, I see his. I've hurt him deeply.

Good.

Then his face goes stiff and unreadable as his hand rises to me once again. "Amawusiakaraseiya was right," Kasim says. "You may be a god, but you will always be a lesser god. The same as all those lesser twins out there, anchors holding society back from its true brilliance." He sighs, as if the burden is something he wishes he didn't have to take on. Humble to the end, I guess. "So . . . I guess it's time we put an end to this nonsense."

His hand trembles at me, then moves over the masses as if he is about to convey some blessing. Scowl-lines crowd Kasim's face. He may be free of vice now, yet I see nothing but pure malice in his heart. The masses cheer him nonetheless. Unsuspecting idiots.

Then the screams come.

Tens of thousands of people below, all at once, let out a monstrous howl. They twist, contort, fall to the ground as if the life is being yanked from them one breath at a time. The winds turn, and I can smell the sick and loosed bowels and blood. I try to avert my gaze, but it is so horrific, so awful. Only no one is actually dying. My vision slips, and though I haven't moved, it's as if I am standing among them. The details become clear upon the back of a shirtless man. His chimeral stripes peel away, rough and ragged like a snakeskin. What's left behind is smooth dark brown. He stands slowly, still pained, confused. Looks over at his twin. They reach for one another in comfort, but upon their touch, agony sets in on their elongated faces. They step apart. The farther they go, the more relief they have from their physical pain, but the emotional pain is painted too clearly upon upturned mouths.

My vision snaps, and I glare at Kasim. "What have you done?"

"Only what needed to be done. What should have been done a long time ago."

A thin part cracks its way through the crowd, growing larger and larger until two distinct groups have formed, amassed on opposite sides of the mountain—like two piles of marbles divided evenly among bratty kids who no longer know how to play nicely. Their numbers are the same, but even without keen vision, it's easy to see that the piles are not truly equal.

Kasim glares at me. "Take your people and all of their vices. They are no longer needed here."

He raises his hand, and the sickness infects me. The sky goes pure white, the thousands of stars now like chips of obsidian. I close my eyes against the pain, and I feel him within me. Every cell of his within my body starts to die. All at once. It takes longer than I would have thought—he makes up so much of me. And I of him. I open my eyes. His teeth are clenched. He was a wisp before, and is even more brittle now.

When the pain recedes, I am half the man I was . . . or rather half the creature I was. I feel so hollow. So . . . free. I take to the air, like a corn husk on the wind.

Kasim stands there smugly, waiting. For what? For me to thank him? For me to apologize? For me to beg him to put things back the right way? I glance back at my people—a collection of misfits and social outcasts—poor, mistreated, tinibru-addicted, barely educated fools trying to make the best of the paltry life they've been given.

I see myself in every single one of their vice-filled faces.

"I know what you're thinking," I say to Kasim. "But this is the best thing you've ever given me."

I catch tears forming in his wide eyes, but I do not care to see if they drop. A new desire burns within my gut . . . one to put as many miles between Kasim and me as I can, as soon as I can. And like one of those bratty kids, I gather my marbles and go home.

TEMPER

The skies open and spring rain falls in big warm drops, turning the backside of Grace Mountain into treacherous slopes of mud. I'd never thought anything of it before, but this side of the mountain seldom appears in paintings or drawings. It's rounded and plump instead of concave and stately. Littered with scraggly brush instead of lush greenery. A long unsightly crag works its way through the ass-end of the mountain, top to bottom, and trails off into the distance. My people and I, we follow it, and finally park ourselves among the mud huts of a sleepy fishing village, overwhelming it with our numbers by several hundredfold. It takes much of my energy to hold human form now, but in the midst of so much change, I need something of my old life to cling to.

Bellies are empty, but there is not enough to eat. Bodies are tired, but there are not enough places to rest, to shit, to cry. The misery is contagious, and their eyes beat at me, bidding me to do something. Anything. While I stand here like an impotent god, a chicken squawks as it is quartered alive, several sets of bloodied hands bringing back fistfuls of meat and feathers and organs. Desperate people squabble over mere scraps, gnashing teeth, pulling hair, gouging eyes. An entire enclave of mud huts is looted and destroyed, torn down to nothing, like we are locusts on the wind.

I imagine Kasim judging us from atop the perch of his mountain, laughing. I clench my fists, feeling the earth tremble beneath my feet, feeling the winds swirl up and around me, feeling my temper roil in my gut with all the strength of a hurricane. These terrible, vice-ridden creatures . . . taken from the dirt and clay and formed by my own hands, cannot be what I'd intended. Something shifts within my anger, subtle vibrations run through me, and an odd stir of power sizzles at my fingertips. I rub my fingers together, and they glow with a soft blue light. I feel tethers—to the earth, the moon, and the planets beyond, as fine as spider silk, but strong enough to move mountains. I think of how Kasim had caused the sun to arc across the sky. I'm tempted to try to do the same, but I stand perfectly still, so as not to snag a line and send the earth crashing into the sun. The sensations subside as quickly as their onset, but my temper remains.

The muscles in my neck twist into a fierce knot as it channels the storm of my voice. "We are not our vices!" I bellow. My people are knocked to their knees, and anything left standing in this wretched town is plowed over in the wake of my words. For a split second, the world stands still in complete silence. I fold down on myself, reining in my power and voice until I can speak in a way that won't kill them. "Forget what you have been told. We have been lied to our whole lives. We are not less than. We are not feral mongrels at each other's throats for a scrap of meat. Now is our time to prove that to ourselves, and to them." I point up to the ridge of Grace Mountain.

I speak my truth, but they all look upon me as if my duplicitous tongue is capable of nothing but cold lies. Perhaps it is not fair of me to expect to change what has been ground into their beings in the course of an afternoon. Perhaps it is unfair for me to expect anything righteous from them at all. But if I cannot mend their souls, the least I can do is mend their bellies.

With a sigh, I shed my cloak and take to the skies, then speed along the coast, flapping over the throng of fishing boats bobbing upon the clear blue ocean. I pierce the water—my wings become fins, my thorny scales become sleek. It doesn't take me long to find what I'm looking for, but I'd underestimated their beauty by several factors. A school of yellowfin tuna. They swarm, movements slick and graceful, eyes full of focus and distrust. I slip into their group as one of them, the clumsy awkward one, for sure. I concentrate, tapping into the rawness of my temper. Invisible tethers sizzle at my fin-tips, and I cautiously tug at the one that binds me to the earth, like it's a kite bobbing at the end of a taut string.

Nothing happens. I take that as a good sign that at least I can't screw things up too easily. I pull harder, more deliberately on the tether. It resonates through me, filling me with a sharp, high-pitched twang that rattles my skull. An achy rumble erupts from below. Bubbles rise, a few at first, but then the tuna school is surrounded, uplifted in a whirling frenzy. Above the surface, cold air catches us as a waterspout furiously spins around us. The tether becomes an unwieldy web of gossamer, and with minute movements and delicate attentiveness, I steer clear of the boats as I maneuver back to the coast with my bounty.

I dump the fish at the feet of my people, then lie back, beyond exhausted. Beyond hungry. A hundred-and-some-odd tons of fresh tuna sit before me, but it is not the type of flesh that will settle my appetite. My eyes stick to my people as they feast, pressing back my own cravings. They dare not approach me, dare not look in my direction, like they are ashamed to have me as their god. Over the course of several hours, the catch dwindles down to scrap and bone without a single thank-you. The sun has taken its toll, the smell of fish rot as rank as the ungrateful attitudes of these people. Kasim was right. It would have been easier to wipe the slate clean. Start from scratch. My mind drifts, imagining the sound the moon would make if it came crashing down on top of us . . . wondering how many times the earth would skip across the surface of the sun if I tossed it at just the right angle.

"Excuse me, Lord," comes the grit of a voice caught between childhood and manhood. Its cadence is familiar, and yet when I look upon the face, the features are only partially recognizable. I stare harder into the eyes and something clicks. The eyes, yes, they are the same.

"Chimwe?" I find myself disengaging from the moon's tether. It resonates from my mindless touch.

"I wanted to thank you." He holds up the bulk of a tuna's head, lightly charred, its dead stare filmed over with white. Testosterone steams off Chimwe like a wet sidewalk on a hot day. Off *him*? All traces of Chiso's feminine genes are gone. His hips are narrow, face angular, chest firm and muscular. He looks as exhausted as I feel, and I recognize the unease of suddenly finding oneself trapped in a foreign body. Chimwe and I are kindred in so many ways.

"I—" My words catch in my throat. I'm not sure what to say. "Are you okay?" I ask him.

"Yeah, sure. I guess." He smiles, as if that will help make me believe the words coming from eir . . . *his* mouth? Either way, I can tell in Chimwe's eyes that this situation is about as okay as waking up with a mouthful of blood.

"What about you?" Chimwe asks. "You look hungry. Perhaps we can share a meal together?" He steps closer. I think that he is about to offer me a taste from the fish head, but instead, he pulls a small knife and pricks his index finger.

He shouldn't have done that.

The temptations I had buried in my gut have now worked their way back to the points of my teeth. My cravings whip me so hard, I can't contain my saliva. I drool like a half-starved street dog, leering at Chimwe as he squeezes his finger until it goes pale. A dollop of blood the size of a large coin rests in his palm. I dip my fingers in and suck them dry.

"Wait!" Chimwe says. "We didn't say . . ." His eyes shift to Grace Mountain.

"Say what?" I coax him. The tether to the moon hums luridly in my ear. I swear, if he gives thanks to *Him* for the food I provided . . .

"Never mind. It's not important." He takes a bite of his fish, swallows. I wait for him to leave, but he doesn't. He comes closer, settles beside me, and offers blood from his other hand. "What you said, do you think it's really true?

That we are not less than? That we can do anything, be any-thing?"

"You're supping with a god. I'm not sure there ever were any rules, but if there were, they're pretty much void at this point." I bite my bottom lip. My entire body throbs to the beat of his heart.

"Good. Because all of this, I think it's a good thing. We have a chance to start over, to do things right this time." I feel what he is saying, not because I want more than any-thing to agree with him, but because his keen aspirations prickle like seltzer upon my tongue. I also taste the cool bit-terness of his fears and uncertainties upon my palate. I'd tasted such things before, when I'd killed, but they'd only filled me with haunted remorse. Now they bind me to my cousin-sibling, our connection thicker than blood.

Suddenly, my senses shift and smells from my past over-whelm me: the sweet scents of stale sanjo smoke and cheap inks. I look up and see Uncle Pabio standing there. My heart bucks, and for a split second, all is right, and none of this is happening, and I'm just a kid in the basement of his doting uncle, waiting for him to amaze me. Without a thought, I go to him, embrace him. Weakness overwhelms me, and I go slack in his arms as my bones threaten to slip to dust.

"Hello, Auben," he says. Uncle Pabio hands me his flask, the same one I'd snuck my first sips of spirits from.

My first instinct is to refuse it, but something charges me as I hold the flask. I unscrew the top, and am warmed back to the point of merely freezing. I take a sip, letting the thick liquid curl upon my tongue before swallowing. The buzz is immediate. Intense. Gratifying. I take another. Longer. Deeper, until only vapors remain. It's not as delectable as those last sweet bits of life force sucked dry from the depths of a desiccated heart, but it satisfies me nicely.

"More," I demand of him, handing back the empty flask. When he takes it, I notice the red bandage around his wrist. It is his blood settling into my stomach. My taste buds swell with the savory-sweet mix of his eccentricity, his creativity, and his perseverance . . . like a good Rashtra chutney.

"I know your mother taught you better manners than that," his voice cracks, clearly irritated. "A thank-you would suffice."

I stiffen at the mention of Mother and my buzz washes clean away. My brow tightens. "And you should mind how you talk to your lord, Pabio," I growl.

"That's *Uncle* Pabio," Uncle Pabio says. "I know who you are and what you are. But none of that stops you from being my nephew." Uncle Pabio sniffs the flask, screws the lid on tight, then pockets it. He lays his arm around me and pulls me in close—no hesitation in his eyes, no uncertainty in his smile. "My favorite nephew," he adds.

Chimwe sighs and turns his jealous gaze to the pieces of fish flesh stuck beneath his fingernails.

Me, I prickle all over with Uncle Pabio's eyes upon me. He's never been one to hide his contempt for religion, and now here I stand before him, a god in the flesh. "You still claim me? Even though you know what I am? A figment of the imagination? An invention to coerce morality?"

"Maybe an invention. Definitely not a figment." His warm hand touches my cheek. "But what does it matter if humanity created the gods, or the gods created humanity? We're both here now, right?" Uncle Pabio says. "What you did today was a miracle. It's seeded hope where there was none. Yes, this is a dark day for us all, but with your help, we can recover. We can thrive."

"Yes, but at what price?" I say. "For how many lives?"

"If blood is your currency, you only need to tell us how much," Chimwe says flatly, as if this is a business transaction.

"More than can fit in Uncle Pabio's flask." I eye the bulging pulse in Chimwe's neck. "More than runs through your veins."

Chimwe nods. He is not perturbed. "I'll need a solid number. Ten pints a day? Twenty?"

I think of what Sesay had said. Three lives per year on average, but that number makes me cringe. I realize what restraint I've shown for all these centuries, nearly starving myself. If I'm going to be any use to anyone, I'm going to need more. Much more.

"A hundred fifty pints. And it needs to be fresh," I say greedily. "Still warm." I become warm myself as embarrassment washes over me. My mind races to the time Uncle Pabio caught me red-handed with his stash of vice mags. He was the one who'd taught me to walk the thin line between pleasure and indulgence, between virtue and vice. He was the one who'd taught me to appreciate all the shades of gray. I turn my mind around this, finding strengths within our weaknesses. Uncle Pabio would give his lifeblood so willingly. And from his confidence, I am sure he is not alone. "This is our communion," I say.

"What's that?" asks Uncle Pabio.

"Your blood. I feel closer to you both now. I thought it was a craving for more . . . but it's not that. Not only that, at least. It connects us." I resist the urge to smack my lips as I savor the robust flavor of their essences lingering upon my tongue. Smoky. Nutty. Firm. With a hint of spice . . . anise, maybe? I'm eager to stretch my palate with the samplings of many more.

Within the span of half an hour, a line forms more than a hundred deep. An ounce at a time, my mind peels open to the infinite resources that my vice-filled people possess. Greed runs hot and harsh within the veins of a comfy mogul who had grown a financial empire despite the odds, and had given hundreds of people jobs to provide for their families. Then there's the tart and grippy vainglory of a talented architect who despite her years of experience, had never risen above a junior title. Her ideas were stolen by her superiors to build three of the most gorgeous buildings upon the Cape's skyline. Then there's the supple creaminess of a streetwalker's lecherous blood, stirring me deep. He's damned good at his job, and proud of it, too. I do nothing to sway him or shame him. There is no judgment. After all, who am I to judge anyone? He works hard, puts in the hours, survives. Thrives, even. When I look out before me, I see my people are all survivors. I see warriors and fathers and mothers and lovers and people who've worked their fingers to the bone to put an extra scrap of meat on the table. Just like my mother had. Whatever she'd done, she'd done it for us.

When my energy is fully restored, I'll take to the skies and spin my gossamer webs, bringing back wood, stone, fresh water, and metal ore. Together we will create a city of vices—an infrastructure built by temper and lechery, an economy fueled by greed and envy, a culture adorned with vainglory and guided by doubt, and as all governments worth their sand, ruled by a leader with a well-intentioned, yet duplicitous tongue.

I look at Chimwe, dutifully at my side, gnawing on the remnants of his fish. A couple months ago, he would have been the last person I thought I could count on for anything. But I've tasted the depths of his work ethic, his aspirations, his guile and creativity and problem solving. Despite his vices, I trust him with my life, and I trust him with the heart of our city. "So, back in our dorm room," I say to him, "were you serious about being capable of running a multimillion-djang corporation?"

Chimwe stops chewing. His eyes brighten, and then we both stare off into the stretches of muddy, underdeveloped land, imagining the possibilities.

I may be a god, but I am not the god they are used to. I do not require sacred monuments or churches or texts or hymnals. I do not listen to prayers. Communions are informal, mostly filled with laughter and raunchy jokes, but the occasional intellectual discourse is not unwelcome. No one is turned away. At the center of Akinyemi, our charmed city, I rest in the plaza, watching the skyline spring to life before my eyes. Science is no longer repressed, and as a result, subsecular groups have come out of hiding and their machinations have allowed the buildings to soar higher than anything before. Money has no meaning. Hunger doesn't exist. Without struggle, without the stigma of lesser twindom hanging over our heads, we are free to create, to innovate, to thrive. Our city is one of unabashed mental masturbations, the architecture luminous and rotund—the sun glinting off violet and indigo glass and polished metal, like our skyline is a collection of gaudy baubles and gems. It steals your gaze, fills you with envy, then sends you on your way. Here, in our charmed city, we live as one—a people born of vices, using them to lift us higher than any virtue ever could.

Thousands visit me each and every day. They stand proudly in line, sometimes for hours at a time, not rushed, not harried, but eager for the opportunity to spill the blood that has built this city. While they wait, they also commune with each other, sharing boisterous laughter and fledgling innovations, savory samosas and fresh-baked mealie bread. Inventors and investors, philosophers and philanderers, gallery artists and con artists—they all come, but it is who doesn't show up that concerns me the most.

Mother.

"She is not ready yet," my uncle Pabio consoles me. Not for the first time. Not for the hundredth. "She needs a little more time to process."

Time is much too slippery for me when it's measured in seconds and minutes and days, but enough of it has passed, I am sure of that.

"I want you to take me to see her," I demand.

"I promised her I wouldn't."

His words sink into my bones, and it's difficult for me not to question where his loyalties lie. I keep Uncle Pabio close, like a moral compass—a moral compass that happens to always point south-southwest, but his eccentricities are easy enough to adjust for. He's right, though. I should respect my mother's wishes. I should keep stepping around the pit she's left in my heart. "Does she hate me?" I ask. "Is she embarrassed of me?"

"Of course not."

"Then why? Why will she not come to visit her own son?" My fist pounds the ground. The earth rumbles, and a narrow crack winds its way across the plaza's manicured lawn. Pigeons take to the air. Childish laughter from a nearby game of freeze tag comes to an abrupt halt.

Uncle Pabio swallows. "I do not wish to put words in her mouth, Auben."

I flinch at the name, like it's the remnant of a past I'd nearly forgotten. If I could will my heart to stone and not care, I would, but beneath the armor of godhood, I pine for Mother's approval. I have always been a disappointment to her, but now look what I have built. How high must these buildings be before she lets me back into her arms? "I need to know, Uncle Pabio. What can I do to make her love me again?"

Uncle Pabio crumbles at my words. He comes to me, rests a comforting hand on my shoulder. "She is fighting her own demons." Uncle Pabio catches himself and flushes at his misspoken word. "You know what I mean. It's tough on her . . . all this time she was so dead set against religion, only to discover she'd carried the very seed of it in her womb. Religion still makes her uncomfortable."

"But this whole city is built upon mental masturbations! There is no religion." I look around us, and under the rolling curves of the plaza's honeycomb pavilion, dozens of children tinker with machinations, brains greedy for knowledge. I watch, completely rapt as they build small automatons that skitter around on their own volition, like they are gods springing life from metal. Never in my eleven years of schooling had I seen so many young minds so motivated, so inspired. So lecherous. Here, there is no one to tie them down to desk chairs and pour globs of misinformation in their heads until they forget how to think.

"I'm sorry, Auben," he says, offering me his flask.

I shove it away. "I'm not in the mood." I already can smell the pity upon his breath. No need for me to taste it as well.

Uncle Pabio nods. "I'll see you tomorrow, then?"

"Mmm . . ." I grumble. I stand, stretch my legs, strum a few tethers, and get ready to uphold my end of the social contract between me and the citizens of Akinyemi.

"Oh! Are you leaving?" says the next girl in line. "I've been waiting forever." My heart swells at the sound of her voice. Nkosazana. I'd nearly forgotten about her after all this time. My eyes run over her, top to bottom. She's still prim and tight, outfitted in a turquoise shweshwe-print dress with stunning black-and-cream accents and a matching beaded necklace, but gone are the false embellishments . . . the luxurious store-bought mane, the layers of makeup, the blue glass contacts. Her hair is pressed and falls lightly upon her shoulders. Her skin is flawless, save for a small, off-colored patch upon her cheek. Her eyes are a warm, reddish-brown. Ruda's imprint on her must have run extremely shallow in her blood, because other than embracing her natural beauty, almost nothing about her has changed.

"I've got time for one more," I say.

She's ripe with nervousness, something I've never seen in her. She'd always been so self-confident and sure. Nkosazana rummages through her purse and pulls out a silver letting thimble. Her hands tremble as she fumbles with it. I take her hands in mine, guide her index finger into the small cup, press it into the spike hidden inside. Gently, I milk her finger until an ounce is drawn, then sip it down with delight. From this taste of her, I learn more than I'd bothered to in all the time we were together. I savor the expanse of her intellect, and am piqued by the decadent creaminess of natural nobility, with a subtle twist of lime that catches me off guard.

"I've missed you," she says, batting unremarkable lashes. They make me flush nonetheless.

"I bet you say that to all the gods."

She smiles at me and my heart flips. "I was hoping we could talk somewhere private?"

I flex my fingers, play a tune on invisible strings, and from the earth erupts a tangle of green vines all around us. They extend up, dome over our heads, sprouting large heart-shaped leaves and floppy-headed yellow flowers.

Nkosazana stares up in awe, nicks of light dappling her face. "You remembered my favorite color."

"Just a lucky guess," I say with a grin. In a society that thrives on duplicity, blatant honesty has become a particularly useful tool to connect with people on a deeper level.

Nkosazana arches a brow. "Really? The Auben I knew would have claimed to have never forgotten a single detail about me, even if a thousand years had passed."

I'd spoken to her like that? Probably. Certainly. I was adept at the game of talking my way into her panties. Memories of us in bed press up against my mind. I'm overcome with warmth, not from the sudden whip of lust coursing through me (though I won't lie, it's quite nice, too), but from the memories of her companionship, the touch of her skin against mine, and the giggles we shared beneath cool sheets. She anchors me to my humanity, like a lifeline to my former self. Both of which I've been losing my grip on with each day that passes. "I'm sorry about that," I mumble.

Nkosazana shrugs me off. "That was the past," she says. "The reason I'm here has more to do with the present."

Ah, so that's why she's here. To rekindle our romance, after all this time. I remember how proud she'd been of dating a comfy rat. I can only imagine how much dating a god would stroke her vainglory. My excitement ebbs, though, as I feel her eyes fork at my body, like it's a cooked sausage about to break through its casing.

"We can be honest, can't we?" she says. "Completely honest. Completely open."

Completely open. I hear what she's saying. She wants to see *me*, the body I keep hidden underneath this fleshy cloak. I stare back at the blemish on her cheek, wondering how many times she'd covered it, keeping that bit of her hidden from me. How often had she worried about her makeup smudging off?

"Nkosazana, I can't . . ." It takes so much effort to keep myself fitting within Auben's skin. I'm constantly folding and refolding myself, trying to squeeze back into a container far too inadequate to accommodate the boundless span of a god. But I do it to protect my followers from the nightmare I've become. And to protect myself from their fickle loyalty.

She leans in close, her breath hot and humid upon the lobe of my ear. "Auben, it's me. You can show me. It's just us in here."

"The last person who I let see the real me betrayed me," I say bitterly.

"I'm not that person." She draws back, crosses her arms over her chest. "I thought we had something, you and I."

"We did!" I blurt out, the seams of Auben's skin burning white-hot as the beast within threatens to jump out. I can't show her. Not yet. She's not ready. I'm not ready. But if I don't give her something, I might lose her again, and with her, the last vestiges of my humanity.

I shift. Not into what I am, but into the monster she has built up in her mind. I force my body into its mold. My skin grows tawny fur, shorn close like velvet so that she can still see the ripples in my muscles across my long, lean body. Claws erupt from my nail beds, a fraction of their actual size. They're sharp, black, and polished, like slivers of onyx— glossy enough to catch my reflection. In them, I see the wide, caring eyes of a baby oryx, and upon my head a noble crown of horns. I wrap my large wings around my body like a satin sheet, playing the part of the shy little thing Nkosazana wants to save.

"Oh, come on now, it's not that awful," she says with a soft smile. "Actually, you're kind of cute. In a beastly sort of way." With a gentle hand, she slides my wing back, and strokes me from shoulder to elbow. I tense at her touch. Arousal grips me, wrenches the logic from my mind. I swell within this flimsy container, the thought of her tongue playfully ringing circles around my navel, of her kissing my chest, my shoulder, my cheek . . . Certainly a vice-ridden girl like Nkosazana knew not to let *me* kiss *her,* but the promise of death upon my lips would only add to the thrill. I'm so taut, so ready, another touch may send the heavens crashing down upon us.

It's a risk I'm willing to take.

"So what do you say we get down to business?" Nkosa-zana says.

"Yes," I breathe, the whisper of a god. The earth hums softly, not just beneath us, but from shore to shore of this whole wretched land. The entire continent has gone aim-lessly adrift. For a moment, I let my mind unfold, spinning my gossamers until we're safely tethered again.

"—once we've established relations, of course. And I want to let you know up front," Nkosazana is saying, her eyes full of seriousness, "if this is going to work, it's going to have to be mutually beneficial."

"I'll do everything in my power to please you," I say. At this point, I'd agree to anything to be able to call her mine again.

"Good. But remember, this isn't charity. Payments would be arranged."

Wait, what? I've missed something. "Payments?"

"Right now we can offer fish, yams, corn, and an assort-ment of handmade crafts. As time passes, we will be able to trade intellectual properties, too, but those are still under development."

"Who's *we*?" I ask.

"Auben, have you even bothered to listen to a word I've said? I swear, some things never change." Her nostrils flare. "We want to establish trade relations between Akinyemi and the camps. We're in desperate need of raw materials."

So not *those* kind of relations. Economic relations. The flowers above us wilt. Green vines dry up and go brittle as my disappointment and embarrassment grip me the way I wish Nkosazana would.

"Oh!" she says, sitting back, gathering herself. "I haven't upset you, have I?"

"No," I say. This can't be it, the only reason she's come to see me. There must be some deeper meaning, some invisible string that still connects us. A string that I could pluck, and Nkosazana would ease right back into my arms, like she'd never left. Unless . . . Unless all this is a game she's playing, and she's using this trade agreement as a convenient excuse to be around me. Yes, well two can play at this. "I'll set up a formal meeting then, and we can discuss the matter with our board," I say coolly.

"That would be fantastic," she says, holding my clawed hands loosely in hers. "It really is good to see you again." She pulls me in close, and her scent plays tricks with my mind. She feels so soft and tiny and wrong in my arms, like a field mouse caught in the embrace of a lion-shaped nebula. I pull her in tighter, wishing for the sensation to subside, and hoping she doesn't feel it, too.

Nkosazana ducks out from my grip, then stands and dusts herself off. I take her cue and open an arched doorway among the brittle vines behind her. The plaza has cleared of people, and she stands alone against the jewel-speckled backdrop of the city. She smiles before she turns to walk away.

That bit of humanity I had left, I think she's taken it with her. The vines go to dust around me, and my bones go to dust as well, my true form revealing the myriad of grotesque incompatibilities that prove my infatuation ridiculous. We are too different, and yet still I pray for her to look back at me one last time, to see *me*. To accept my blemishes.

She doesn't look back, and if we are indeed playing a game, she is definitely winning.

"They need infrastructure," Chimwe whispers to me as Nkosazana leads us through the meandering roads of the camp. It's been years since I'd last stepped foot here. It was the predecessor to our charmed city—built of scraps and sweat and blood, haphazard shanties and shebeens selling much-needed goods. They have made progress. Only around 10,000 residents remain in what had once housed all 300,000 of us. There is purpose now, cobbled streets, community gardens, schools.

"Of course they need infrastructure," I hiss under my breath so only Chimwe can hear. "And we have it. I don't understand why they can't move into the city. There are plenty of empty flats to accommodate them all."

"It's not what you have. It's what you don't have," Nkosazana says. Apparently, I hadn't spoken softly enough. She presses her hand on the tin siding of a shanty. Graffiti adorns its surface, big-headed stick figures that must have been painted by a four-year-old, though they extend much higher than a kid could possibly reach.

"We have everything you could want!" I plead. "There are jobs to be had, all the luxuries of life."

"I think she's talking about community," Chimwe offers. "They've been uprooted once already. We have room, but spread over a half dozen different districts."

Nkosazana nods. "It's exactly that. We're making progress of our own, but if we open trade relations, we can—"

I shake my head. "We are one city. I will make sure you

have what you need. Trade is not necessary." Despite my best efforts to be humble, my words echo with pretension off the tin walls of this shantytown. I soften my shoulders, narrow my chest, try to make Nkosazana feel like I'm taking her seriously, but it pains me to see our city separated like this. I've lived my whole life in a segregated city. I can't stand for it to continue, not if I have the ability to stop it.

Nkosazana glowers at me. "Chimwe gets it. Why don't you?" She steps close to me, so close, we're nearly touching. Her scent overwhelms me, her anger and frustration adding a smoky edge to her essence, accompanied by a ginger so spicy, it makes my lips pucker. The tension between us is so acute, my coarse scales erupt through my cloak. Nkosazana doesn't flinch, doesn't look away from my gaze.

"You're the ones who don't get it," I say. "We can't stay divided like this. You saw how we were split up and separated before. By vice and virtue, by gender, by class. We were cut up and pitted against each other in so many ways. Now here in Akinyemi, we have a chance to do it right."

I'm so gutted, I'm trembling. Everything I've tried to love has been torn away from me—a hole in my heart where a father should have been, a mother who disowned me, and my brother, the only person I could depend on, who cast me away like garbage. I *need* this city to work.

"Trust me, I know all about divisions," Nkosazana says, glowering at me. I know that look. It's something I said. "There are a few purists who think it unwise to put ourselves in your debt. However, most of us aren't so shortsighted and see trade with Akinyemi as a *necessary evil*." Her words are sharper than my claws, and she's not apologetic in the slightest. But something else lurks beneath her complete

314 / NICKY DRAYDEN

openness . . . a message hiding in plain sight. There are a few who do not want to be in my debt. A few who want nothing to do with me. I get a sudden, sinking feeling I know who these "few" people are.

My nostrils flare, ears perk. I tune out Nkosazana's overwhelming scent, and focus on the subtle aromas that lie beneath. I unfold them, and my world of muted sensations becomes a rich, vibrant web of colors, sounds, and smells. I catch a fragrant whiff of citrus blossoms, polished and powerful, with the faintest trace of cleaning chemicals that never worked their way from flesh, even after all this time. I breathe her in, my mother, somewhere close.

"Where are you going?" Nkosazana says, running after me. "You can't go that way . . . that's—"

"Sometimes I think you forget who—and what—I am," I say. "You don't tell *me* what to do."

I follow the scent, until I reach an outcropping among the shanties. In its center, a two-story building with blacked-out windows. Two guards stand at the double doors leading inside. They immediately lock eyes with me, and their postures become erect. The beating of their hearts turns staccato in the course of a second. From inside the building I hear metal crashing, drills screeching, saws buzzing.

"My mother," I growl. "She is inside."

Nkosazana scrambles around me, putting her hand to my chest as if she could stop me. "I wanted to tell you, Auben," she says. "I really did. But you can't go in there."

"I can go anywhere I damn please," I say.

Nkosazana gawks at me, her eyes haunted. I've shed Auben's skin completely. This is the body she was begging me to show her. She stares for a long moment, at all my impressive wretchedness, probably trying to figure out what part repulses her the most.

"Here's what you wanted. 'Complete honesty and complete openness,'" I say, completely and utterly unashamed of each and every damned blemish upon my body. No longer will I hide who I am. No longer will I pretend to be something I'm not. "Now it's your turn."

Nkosazana is trapped by her own words. She leans against the door, and slowly she presses the latch down on the handle. I suck in a shameful breath as it clicks and the door cracks open. It tastes like the future inside—sweet, brassy smoke, and sparks from metal kissing metal.

My hooves clack against the concrete as I walk deeper and deeper into the building. Subsecular inventions crowd the space like a clockwork forest. Daylight filters in through a dusty green skylight, doing its best to hold the creepy red glow of dozens of boilers at bay. Gears are stacked high and thick like tree trunks, iron chains and brass piping form a maze across the ceiling, like vines and branches of a canopy, and hanging diagrams and blueprints flutter about whenever one of the workers walks past. One by one, they notice me, and the buzz of ingenuity slowly grinds to a halt. The smoke dissipates, and I see her, my mother in her immaculate white lab cloak, nearly half her face obscured by big brassy goggles with mirrored lenses. She's yelling at some poor ingrate.

"There's no excuse for this kind of error!" Mother says to a woman cowering behind a large sheet of paper like it's an impervious shield. Detailed drawings adorn it, in blue and brown ink, numbers and symbols and signs, and I'm immediately reminded of the pamphlet that had fallen out of Mother's posh magazine on our way to narrow season dinner.

"It's these Mzansi-made instruments," the woman complains. "Only one out of fifty of them will hold precision. I waste half my day checking and rechecking my measurements. All I need is a solid Rashtrakutan panel gauge that won't slip up on me."

Something odd happens at the mention of Rashtrakutan fare—a craving swells on my tongue, and for the first time in a long time, that craving is not for blood. It's for curried chicken and mango chutney. I cling to it, coddle it, try to stoke that little smolder of my humanity into a flame, but it slips past me, and my fangs once again itch only for the lifeblood of my subjects.

"You will use the tools we have," my mother snaps. "And you will find a way for them to work. If your measurements are off by even one—" Mother's body tightens. She wraps herself up in her coat to ward herself from the sudden chill and then turns to me.

"Hello, Mother," I say.

Of the hundreds of awkward situations I've brought upon myself, none compare to standing here before my mother, the mirrored lenses of her goggles aiming at me like small cannons. Slowly, she removes them, letting them hang around her neck, and things become much, much worse. That stare could make a god lose hold of his bladder, just a little. And the workers, they're all as terrified of me as I am of Mother. She's not scared, though. Rather, her eyes are hooked into mine, holding a burning fury that I cannot break away from.

"Can someone tell me why my damned devil of a son is standing before me?" She spits these words, but I cannot help but feel a smoldering of pride that she still claims me as her own.

Nkosazana skitters up between us, breaking the line of sight and the power Mother exudes over me. "Enna Zeogwu, I can explain . . ." she stammers. "We need more material. If other cities won't trade with us, then we have to accept alternate means."

"What place do you have telling me what we need? How dare you go against my word?" Mother smolders. She is a woman who held gods in her womb, and every bone in her body embraces this truth, no matter how much she'd like to deny it. Anyone else would crumble before her, but not Nkosazana.

"No matter how keen your vision is, the reality is that we can't harbor invention here, sharing faulty tools and bickering over each other's scraps." Nkosazana steps forward to my mother. They're like twin stars entangled by each other's pull. "Your words can move our minds toward invention, but they can't make resources out of thin air. We *need* him."

"We'll manage getting our own resources soon enough. You have no patience!" Mother yells.

Their quarreling makes me go faint. As I steady myself, my eyes drift, taking in the scene around me. Tinkerings pile up like snowdrifts against walls, machinations of all sorts. Broken gears litter the floor. A large brass telescope points to the filthy skylight. And in the far corner sits a giant rotund machination painted yellow with polished gold trim, and six legs cinched close to its sides like some desiccated spider. Its eyes are twin furnaces, unlit and achingly cold, and I can't help but notice the resemblance to those mechanical bugs Mother had stashed in the secret compartment of her desk. I'm staring. Everyone notices that I'm staring. The tension in the room suddenly doubles, and before I can utter a word, Nkosazana's hand is on my arm, and she's pulling me away.

"Please come," she whispers. "I'm in enough trouble as it is."

My hooves stand firm, but the entire building wobbles. I worry that I've snagged a tether, and have sent the earth spinning off-kilter, but no one else seems affected. It's all in my head. Still, somehow I manage to fall in step with Nkosazana, out into the dusty air of the camps. Chimwe is immediately at my side, catches me in his arms and helps me down to the ground.

"I saw her," I heave, watching the fog of my cousin's breath thicken with each moment that passes. He holds me tightly, despite the frost growing around us.

Chimwe nods. "And how is my dear aunt Daia?"

"About as charming as a riled beehive," I say.

"Sounds about right." Chimwe squeezes my hand. "So is everything okay with you?" His eyes flick skyward, toward the half moon hanging in the midmorning sky. Closer, it seems. Too close.

I realize I've been clinging to it like a crutch, and I release my grip on the tether, ignoring the thick jagged trench now running along the moon's surface. "Everything's fine," I say to Chimwe. "Everything's just fine." I try to ignore all the connections I have to the cosmos, and focus on the ones I'm trying to make here.

"I'm sorry I got you mixed up in this," Nkosazana mumbles, oblivious to my celestial manipulations. "With the trade embargoes, we've got limited supplies and opportunities, and all of the sect's instruments were left behind with the split. Your mother thinks we can manage, but our innovations will never get recognition within the greater science com-munity unless we can shake off this stigma that we're just bumbling hobbyists. We *need* the right tools. If only there were a way . . ."

My mind must still be spinning, because I've got a new scheme percolating in the back of my brain. A crazy scheme, sure, but really, am I capable of any other kind? I can get my mother the equipment she needs, *and* make sure Nkosazana gets all the credit.

"If I get you those tools," I say to Nkosazana, "will you promise to help convince the sect to join Akinyemi? We'll make room for your entire community, provide you with state-of-the-art—"

"Your mother won't allow it. She's furious even about the idea of trading with you. If she knew you were involved in getting our instruments back, she'd have nothing to do with them."

"Well, what she doesn't know won't hurt her," I say, raising a brow. "Me and you. We go back into the old city, grab your tools, and slip out before anyone notices."

"Do you think we've never considered that? They shunned us once, kicked us from our homes, pried us from our families. What do you think they'd do if they caught us in their precious city? Besides, it's not like everything we need is locked up together in some secret subsecular ware-house. We're talking dozens of hidden locations, all over the place. It's impossible."

"Impossible for humans, maybe." I arch a scaled brow.

"Impossible for humans. Inadvisable for gods," Chimwe says, stepping in. "If you're caught, what will happen to Akinyemi? What if Grace's wrath befalls us?"

"We'll have to be stealthy, then, won't we?" I boast. "Stick to the shadows. Blend in. We can use the comfy burrows to travel from one location to the next. They have to all be abandoned now." I touch Nkosazana's shoulder. "Just imagine what Enna Zeogwu will think when you come back to her with those tools. She'll never doubt you again." The words singe my throat—not quite the truth, almost spoken in anger, and envious as all hell. But Mother would be so proud of Nkosazana, and if I can align myself just right, maybe some of that pride would rub off on me by association.

"Well . . . I guess we could—" Nkosazana starts.

"Wait." Chimwe's eyes light up. "You can't actually be entertaining these delusions. What are you going to do? Just hike back across no-man's-land, over Grace Mountain, and back into the city that rejected us?"

"Well, something like that. Except we're flying," I say, unfurling my wings and flapping them, "not hiking." Nkosazana's hair flips up in my wings' wake. I extend my clawtips gently toward her. "Care to join me?" Her fingers press into my palm with more certainty than I'd anticipated. I pull her close. She straddles my thigh, and wraps her arms around my neck, prepared for the adventure of a lifetime. I can't deny, I'm hoping this little adventure of ours will bring us closer together—

"Where do I get on?" Chimwe says, butting his way into the thick of my fantasy.

"What?" I ask.

"I'm going, too. If the both of you think this is in any way a good idea, then you're going to need someone sane to accompany you."

"Fine." I nod to my back, and try not to wince at his

heft upon me. I flap my wings, once or twice, preparing for liftoff. But then Nkosazana squeezes me tighter, her cheek pressed squarely against mine, and my heart stutters and goes weak, and my mind . . . oh, my mind skips back to all those nights I'd spent in her bed, how many times we'd nearly been given away by too loud of a moan or too shrill of a squeal, while her father tinkered away in his study, just the next room over. The thrill of being so young, so reckless, so mortal, it sort of *infects* me. We're a couple inches off the ground when my powers give out, and my wings revert to wimpy chicken winglets.

"I swear, that's never happened before," I stutter as I touch back down, feeling like a moth tossed around by a windstorm. "Let me . . . let me get a moment to compose myself." And maybe take a cold shower.

"How about we take a carriage?" Nkosazana offers. "I can get us one. Meet me at the city's edge, right after sundown."

"You know, you really don't have to accompany us," I say to Chimwe as we wait for Nkosazana to arrive. I pace back and forth, wearing my best Auben suit, checking that my hair is symmetrical, and that my skin isn't bunching, and that my claws and fangs are nicely retracted into brittle, useless nails and teeth. "The city needs you."

"The city can run itself now. *You* need me."

I scoff. But he's right. Without him, none of our charmed city's successes would have been possible. It stands to reason that this excursion of ours won't be successful without him either. But still, I can't help but imagine how this would play out with just Nkosazana and me. I practice my smile, wondering if we'd be better off making the hike after all. It'd take forever, but we'd certainly draw less attention than clomping around in an oryx-drawn carriage.

"Hey!" Nkosazana says, startling me, and making the seams of my suit go wonky. I quickly tidy myself, but get lost in the beauty I see before me. There was no clopping of oryx hooves to warn me of her coming, no smell of beastly excrement, only that sweet, brassy smoke and the faint purr of a mechanical engine. It's an oryxless carriage, supple and curving, big bold wheels, chassis boasting warm wood tones that blend into the landscape, and a cloth top made of what looks like chameleon scales. If I wasn't looking right at it, I'd have a hard time believing it was sitting in front of me.

Nkosazana gets out of the carriage, looking so pleased with herself. "Oh, man, they're going to have my hide if we don't get her back before they notice she's missing. We can take her most of the way, then hike the rest. That should leave us with three or four hours to get the goods." She looks up at me, realizes that I'm staring at her. "What?"

"Nothing. It's just reminding me of old times. Us sneaking around your house after everyone had gone to sleep."

"Well, that was a long time ago," Nkosazana says, laying out a map of the city before us. "Right now, we need the power of a god, not the musings of a horny teenager. If you can't handle that, we're calling this off right now."

"No, you're right," I say, groveling like a kicked dog. This is business. I need to step up. I need to focus. "First and foremost, we need to make sure we avoid our twins. Mine especially. You feel even the slightest pain of proximity, we reverse course."

Chimwe nods, pointing at a dot on the map. "We should start here, farthest from the Sanctuary, and work our way around." His finger traces a lazy path between the dozen or so dots marking the locations of subsecular tech, but then abruptly comes to a halt. "Ohhh," he heaves, like someone's kicked the wind out of him. I look at his finger. I recognize the street name immediately, one we'd passed dozens of times on our way to visit Chimwe and his family.

"Oh, what?" asks Nkosazana.

"That proximity thing——" I say "——is probably going to be an issue with that one. That's two streets over from Chimwe's house."

"Well, he can hang behind on that run, right? Shouldn't be an issue," Nkosazana offers, but looking in Chimwe's eyes, I can see it is too late. This change has been much harder on him than he lets on, and separation from Chiso has made his soul brittle. Chimwe and Chiso were bound so closely, so perfectly, that love and hate became indistinguishable and meaningless, and seeing that street name has broken the dam that was holding it all back.

I hang an arm around my cousin-sibling, hoping that our own bond is strong enough that I can temper some of his pain. He shakes beneath me, ever so slightly. "I'm fine. I can stay back," he says, nodding to make us believe his lie, and maybe to make himself believe it as well. Deception, including self-deception, is the most vital tool we'll need to make this plan work, and yet I get the sinking feeling that sneaking our way into the city is going to be the easy part. I should order him to stay home, but at this point, I'm selfish and realize how much I need him with me.

So I say nothing.

We tuck into the carriage, and it eats up the distance between our charmed city and the backside of Grace Mountain, big fat tires rolling over the ragged landscape like a stroll along the beach. We stash the carriage in overgrowth, then look up, preparing for our climb. The darkness presses upon us, but I lead the way, my vision as keen as a night predator's. Nkosazana trudges close behind me, not missing a step, and Chimwe lags, carrying our gear like he's a damned martyr.

I lose my breath when the Sanctuary breaks into view. We are about as far from it as we can get, and yet I feel a twinge in my gut, ever so slight. Maybe it's just nerves. I hope it's just nerves, or our adventure will be over sooner than we'd anticipated. Twenty minutes later, the city bowl itself comes into view. We stop. We stare.

In a little over three years, we'd scraped together a living, thriving city out of nothing but mud and our vices. Here, it seems the city that cast us out has crippled under the weight of its own virtue. A yellow-brown haze carpets the city bowl, buildings have been gutted, and everything is lit by the brazen flames from several smoldering trash heaps. The smell is so awful, so potent that even Chimwe and Nkosazana cover their noses.

It isn't what I'd expected by a long shot. All this time I'd envied the kind of lives they'd have without us, but the Cape practically sits in ruins now.

"Oh, this is so awful," Chimwe says, losing his balance. Nkosazana wedges a shoulder under his armpit and manages to keep them both from toppling down the mountain.

"Don't go feeling sorry for them," I say. "They're the ones that kicked us out."

"Your brother kicked us out," Nkosazana says. "*They* didn't do anything."

"Well, they certainly didn't come looking for us, begging us to come back," I huff, then head down, feet trudging through the undergrowth, my eye on the Eastern Palades. Dassie rats and slithering things skitter out of my way when they hear me coming. I hiss at them, irritated and focused on the task at hand. It takes me a moment for it to sink in, but these prey animals are usually long gone before I can get anywhere near them. I step faster, putting a little extra distance between Nkosazana and me. I'm sure it's probably nothing. Probably. Not worth the worry now, anyway, because all of a sudden, we're in the thick of the city outskirts.

We wear dark cikis, the color of shadows, but still we stand out in this place. Chimwe scoops up a handful of dirt and ash and rubs it over his face, his clothes, his hair, until he becomes one with the filth that surrounds us. We follow suit, then step softly through the dead-quiet streets.

"Here," Nkosazana says, pointing down a street to a building made of skeletal remains of chipped brick and crumbled mortar. I lead the way, keeping my eyes and ears peeled for danger. We step over the rubble that used to be a wall, and into a living room with furniture strewn and covered in soot. The ceiling is caved in, revealing another living room above. "Up there."

"Of course it's up there," I moan. We poke around a bit, but can't find a clear path to any stairs, so this is it.

"Give me a boost," Nkosazana says. I kneel, so relieved that no one asked me to fly up there and get it. If I have to suffer through the humiliation of those little chicken wings one more time . . .

"I've got this," Chimwe says, being so helpful. So annoying. He grabs Nkosazana by the waist. She gasps in surprise as she's hoisted up onto Chimwe's shoulders. She scrambles up into the living room, then looks back down at my cousin-sibling, as impressed as I am aggravated.

"Thanks," she says quickly. "I'll just be a moment. I think I see it." Then she disappears into the darkness.

"She shouldn't be up there alone," I say.

"She probably shouldn't," Chimwe says to me, dragging an upturned sofa under the gape in the ceiling. "I'll go check on her."

"I should be the one checking on her," I say. "What if there's some creeper up there, waiting in the shadows for a victim?"

"Nobody needs to check on me!" comes Nkosazana's voice from the pit of darkness. "I'll be down in a minute."

Chimwe and I stand face-to-face, the tension between us as thick as spit. Maybe he's not tagging along from the goodness of his own heart. "You like her, don't you?" I whisper. "All of a sudden, you're a man, and are having feelings for a woman, and now you want to steal her away from me."

Chimwe sucks his teeth so hard, I'm surprised he has any enamel left. "You know I love and respect you, but you need to stop being such an asshole." Chimwe quickly adds a submissive "my Lord," without breaking the intensity of his stare. "For one, that's not how *any* of this works. Two, my love life, and yes I have one, is not up for discussion. And three, I *have* to be here, running interference because you're so desperate for affection, you can't control your damned powers, and if this continues, it's going to mean bad things for Akinyemi. So just act like the god we need, okay?"

"I thought you were different, Chimwe, but you're just as greedy as the rest of them. What use am I if I can't provide you with raw materials, is that it? You tolerate me as long as your bellies are fed and your city sparkles like a pretty jewel? And you think if I fall in love, I'll be reduced to a sniveling wreck that's no good to anyone?"

"I don't know. Maybe!" Chimwe gestures wildly. "But if it does happen, and if you're truly happy, there's nothing more I'd want for you. Akinyemi would be fine, I suppose. It's just that I worry . . ."

"What?" I demand.

"I worry more about what will happen if you fall *out* of love."

I don't even have time to flinch, when from behind me a deep growling sets my hairs on edge. I jump and let my bones go to dust, landing on four paws, ready to eviscerate what I should have smelled coming. A demon dog. Frothy-mouthed, teeth like gleaming white sabers, eager to drag me back to the hell it's escaped from. I tense my haunches, ready to pounce, only they're not haunches, just Auben's hairy thighs. Slowly, I stand, keeping my eyes locked into those demon-filled ones, seeing myself. What it must see in my eyes is not nearly as menacing, as it approaches, closer and closer. I press up against Chimwe, arms spread wide to protect him.

"I'm going to make a run for it," I say. "While it's distracted, you get Nkosazana out of here."

Chimwe pushes himself in front of me. "No, Lord. I'll distract it. If you've lost your powers . . ."

"I haven't lost them. They're just muddled." We step back farther until the wall catches us, and there is nowhere

else to go except through jaws and teeth. "I just need to concentrate."

But before I can try again, the growling gets deeper.
Darker. This can't be it. The end. I mean, I knew coming
into this that I'd have to face my demons. I just never expected for them to have such awful breath. Teeth gleam,
then they're upon my arm. The pain burns hot, and before
I can scream, there's a flash of gray, and a thud, and a sharp
whine. I clutch my arm and I turn into Chimwe's chest,
flinching at the smell of blood.

Chimwe and I pull back from our shivering embrace.
Look each other over, then down at that demon dog, a large
chunk of concrete wedged right into its neck. We look up,
and see Nkosazana standing solidly on the fulcrum of a lever
made from a wood post that likely used to be a part of someone's bed frame.

"What's wrong with you two?" she asks. "It was a street
dog. Maybe a little rabid. A few years living in the camps,
you learn to handle yourself. Guess you're both just soft
from city living. Can I get a hand, here?"

Chimwe and I step around the pile of bone and fur that
used to be a dog, then help Nkosazana down to the first floor.
She takes one look at my bloody arm, then pulls out a swath
of linen and tosses it at me.

"You're going to want to wrap that up," she says, then
opens her satchel to reveal a metal doodad that looks like
some sort of torture device. "Got the calipers. Fourteen stops
to go. I hope they're all this easy."

"Me, too," I say. And it scares me that I mean it.

We step back into the night, and I can't help but replay
the words Chimwe had said. I've had my fair share of break-

ups, and none of them ever went over well. Temper has never been my friend on these occasions, and I would be lying if I said my fist hadn't put holes in a few unsuspecting walls. What damage would I do with the fist of a god? Fists that can break open the earth and strangle the life out of stars?

By the sixth grab, we stop sneaking, stop gripping the shadows, stop trying to be inconspicuous. The three of us walk down the middle of the street, feet crunching through debris and trash. We're still in the thick of night, and no one is about, save for the odd pile of clothes and dirt scavenging alleyways for scraps. They scatter like feral animals when they see us coming.

"I don't get how things could have gone so bad, so fast," says Nkosazana.

"It doesn't matter. We'll be home soon," I say. "What's next on the list?"

"Three blocks down, two to the left," she says after consulting her map.

Chimwe is uncharacteristically quiet, then I see it, to the right, looming over the buildings that surround it. His father's corporation. The building that was once his future. All that beautiful glass has been busted out, leaving a skeleton of metal.

"You okay?" I ask.

Chimwe nods.

"Do . . ." I pull him into a one-armed hug. "Do you want to go see it? I'm sure we can spare a little time." I glance at Nkosazana.

"We really need to stick to the plan," she says.

"But we're already here," I plead, like she's the god and I'm one of her followers.

"Fine. If you're quick about it," Nkosazana concedes. She pulls her water canteen, takes a long swig, then offers it to me.

I guzzle, washing down the soot that's settled at the back of my throat. "Chimwe, you ready?"

Chimwe doesn't say yes, but he doesn't flinch at the idea either, so I nudge him in that direction, and he goes willingly. Nkosazana hangs back a bit, following at a respectable distance—far enough to give us some privacy, not quite close enough to expose her to additional risks. We make our way into the building, stepping carefully over sea blue piles of glass in the foyer. Clothes piles scatter like hermit crabs, leaving campfires smoldering. We make our way up the stairs, and soon we are standing in my uncle-father's office, glass wall still mostly intact, overlooking despair and darkness. The portraits of Chimwe's family hang on the wall, covered in layers of grime. Chimwe smudges his hand through the family portrait, revealing their smiling faces.

His fingers tremble, then he doubles over abruptly, starts heaving. I bite my lip, wondering if it was wrong to bring him here. He falls to the floor, moaning and writhing in pain.

"Help me up," he rasps.

"No, you rest," I say, taking a step toward our father's gin closet to help him self-medicate. Chimwe snatches my hand.

"Help me up!" he demands this time. So I wedge myself under his arm and lift. He takes a few steps toward the doorway. I look up and see her, clinging to the doorframe like the world is about to slip from under her feet. She's wrapped in layers of dingy cloth, head to toe, but the ones at her face hang loose. Her face is thinner, chin and cheekbones are prominent—not just from the split, but also from malnourishment. I smile, maybe more of a grimace, but she smiles back, even through the pain.

"Hello, cousin," I say to Chiso, when I realize Chimwe is too bent for words.

She exhales something, then tries again. "Cousin," she greets me. Then, "Brother . . ." I swear it sounds like a foreign word coming off her tongue.

"Sister," Chimwe manages, still stepping forward.

"Maybe we should stop here," I suggest. The pain is only getting worse the closer they get, but they'll have none of it. The agony of proximity causes Chimwe to crumple, and there's nothing I can do but watch. He hits the floor and wails out. Chiso presses her hands to her stomach, then totters forth as if a single misstep would cause her entire being to shatter. The determination in her eyes is haunting. Finally, the siblings' fingers touch, but it is not enough. Not after so long. Not after so much. They manage an embrace. There is panting and hissing and moaning and wailing, as if together they are birthing their relationship anew. Chimwe passes out. I run to my cousin, dragging him away to the other side of the room until his shallow breathing strengthens.

"What the hell is going on here?" I ask Chiso. "Buildings are crumbling, people have turned feral, there's trash burning in the streets."

Chiso grimaces, then gropes her way across the floor, and piles herself into our father's office chair. Her dingy wraps smell of garlic and licorice permeating through and through. "It's not trash that's burning," Chiso mutters.

"What is it then?" I ask a moment before the truth turns my throat stone cold. Bodies. They're burning bodies.

"There's been a sickness plaguing us, nearly four months now, but the city was in bad shape well before that. It was our virtues that did us in. Our humility crippled us. People flocked freely to fill the void of menial laborers. Former CEOs worked the mailroom. Accomplished chefs washed dishes. If that wasn't enough, charitable traders started selling our exports at a loss, and the council got so caught up by their unchecked consciences that they niggled over every single possible way some issue could offend someone, somewhere, sometime. Our city was slowly sinking. We needed you. We needed you all along, and we sent you away. Nobody wanted to admit how much of our worth depended on standing upon the backs of those lesser than us."

Chimwe and I flinch at the word *lesser,* like a small bolt of lightning has pierced our hearts. It never used to bother me, but after going so long without hearing it, it sears fresh all over again. Chiso catches herself, looks out at the murky horizon.

"And now Father is sick. This plague has been taking its time with him. I don't know whether to be thankful for that, or resentful. Either way, I can't stand the howls of his pain, so I spend most nights here. I know it's awful of me, leaving him there with Mother, all alone like that, but . . ."

"I want to see him," Chimwe mumbles.

"I hate to break up this little reunion," Nkosazana says, edging into the room and into the conversation like she's always been here. Maybe she hadn't given us as much privacy as I'd thought. "We're already behind schedule. Besides, you can't just walk in there and expose yourself to the sickness like that!"

"He's my father," Chimwe says. "I *have* to see him."

"If you catch the disease and bring it back to Akinyemi . . ." Nkosazana warns.

Chimwe stares at me for a moment. Mind grinding. I shake my head, begging him not to say it, but he does anyway. "Then I'll stay here."

"No," I rasp. Akinyemi needs Chimwe. I need Chimwe. Without him—without his advice, his encouragement, without his fortitude, without his love—there's no way I could have made it through these past few years. "You're mine, too," I tell him. "Nearly as much mine as you are hers."

Chiso's eyes cut to mine. "You know?"

"Know what?" Chimwe asks.

"We're siblings," Chiso says without pomp, as if she were relaying the weather. Terribly bland weather. "You and me and Auben and Kasim."

"I . . . How long have you known?" I ask, dumbfounded.

"I don't know. About since I was really able to look into a mirror. Eight, maybe nine? I studied our features—all four of us—for hours on end, comparing them with the old portraits of Dad hanging at our grandmother's house until I was certain. I worked up the nerve to ask him about it. Got this in return." Chiso turns her chin up, points to a small scar right above the smooth jawline once covered in stubble. "His Gabadamosi ring caught me here. Never brought it up again. To anyone." Chiso's eyes are apologetic, but relieved. I guess it makes sense, looking back. Eight or nine is when Chimwe and Chiso turned from our cousins into our tormentors. I remember the weird staring.

"You should have told me," Chimwe snivels, then locks his eyes with mine. "*You* should have told me." He pulls away from me, like mine is the bigger betrayal. He gets up, makes a pronounced curve away from Chiso as he walks to the door. "I'm going to see my father."

"Wait," Chiso says. "You'll need some of these." She tugs a couple of layers of garlic-wrap off, and the smell . . . I tell you, the smell is not pleasant. A few moldy-looking cloves tumble onto the ground. Chiso wads the rags up and tosses them to her brother. "Wrap that against your skin. Probably best to wet it first. It'll keep the sickness from spreading. When we're back at the house, you'll want to cover your face really well."

Chimwe nods, as if he's just gotten instructions on how to bake a proper milk tart and not to save his life from plague, then disappears through the door. Chiso waits thirty seconds, then follows, leaving Nkosazana and me alone.

"I guess we should finish up, then start on our way back," she says. She takes a sip from her canteen before offering it to me. I shake my head. "We'll have to quarantine ourselves for a few days when we get back, just in case."

I hear what she is saying, but the words breeze between my ears. My father is sick. Dying. His is the fabric that has run silently through my life, at least the human part of it. It sits in tatters now, loose, severed threads that could have been something beautiful that connected us all. I try to hate him for the ill he has brought to our family, but my temper refuses to roil, and this time, in the pits of my bones, I know it has nothing to do with Nkosazana's proximity tempering the god within me.

"Hello?" She knocks on my skull. "Anybody home? I said we need to get the rest of the supplies and ditch this hellhole. We've got four more stops."

I nod. "You've got four more stops. You can handle it yourself, right?"

"What? Wait—" she calls after me, but I'm already bolting toward what's left of a cracked pane of glass overlooking this gray and decrepit city. "You can't—"

"I'll meet you in two hours, back at the school," I yell at her. Glass breaks and rains down with me as I'm falling and the demon within stirs. Right before I kiss pavement, the fog in my mind clears and the skin at my shoulder blades rips apart, making way for wings to unfurl. The winds catch me and soon the clouds embrace me, and I soar above the devastation, back to the home that has brought me so much hurt, and promises that it is not yet done.

The pristine white brickwork has gone gray, drifts of ash bank in the multicolored glass windows. I fold my wings nicely, and out of habit, I wipe my claws on the front mat, but do not bother to hide myself. Aunt Cisse would see straight through the facade anyway, and Father—I *want* him to see me.

I knock. I wait. Chiso and Chimwe are still a good thirty minutes away by foot. Aunt Cisse answers, a mere sliver of the woman she once was, mummified in the same smelly sashes Chiso had worn, cheeks sunken, eyes dull, hair graying with worry at the temples. She tenses at the sight of me, for the briefest of moments, then steps aside to let me in. "I've been allowing the devil into my home all these years. No reason to start denying him now. You're here to see your father, I take it?"

I stare at her, mouth agape. "Are there no secrets left in this family?"

Aunt Cisse sucks her teeth. "They say it's bad luck for the groom to see the bride on the day they get married. You know what's worse luck?" She stares at me. This isn't a rhetorical question.

"What?" I ask, not sure if I want to know.

"The bride seeing the groom atop her sister twenty minutes before she's supposed to walk down the aisle wearing the most spectacular designer gown in front of three hundred of her closest friends and family, that's what. Stood there a whole thirty seconds, and neither one of them noticed. I always thought you were their punishment. No offense."

"None taken," I mutter. The house looked bad from outside, but inside it's a crypt. Quiet. Cavernous. Walls that had born witness to celebrations and fighting sit silently now, like dead bones holding up the structure that once teemed with life.

"He's back there. You should go now, if you want to see him." While he's still alive, she's implying. Aunt Cisse moves to offer me a garlic-scented sash, but decides against it. I'm sure I'm above such illnesses, and if I'm not, I totally deserve to catch it. I'm guessing she thinks the same thing.

I stand still in the doorway, looking around the room— curtains drawn, lights dimmed, curling wisps of smoke rising from shallow bowls filled with obi powder, supposedly meant to deter the demons that brought sickness and death.

"Oh," Aunt Cisse says, following my gaze to the loose incense. "Should I put those out?"

I shake my head. Obi powder is not what is keeping me from crossing over the threshold. It makes me sniffle, but that's about it. I'd inhaled a whole jar of it back in that other life, when all my problems consisted of trying to impress a girl with wu dolls. It's the smell of what lies beneath that ragged, cloying scent that worries me. I smell *him*, my father . . . but it's all wrong. Bent and bruised and battered. Like fruit gone to rot.

I'm trembling as I take his bedside. His eyes are crusted over. At first I think that I am too late, but then his head turns, and he smiles like he's glad to see me. "Finally," he rasps, his voice like wind in the reeds. "Death comes."

"I'm not here for that," I say. "It's me. Auben. Your son. This is what I am. This is what the truth looks like."

"No . . ." My father wails. Flails. "Icy Blue," he screams. "Take me! Take me!" Aunt Cisse runs in and holds his wrists. Father is frail, but there is more fight left within him than I'd guessed. He pants like a rabid mongrel, then bays into the bitter full-moon night.

"Can you hold him?" Aunt Cisse says. My hands swap with hers, and she wets cloths and presses them to his feverish skin until the baying subsides. Finally, he slips into a deep sleep, then his breathing shallows. His pulse goes thread thin. He no longer needs restraining, and yet, I can't let go.

"He was the first one to hold you, you know," my aunt says, not bothering to look up from her nurse duties. "The midwife wiped you off, took one look at you, and handed you to him before going back to deliver Kasim. I stopped hating him in that moment. Good Grace, the way he smiled at you. You were perfection. The way you glowed. The way *he* glowed. It was all so serene, so . . . so perfect, and I knew no child I could give him would match the intensity of that moment. The mind does certain things to protect itself. To delude itself. I turned my blame to Pabio. If he hadn't been running late to the ceremony, his presence would have tempered your father's lechery. I hated him more for it each and every day."

"Why are you telling me all of this?" I ask my aunt Cisse. Never in my life had I seen her go two sentences without breaking into a yelling fit.

She looks at me, smiles balefully, then coughs daintily into a lace handkerchief. She opens it up to reveal a spot of blood. I shake my head. And with that, she steps closer to me, tips up onto her toes, and she kisses me full on. I try to hold it back, but the cold slips over my lips, then over hers. Her body goes rigid in my arms, her shallow breath turns to crystals at the edges of her mouth. I move her into bed, next to my father.

Then I sit with him for half an hour, pressing cold towels to his forehead as he mumbles incoherently, interspersed with writhing and howling and spitting. I cannot let my cousin see him like this. I cannot let this image be the last thing Chimwe remembers of his father. Our father. My uncle Yeboah, the man who first held me in his arms, who loved me in the best way he could. I break his fever with a single kiss.

I'm still standing over him when I hear Chimwe's cries. "What did you do to them?" he says, pounding his fists into my back. "What did you do?"

Chiso hovers in the doorway for a moment, then decides to risk the pain. She's at her mother's side, fingers crunching the ice crystals formed over her skin, hoping her touch would force life back into that cold, cold corpse. Chiso crumples from the pain of proximity, and Chimwe falls to my feet, begging me to fix it. To put things back to how they were.

"We have nothing!" Chimwe cries. But he is wrong. They still have each other. I cannot give life, but I can re-arrange it. I raise my hands, feel intently for the gossamer strings that tie Chiso and Chimwe together. They are fine, much finer than the webs that hold the universe together. A billion strands could take up the fraction of the width of spider's silk. I feel for them, and then I begin to knot them, weaving them together with such intricacy that no one, not even Kasim, would be able to unravel them again. There is screaming, and lots of it, some of it coming from my own agape mouth, but when I am done, when the fabric Chiso and Chimwe share is whole and right again, I exhale, and fall to the floor.

Half-lidded and drained of energy, I watch them as they realize what I've done. Immediately, they hug each other, making me aware of my own tattered fabric. I feel a loss. Chimwe was almost mine. Almost. But almost is not enough. Not for em, nor for me.

Sooner or later, I will have to face Kasim.

I can't cry. It's not some dumb macho thing, either. I hurt like hell right now, my heart rubbed raw. My father, gone. My aunt, too. I still taste her on my lips, breath foul from worry and regret and bitterness. Just traces of my saliva had frozen her over, head to toe, but death by Icy Blue's kiss pales in comparison to the schoolyard rhymes about the damage my tears cause. Of course, they might not be true. But they probably are.

So I repress. Pretend it's not that big of a deal. Just a couple more deaths to add to my tally. I whistle as I walk the desolate streets to keep the images at bay. The rheumy eyes swollen in their sockets like marbles. The pattern of burst blood vessels like red lace doilies sitting upon their skin. The sound of icy slush forcing its way through their veins. Despite the risk of being noticed, I whistle a little louder.

When I arrive at our old school, I cringe at how much it's degraded. The windows are boarded up. The tangle reeds Nkosazana and I used to sneak kisses behind have turned to rotten mush. The awnings have collapsed in several places. The door is ajar. Nkosazana must have gotten here first. Inside is dark and musty, rodents scatter past my feet.

Past the doors to the drama department, a chill sets my arm hairs on end. Of course, I dare not go in, but the entirety of this school, the entirety of this whole city reminds me of the demon-studded disaster that happened backstage that day with Ruda, so long ago now. I hurry past, the clack of my loafers echoing through the halls.

"Auben?" I hear Nkosazana's voice, and immediately my fears are laid to rest. She's calling from the cafeteria. I duck inside the double doors, and enter the gray expanse of shadows. Tables where students once clamored for a seat to inhale whatever slop the servers had tossed upon their trays now sit uncomfortably vacant.

Nkosazana takes one look at me and laughs. "Oh my, where did you find this?" She touches the sleeve of my school ciki, but it dissolves away, revealing smooth human flesh beneath. She withdraws her hand, watching curiously as clouds of silk threads reform my sleeve again.

I shrug. "I don't know. It felt right, I guess. For old time's sake."

Nkosazana grins. "Too bad you couldn't do that trick back in school. Would have saved your mother a fortune in uniform fees."

"Nah, she would have just found something else to complain about. It was rough being her son. I can't imagine how awful it'd be to work with her."

"She's . . . *headstrong*," Nkosazana says after the slightest hesitation.

"In the same way a typhoon is headstrong," I laugh. "If you tell her she's being stubborn, she takes it as a compliment!"

"Ha! Remember the time she decided to drop her voice an octave because she thought she'd be taken more seriously, and she went hoarse after three days?"

"Yes! Not complaining. It was nice having a break from being yelled at for leaving the mafi carton out on the counter. 'All I'm asking is for you boys to put it back in the icebox so it doesn't spoil!'" I say, mimicking Mother's horrid falsetto. I've got tears rolling down my cheeks, and Nkosazana's laughing so hard, she's holding her side. Her guard is down, and it's really nice, just enjoying her company.

"Oh, honey, come here," she says, pulling a handkerchief from her pocket and dabbing at the corners of my eyes. But then my mind starts churning, memories align, and I stop laughing.

"Wait a minute. That happened before I met you."

Nkosazana blinks a few times, then stiffens. "I *know*. You told me all about it. Went into so much detail, it was like I was there."

"I'm sure I didn't," I say. Nkosazana used to always change the subject when my mother came up. Never cared to even meet her, even though I'd met her parents a dozen times.

"I promise *you did*," Nkosazana says resolutely, then pats her duffel bag sitting on the lunch counter, suddenly all business. "I got all the items on the list. So did things go okay with your dad?"

"It went okay," I lie, trying to ignore the weird air now between us.

"If you want to talk about it . . ."

"I don't. I just need to rest for a moment. I'm famished." I turn from her, and rummage through the empty kitchen cabinets, finding nothing but cobwebs and dust. The whole place has been scavenged over. Then I see it. An old dented can tucked beside the industrial ovens. I run to it, wipe my hand through the dusty label. Curry Paste, it reads. A year and a half past its expiration. I flex a claw and turn the lid to metal shards. I dip in, slurp it down, ravenous. Like a beast.

"Auben!" Nkosazana cries.

I straighten up, alert. Suddenly aware that she'd called me several times. I stare at her.

"What?" I say, realizing how foolish I must look. "Sorry, did you want any? It's just paste. Only gone a bit off."

She shakes her head then nods toward me. I look down at myself, pristine ciki now covered in bright red sauce, like I'd been in some sort of bloodbath. *Blood.*

"I'm not craving blood," I tell her. No craving for blood,

but the hunger is still as savage, like someone is trying to rip my stomach through my throat.

"What does that mean?" she asks.

My hand is back in the can before I can answer. I scoop a few more times, but then find it easier to chug the whole thing. Hunger releases its grip, just enough for me to compose myself. Nkosazana comes to my aid with a stack of napkins, carefully wipes my face, my lips, and uses several more to clean my clothes. She laughs as she wipes, cloth briefly going to skin everywhere she touches. Devil turning human.

Everywhere she touches. I look down, thread clouds swirling between my thighs. All those thorns and barbs that made physical intimacy between us impossible are gone, replaced with a respectable shaft of thin, veined skin. Her hand lingers, a moment too long, then she licks her napkin and goes after a spot of sauce on my lapel.

"I thought you wanted to stay focused on the job," I manage to eke out as fabric returns, along with the barbs it conceals. *Concealed*. It's not doing such a great job of it now.

"Job's over. Or nearly," she says. "Remember how we used to talk about sneaking back here, and you know . . ."

"What, eating our weight in samp and beans?" I tease.

"No!" She pinches me in the side. "You know what I'm talking about."

"Stealing all the hairnets on mala mogodu day so we'd have to go off campus to eat? Spiking an entire tub of that drab beef stew with chili powder?" I make the mistake of looking into the serving tray nearest me. The carcass of a dead rat is curled up in one corner. I cringe, and when I look back at Nkosazana, her shirt is off, and I feel like I'm not the only one that's capable of turning clothing to vapor. She holds her weight like a woman now, fuller, rounder. Softer in the places that need to be soft, and firmer in those where life in the camps demands it.

"We've still got a couple hours before we need to worry about daybreak." Her hand touches my chest. She presses until I'm backed up against the iceboxes. She eases her body up against mine, and all of a sudden, I'm Auben all over. Naked, fragile, and half-starved of love as well.

Hands that have pulled the tethers of the moon tremble at the magnificent curve of her breasts. Skin that has withstood the fires of suns burns hot where her flesh touches mine, and the vacuum of space could only wish to be as cold as when her lips pull away from me, again, again, and again, in a rhythm that throbs to the beat of the universe. Expanding ever farther into the nothing. Faster. And faster. And . . .

Time stops. Days, weeks, a millennium passes in that moment, our bodies entwined, a million thoughts pass through my mind, and every single one of them obsesses over how much I love Nkosazana. How could I not? The only person in the world who could make me feel—

This.

Damned.

Good.

And not just here, about to cross the precipice. I mean, all the time. Forever.

"I love you!" I scream, grit my teeth, clinch my eyes, as gravity returns, and all the laws of nature with it. The ride down is a swift one. I tingle all over. Splayed over the tile floor like a puddle of jelly, I take a moment to savor the feeling, then open my eyes. Nkosazana's already up, tucking her shirt into her pants.

"That was nice," she says with a wink.

"Nice?" I ask. There must be a fair amount of disappointment in my voice, because she smiles warmly at me.

"*Very* nice," she says.

Yeah, okay. I'll roll with it. "It was pretty good." I peel myself up, resting back on my elbows. I take a deep breath, and roll my skin into the drab gray swatches of fabric that Chiso had worn. "Just like old times."

"Definitely." She nods to herself, eyeing me suspiciously. I tense, puff my chest, trying not to look like a kicked pup, but I'm failing so hard. "Wait . . . you're not . . . *into* me, are you?"

"No, I mean. I just thought. I dunno. Maybe?" Hope springs.

"Auben Mtuze," she says my name, my old name, like it's a cuss. She smiles, and no longer in a rush, comes over to me, looks me square in the eyes. "Don't tell me becoming a god has softened your heart."

"I've come to some realizations. About what's important."

"Like?" She arches a brow.

"Like family. Friendship. Love."

"Friendship, I'll take. I like you, Auben. I really do. I always have." She pecks me on the cheek. "I've gotta piss," she says, and like that, she's off.

A thousand glass shards pierce my heart, searing pain for a long moment, but it goes completely numb. Breathe. Breathe, damn it. I force the breath out of me, my eyes burning red-hot in their sockets. I tremble all over. I try to restrain my temper, but soon the earth starts humming along with me.

BREATHE.

In and out, in and out. I think about what Chimwe had

said, fearing what would happen to a god whose love goes unrequited. But eir fear was unfounded. I can control this. Light fixtures above sway like pendulums. Doors to empty cabinets swing on their hinges. Layers of dust and dirt stir up into the air.

Fucking breathe, Auben, I grate through my mind like a saw, until finally the tremors subside. See. Nothing to fear. It's still hurts to get rejected, but at least the seas are not boiling off, and the sky's not burning.

Nkosazana's bag has fallen off the counter from all the commotion, zipper busted, contents strewn wide. I grit my teeth, hoping that my infatuation hasn't ruined all that delicate equipment. I check the devices over, they're dented, busted, rusted. Not something a little fall would have caused. It's all scrap, not the precision-crafted tools I'd expected.

"Auben, what was—" Nkosazana says as she runs back into the cafeteria. She sees what I'm holding. Stops where she stands.

"What is this?" I demand of her. "It's just a bag of junk."

"It's nothing you need to worry over," she says, then bends down and starts shoving the busted tools back into her bag. Finally, when it's all packed, she takes another swig of water before offering me her canteen.

"No, thanks. My bladder is about to burst as it is."

"Better take care of that then. It's a long ride back."

"Yeah. Maybe I'd better," I somehow manage to say this without belying the burning suspicion braiding through my mind.

We chat the entire trip back, wind whipping at our faces as the skitter-scat engine rumbles away from the ass-end of Grace Mountain. I laugh when Nkosazana laughs, sigh when she sighs, blink when she blinks. We connect on a deeply platonic level. It's like we're best friends. Like we're siblings. Like we're the same person. I absorb the cadence of her stories, feel the tension of her voice right before she delivers the punch line to a joke, calculate the angles of her hand gestures.

"Auben, I'm really glad we had this time together," she says as the familiar shape of Akinyemi rises above the horizon. The oryxless carriage slows.

"Auben, I'm really glad we had this time together," I mimic. She looks at me, smolders.

"Why are you mocking me?" she says.

"Why are you mocking me?" I repeat, putting my hand on my hip to match hers.

"Funny. Here I was thinking you were beyond these childish games."

I grin at her. Finally, finally . . . I get the rules of the game she's playing, and I'm about to rewrite them. I get out of the carriage, and round the back where Nkosazana had stuffed her bag. There's a big gold lock. I put my fist to it and extend a claw, slice it to pieces. The trunk pops open, revealing a nice, velvet-lined compartment, just big enough to fit a body in.

"What are you doing?" Nkosazana screams at me. She jumps out of the carriage, takes one look at me, and faints.

Nkosazana struts into the subsecular warehouse, bag slung over her shoulder like she's bearing the spoils of war. The whole place swarms with goggle-eyed machinists bent over their work, torches sparking, saws buzzing, the steady churn of steam fogging up the room. She sees Enna Zeogwu inspecting the welding seams on a giant machination, a spider-like thing come to life from hunks of metal. A large furnace burns where a mouth should be, twin red-hot eyes and steam petering out from the smokestacks.

"We still need more power," Enna Zeogwu says, looking into the furnace, the lenses of her goggles reflecting the fire inside. "If we can barely scrape together enough fuel for this prototype, what hope do we have for a fleet? A four-person team with a pickax and an oryx-drawn cart could harvest more wood and ore than this contraption!"

Standing fully upright, the machination does a slow dance on its mighty haunches while the undercarriage pivots, revealing a thick protrusion that neatly houses industrial-sized drills, saws, and hammers.

"We're working on it, Enna Zeogwu!" says one of the other machinists.

Nkosazana approaches the leader of the sect, ready to share her bounty and claim her congratulations on the collection of junk she'd reclaimed from the Cape, but a hand comes down on her shoulder and spins her around.

"What are you doing?" Ruda whispers. Her is hair thinly plaited and pulled up into a knot atop her head, and she's wearing the same blue-gray worksuit the other machinists are sporting, streaked over by three different hues of grease stains. Nkosazana loses her balance, but Ruda pulls her back up. "Whoa, there. Do you need to sit down? You look a little dizzy."

"Ruda? What are you doing here?"

"Saving your ass from ruining four years' worth of work, that's what! Were you just about to hand everything over to Enna Zeogwu?" Ruda doesn't wait for an answer and whisks Nkosazana away to a dark corner. "Did you get it all?"

Nkosazana nods.

"All five of them?" Ruda arcs an awestruck brow.

Nkosazana nods again, sets the bag atop a worktop covered in metal shavings, and then zips open the bag, revealing the rusted instruments.

Ruda sucks her teeth. "Not those." She grabs the bag, dumps the contents onto the floor, then rifles through an internal pocket. She pulls out a metallic envelope and looks inside. "Saliva, blood, tears." She pauses. "Urine. Semen . . . I'm not even going to ask how you got those." She stares into Nkosazana's eyes—stares hard, too hard, as if she's penetrating the privacy of her very thoughts. "You know you didn't have to. Blood and saliva work just fine."

"What can I say?" Nkosazana boldly lifts a brow. "Dedicated to the cause."

"Lwazi!" Ruda says in a harsh whisper. Seconds later, Nkosazana and Ruda's father is there, armed with a leaded apron full of scientific instruments.

"You got them?" he asks, taking the metallic envelope and reaching in with a pair of tongs. He pulls out five handkerchiefs, each drenched in body fluids that glow blue-white. Ruda and Lwazi don their goggles and stare as Lwazi takes readings with a metered device.

"I think we've done it. Definitely potent enough now," he says, then he looks Nkosazana up and down. "Are you okay? You look like you've seen a demon."

Ruda snorts. "Lwazi! She's been through enough."

"It wasn't my idea for her to go around sleeping with the

devil!" he whispers, and suddenly there's a pained look in his eyes before he grabs the envelope and rushes away.

"Ugh," Ruda says, rolling her eyes. "He played the role of our father so long, now he's really acting like one. I'm just glad we're done with all of that, pretending to be those awful sisters. And when Enna Zeogwu sees what we've done, how we've solved all of our power problems forever, she won't be able to overlook us anymore."

"Singletons . . ." Nkosazana breathes.

"Changing the world for the better! But you know, if I did have a sister, I'd like for her to be just like you. Confident. Charming. More dedicated to the cause than anyone has a right to ask."

Nkosazana wraps her arms around Ruda, pulls her body in tight. Natural, at first, but then it stretches on too long. Much longer than a hug should last between sisters. Between artists of deception. Between anybody, really.

"Come on," Ruda says as she struggles to free herself. "Let's go give Lwazi a hand with the distillation before he wrecks everything." She tries to laugh off the awkwardness, but makes the mistake of looking into Nkosazana's eyes. "What, why are you staring at me like that?" Her lips open into a perfect circle, about to scream a name, but Nkosazana's mouth is upon them so fast, Ruda doesn't get the chance to utter a syllable. The kiss is wild, deep. The flavor is nutty and sweet, sucked over the tongue, and smooth going down, like a good malt. Exactly as expected, only it ends entirely too soon.

There is nothing left to taste but ice.

Someone screams. Nkosazana startles, bumps Ruda who falls back, a sculpture of pure perfection right up until the instant she collides with the floor. Millions of ice shards explode on the concrete.

In the span of seconds, the room's temperature drops to below freezing. Nervous puffs of smoke rise from the sect workers' mouths, all eyes trained on me. On all the facets of my godhood. They shiver. Teeth chatter. Probably from the cold.

"Mother!" I cry out. The entire building shakes, metal clatters, gear stacks topple, people are brought to their knees.

She comes to me, her white lab coat flapping behind her like a full-length cape, pristine, despite the piles of coke coals and black dust littering the entire floor. She doesn't bat an eyelash at the beast standing before her.

"Why, Mother?" is all I can manage. All I can say without turning into a stream of tears.

She looks down at the splinters of crystal ice that used to be Ruda. "I warned her not to get too close," she says solemnly.

"Just like you refused to get too close?" I say. "Like you refused to be our mother, and for what? Because you need a little bit of my blood to power your big, powerful resource-fetching machination?"

Something like compassion flashes in her eyes, something I can barely remember from our early childhood, but it passes as she covers them up again with her bulky goggles. "We don't need your blood," she says. "We just need you to stay out of our way. We've fought against the religious sects so long, they've stifled our work. Plotted against our advancements. Imagine where we'd be as a people if we'd been allowed to delve into science without restrictions! We'd be walking on the moon instead of staring at it through tele-scopes."

"But I encourage science! Akinyemi is built upon science."

"True, but your celestial manipulations wreak havoc on our data. You, son, were chaos as soon as you erupted from my womb."

I shake my head. "Aunt Cisse said I was perfection." I hold my late aunt's words in front of me like a shield.

Mother's mouth twitches at the mention of Cisse's name. I've struck a nerve. "*Chaos.* From that first moment I held you in my arms, I knew what you were. I should have told the sect then, but I was stubborn. I thought I could change you, or at least stop you from becoming what you were meant to be."

"You could have killed us, Mother. When we were weak and vulnerable. But you couldn't because you needed us. You loved us."

"I was doing my job. And you can't kill a god. Only break their vessel, if you've got someone foolish enough, someone strong-headed enough to try. But the souls of gods would only find another vessel." Mother's hand hovers over the womb Kasim and I had once shared. "Then things started happening. Bathwater started turning ice-cold, sitters complained about bite marks and blackouts. I put you and Kasim through Discernment early, and had the practi-tioner do everything he could to prevent you from accessing your powers. Then I spent the next twelve years hoping it'd worked."

"What about the bedtime stories? What about when you tucked us in at night and made us our favorite meals for our birthday dinners? Was that just a part of the job?"

She stares, says nothing.

"You loved us!" I yell at her. "You love me, and you need me." I plead with everything I have in me. I hold out one arm and use a claw to slice from the inside of my elbow to my wrist. A blinding flash of white light spills from the wound, causing all the machinists to shield their eyes, even those with protective goggles. Mother doesn't look away.

"Take my blood," I tell her. "Take all of it. Power every machination in this whole wretched city. Just tell me you need me." Before I know it, I'm standing in a pool of molten blood.

Mother steps back, maybe from the searing heat, maybe because she's repulsed by the thought of being near me. "I think you should leave now," she says.

I go, feet pounding the earth, dirt and stone splitting with each step. There's so much blood, so much it doesn't even seem possible that this body has contained it all, but it keeps flowing down behind me.

Above hangs the moon—the impossibly distant moon Mother would rather coddle than spend an instant thinking about the son who's been right here just out of arm's reach his whole life. I stare hard at the moon, connect with it, the gossamers in my mind a terrible, tangled mess. My temper bucks and a violent charge whips through me, a soundless explosion so intense, I bite down on my fist to keep my teeth from shattering.

When I look up, the sky is changed. Most of the moon is now a haze of insignificant dust that used to make up something magnificent, something seemingly impervious and unexpectedly fragile.

My temper has not been mollified and nothing is safe

from my touch. I breathe in, breathe out—tethers humming at my fingertips like angry wasps, waiting impatiently for my next command. Those commands are foreign, and wrong, and much, much too easy to give. It is truly unfair that the only person capable of healing my fury is the one who has given me my deepest, coldest scars. Still, I must find him, and if I can keep calm enough not to rip him to shreds, then maybe he can help.

I stand at the tip of Grace Mountain, at the doors of the Sanctuary—or what used to be the doors of the Sanctuary. They've come unhinged, centuries-old tarred wood burnt down to a collection of blackened splinters. Inside is worse. Scattered light shines through broken stained glass. Enormous defting sticks lie strewn across the pulpit, like an entire forest toppled by a storm.

But I don't see Kasim. Don't *feel* him anywhere. I keep looking, beneath overturned pews, behind broken doors. I yell out Kasim's name over and over, my words echoing back at me, so angry and bitter. Maybe he's not here, but I do have one way I can reach him. I'm weak, dizzy from losing so much blood, but I still find the strength to maneuver the defting sticks. They're charred and burnt like the rest of this place, but most of the gold-inset inscriptions are legible.

"Kasim, if you can hear me, tell me where you are." I look dubiously at the sticks. I'd had enough trouble with the defting trainers, but I have to try at least. I tent two sticks together, and they come easily to a point. They stand solidly, to my surprise, but the second pair I set opposite the first nearly collapse on top of me. I try again. And again. I get the feeling that someone is watching, and I'm creeped out by the gaggle of broken, battered zekwenusi statues staring back at me with their menacing marbled eyes. I swallow back my unease and try the sticks again with no luck.

The original pair stands dutifully, though. Not even a hard shove disturbs it. I step up onto an overturned pew and dust off the gilded script inset where the sticks meet.

"Stacks," it says.

"Stacks?" I say to myself. If I could stack these things any higher, I wouldn't be standing here, wondering where the hell my brother is hiding. If I had more of the message . . . but, but what if this was it? What if this was Kasim's answer? "Stacks. Like library stacks?"

"Shhh. The walls have ears," says a voice from behind me. "Even burnt-out ones."

On pure instinct, I turn, flex claws that refuse to erupt. Bare fangs that would impress no one. Sesay stands there, face haunting me, a reminder of her betrayal a final wound that my heart can't bear. I'm too weak to slice her to pieces, but my hands still work, and are strong enough to squeeze the life out of a traitor. So I snatch her by the throat.

She squeaks at me. I squeeze harder, and glare into the face that betrayed me.

"I'll take you to him," she manages to rasp as her fingernails pry futilely against my grip. "No tricks this time."

"Why should I trust you?" I demand, but there's no response, just her mouth gasping for air, and those once too-cute eyes bulging and bloodshot. I wait another second, another. Nothing she can say will erase her treachery—the memory of her pulling out her doubt signet, of those incantations in that awful, ancient tongue—but finally reason strikes me as I realize it'll be nearly impossible to get answers from a corpse. I release her, and she falls to the ground, sucks in rapid breaths until she regains composure.

"We need to wait until sunset." She springs to her feet and steps over to the defting sticks. "Here, help me push this over. Don't want to leave any evidence." She leans against a stick. Finally, it topples, stirring up dust and ash.

"Stay here if you want. I'm leaving now," I tell her.

"You can't just walk out there, traipsing down the mountainside! If someone sees you . . ." she says, eyeing the blood still weeping from my arm. "Besides, if you don't mind my saying, you look like you could use a little rest."

That's true enough. The silence stretches, and I decide to pass the time by plotting my revenge on her, each iteration of her death more calculated and cruel.

"Auben," she finally says, eyes digging into mine, as if she could feel the thoughts of her sour heart being squeezed like a lemon in my fist. "I feel like I owe you an explanation—"

"You don't owe me anything," I snap back at her. I strum nonexistent tethers, wishing the earth would swallow her whole.

"I deceived you, but I thought . . . I thought I was doing the right thing, following Kasim. But then, we kind of connected, you know? You accepted me, I accepted you. Neither of us even flinched." She pauses for a response I have no intention of giving, then she continues. "You know what it's like, being from the comfy. I already had one strike against me. And Daki had two, being a lesser twin."

I growl at her, low, deep, and throaty.

"That's not my term, it's society's. I couldn't care less how many vices a person has."

Heat buds in my eyes. My jaw clenches tightly, trying to contain my anger, but my tongue refuses to let her privilege pass. "That's because you've never had to care! You don't know what it's like to be constantly underestimated, written off. Completely ignored just because of what's branded into your arm!"

"True, but I can imagine." She casts her gaze down to her feet, twiddles her thumbs. "Society isn't exactly kind to kigens either."

Oh, yeah. There was that. Cute little Sesay. The split has changed her, but differences are subtle—the added musculature, the set of her bones, the pitch of her voice. But when half the population is kigen, you get good at spotting these things, or else you get used to getting corrected, or yelled at, or worse. She was born a kigen, but even now with all her female genes back with Daki, Sesay still exudes her girlish charm. Maybe there's more to self than science.

Lesser twins, kigens, comfy stock, singletons, we all suffer silently, we all go ignored. It should be easier for me to empathize with her, but no matter how hard I try, all I can see are the lines drawn between us.

"It wasn't always like this, you know," Sesay says. "Back before religion, before vice and virtue. Maybe even before gods, the genders were fluid, each person a drop in an ocean with their own way to be. I've read some of the old greats of literature—Okpara, Balik—"

"Don't you dare say Biobaku," I grumble.

"Heh, his work is derivative at best. He copied off Nambota, who copied off Naidu. You go read Naidu, and tell me you don't wish you could have been alive then, when humanity was a simple extension of nature—before lines were drawn

between men and women and kigen, before borders defined
who we were, before schools told us what we should be."

"It does sound nice . . ." I bite back the smile trying to
worm its way onto my face. "We have to find a way to get
back to that sort of life, but that doesn't mean I don't still
hate you," I growl at her. "But it's for what you did, not who
you are."

"I know. This isn't right, us being separated from our
twins. You can't even imagine how sorry I am." She bites her
lips, then looks up at me with those innocent eyes.

I can't take it anymore. If I sit here, listening to her
babble, I'll start trusting her again, and I can't afford that.
"Come on, it's time to go," I demand.

"But it's not dark—"

"We're going."

We stick to ditches and trenches and tunnels as the sun
starts to set. The debris of the moon becomes more notice-
able, stretching out wider and wider, like wings straddling
the chunk that's still intact. I keep my temper gripped tight,
because even though I can no longer break moons, I can
still break bones, and every bit of me still insists that I
teach Sesay one last lesson. But she proves true, leading
us through overgrown shrubbery, through another drainpipe, up through a copper floor grating and into the long-
abandoned stacks of the Gabadamosi library.

It'd been dusty before, but it's caked in filth now. Gone
are the patrons, the acrobrarians. Sesay lets loose a whistle.
One comes back from the rafters. I look up, see him. I take a
few steps nearer and I feel him.

"That's close enough," he calls out. His voice is a rasp,

but still jovial, and I can tell from here he is weak. Weaker than me. He's exhausted, starving, and dehydrated, and I can almost *feel* how his bones are poking at his skin. "Sesay told me about your handiwork with the moon. Temper got the best of you?"

"Something like that," I mumble. "What about you? You look like shit."

"Being Grace is hard work. And I apparently kind of suck at it." He looks off for a moment, caught in a web of thought, then laughs the laugh of a fool. "I think I'm as awful at healing as you are at killing."

I'm not *so* awful at it. My most recent kill swamps my mind, and I grit my teeth. I dare not tell him of Ruda's fate. He's precariously perched up on a third-story shelf, and if he lost his balance . . . I shake the thought. Why the hell should I care about what happens to him?

"We're pathetic, aren't we?" Kasim says. "I tried to keep up, to keep the plague at bay, but there were just so many people asking for so much. Humans are just so fragile and needy." He looks down at Sesay. "No offense."

Sesay shrugs, and turns her attention to flipping through the pages of her giant three-ring binder, the very same one she'd accused me with so long ago. I scowl in her direction, but it goes unnoticed and unappreciated. "You're sure we're safe here?" I ask.

"For now. No one goes looking for god in a library. Plus, it's nice here. Quiet. No more prayers to deal with, at least."

"You answered mine," I say.

"I was holding out, focusing all my energy listening for you. Clinging to hope that you'd reach out." And as bad as he looks, I'd guess that stubbornness nearly destroyed him. Kasim can cling to whatever hope he wants. Still won't buy him an ounce of pity from me.

"Well, I'm here now," I say. "I've got nowhere else to be. Mother . . . she wants nothing to do with me. All she cares about is that machination of hers. You know, she knew about us, all along. She admitted to paying some guy to swap our greed and charity so we wouldn't discover our powers. Sesay knows about him."

"Sall Iweala is the man who performed your Discernment," Sesay says with a nod. "His registers were submitted as evidence during his trial, and I got ahold of them. Of the hundred and twenty-seven Discernments he performed that year, only one of them lasted longer than an hour. Yours." She looks pointedly at me, like she's waiting for me to connect the dots. Aunt Cisse's words come flowing back to me, how I was born so perfect.

"Mother said she had him do everything he could. Do you think he switched *all* of our vices and virtues?" I ask. "All of them *except* greed and charity?"

"I suspect he switched a lot more than that. Eleven hours is how long your Discernment lasted. I thought it was a mistake on the paperwork. But now . . ."

"Maybe that's how we ended up with a prayer-intolerant Grace and a blood-repulsed Icy Blue," I say, trying to wrap my head around the possibility. I've spent so much time denying Grace, hating Grace, forsaking Grace, that the thought of actually *being* him has me grasping at my vices just to make sure they're still all there.

"Shit," Kasim says. "We were doomed from the start. All that holier-than-thou bullshit I pulled all those years. I was awful to you. Judging your every vice when the whole time it was me who—"

"Hey, I've seen vices build an entire city, one brimming with innovation and community. We both made mistakes." The words slip out of my mouth so effortlessly. I'd been clutching my anger so tightly, it takes a moment to realize that all this time, I'd been so desperate to finally let it go. A weight lifts from my chest. Kasim smiles, and kicks his feet like a child, like he'd jump down and hug me if he weren't sure the resulting proximity pains would kill us both. Something dark sweeps over my mind, though, the image of me lying in a pile of broken glass, Kasim's breath still hot and wrong against my lips, shivering so hard, I could have brought all the stars crashing down on us. It still cuts, deeper than I'll ever admit, but I can't hold on to those other wrongs, either, not if we're going to restart our brotherhood anew. "I forgive you for everything . . . including Ruda." Her name comes out in a pained rasp.

Kasim stops kicking, looks down at me with a smoldering of temper in his eyes. "What do you mean, 'For Ruda'?"

I bite my lip, feeling like coming here was a big mistake. "Never mind. Forget I said anything."

Kasim shakes his head. "No, I want to know what you mean by that." He leans forward, his balance even more precarious now. "Because I can certainly tell you why *I* forgave *you* for Ruda. I was there, Auben, sitting in the back of the auditorium during her audition, arms full of flowers. I was going to ask her out. When she didn't come out from the dressing room afterward, I went backstage looking for her. I saw you, heard how she laughed at me. The revulsion on her face when you mentioned my name killed a part of me."

I recall my compulsion that night, how my will to kiss her had bent so hard, so suddenly, and how it would have broken completely if I hadn't jabbed a rusty nail through my palm. But it wasn't Icy Blue driving that time. "You used your mind tricks and tried to make me kiss her. And you knew . . . *knew* what that would do!"

"I wanted to destroy her, and you in that moment. I'm not proud of my actions. It took a long time, but I built up my distance. I forgot about Ruda, and what she did to my heart. Maybe I had to put some distance between me and you as well, but I forgave you. Then I buried myself in virtues. Everything I could do to live, breathe, and eat for the good of all."

I close my eyes, realizing now what I'd done. What I'd undone.

"Then when I saw Ruda strut into Kalukenzua House . . . for a split second, I was fooled. Auben, that split second was the absolute best moment of my life. I thought I'd locked away my heart from everyone, but I swear, it nearly burst out of my chest. And my pants, I won't even mention what was going on in my pants, but I shed my virtue in that instant. By the time I realized the truth, it was too late. What you unleashed, my dear brother, could not be put back into its box. And now here you are, forgiving me . . ." His eyes flash, and suddenly he's lurching toward me, falling through the air. I'm caught between the urge to protect myself and to soften his fall, but I don't get the chance to do either as the pain of proximity ratchets up, causing me to crumple. Kasim screams. His torso lands on mine, his limbs thump against concrete. I hear something break, and when he looks up, the pain I see runs so much deeper than fractured human bone.

Sesay gets up, tries to pull us apart, but she's swatted away. We grapple, bite, scratch. He pounds his fist into ribs I'm sure are already broken. We're bitter, petty. Fighting like five-year-olds, only I'm damn sure hugs and candy aren't going to smooth this one over.

There is a boom like thunder that shakes the sense back into me, and suddenly it's snowing. No, not snow. Tiny bits of paper. Kasim and I stop struggling long enough to see the gaping hole in the bookshelf inches away from our heads. Sesay stands nearby, mouth in a perfect O. I follow her gaze down the stacks, and see Nkosazana's father, or the man who'd pretended to be her father, holding a big brass gun. Wisps of smoke curl up from the end of a barrel so thick, so long, it's more like a portable cannon. He braces himself, steadies his footing, then fires again. We scramble around the endcaps, and watch as the shot sails past us.

"Someone must have followed us," I say, my shoulder pressed hard into Sesay's, clutching my bruised side.

"No shit," Kasim says from the next aisle over. He holds his arm close to his body, wincing.

"So, Auben, you thought you could get rid of me by locking me in the trunk of a carriage?" comes Nkosazana's voice ringing throughout the library. "These hands *built* that carriage." Her shoes tap up the aisle that separates us.

"Come on," Sesay whispers. "I know another way out." She tugs at my shirt, and waves for Kasim to join us. He peeks his head around into the aisle, but is met with another cannon blast. He backs up and runs the other way.

"Kasim!" I yell, but it's too late. Nkosazana is almost upon us. Sesay practically drags me away. She and I cut back up two aisles over, but another sect member spots us.

Sesay cusses and pivots. Runs smack into my chest. She pushes me backward, nearly knocks the wind out of me. "Go up that aisle and hang a hard left!" I do as she says, and she sprints past me, then ducks down, pulling at the spines of several large books. I think she's making some sort of obstacle, when I notice the dark recess behind the shelving. She waves me forward, and I squeeze myself in, shouldering past the rubble of scattered books. The crawl space is tight, leading left and right, with a wider path in front of me that leads to safety. I turn around and grab through the shelving for Sesay's arm. "Come on," I yell. She slides her binder in. I push it to the side, then reach for her arm, but her eyes go wide. I tug, but something's tugging her back.

"Go!" she yells. "Save yourself." Her fingers slip from mine. "I'm sorry. I really am." And then like that, she's gone. I hear her fighting and flailing.

I glance back, considering the dimly lit hallway that leads to my freedom. The temptation is real, I can't deny. I could go off to Nri, or travel the world. Or anything. No one to tie me down. No one to let me down. But I draw away from the thought of such an empty existence. There would be no one to be tied to, no one for me to worry about letting down. I can see proximity as a gift or a curse. I can see it as both, but no matter what, it's worth fighting for. I grab Sesay's binder and duck into the narrow passageway to my left—the reverse side of the shelving, sprawling with pages and pages of nondescript books. I sidestep softly, trying to keep a mental count of where I am. I pull a couple books from the shelf and peek through.

"Come out, Auben," Nkosazana says. "We've got Kasim

and your little friend. Don't want to show up late to your own farewell party."

Out of nervousness, my fingers strum nonexistent tethers. I haven't heard any more shots. Maybe I could reason with her.

An eye peeks through the opening in the books, disappears, and then is replaced by the round lip of the gun. I duck, banging my forehead on the shelf in front of me. The blast throws me back, nearly knocks me unconscious. I look down, feeling my chest for a hole, but Sesay's binder stopped the bullet. My brain has taken a beating, though, and I'm sure my ears are bleeding. I turn to run, but a hand reaches through, grabs me, pulling the entire shelf section along, too. Stunned and disoriented, my life wobbles before my eyes.

"You'll pay for what you did to Ruda," Lwazi grates, sounding like his words are coming up from a very deep well. I shake my head, trying to process what's going on, but it's too damn hard. I can't stop seeing Nkosazana and her father together, feeling like I'm supposed to be getting yelled at for keeping her out too late, for causing her grades to slip . . . anything but this.

Kasim looks up at me with a swollen lip, still clutching his busted arm.

"It was an accident," I plead. I know damn well it wasn't. I had fully intended to put my lips upon Ruda's, to turn her to ice, to make her feel as cold as their charade had left me. But that revenge had proven bitter instead of sweet.

"Well, I can promise your deaths won't be nearly as pleasant," Lwazi says.

"Or as quick," Nkosazana adds. "We're going to drain

every ounce of blood in your veins first." She grins, eyes spitefully hidden behind her sect-issued, mirrored goggles. "An event like this deserves a spectacle. It deserves an audience!"

The ground shakes. Bookshelves shudder. Pages flap and flutter all about. Steam rises above the stacks. Then I see it round the corner. That yellow machination, a clockwork god, powering forward on three sets of steel haunches, springs and cogs working and grinding together. Red eyes flicker. The tool armory jutting from its undercarriage swivels back and forth, keeping time like a metronome. This close, *too* close, the armory is definitely phallic in nature, no doubt a resolute "fuck off" to the institutions that repressed knowledge for so long. The machination hunches down in a defensive stance. It was built for breaking rock and chopping down trees, but it definitely looks like it could hold its own in a fight.

"What you're looking at is your replacement," Nkosazana says. "We're making technological leaps faster than you can imagine. The future won't need gods. Just blood, sweat, and ingenuity." Outside, in the distance, the bells of the Sanctuary play off tune, grating to my ears, calling the devout to worship. Nkosazana clears her throat, then speaks over them. "Soon, everyone will trek up Grace Mountain to see one last exhibition. Your deaths, and with them the ushering in of a new age, and—"

"Nkosazana," comes a meek voice of a machinist. Nkosazana nearly rips her face off for interrupting.

"What is it!" she yells.

"It's the convoy. The roads to the Sanctuary are blocked with debris, and they can't get through."

"Keep an eye on these fools," she says to Lwazi. He looks

at me the way he had that night I'd had dinner over at his home—overprotective and angry—and desperate enough to do something stupid. I find myself more scared of him than I am of being squished by this giant bug.

I shift my attention to the mechanical phallus, mesmerized by its suggestive sway. Something clicks. My eyes travel up to the fury of smoke those furnaces put out. A mechanical penis for lechery. Smokestacks for temper. Gilded trim, that's got to count for greed. My eyes dart to Lwazi and his duplicitous tongue. For a couple years, his whole life had been a lie.

"Sesay," I mumble, trying to get her attention.

"No talking," Lwazi shouts, swiveling his gun in my direction.

Sesay looks up from her pouting. I nod at her binder over against the wall, in tattered pieces, then at the metal penis. Jut my head at the steam spouting from the machination's smokestacks. Flick my tongue at Lwazi. She looks blankly at me for a long moment, then a wave of understanding washes over her. She pulls her doubt signet tucked beneath her ciki's collar. We still need envy and vainglory to make this work, but it's a start.

Sesay may be cute and petite, but she's got comfy wiles up to here. She calls Lwazi over, mewing like an injured cat. Big brown eyes that are virtually impossible to say no to.

Her hands are fast, hard. There's the gnarly sound of ripping flesh followed by a spray of blood. Before I can even process what's happened, she's holding Lwazi's tongue in her hand, and he's holding his hands to his mouth. Sesay doesn't even flinch. She'd cleaned up slaughterhouse floors, after all. Last thing she's afraid of is a little blood. I notice Lwazi's gun on the floor.

"What's going on?" Kasim yells.

"I know how to get us out of this," I say. I grab the gun as Sesay boots Lwazi in the ass, and he goes stumbling into a pile of books. Sesay darts for her binder, leafing through page after page, until she finds what she's after. She pokes her finger through a gaping hole in the page, rimmed by flaky burnt ruin. The stupid machination observes the entire situation, but does nothing. Some kind of replacement god.

"It's okay," she says. "It's here. Enough of it, anyway. No words missing, just illustrations."

Good. I take aim at the machination's clockwork phallus. Lwazi screams, clamoring toward me. He's a bloody, frothy mess. I nudge him out of the way and pull the trigger. The kickback sends me careening into the stacks. Books tumble forth, raining down into a massive mound of leather binding and yellowed pages. My hand throbs, the bone in my arm aches something fierce, and the gun is nowhere to be found. When the smoke clears, when my senses congeal, I see the metallic dongle lying on the floor between the machination's legs, viscous fluid leaking from where it'd been severed. I can't help but wince.

"Sorry about that," I say to the mechanical god as I grab its severed rod. The metal is still hot as I twist off gold-plated bolts and stack my winnings around Sesay's circle. Bolts for greed, phallus for lechery, Sesay's doubt signet, a slab of tongue meat for duplicity. And sitting at the center of it all, that machination, steaming . . .

Steaming.

The sound of the gun blast has brought Nkosazana back into the room. "No!" she screams, ignoring me, ignoring poor Lwazi writhing desperately in pain. "This is our only chance!" She goes to the machination, immediately pulls a slim tool satchel from a pocket in her jacket, and starts her frantic repairs. The leaking white-hot fluid slows, but doesn't stop. Silently, I slip next to her as she works, hell-bent on fixing the machination. Lwazi helps the best he can, one hand holding gauze up to his mouth, the other handing her tools from her satchel as she demands them. I can see how badly they're hurting, how badly they want to prove themselves worthy as singletons. So badly that they'd put their lives within reach of a god. *That* . . . was a mistake.

She startles when she sees me and stumbles backward, screaming. Enough of my strength has returned for claws erupt from my nail beds. I flex them, sharp as steel blades. "Please, please," she begs, staring up at me behind those mirrored lenses, trying to scramble out of my reach. Lwazi drives his elbow into the side of my face, but I flick him off like an insect.

She cowers as I move my claw to her temple. I slice down, and the strap on her goggles snaps. I toss them to Sesay.

Vainglory down.

"If you're squeamish about gouged eyes, look away now," she says, taking a step toward Lwazi, her fingernails looking more and more like weapons.

"Sesay, please. Don't!" I command. I've got an idea, probably a horrible idea, but Sesay is so focused on plucking eyeballs that my words barely register. I grab her shoulder, stopping her before more blood is shed. "Can you perform the ceremony without envy? What would happen if we just used six vice talismans?"

"It's hard to say. Probably nothing, but maybe . . ." Her eyes go glassy and wide. She sees what I'm getting at. "Ahhh . . ." she says, nodding.

The large majority of twins are four-and-three in pairing of their virtues and vices. If we put things back together the way they were, minus a vice and virtue, most pairings would be three-and-three, meaning for the most part, there wouldn't be the means to oppress half the population. Sure, there'd still be four-and-twos and some five-and-ones. And of course, that does nothing to address all the singletons born after the split, but we can't expect a single incantation to fix all of society's ills overnight.

I look Lwazi in the eyes. Then Nkosazana. Maybe I was born with grace, but I have absolutely no need for it now. Taking their lives would be easy. I growl at them, letting the venom of their betrayal drip from my jowls. "Go," I say. "Go as far from Mzansi as your feet will take you. If I ever as much as catch a whiff of your blood again, I will hunt you down and devour your entrails while you watch."

Nkosazana and Lwazi scramble up to their feet, and I gnash my teeth at them, ensuring their hasty exit.

"Okay, Sesay," I say after my nerves have steadied some. "Let's do this."

"You're sure?"

Am I sure? How could I be any less sure of anything? But in my heart, I know it must be this way. It's the way it's meant to be. A wrong needs to be righted, but this is going to hurt as many people as it helps. With Aunt Cisse gone, Mother will suffer, go insane, or worse. I think I can deal with that, but then there's Uncle Pabio, who's never hurt a soul . . . what will become of him with Uncle Yeboah gone?

I nod. Barely a nod, but it's all Sesay needs, and she starts reading off the incantations. Her words are choppy at first, not just weird in my ear because of the foreignness of the ancient language, but because she's improvising along the way, editing out the references to envy, I'm guessing.

There's a whole lot of chanting, time slips in and out, and for a long, long time, I'm watching Kasim struggle on the other side of the room, the both of us trying to push through the pain. Finally, something changes in the air. There's dust . . . different than the dust of aged books . . . an ephemeral dust that glows ever so slightly, like embers struggling to catch fire. Instinctually, I hold my breath so as not to extinguish them. They start to smolder, tiny wisps of smoke snaking around the talismans.

Sesay chants harder.

I'm dizzy with pain, barely conscious when something clicks. Kasim's proximity is no longer a burden. But he's barely there. It's as if my insides are grasping for him, and he keeps slipping through my fingers like sand. I think maybe it's just an effect of the improvised chants, but when I look over at him, there's not much life left. He's dying.

"Kasim," I whisper. I clear my throat and try again. "Kasim," I say with a rasp that's no better.

I crawl over to him, dragging myself, inch by inch. Carefully, I pull him into my arms, kiss his forehead. My kiss doesn't kill him, doesn't make him stronger either, but it lets him know that I'm here, and that I love him, and that if he holds on just a little longer, we can survive this together.

He slowly pries his eyes open, and I flinch at how red they are. "You look like shit," he says. "Please don't go dying on me."

"Me? You're the one that looks like he's about to take his last breath."

"I'm fine."

"I'll have that written on your tombstone then. 'Here lies Kasim Mtuze. He was fine.'"

Kasim laughs a phlegmy, painful laugh. Eyes close. I shake him, trying to rouse him again, but there's nothing but slow, shallow breathing. Sesay joins us, nearly doubled over from the pain of her own broken proximity. "Is he getting any better?" she asks, though clearly, he's not. It's just a lot easier to say than "Is it too late?"

I shake my head, but Sesay just stares at me, like she's expecting me to do something. Like I know how to fix this.

Kasim inhales. It's not loud, but I notice because it's the first breath he's taken in a while. Nearly thirty seconds pass before he lets the breath go with an unceremonious heave. His last breath coalesces before me, a swirl of silver dust. I'm both shocked and mesmerized. I'm seeing things. Maybe that means my last breath is drawing near as well.

Please, Grace, do something, comes Sesay's voice. But it buzzes oddly in my ears. Like her words were stretched upon the wings of a gnat, and released directly into my mind.

I look at her. Her eyes spark. *Please,* she says again, but her lips don't part.

"How—" I start to ask, but then I notice the swirl of Kasim's breath is dissipating. I rake my fingers through the air, balling the wispy tendrils back together like tussled yarn until I hold it all in the palms of my hands. I concentrate, strengthening it with every spare bit of energy I have left, before pouring his life force back into him.

He's breathing. I'm breathing.

Sesay smiles, though the pain of broken proximity rims her eyes. "I wasn't sure it would work."

"What did you do, Sesay?"

"I wanted to fix things between you two, to put it all back the way it's supposed to be. And then I got to thinking about how the six virtue-vice pairs would help even out things among a lot of twins, but not pairs where the lesser twin had envy, and not twins like Daki and me. So I improvised a bit with the incantation, and switched the greater/lesser twins in the pairing. I figured having walked in each other's shoes would offer more insight into our relationships." She shrugs, as if she'd decided to experiment with a new herb in a favorite dish. She taps her fingers, and smiles again. "Would it be okay if I leave, now? I really need to find my sister."

"Of course," I say, holding Kasim even closer. His breathing grows stronger. He's going to be okay.

Before I can start to process what's happened, Sesay's out the door, her battle-worn binder still lying splayed open where it'd fallen.

"Kasim," I say, nudging him. "Kasim, it's me. It's over."

His eyes flutter once, twice. Then they pop wide open. It takes him a good minute to finally focus on me, but when he does, his gaze softens with relief. He smiles, and starts to say something, but then his mouth goes rigid. Bulges. He keeps his lips pressed together until it becomes impossible to contain what's growing inside. Fangs erupt, and a muzzle presses itself out of his jaws to accommodate them.

"Blood," he says, nearly a howl. Muscles pop and tense. His maimed arm straightens out with a spine-scraping snap. Joints turn inward, tawny fur erupts from his smooth brown skin, glistening like gold all over. My once frail and injured brother pounces onto all fours, sniffs the air. Growls. He's caught Sesay's scent. I move to restrain him, but he's already slipped away. I follow him as fast as I can, but it won't be fast enough. To make matters worse, more and more prayers buzz in my ears. I keep swatting at them, dozens now, and it's only slowing me down further.

When I catch up outside the library, Kasim's got Sesay pinned to the grass. She screams, bashing his snout with her fists. A long strand of drool hangs from his muzzle.

"Kasim!" I command like he's my dog. He doesn't heel, but if he hasn't devoured Sesay already, there must be some part of him left that's open to reason. "I get it. The need for blood. But there are other ways. You don't have to kill."

His jaw shifts back and forth, like he's trying to get a good sense of exactly how big of a bite he could handle. The need is real.

"I remember my first time," I say hurriedly. "I'm not going to lie, it was decadent, completely overwhelming. And that taste never goes away. But neither does the look on your victim's face as they take their last breath, as they utter their last words. Do you really want this moment to be with you for all eternity?"

Kasim breathes deeply, like he hears me, like he's trying to compose himself. He rears back, enough for me to reach for Sesay. She sees the opportunity, and scrambles over to me, but the sudden movement catches the predator's instincts. Kasim fights them and pulls back, but his claw catches her skin just right. Blood blooms through her shirt. No words could convince him to bite back his instincts now. Hell, I'm practically salivating over the memory of the craving.

I pull Sesay into my arms, yank her bloody sleeve off, and toss it directly into Kasim's gaping maw. He doesn't bother to suck the fabric clean, just swallows it whole.

Sesay's bleeding badly, but she's going to have worse problems if Kasim decides to sink his teeth into her. Instead of pressing at the wound, encouraging it to clot, I let the blood dribble freely into my cupped hand. Kasim stares me down. Those big caracal ears like horns. Fangs bared. Maw trembling with hunger, salivating. I stare back, as petrified as I was that night I'd decided to scale Grace Mountain alone.

But I'm not alone, now . . . for better or worse, I've got my brother with me.

I extend my arm toward him. A peace offering. The blood in my hand is gone before I can blink, then Kasim wedges his way closer to us, like a feral critter looking for a handout, lapping gently at Sesay's skin. I lay aside my worry, having faith that he'll stop before he's taken too much. Sesay's lost consciousness by the time he's finally done, but I press my hand to her arm, mending the wound and willing her body to flourish with a simple thought. Kasim purrs contently. It's all I can do to stop myself from petting him between the ears and asking him "Who's a good boy?"

"Will you come to Akinyemi?" I say to him instead, an invitation not just meant for him, but for all the people left here in the Cape. This place is too close, too broken.

"Of course," he says, his gaze still distant. His blood-thirst constantly demands his attention, but after a moment, he nuzzles underneath my arms and purrs a deep purr that winds itself into my soul, and we settle into this connection that is our brotherhood redefined. "Look," he says, his half paw, half hand pointing up at the sky.

A meteor shower, hot streaks of white searing the atmosphere. The prayer gnats start swarming again, but I embrace them. No rest for weary gods. I pull myself up from the comfort of Kasim's proximity and begin to answer them. They appear like dust motes in front of me, thousands of them, shimmering in the air. I touch one, and instantly, I am connected to a middle-aged man, and through his eyes, I see his son lying upon his bed, wrapped in layers of blankets, feverish and delirious. With Hallowed Hands, I reach out and touch him with the light that resides within me. Soon, his fever will break and the child will be running the halls, whooping and hollering and tormenting his thankful parents once again.

The act does not drain me in the slightest, but instead, fills me with invigorating buoyancy. After a few more, I find myself caught in the air, a few inches above the ground, and for nearly an hour, I play my fingers across the motes, answering every single prayer, virtue- and vice-ridden alike. I take special pleasure in crafting inspirational vagaries, and balancing those words upon hundreds of sets of defting sticks, whether they're made from ivory or the cheapest of splintering woods. Many of my followers, nearly the entirety of the city, are making their way up Grace Mountain, called by Nkosazana's false bells. Their prayers are full of excitement, anticipation as the bells ring, as my tears continue to streak across the sky above.

So many tears . . .

The meteor shower hasn't slowed. It's intensifying. The ground trembles in the far distance, and before I can register it as an impact, a meteor slams into the Cape. The entire mountain quakes, and the city bowl becomes a blaze. It's not a meteor shower . . . it's pieces of moon crashing down upon us. Immediately I flex my gossamers, hoping I have enough power to stop the destruction. I let my mind unfold to the cosmic scale. I brace myself, steady my nerves, then concentrate with all my might, folding my attention on the rocks and dust decaying in Earth's orbit. My gossamers sprawl out like a spider's web, vibrations of silken threads drawing my attention to each and every fragment. I move slowly, meticulously, gathering the pieces, rolling them like a soft bit of clay between my fingertips, until the moon is whole and beautiful again.

Then I keep folding, until I'm tucked into the flimsy paper sleeve that is Auben's body. I'd spent seconds, maybe a minute on the cosmic scale, but when I open my eyes, I'm surrounded by hundreds of amazed onlookers. Thousands. Kasim extends a hand up to me. I take it, and carefully step down through the ether until I'm once again on firm ground.

Above, the moon hangs differently than before, like a smooth white marble—no pitting, no craters, no seas of gritty, gray dust. Untouched and pristine, compared to the ruin below—the city bowl burnt down to embers. Smoldering. For all the scorn I have for this place, it doesn't stop my heart from lurching. So many memories were made inside the walls of our comfy.

"Don't worry," Sesay says, her small hand pressing firmly against my back. "The casualties are few. Most everyone was already halfway up Grace Mountain, ready to witness a miracle. You did not disappoint."

I blink her into focus, noticing that while one hand still reassures me with her touch, the other is held in the tight grip of her twin, Daki. I notice Kasim's hand still clutching mine. I notice my congregation, the majority of them paired off, standing shoulder to shoulder, basking in the pleasure that is absolute proximity. I see so many faces that I've shared countless communions with. How much time has passed for nearly all of Akinyemi to be here?

As much as Akinyemi draws me, I get the creeping feeling that this is where we truly belong. The city bowl is a carpet of smoldering ruins—shattered streets, broken buildings, comfy walls reduced to stacks of rubble, and whatever foul memories had haunted this place . . . they've been destroyed, too. I'm eager to build something here, something that'll surpass even the greatness of our charmed city. But a foundation of trust must be laid before we can construct new homes and communities. Respect needs to be repaired before we can repair the ruin of our schools and businesses. Faith must be restored—but not faith in me. Even a poor, secular-raised, self-important kid from the poorest comfy in the Cape could plainly see that I just made a giant space marble out of moon dust.

No, I need them to have faith in each other.

I open my mouth, and with a bellow that will cause nothing more than their hearts to stir, nothing more than their convictions to tremble, I say, "My people, we have work to do."

"Thanks for coming," Chimwe says, pressing me through the security doors of the Diligence Care Facility for the Terminally Separated. Except for the guards posted at the doors, you'd never know it was an institution. Inside is bright and cheery, lots of natural light, and the entrances to the residents' rooms resemble the exteriors of little beach cottages. It's quiet, quaint, cute. It helps with morale. Not as much as we'd hoped—Death isn't one to be deterred by a few copper planters and a fresh coat of paint, but sometimes, sometimes, he'll at least get a little distracted by such things, buying a few weeks, months, even years for loved ones who aren't quite ready to say goodbye.

Chimwe knocks on the door of one of the cottages, then lets himself in. Stacks of used canvasses, towers of clay pots, and buckets of dried paint all stand tall in the cramped living room. The sweet smell of ink stings my nose. A figure in a ragged patchwork jacket crumples over a desk, working. Diligently, of course. We weren't quiet entering, and yet he still hasn't looked up.

"Uncle Pabio?" I call, his name like a rusted razor cutting through the flesh of my throat. I've been away. I've been busy. Answering prayers, healing the sick and wounded, balancing my words upon defting sticks at all hours. And it seems that I've overlooked that there'd be some six-and-zero pairings, former six-and-one twins with envy being their lone vice. Basically, the Cape is lousy with bratty little godlings, always underfoot, watching Kasim and me closely, and creating havoc when we let the leash slack. But we need their help. There is yet so much work to do, bandaging together cultures and subcultures upon subcultures so that they can heal together and emerge as something stronger than before.

Like I said, I've been busy, but I still should have made time for this.

Uncle Pabio looks up, he turns and his visage lights up like the iridescent feathers of a peacock. He smiles. "Auben," his voice scratches.

I look to Chimwe for reassurance. Ey nods, and looks markedly more relieved than when ey'd come calling for me. Ey hadn't been able to get Uncle Pabio to eat or drink or even acknowledge em for the last few days. The death spiral was starting, and if Uncle Pabio didn't eat soon, his diligence would consume him instead.

I step toward the figure my mind still has trouble recognizing as my uncle. His smile has become an expanse of pitted gum line, but it still warms me like nothing else. "Show me what you've been up to," I say, keeping the small sack of food I'm holding just out of his sight. I don't want to spook him.

"Yes, yes!" he says. He tries to stand, but hasn't the strength to keep his legs under him. "Come. Come. Come see my latest." He turns his arm for me to see. Detailed tattoos of his characters light up his forearm, iridescent inks standing brilliantly against his brown skin.

"It's magnificent." I bide my time as he explains his creations to me, and only once his eyes have softened do I attempt to make my move. "Chimwe says that you promised to eat if he got you these inks."

"Yes," Uncle Pabio says, a nod of his head. "I did eat."

"I don't think he meant eating just the once," I say.

Uncle Pabio nods, but I'm already losing him. He's picked up his needle again and dips it into a striking metallic green ink.

You're wasting away, I want to tell him. *Eat, please, for me and Kasim. For Chimwe and Chiso. Eat because we still need you, and because it's just too soon for any of us to have to say goodbye to a loved one again.* But that is not how you reason with someone driven to the brink of madness by the compulsion to create. I must speak to him through his art.

"Uncle Pabio, if you were choosing a canvas, would you not take care that it was properly stretched, adequately primed?"

"Of course," he says, listening, but not looking up.

"Well, your skin is your canvas now, and you must care for it as such," I say. "Water to keep it hydrated and supple, and food to keep the muscle firm and taut beneath."

"And fresh air," Chimwe says, catching on. "So that the art may be appreciated by the world, and not confined between these walls."

"Mmpph," Uncle Pabio says, not an overwhelmingly positive response, but it was a response nevertheless.

I rummage through his art supplies and find a tin cup full of dry brushes. After removing the brushes, I pour water from his pitcher into the cup and set it beside him. Then I pull a still-warm samosa from my sack and set it upon a mostly clean paint palette. I watch carefully as Uncle Pabio begins to work sips and small bites into his creative process.

Chimwe lays eir hand on my shoulder. "Thank you," ey whispers into my ear, and I feel the need in eir voice as deeply as I do in my own.

"I'll sit with him awhile, if that's okay," I say to Chimwe. "You can get back to work, if you need to."

"You're sure?" Ey raises a weary eyebrow. My poor cousin can barely keep eir eyelids propped open, ey's so exhausted. All those years ago, back in our dorm room, Chimwe had claimed to be able to run a business in eir sleep, and between running our city by day and parenting eir sweet-but-unruly six-month-old twins by night, some days it seems like ey's doing just that.

I nod. "We have some catching up to do," I say.

But just as Chimwe is about to leave, the door creaks open.

Kasim enters, carrying a greasy lunch sack. We lock eyes, and though it's been ages since I've harbored Icy Blue's power, I freeze up all over. Things between us have been . . . *awkward*. And not just *I'm a god, you're a god* kind of awkward.

"Oh," Kasim says. "Chimwe told me Uncle Pabio wasn't eating."

Uncle Pabio smiles and fully opens his mouth, revealing a mash of potatoes, onions, neon paint flecks, and what looks like brush bristles.

"Um," Chimwe says, brows nearly reaching eir hairline. "I've really gotta go. Those diapers aren't going to change themselves!" And then ey's gone, door swinging closed behind em.

"I'll come back later," Kasim says, looking so uncomfortable in his skin. I wonder if it's from the ill fit of his human suit, or from being trapped in the same room with me.

"No," I say. "It's okay. Sit."

Kasim does, carefully. We both feel it, the draw to each other, like those two yam halves yearning to be whole. The need is there. Hands to Grace, the need is there, but there can't be a true connection yet, because our edges are too ragged, and we've still got rotten spots to root out. For right now, close is close enough. I break a wad of red clay in half and lay a piece in front of Kasim.

Along with our uncle Pabio, the man who both inspires me and keeps me grounded, we sit shoulder to shoulder to shoulder at his cramped little desk. I press my fingers into the clay, warm it in my hands, and then, together, we create.

ACKNOWLEDGMENTS

To my super-secret writing group, Crytopolis. Maybe it really exists. Or maybe it's a figment of the imagination. Maybe they read an early draft of *Temper* and helped make it shine. Maybe they're just a bunch of thread-worn sock puppets I carry around with me in a duffel bag. So to Julia, Patrick, Patrice, David, Jane, Elle, Sharon, Fred, Rebecca, Steve, and Matthew, a very special thanks to you. Maybe their names have been changed to protect the innocent. Or maybe they haven't.

Thanks to Gabby, Bogi, Chinelo, and Yewande for allowing me a peek at the world through their eyes. Thanks to Dan for the history lessons on Twitter and a nice chat on alternate histories.

To Dad for becoming a wonderful beta reader, and Mom for being my personal cheer section. To Tony for the wonderful Plated meals, especially on days when it's hard to find time to eat. To Alex, my wonderful writing partner. To Dana the dog for spending fifteen-and-a-half years right by my side. And to all my family and friends, thank you for your encouragement and patience through my transition from a writer to a published author. It's been a ridiculously wild ride, and having you in my corner has kept me on the tracks.

To Jennifer, my amazing agent, and David and the crew at Harper Voyager for turning my words into an actual thing I can hold in my hands. You are all magic workers.

ABOUT THE AUTHOR

Nicky Drayden's writing credentials include more than thirty short fiction sales to magazines such as *Shimmer* and *Space and Time Magazine,* and she is the author of the critically acclaimed novel *The Prey of Gods.* She is a Systems Analyst and resides in Austin, Texas, where being weird is highly encouraged, if not required.

ALSO BY
NICKY DRAYDEN

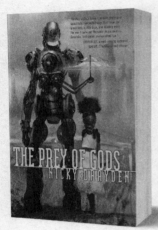

THE PREY OF GODS
A Novel
Winner of the Compton Crook Award

Fun and fantastic, Nicky Drayden takes her brilliance as a short story writer and weaves together an elaborate tale that will capture your heart...even as one particular demigoddess threatens to rip it out.

"Fans of Nnedi Okorafor, Lauren Beukes, and Neil Gaiman better add *The Prey of Gods* to their reading lists! This addicting new novel combines all the best elements of science fiction and fantasy"

—*RT Book Reviews*
(June 2017 Seal of Excellence—Best of the Month)

TEMPER
A Novel

Two brothers. Seven vices.
One demonic possession.
Can this relationship survive?

VE OFFERS, AND MORE AT HC.COM.

TAL AUDIO WHEREVER BOOKS ARE SOLD.